Steven Knight was born in Marlborough in 1959 and grew up in Birmingham. After studying English Literature at University College London, he worked as a radio producer and then as an advertising copywriter, winning several major industry awards. In 1987 he began his career as a television scriptwriter and has written extensively for some of Britain's leading performers, both alternative and established, and he has also devised a series of successful TV game shows. He now runs his own TV production company in Covent Garden, writing and producing comedy and drama for the BBC and the independent networks.

STEVEN KNIGHT

THE MOVIE HOUSE

PENGUIN BOOKS

PENGUIN BOOKS

Published by the Penguin Group
Penguin Books Ltd, 27 Wrights Lane, London W8 5TZ, England
Penguin Books USA Inc., 375 Hudson Street, New York, New York 10014, USA
Penguin Books Australia Ltd, Ringwood, Victoria, Australia
Penguin Books Canada Ltd, 10 Alcorn Avenue, Toronto, Ontario, Canada M4V 3B2
Penguin Books (NZ) Ltd, 182–190 Wairau Road, Auckland 10, New Zealand

Penguin Books Ltd, Registered Offices: Harmondsworth, Middlesex, England

Published in Penguin Books 1994
1 3 5 7 9 10 8 6 4 2

Typeset by Datix International Limited, Bungay, Suffolk
Filmset in 10.5/12 pt Monotype Ehrhardt
Printed in England

PART ONE

CHAPTER ONE

If this had been a movie, Baxter wouldn't have been the man I would have cast in the role of chief of police.

He was in charge of the whole southern half of the Florida Keys, from Big Pine Key to Key West. In the movie, he would have been a fat guy, with a square cut of blond/grey hair and with sweat patches the size of dinner plates around his armpits and, around the sweat patches, a halo of dried-on salt. He would have had meaty hands and his tan leather holster would have been slung low underneath his paunch, straining the buttons of a shirt that gaped at the neck and at the belt buckle. Instead, I was introduced to an owlish, pale-skinned college graduate who looked as if he had just stepped off an executive jet from Boston and hadn't yet got used to the climate. He wore a heavy woollen tweed jacket and neatly pressed cotton trousers and shoes that were real shoes, black and shiny, the kind you rarely saw down here where the United States dipped its toe into the sub-equatorial waters of the Gulf of Mexico.

I decided, when I shook his hand and saw the sly intelligence focused behind his round-rimmed spectacles, that the real Baxter wouldn't do at all.

'You the movie guy?' he said as if the answer didn't concern him in the slightest. I said that I was and he shrugged his shoulders. He stroked an eyebrow with his ring finger and sighed, and said that if I hadn't seen the inside of a prison before, an American prison, then I should take a deep breath and prepare myself for something of a shock.

I had been waiting for Baxter for over an hour. My appointment was for three o'clock, but the female police lieutenant who met me outside the secure area (she called it 'the tank' and I made a note) told me that Baxter had been held up. I had already been waiting for half an hour before I asked her again. She was sitting at a typewriter and she didn't even look up.

'I guess he's still with Silus,' she said, dabbing a mistake with Snopake.

'Silus?'

'Murder investigation. They sometimes take a while. He's probably still trying to find out why Silus chose to put kerosene in his baby's bottle instead of milk.'

She rolled a sheet of paper round the platen of her IBM manual and then cursed because she'd put only one r in 'arraign'.

Baxter took me through three secure doors, all of them heavy metal and painted milky blue. The smell of detergent and urine got stronger with each door, until by the time we were in the holding area ('the pit' – another note) the smell had become a taste. The air in here was as hot as an incubator, and I could hear the gentle hum of a generator, somewhere, high above or deep down below. This place had no up and no down, no left or right, just doors and corners and the certainty of solid steel. Baxter's voice echoed as we walked, and behind his voice there was a constant chorus of yelps and grunts and whistles that came from the cages, the soundtrack of a tropical jungle. The cages were in the distance, and then they were right there in my face and the jungle noises got louder. Somewhere behind me there was a hand reaching out from between the bars.

'If they don't like you,' Baxter was saying, 'then there's not a sweet thing you can do about it. It's something like a

4

smell that you've got and if they don't like your smell then you're in trouble. If they like you, then you're OK, at least for a while. But if they really *really* like you, then you're in more trouble than if they hate you. Know what I'm saying?'

Baxter didn't smile as he turned to check that I knew what he was saying. I heard a soft mumbling sound from somewhere not far away, the sound of someone praying in Spanish close by in the darkness. Baxter unlocked another door and allowed me to walk through it ahead of him.

'These guys in here are mostly Cubans,' he said, locking the door behind him. Suddenly there was crackle from the mechanism of the lock, and Baxter spoke into it.

'Baxter and one civilian,' he murmured.

'OK, go ahead,' said the lock.

'These are the guys we pick up in the Gulf trying to make it up to Mud Key. Refugees. They're mostly farmers and, let me tell you, farmers don't make great sailors. No sir. We pick 'em up hanging on to oil drums, floating around on orange crates, some of 'em in old fishing skips that got washed up on the shore and beaten to hell by the hurricanes. I guess it must be pretty hard down in Cuba. Especially for guys like these. You see, ole Fidel has a tendency to only send us his bad guys, murderers, rapists, hoodlums, all the refuse. We have to be pretty careful. We never know who they are because Fidel don't attach green slips to 'em when he sets them out to sea.'

'Green slips?'

'The details of their criminal history.'

'Oh, right.' (Another note.)

Baxter took off his spectacles and rubbed his eyes. His naked face looked more human, and more fatigued. I knew that giving guided tours to 'civilians' at the end of a sixteen-hour shift wasn't his idea of an afternoon well

5

spent. I decided to take a short cut to where I wanted to be, for his benefit as well as my own.

'So if the hero in my movie commits a murder, this is where you would bring him,' I said.

'No sir. If he was suspected of a first degree, he'd go straight through to the blue area.'

'The blue area?'

'Straight through that door ahead of you.'

The door seemed to vibrate at the mention of it. It was a blue door, chunky and mean, wired up and impregnable. It looked like the door on a space ship.

'Can we go through?' I asked. Baxter put his spectacles back on and his face became the face of an official again. He had no expression.

'Afraid not, Mr Stone. We're kinda busy in there at the moment.' He walked by me, heading back for the door we'd just come through as if there were no possibility of argument. 'Besides,' he said, 'you really wouldn't want to put the blue area in your movie. No sir. It's sort of . . . de-pressing.'

The light outside was so bright that it made my eyes water. Out beyond the outer perimeter fence, I could see a long strip of white sand, like a line in crayon around the electric blue of the ocean. The sea breeze smelt of freedom, and the seagulls wheeled above our heads just to make the point. The distance between freedom and hell was just a few inches, just one footstep from the inside of the tank to the wide open, salty vista of Smathers Beach. Baxter seemed to think that it was his duty to make small talk as he showed me out.

'So, what kind of movie is it, Mr Stone?' he said, utterly devoid of curiosity.

'It's a kind of thriller,' I said. 'I guess that's what it is. It's still sort of up in the air.'

6

'You must know what sort of movie it is, Mr Stone. You're the writer.'

Baxter didn't like vagueness in any area. Even though he had no interest in my movie, he wanted this thing sorted out. It was instinct verging on compulsion.

'I don't know,' I said. 'It's still changing.'

Baxter thought for a moment. His indifference beat his curiosity to the line by inches. He let it pass. But then he said, 'And do you have someone in mind to play the hero?'

'Yes. I suppose I do.'

'Who?'

'Who? Well, I'm not sure yet. Like I say, it's changing.'

Baxter handed me a release form to sign so that my signature could be checked against the signature I'd written on the way in. In some part of his mind, Baxter had begun to think that something wasn't right.

'So you don't know what kind of movie it's going to be and you don't have a star. Have you got a director for your picture, Mr Stone?'

I signed quickly and my hand shook a little. Baxter never missed a thing. He was looking me in the eye. I began to feel his stare like heat on my face.

'We have a lot of options,' I said. 'But just at present it's all . . .'

'Changing?'

'Yes, changing.'

Baxter nodded. I guessed that his work made him compulsively suspicious, attracted to evasion and equivocation like a moth to a hurricane lamp. The lady lieutenant had told me already that they'd waived a lot of security procedures when they heard that I was just a writer looking for some background for a screenplay, and that I didn't actually need to see inside any of the cells or speak

7

to any of the prisoners. Suddenly, the look on Baxter's face told me that he wasn't so sure any more. I wondered what he thought I could possibly be if I wasn't who I said I was. I decided that I really ought to put his mind at rest.

'You see, Mr Baxter, I'm pretty new to this business myself,' I said. 'I only got here from London a few weeks ago and I just do what they tell me to do. The studio I mean. I'm just a writer, and sometimes the writer is the last person to know how his story is going to turn out.'

Baxter looked at me as if to say, 'I hear what you say, buddy, but, hell, I don't know . . .'

As I turned to leave he said, 'Remember what I said about people having a smell, Mr Stone?'

I said that I did, not wanting to turn around and face him.

'Well, I guess I got a pretty good sense of smell myself. That wasn't the first time you've been inside a prison, was it, Mr Stone?'

I began to walk away towards the South Roosevelt Boulevard and the ocean a little too quickly, saying out loud that I had no idea what he meant.

That night, I tried to write up the notes I'd made on my tour of the tank, first in longhand, and then, to get the juices flowing, on my old faithful Singer typewriter. But the chopping of the keys had no effect.

I had often thought, in the time between waking and sleeping, and between sleeping and waking, that it was possible that your past deeds left marks on your body, marks that were visible to the whole world, or, as Baxter had said, a certain smell. Of course it was absurd, except when dealing with men like Baxter, whose inner receptors were as sensitive as the nostrils of a bloodhound.

In the three weeks before I went to visit Baxter at the

tank, I hadn't written a single word. At least, none that wasn't screwed up and thrown on to the bare floorboards a minute after it was put on to the page. The idea was that the second draft of the screenplay I was writing would be completed by January, which gave me four months. The studio had paid my rent in Key West for long enough for me to complete the first rewrite, and then I would return to London to do the third and fourth drafts. Most of the dialogue was already in place and the second draft should have been little more than a housekeeping exercise. Throwing away the excess, tidying up the characters, cutting off the loose ends or at least putting them out of harm's way.

Since my movie was set in Key West, I had imagined that moving out to Florida would be like switching on the current of an electrical appliance. The mechanism was set up, but now I would have the juice, the sunlight and sea and salt air, to really make it work, to make the characters move around and crash into each other. In fact, my three weeks in Mallory Street had had the opposite effect, and it was only in the brightest hour before breakfast that I could raise any kind of enthusiasm for it. My enthusiasm was like those dumb, wake-up erections that seem to exist just because they exist, just because *you* exist. The moment I began to think things through, the impetus drained away.

I knew even then that the script was the worst thing I'd ever written. The story, the characterization, the mood, the whole baggage of the movie appalled me. It didn't even feel like my idea any more, and it didn't read as if I had written it. But it had taken me out of London, right at the time when I knew I had to either get out and start all over again, or burn up from the inside. I'd spent ten years in TV, writing comedy, and I'd done pretty well and made some TV I was pleased with, a little less that I was proud of, but then some god or some devil somewhere in the sky had pulled out my file and smiled and said, 'Let's change this guy's life.' When I thought about how I left London, and why, I thought of a man leaving a burning building, with his clothes on fire.

After the sun had set, after the walls of my room had changed from orange to red and finally to dark blue, the noises started up above my head and the ceiling began to shake. Every evening for three weeks, the same thing happened. The moment the sun dissolved into the ocean, the lady in the attic room above launched herself into the final session of her insane daily workout routine.

'For Christ's sake will you stop punishing yourself,' I said out loud to the ceiling, eyes closed, hands locked together under my pillow. 'Why don't you just accept the laws of fucking gravity and let it all slide!'

Since I had moved into my room in 1131 Mallory Street, Ms Lisson had worked out for seven hours a day every day; three hours in the morning, three hours after lunch and one hour in the evening, directly above my head. I had hardly spoken to her except to exchange greetings on the stairs, and if I said hello to her in the morning, she would ignore me for the rest of the day, as if the business of greeting had been discharged for exactly twenty-four hours. She was in her early forties, well kept and tightly muscled, with that kind of sparkling olive complexion that comes from frugal sunbathing and too much exercise. She had long auburn hair and deep, black eyes, and the kind of floaty, lazy-camel walk that made me think that maybe she had been a fashion model some time before age had taken over and made her fight for every inch. She had a look of nervous incomprehension, a look that said that she was afraid but she was ready because she expected the worst to happen anyway. It was a fleeting impression I got sometimes when I said hello to her from the top of the stairs and she didn't know I was there. I thought back then that maybe I was imagining it, or worse, projecting my own feelings on to her blank features. I found out her name from looking at her mail, which I'd see when I was checking the communal mailbox. Her mail was always addressed to her as Ms Lisson, or Mrs Lisson, or sometimes just 'Lisson', and I'd become curious about her first name. Every Wednesday she got a rolled-up copy of a magazine called *Workout* wrapped up in a brown paper tube, and twice in the three weeks I'd been in the house she'd had letters from the Chase Manhattan bank in Chicago, marked 'Strictly Confidential'.

I'd become curious about Ms Lisson for reasons I couldn't quite explain to myself. When I watched her out of my window, floating through the overgrowth on the front drive into Mallory Street, I would have said that she was some kind of glamorous Palm Beach housewife, bored maybe, possibly unfaithful, married to some dumpy, potato-headed business-man who picked her up when she was still the beauty of the islands. That was how I would have cast her. Faded but still fighting. But if that was the case, what was she doing living alone, renting an attic room in a rotting colonial mansion house on the middle-rent side of town? Maybe this was where the Florida princesses wound up when their bodies began to subside. Maybe that explained the look in her eye, that look of being pursued by something. When she turned her head at the sound of my voice it was the monstrous twin heads of middle age and cellulite she expected to see. But I suppose that the real reason I had begun to spy on her through my window, snoop through her mail in search of a first name, have these whimsical, wisecracking dialogues with her through the plaster of the ceiling, was that I had convinced myself that I'd seen her somewhere before.

Maybe I was imagining it. Since I'd arrived in the Keys, I'd begun to imagine a lot of things.

The house at 1131 was divided into three apartments. Ms Lisson had the attic, I had the room below, and across the hall there was a gay realtor called Clark, who worked for the agency that rented the house. It was Clark who had first shown me across the threshold of the place, one early evening when the sky was glowering. I had arrived from London in the middle of the Florida hurricane season, but Clark had been anxious to let me know that if the hurricane hit hard, real hard, then I shouldn't be concerned because my new home had been around for a hundred years and there was no reason why it should fall to pieces now. He said some of the other places over at Mallory Docks had been sucked out of their foundations like rotten teeth just three years ago when Hurricane Jane had hit, but he assured me that there was nothing to worry about at 1131. He tapped the banister of the rickety wooden staircase with his fist and smiled.

'I guess a hundred years isn't so old for a European,' he said as he led me upstairs to my room, 'but over here, a hundred years is just for ever. You know? Looky here, Mr Stone. Look at your beautiful new home.'

Clark had opened the door to my room with a theatrical flourish. He was lithe and tanned, with bleach-blond hair and a round freckled face that looked like a gull's egg. He wore tiny white tennis shorts and a torn T-shirt and when he smiled his eyes oiled up and swooped from my face to my belt buckle and then back to my face again. He led me into the kitchen and pulled open the blinds with a cascade of dust to show me my view of the famous Gulf of Mexico sunset.

We both stared out across the ocean for a long time before Clark said, 'OK, so today isn't great but, come on,

Mr Stone, you've got yourself the best damn vista on the island.'

He would have tried to sell it harder but he knew that the rental deal had already been signed by the studio and it was a little late for me to change my mind. The sky had been low and smouldering, the sun a streak of light green and purple, the ocean troubled and grey. As he headed for the door he paused and said that if the wind got up, I should lock up the storm shutters on all my windows or the hurricane might come right into my room and suck me all the way out to Cuba. Then he peered at me and I guess he decided that while he was here he really ought to test the waters. After all, I was a man alone, middle thirties, pretty quiet, not so bad looking.

'But think of it this way, Mr Stone,' he said with half a smile, framed in the crooked doorway. 'Maybe that old hurricane'll pick up some big Cuban guy down in Havana, and bring him all the way up here and push him through your window the other way. That's how I think of it. Now what would you say if something crazy like that happened?'

I laughed and said that if that happened, I'd be pretty surprised.

Since that first night (the hurricane never came) I'd got used to the house at 1131, to the delicate smell of decaying wood and turpentine that oozed up from the cellar, to the patter and scratching of mice under the floorboards, even to the way the whole ceiling creaked and groaned when Ms Lisson fought for her youth. As I lay on my bed, watching my naked light bulb swing to her frantic rhythm, feeling bad about not working, feeling bad about Baxter and the way he had looked through me, I decided that the house suited my mood. This house had a feeling in it, a vapour in its wooden bones, that was all

13

about regret. Sometimes it felt oppressive, other times it felt like I'd lived there all my life. I said goodnight to Ms Lisson through the ceiling, and spent the night in a familiar place, a place of terror, somewhere behind Baxter's heavy blue door.

CHAPTER TWO

I spent the next morning waiting in my room for a call from G. F. Benelli, the acquisition producer who had commissioned my script. It was Benelli who had arranged my visit to Baxter's tank, and he had told me he would call the next day to see how I had made out. In the three weeks since I'd been in Key West Benelli had promised to call many times, and sometimes he called and sometimes the phone didn't ring. When his calls failed to come through, when I was left for two or three days with no word from him or from anyone at the studio, then I would become anxious. If I didn't get regular word from the studio I'd begin to wonder if maybe this whole commission wasn't just a figment of my imagination. So far, I'd been given no word on which direction the script should take, no cuts or casting ideas. This whole project had only ever been sealed by a handshake, the 'commission' had been nothing more than a short conversation over lunch in London and the contract I'd been promised still hadn't arrived. The only solid information I had been given by Benelli was that maybe some people at Warner Brothers were interested in buying the option.

I'd written the script with Benelli in mind. I wrote it as a thriller and I'd sent it to him even though I knew that he'd built his reputation in comedy. I'd been given his name by a friend of mine, a director who had spent some time working for a subsidiary of S-Productions in Santa Monica, where Benelli was head of acquisitions. He told me that he'd spoken to Benelli at some end-of-shoot cocktail party, and that my name had come up in conversation. It had been Benelli who had mentioned my name first, saying he'd seen one of my shows when he was last in London and it had made him laugh out loud because it was so crazy. My friend told me that Benelli's exact words were 'I guess a guy who writes stuff like that must be pretty crazy himself,' and my friend had said that yes, Karl Stone was pretty crazy.

For ten years, I'd had this dream of writing a Hollywood feature, a dream that had always been a twinkling presence on the horizon, something to look at when I closed my eyes. When I heard that someone in Hollywood actually knew my name and liked my work, I dug out a pretty awful half-finished movie script that I'd abandoned a long time before, reworked it and sent it to Benelli. I also mentioned the TV show that he'd thought was so crazy. I got a rejection slip back from S-Productions, not even signed by Benelli, but two months later, out of an empty grey sky, Benelli called me up, told me that he was in town and said it would be a good idea if I took him to lunch. He said he wanted to talk to me about my script because the way he saw it, my work had feeling.

'You've got feeling,' Benelli said. 'You take that old guy. What's his name?'

'Max' (the murderer in my screenplay).

'Sure. Max. He could have been funny. I mean he says funny things. Then you go and turn him into a creep. A murderer! I showed it to this guy, a friend of mine, a writer (you believe I got a friend who's a writer?) and he says the same thing. He says it was a wasted opportunity. He says if you're going to write for a killer you've got to know about killing. I don't believe you know about killing. Not from the inside.'

I had arranged to meet Benelli in a restaurant in Covent

Garden. He showed up half an hour late and I'd arrived half an hour early, so by the time he waddled into the restaurant with my script under his arm, I had already drunk five glasses of strong beer. I had decided in absolute sobriety that I couldn't face Benelli without something to wash the tension out of my face. It wasn't just that Benelli represented a chance to break into the movies, he was also an escape route, a fast exit that had suddenly and miraculously opened up right at the moment when I needed it most – his call had come on the morning my wife had left me for ever. For ever and ever, no question. When the phone rang two of Sarah's friends were sifting through my belongings upstairs, my papers, my clothes, my scripts, as if they were soiled tissues, delicately extracting her life from mine and putting it into plastic bags. Two guys in orange overalls were emptying the kitchen and a friend of a friend had taken the keys to Sarah's car from my pocket and driven it away without a word. When Benelli had finally arrived at the restaurant and sat down, I shook his hand just to make sure he was real.

'You see, this stuff is shit if you'll forgive me,' Benelli had whispered, waving a copy of my script at me, 'but it's got feeling. I read shit all day. That's my job, to wade through the shit. Sometimes you see some piece of shit that isn't quite so bad as all the rest. So you pick it up. You shine it up a little. You wash it in your bowl. You put it here, in your pocket, you think, well, maybe some day . . . And you say to yourself, where did this come from? Is there some more that's like it, or better? Don't get too excited, Karl, but I think you've got some feeling. And I only say that to a new writer maybe once, twice a year.'

There was a picture in my mind of the house I'd left behind, empty inside except for the echo of a closing door. I knew that I couldn't return there, and there was nowhere else in London where I could possibly go. Everyone I knew was either afraid of me or angry with me. I ordered more beer to quieten the voices which were whispering in my head that Benelli was an angel sent from heaven to save me. And other voices which told me that even if he was, I could still fuck this thing up if I made the wrong moves. When I ordered my drink, Benelli said that he didn't drink beer and ordered himself one of those absurd bucket cocktails that Americans drink to kid themselves they're not drinking alcohol.

'So,' Benelli said, sucking his purple liquid through a straw, 'maybe we can do something with this shit.' He tapped the script with his knuckles and then stared into my eyes.

'You married?' he asked. I took a long swig of beer and lit a cigarette, hoping that the question might go away. Benelli suddenly seemed angry, and I had the absurd notion that maybe he knew something about Sarah and me. I imagined that somehow he had heard the whole story. Then I realized he was angry because I had lit a cigarette. I stubbed it out.

'Separated,' I said at last. 'Just. I mean today, this morning.'

I thought that Benelli would at least give me a few seconds of reverential silence, that he would delicately change the subject or offer me an embarrassed word of sympathy. Instead, he just stared at me, apparently neither surprised nor concerned.

'You got kids?' he said.

'No.'

'Funny. You write like a guy with kids. What happened?'

'What happened to what?'

'To your marriage?'

18

'She left me.'

'Sure.'

Benelli pushed the straw away from his mouth and closed his eyes.

'She left you for another guy,' he said, like a fairground mind-reader.

'That's right,' I said, a little shocked, peering at his closed eyes.

'And the guy who stole your wife was a friend of yours.'

I remembered what my friend had told me about Benelli. He said that he'd heard rumours around the S-Productions offices that he consulted his own personal shaman before he commissioned scripts, and that he always spoke to his astrologer before he booked air tickets. My friend said that Benelli liked to put it around that he had some kind of power to predict which projects would make it and which would bomb. But he also said that in LA, in the movie business, stuff like that wasn't so unusual. Benelli opened his eyes and fixed me with his unblinking gaze.

'So, am I right?' he said.

'As a matter of fact, the guy wasn't a friend of mine,' I said. 'Far from it.'

Benelli shrugged. His eyes could harden quickly and then he looked like a man built for anger. His face had the look of a piece of burnished metal that had been beaten roughly into shape, and his bald head had been burnt tomato red by the Californian sun. He was overweight but healthy-looking, and beneath the pudges of flesh he exuded energy. I thought that I should maybe become angry with Benelli for playing games with me like this, on a day like this, but I knew that it was no time to let my anger loose. And there were other reasons for being careful with a man like Benelli. The other rumour my friend had heard

19

in LA was that sometimes, when Benelli needed finance for a movie, he used what were known as his 'excellent Italian connections'. But taking money from the Mob wasn't so unusual either in Hollywood.

'Sometimes when a guy feels strongly about something, he gives off waves,' Benelli said, to explain himself. 'Sometimes I pick up a picture in my mind. Got to be a strong feeling to make a picture. You got a strong feeling about the guy who stole your wife?'

'Yes.'

Benelli nodded and tapped the side of his glass. I wanted him to get back to talking about the script, but instead he peered deeply into my eyes again.

'So who was he?' Benelli said.

'Who?'

'Who was the guy who stole your wife?'

'He was an advertising copywriter.'

'That's too bad.'

'Yes it is too bad. It's just that.'

'So what happened? Come on, talk. It's fate that I call you on the day your wife dumps you, so we should make the most of what fate gives us. You want us to work together, I've got to know you. I've got to know your insides.'

Benelli sucked up the last of his cocktail and the ice and bubbles at the bottom of his glass made an obscene gurgling sound. Had he really said that he and I might work together? So far his only reference to the script was to say that it was shit.

'I believe in feeling,' Benelli said, before I had a chance to speak. 'Sure I do. I'm in comedy, but I work with feelings. You're in comedy too but this piece of shit you sent me is a thriller and I say well, OK, sure, but if a guy is going to write thrillers he's got to deal with the serious stuff. Love and pain. I don't think a guy like you can write love and pain, but who the fuck knows? So tell me about this guy who stole your wife and I'll see if you've got feeling.'

Benelli shifted in his seat, like a kid waiting for a movie to start. I considered the possibility that this whole thing was a joke, that I had been set up in some way. It would explain the uncanny timing. Maybe Benelli really did know the whole story and this was just his way of making me tell him about it. He waited for a few moments and then told me he wanted to hear the whole thing. I decided quickly I would only tell him part of it. Just the first act. The second and the third would have to remain hidden, for his sake but also for my own.

'I used to drink a lot,' I said. 'I was drinking a lot and staying out and working too much. I got pretty famous for a while. When I was writing the TV comedy. Then there was this other guy. This copywriter who wrote commercials. Did you ever see the TV ad for fake cream? With the cows that skip and go "la, la, la"?'

Benelli shrugged. This was my favourite and least favourite topic of conversation.

'Sarah's new boyfriend wrote that. She's been having an affair with the man who wrote that. It was an impressive piece of work, Mr Benelli. And now she's so impressed with him she's decided to go and live with him. And that's why I've been a little crazy lately. I had some problems and that's why I need to get away. And stop drinking. I only drink beer now. Mostly. I cheat sometimes. In everything.'

Benelli didn't say anything for a long time and I guessed that I had said too much and that Benelli would be embarrassed. But then he closed his eyes again and smiled.

21

'You're pretty angry,' he said.

'Yes I am. Fucking cows.'

'And you're pretty honest too.'

'I'm feeling pretty honest today,' I said. 'And I think if we are going to work together, Mr Benelli, it's important that we should both be honest with each other.'

'Sure,' he said, 'I think we should be honest. So I'll be honest with you. When I say that this shit has got feeling I mean that sometimes when I pick something up I get a feeling from it and that's what is important. The rest I can fix. It's like sometimes I get an omen. I get a sign. You believe in fate, Mr Stone?'

I told him that I hadn't ever believed in fate before but that as of two hours ago, maybe I did. That made Benelli laugh out loud and all the intensity vanished from his eyes. He stood up with my script in his hand and suddenly he looked like just any other guy.

'Hey, I just remembered,' he said, waving at the waiter, 'you got a cow going "la, la, la" in your script.'

'Yes.'

'That's good, Karl. That's smart. I like to know a guy is suffering for his art.' He laughed because he thought it was funny. I laughed because he thought it was funny.

I asked a waiter to call a taxi and I waited with Benelli in the doorway of the restaurant. It was raining and the sky had turned purple above our heads. Benelli had a disgruntled look on his face.

I could see Benelli detested London and I knew why. As we stood waiting in that doorway, the pavement steaming in front of us, I could almost hear him condemning the place in his own mind for being so serious and melancholy, and for making everything such hard work. A wet city soaking and rotting in its own brine. I was familiar enough with California to imagine the misery and disgust felt by someone like Benelli when confronted with a wet and dark English afternoon. I understood how he felt because I felt the same way, for different reasons. We stood in silence for a long time before he spoke.

'So do we have a deal?' he said.

'A deal?'

'You come out to Florida and we get the feeling out of this.' Benelli flicked the script with his middle finger. I saw a taxi pulling up on the other side of the street and I waved at the driver. I didn't want to ask Benelli to repeat what he had just said in case it had been a joke. After all, Benelli had built his reputation in comedy.

'Sure,' he whispered. 'I got a place on the shoreline. A place where a writer can write. A place where you can see the sun go down. You can't write in a place like this, Karl. It's like Dante's Inferno but cold. That your fucking taxi?'

'Yes, I think it must be . . .'

'You think that's him? Jees, he's smoking a cigarette. You can't write in a place like this. You come out to the States, Karl, and dry out a little. You know what I mean?'

Benelli looked deep into my eyes one last time and he shook my hand. He squeezed it hard, to let me know that his handshake meant something. Then he dashed into the rain to the taxi. As he opened the cab door he turned back to me and called out, 'I'll have my people mail you an air ticket to Tampa. You fly out maybe Monday or Tuesday next week. I got to speak to some people first. You want one way or return?'

'Return,' I shouted. Benelli ducked into the taxi. Just as the cab was pulling out into the traffic, Benelli wound down his window. I stepped out into the rain, the water turning to something like tears in my eyes.

'Things will work out fine,' Benelli said as the cab splashed by me. 'I had an omen.'

The next day, a first-class air ticket was delivered to my house by courier. So I rented out the house and my office, wrote a long letter to Sarah, packed my old Singer typewriter and some clothes, and then flew out to Tampa Bay. At the airport, I discovered there was a red Pontiac Firebird hired in my name and paid for for three months. There was also a message in the rental office, giving me the address of my new apartment. I drove two hundred miles down Highway One, heading south and west over a dozen bridges across the ocean, until the highway finally ran out on the island of Key West.

Benelli finally phoned me in my room at noon. Ms Lisson was already halfway through her morning workout above my head, and I had to plug my ear to hear Benelli's voice.

'So you went and took a look around the penitentiary,' he said. Benelli was calling from his office, and I was having trouble making out what he was saying. The lines out of Key West aren't the best – someone told me that they get nibbled by grunt fish – and Ms Lisson was making the whole house rock on its foundations. I told Benelli that I'd seen the penitentiary and made lots of notes.

'So when Max gets nailed for the murder, you got a place to put him,' Benelli said.

'Yes.'

'And you talked with the cop?'

'Baxter?'

'Yeah, Baxter. He looked after you OK?'

I told Benelli that Baxter had told me everything that I needed to know. A little shower of grey plaster fell from the ceiling under the weight of one of Ms Lisson's footfalls.

'So you're doing OK and you're getting the feeling,'

Benelli said. 'Hell of a feeling that house has got, hasn't it, Karl?'

'It really does have something special about it,' I said, knowing that Benelli was immune to irony. 'The house is fine and the car is fine and the feeling is fine, but I really would like to see my contract soon.'

There was a long silence.

'Mr Benelli? You said that I'd have the contract and the waivers in my hand by last Tuesday latest.'

The phone line quivered. Ms Lisson took a break. Finally: 'Is it money you need, Karl?'

'No, I'm OK for money for the moment, Mr Benelli. But I really would like to see the contract.'

'Sure, sure . . .' The voice was swallowed again. Then it came back louder.

'You see, Karl,' he said, 'things are moving pretty quick at this end so maybe you can give me a little slack on the contract. The important part is that you're getting the thing on track and working on the feeling. Hell of a feeling that place has got, hasn't it? Seen the sunset?'

'Yes, I've seen the sunset.'

Clark had been right about the Gulf of Mexico sunset, and about the room having the best damn vista on the island. He'd also been right about Ms Lisson, who, he had explained one morning without me asking, was 'real serious about getting into shape'. She was back in the traces and pulling hard. Benelli said something but the howling on the line swallowed it.

'What was that, Mr Benelli?'

'I said I guess I can mail you your contract today. Right away. But when you get it, there'll be some stuff you'll want to talk to me about but you don't need to call me because I'm coming down there in person.'

Another howl, another crash from up above. I didn't

like the note of apology in Benelli's voice, nor did I like his certainty that I'd want to discuss the contract. Most of all, I didn't like the idea of Benelli turning up on my doorstep.

'I got to tie up some things here, then I'm taking a plane,' he said. 'Give me two days, or maybe three. I got a lot of things I need to explain. About the contract and the murder in the second act. You see, Karl, I got some ideas of my own. But remember, Karl, it's the feeling that counts. You get the feeling of the place and we'll have ourselves a movie. Oh yeah, I was just telling the girls here in the office, I had another omen. Looks like this thing is going to go all the way.'

'That's nice.'

'Sure it's nice. But I guess you want to get back to your typewriter. Write up the scene in the pen. Maybe put that cop in it too. I'll see you in two days, Karl. Maybe three.'

After that, either the line went dead or Benelli hung up.

Before I left London, I'd asked a few of the friends who were still speaking to me and who were in the business about the kind of procedures I should expect in dealing with a Hollywood studio. Benelli had fitted their description of a Hollywood producer perfectly, almost too well: talking like a sawn-off machine-gun, restless, insensitive and ambitious, not just for himself but for everyone he dealt with. If I had wanted to cast a studio executive, Benelli would have been it. But I'd also been warned that at every stage of the script's development there'd be a whole crowd of people who'd want to touch the ball, who would want to put their blue pencils through characters and scenes and directions, even people who weren't writers. *Especially* people who weren't writers. I had been told that the development of a movie was a team effort, with the writer working alongside the director and the casting people and studio executives and producers. But the way things had worked out so far, it was just me and Benelli and a few conversations and nothing at all on paper. I'd not had so much as a script meeting. There didn't seem to be anyone to have a script meeting with.

After I put the phone down, I knew I had no choice but to wait around and get the feeling, as Benelli had instructed. I had developed a daily routine of leaving the house at eleven and walking down to the shrimp docks where the fishing boats were moored. There were two docks on the island, one for pleasure cruisers and sports fishermen, and one for the commercial fleet. I preferred the commercial area, where the smell of rotten fish and oak smoke made the coffee taste better, and there was always a place to sit because all the fishermen (Cubans, Jamaicans, some of them smugglers) were out at sea. Since I had arrived in Key West, I had decided to rewrite the final scene and set it in the shrimp docks, so I told myself that my foggy-headed visits were some kind of research. The final scene would have Max and Laura, newly divorced, leaping into the ocean right in front of the café where I normally ate breakfast, screaming and naked and realizing at last that they really were in love with each other after all. (All the scenes were awful, but at least this scene had some dialogue that I believed in.) They'd kiss and say they were sorry and they didn't mean any of it, and they'd splash in the water, crimson with the sunset, Laura shouting that she'd never loved that dumb copywriter anyway. All the people in the café where I sat would laugh and say 'Isn't that the sweetest thing?' as Max sang 'la, la, la'.

Most mornings, as I ate my fish soup, drank my coffee and read my copy of the *Key Wester*, the café was

27

empty, except for the Cuban owner and a blond lady who seemed about as lost for something to do as I was.

The morning of Benelli's phone call, she came over to my table and asked if she could borrow my newspaper. I said, 'Sure, go ahead,' and realized she was the first person I'd spoken to on the island apart from Clark and Baxter and Ms Lisson in the entire time I'd been there. The only other time I'd opened my mouth to speak were when I walked over to the dockside some mornings, shading my eyes from the glare, looking into the water at the naked, refracted figures of Max and Laura splashing around in the ethereal silence, saying half out loud to myself, 'Are you happy now, Max? Really happy? Tell me, how does it *feel*?'

CHAPTER THREE

The next person I spoke to on the island was the postman who delivered the Mallory Street mail and who told me his name was Crazy Jimmy. I beat him to the mailbox the morning after Benelli's phone call, as he wheezed up through the thistles and vines that choked the front drive, waving a large brown envelope at me and saying, 'You're fifteen seconds late one morning and already folks are mooching through their mailboxes saying where the hell is that crazy postman.' He asked me if my name was Karl Stone and I told him that it was.

'Ain't that weird?' he said as he handed me the envelope. It was postmarked New York and I felt the plastic ring binding inside. I guessed that at last it was the contract Benelli had promised me.

'What's weird?' I said with a laugh, suddenly buoyant and filled with hope.

'It's weird that you are Karl Stone,' he said. 'You see I know the name of every man, woman and child on my beat and then I see this name "Karl Stone" at 1131 Mallory Street and I think now either somebody's got it wrong or somebody's moved in. And I've been rolling it around in my mind all morning and thinking, I wonder who this new guy is at the movie house. And then, just when I'm about to put the letter in the mailbox, here you are in person. Now *that* is crazy.'

I nodded my head and said it really was crazy.

'Guess you're wondering why I call it the "movie house",' the postman said.

'The what?'

'The movie house. I call this the movie house. Guess you want to know why.'

The postman, short, grey, grizzled, seemed to find everything amusing in some secret way. He'd taken off his blue and yellow cap and was scratching his head.

'Didn't you know, Mr Stone?' he said. 'They call this the movie house because it's where Bogart and Bacall stayed when they were shooting *Key Largo*. Used to belong to Warner Brothers Pictures. Monroe stayed here once too, when she was going crazy. And that little Italian fella. Edward G.'

I was anxious to get down to the shrimp docks and start poring over the contract but the mention of the movie *Key Largo* took my attention. It was my favourite movie of all time, the movie that had made me want to write screenplays in the first place. But before I could raise my eyebrows and say, 'Now that really *is* crazy,' Crazy Jimmy handed me another envelope. It was a letter from the Chase Manhattan bank and it was addressed to Ms Lisson.

'And I guess you don't even know about her either, do you?' he said, as if I'd agreed to play a guessing game.

'Who?'

'The lady on the envelope. Miss Lisson.'

'What about her?'

Crazy Jimmy liked my ignorance. He chuckled and flicked his cap back on his head.

'Why, she's a movie star. At least she was. Back in '71, '72. I saw the picture over in Marathon. Called *The Last of Love*. Comedy. Didn't make me laugh too much. She was cute though. Tough-looking but cute. It was with old Tony Curtis. She whacked him one across the face. That was the funniest part.'

'She was an actress?'

'Sure. Still looks pretty hot to me. Guess you're the lucky one.'

The postman sifted through his other letters and handed me a bill from Florida Electric for Clark. I put it in the mailbox, along with the letter addressed to Ms Lisson.

'I'm a kind of a movie fanatic,' Crazy Jimmy said as if this were a great confidence. 'I keep video tapes of all those old pictures. Scarlet was her name. Before it was Lisson. Scarlet Timberley. Weird name if you ask me. Weird name for a kike.'

The postman grinned some more and then walked back down the path. Ms Lisson a movie star? Maybe I had seen her face somewhere before after all. I walked quickly along the bleached sidewalk of Duvall Street, past the bars and cafés where doors were being flung open and debris broomed out into the street. Duvall Street could be a pretty wild place in the evening, with its uneasy mix of beach bums and weekenders from Miami and serious, serious gays: moustaches, tans, the smell of cologne and recklessness. The contract under my arm was making me walk fast, making the sun ten degrees hotter. Things were opening up. Maybe the shadow I had been living under for three weeks was beginning to lift. Ms Lisson was a faded movie star and all that working out above my head made sense because that was the kind of thing that faded movie stars did. In the movies. And that old house had given me the shivers because Bacall and Bogart had stayed there once, and maybe they'd left their black and white images somewhere between the eaves and the walls and the rotten gable ends.

When I reached the café, I ordered my usual bowl of fish soup and pot of coffee. The Cuban bar owner gave me a smile that morning, and from the corner of my eye I could see the blond lady writing a postcard. I opened the brown envelope and saw that the contract was accompanied by a letter from Benelli:

KARL,
I've had some trouble with the studio. Personal stuff. I've been working for some time on ways of setting up my own operation and the studio have started to reel me in. I told them to go to hel [sic]. What this means is that I'm making my own contracts and the contract inclosed [sic] is between you and G. F. Benelli. I'm getting registered this week with the Union and the Writers' Guild and I'll be working out of the Delancey Street office for a while. After that, I'll be at home. The phone and fax numbers are on the contract.

Everything else is the same as before. I'll pay the rent on your place out of expenses. I need to see a second draft quick so get it as near finished as you can by the time I get down there which will be tomorrow or maybe the day after. By the way, I got the perfect person to play Laura. Best wishes,

G. F. BENELLI

The contract itself was a standard S-Productions contract with the name of the studio Snopaqued out and 'G. F. Benelli' typed over it. I lit a cigarette and found that my appetite had subsided. I suddenly felt a little seasick.

'You finished?' the bar owner said, wiping his hands on his apron. The blond lady was just getting up to leave.

'Sure,' I said. 'I'm really finished.'

'You want to go fishing? Real cheap. Good boat. Skipper's real lucky.'

'No. I don't fish.'

'You should. Good day for sharks today. Nice and hot.'

The Cuban bar owner must have seen a lot of gringo

customers in his life. He didn't even remember that he'd said exactly the same thing to me the day before, and the day before that. Every day he waited for longer than was comfortable, and every day I shook my head. This day was no different, but I had more to feel negative about.

Somebody had told me before I left London that there was a natural career progression for Hollywood producers. They nearly all started as agents for stars before they became producers, then, when they were spent as producers, they became 'indie producers'. Which meant that they left whichever studio they were working for and tried to go it alone. 'Going indie' was almost always a euphemism for being fired. And after 'indie producer' the next step could be anything from window cleaner to swimming-pool salesman to bar-room bore. Indie producers hardly ever made it, except in their dreams. The Cuban bar owner was still standing over me and he was grinning.

'Maybe you don't wanna go fish for sharks,' he said. 'Maybe you wanna go fish for ladies.'

I thought that it might be a general observation, the sort of thing two guys might say to each other on a hot day. Maybe the first step towards familiarity. If that was what he wanted, he'd picked the wrong moment. But he was looking at me in a peculiar way, and pointing with his chin.

'You see that blond lady,' he said, 'the blond lady just walking over to the dock?'

I looked up at him and the glare from the ocean made me squint. The sunlight, which only a few minutes before had been filled with hope, had suddenly become glaring and uncomfortable. The blond lady had left her table and was heading for the line of moored fishing skips in the dock, hitching up her shoulder-bag as she walked. She was lean and angular, and she moved with forced casualness, as if she knew we were looking at her. The bar owner had his hand on my shoulder and I thought he was going to make some remark about her body.

'She's very attractive,' I said, turning back to my contract.

'Sure. Sure she is. And I think she likes your ass.'

'She what?'

The bar owner was shading his eyes, watching her shadow slip behind the boat.

'I say I think she likes your ass. I think you made a hit. She asks all kinda questions. Asks me if I ever talk with you about your work. I say, "No, ma'am, the guy's a quiet kinda guy," and she says "oh", like that. Asks if you drink brandy or coffee. I think she likes your ass.'

The bar owner's grin turned into a prim and elaborate wink. As he disappeared back into the bar, he called out, 'If it was me, man, I'd be going fishing right away. And I wouldn't need no boat.'

It was at two that morning, after I'd finished chomping on the manual keys of my typewriter, that I first spoke to Ms Lisson.

I had gone out on to the stairs to take a breath of clean air because my room was full of cigarette smoke. Just after sunset, the mechanism of the script had miraculously freed itself, and I had been working for eight hours without a break, trying to get some sort of structure together that I could show Benelli when he arrived. The new contract was perplexing; it was almost certainly bad news, but I had managed to bury the problem. I hoped that by applying myself to the work, I could make it seem more real, and my anxiety had served to kickstart the writing process. I hadn't thought about Benelli or the new contract, or Sarah or the cows that skip and go 'La, la, la,' at all. Then I heard

34

the front door slam and heard Ms Lisson walking up the stairs.

She came up slowly, as if she were limping, and when she appeared on the landing, in a strip of yellow light from the street lamp outside, I could see that she was drunk. Her eyes were half closed and she was resting heavily on the banister for support. I could smell the booze on her breath and on her clothes. I couldn't see her too clearly, but I could see that her face was grey.

'Hello, Miss Lisson,' I said quietly.

'Who the hell is that? Oh Christ. It's you.'

She tried to edge her way around me but the landing was narrow and she stumbled into my chest. She swayed around the banister and sighed heavily.

'You wouldn't want to help a lady to her room, would you?' she said.

I pretended not to hear and stared at her in silence. After eight hours of writing, everything is fictional.

'I said would you mind helping a lady to her room.' She blinked slowly '. . . Ah forget it. I'll be OK. Little fucking shit. Not you, the other guy. Don't you trouble yourself. I'll make it. If you can run fifteen miles clean around an island you can make it up a few little stairs, isn't that right?'

'Miss Lisson,' I said as she took the first step. 'My name is Karl. Karl Stone. I'm your neighbour.'

I stretched out my hand but she didn't turn around.

'I understand that you and I are in the same business,' I said.

She carried on up, taking the last few steps on her hands and knees. She was wearing a tight-fitting woollen dress that climbed up the back of her thighs as she bent over, and I glimpsed the tight muscles flexing as she rose to her feet.

'You didn't see me like this, OK?' she whispered, and

put her fingers to her lips. 'Not like this. It's a secret. You understand, Mr Stone? Secret.'

She smiled down the stairs at thin air and then fumbled for a key. Her body was deflated, crumpled. She unlocked her door and disappeared and as the sound of the door closing fell away, a chill ran through the house. The shadows of branches and leaves moved silently across the skylight on the landing outside her door, and something made me turn away, like a child not daring to look into the darkness. I thought about the black and white images that might have been left behind in the house, stuck between the plaster and the walls, and I remembered the way Clark's eyes had glistened when he led me up the stairs. A few days after I had moved into the movie house, I had met Clark on the landing and, for no reason, he had told me that the old colonial houses on the Keys often have huge snakes living in the cellars. Sometimes fifty feet long. I could hear his voice in the darkness, telling me how those old snakes get stuck under the floorboards because once they get inside the cellars there are so many rats and mice down there they get just too damn fat to slide back out again. After Ms Lisson had closed her door, I thought I could hear the serpent shifting beneath my feet.

An idea came to me. Back in my room, I tore up the sheet of paper that was still in the typewriter and I began to write a new scene. In the script as I had it, Laura worked out every day and preached a lot about eating the right food and staying in shape. She was English. In the new scene, I wrote Laura as an American. And I wrote her coming up the stairs of the family home stone drunk. I had her pausing on the landing to scream as loudly as she could that she was drunk and glad of it. Then I had her heaving a large and ugly Grecian urn down the staircase. Then I tore this page up too and instead I had Laura confessing to Max that she'd been drinking Portuguese rum out of the kitchen cabinet for the past ten years and that she hadn't been sober for five. It was a straight scene, filled with tender confessions and declarations of love, and when I read it back, I realized I had achieved new levels of awfulness. It was, without doubt, the worst thing I had ever written. Possibly the worst thing that anyone had ever written. Benelli was right. I couldn't write pain and love to save my life. And now wasn't the time to be making these kinds of changes to the characters. It was four in the morning. Upstairs, Ms Lisson had begun to tramp on the floorboards again. I heard her lie down on the floor and the unmistakable grunt of her sit-ups. There was a new poignancy to the sounds. But what really mattered was that Benelli was on his way from New York and my script was still half unfinished. That and the fact that for the first time in over a year, someone, somewhere (blond, shy, angular), had actually liked my ass.

CHAPTER FOUR

'I got the perfect person to play Laura,' Benelli said as he pushed past me into the hallway. 'And I think you already know who she is.'

I showed Benelli up the stairs, which he took three at a time. His energy and the loudness of his voice felt out of place in the gloom of the old house, as if his exuberance would blow out the walls. It wasn't until I saw him bounding up the stairs that I realized the damp, musty air in the place had been having a narcotic effect on me.

'Jesus Christ,' Benelli said when he showed him into my room, 'what have you been doing in here, burning the bedding, what?'

I opened a window to let out some of the stale cigarette smoke. Benelli looked well scrubbed and neatly turned out in a pink tennis shirt, dark grey slacks and leather loafers with white tassels. Even his clothes looked out of place in amongst the run-down and beaten-up furniture.

I offered him coffee.

'I don't drink coffee,' he said, though I'd seen him drink it in London. 'Got water?'

I ran him a glass of tap water, which he took with half a smile.

'Very funny,' he said.

'What is?'

'You drink water from the faucet? This stuff comes straight out of the swamp. Still got alligator piss in it.'

I handed Benelli a handful of papers, the parts of the script I'd managed to complete the previous night. He took them on his knee and began to flick through them as he talked. He didn't look at any of the pages for longer than a few seconds, long enough to read two or three words. He shuffled them as if they were playing-cards, or photographs of strangers.

'I said I've got the perfect person to play Laura. She's everything we need . . . what's this?'

I angled my head to read the page he was holding up.

'That's just an idea,' I said. 'It's nothing. I just thought maybe that Laura could be something more than just . . . I thought that maybe she could have a problem. Something . . . I don't know, like a drink problem. Even though she pretends to be a health freak.'

Benelli tightened his lips and shook the piece of paper in his hand. His face reddened.

'You see, Karl! You see! This is fucking fate, isn't it! I told you I got an omen.'

Benelli reached into his pocket and produced a pair of spectacles. He put them on and began to read furiously. He looked older and kinder in his glasses. He kept murmuring 'beautiful' under his breath as he read. I felt embarrassed, because I knew that it wasn't.

'So she's American and she's a lush,' Benelli said, returning his spectacles to his pocket. 'That's perfect. You'll see that it's perfect when you hear who I've got in mind to play the part.'

Somehow, Benelli's enthusiasm confirmed my suspicions about him. I decided I would have to speak bluntly, right now, before this thing got any further.

'What about Warner Brothers?' I asked.

'What *about* Warner Brothers?'

'It is Warner Brothers who are interested in the script, isn't it? This would be a radical shift, wouldn't it? Shouldn't you check it out with someone?'

Benelli looked offended. I knew straight away that he knew what I was getting at.

'What, don't you trust me to deliver, Karl?'

'I trust you, Mr Benelli. But this business with the studio. This new contract.'

'What about it? You don't want to sign?'

I had been working as a writer for ten years. I should have been wise enough and direct enough to have dealt with the situation. Benelli's stare was unnerving.

'You obviously don't understand the movie business,' Benelli said. 'People move around all the time. So I leave S-Productions. So what? That's just a mailing address. It's Benelli you're dealing with. I know people. Hey, listen to me, Karl. Who's paying for this apartment? Huh? Who got you over here? I got plans, Karl. Big fucking plans. You want to deal with Warner Brothers direct you call them up right now and offer them your script. See what they say. You listening to me, Karl?'

When he was angry his chest puffed up like a bullfrog. I found myself retreating from him, since I was unfamiliar with this kind of rage. I'd always found it impossible to lose my temper, except when I was very drunk. I hadn't lost my temper without a belly full of alcohol since I was eight or nine years old. The absence of fury can make life hard and dull. That was why I had taken to drinking in London. It was pure distilled fury that in the end had come out once too often and turned the tables on me. Benelli's temples were pulsating and he reminded me of Broderick Crawford playing an angry sheriff in some movie I thought I'd forgotten.

'I'm not saying that I don't trust you. It's just . . .'

'You listen to me, Karl,' Benelli hissed. 'This script of yours. It's nothing. There are a million scripts out there, just blowing around in the breeze. And if you want it straight this script of yours ain't the best of them. You just got lucky it was me who saw it and it was me who got the feeling out of it. Things change all the time in this business, Mr Stone. This ain't real estate. And if you put this pile of shit to Warner Brothers without me they'd laugh at you. Or maybe they wouldn't. They'd say, "What's this? Comedy?" You got a lucky break meeting me, Karl, and maybe you should remember that.'

'I didn't mean that you aren't somebody in the movie business,' I said. 'It's just that if you aren't representing S-Productions then who are you representing?'

Benelli began to chuckle. His eyes were hard and glassy.

'This is a joke, right?'

'No, it's not a joke. It's just all a bit confusing, that's all. When we spoke, I thought I was dealing with a . . . studio. But now, it seems that it's just me and you.'

Benelli walked past me into the kitchen. He found the telephone as if he'd lived in the apartment all his life.

'Who are you calling?'

'My secretary in New York. To tell her it's all off.'

'No. Wait.'

'Hello, Grace . . . it's Giorgio . . .'

'Mr Benelli, wait. I didn't mean that . . .'

'Sure, Grace, I'll hold.'

Benelli put his hand over the receiver and gave me a dead-eyed stare.

'What's it to be?' Benelli hissed. 'Stick with me or throw the whole fucking thing out the window?'

The stories I'd heard in London were coming true, and I didn't like it. I didn't like it at all. I had heard of the Hollywood tradition of corporate cruelty. The acquisitiveness and the duplicity and the greed, as well as the unseemly directness. So far, Benelli had struck me as

41

eccentric but manageable. Now he was acting like a madman. I cut Benelli off by pushing the recall button on the phone, an action which I felt to be daring but in keeping.

'So what? You want to sign the contract?' Benelli said, looking at my hand on the phone.

'I never said I didn't want to sign,' I said. 'You got the wrong impression. I just need to be sure that I'm dealing with . . . with a proper company.'

Benelli imitated my English accent and said 'proper' in a ludicrous way. This made him laugh.

'I didn't mean to offend you,' I continued. 'But this is all new to me. This whole business. And I thought that maybe I would be doing all this work for nothing.'

'Nothing?'

'OK, so you pay the rent.'

'Sure I pay the rent. And what's this? Huh?' Benelli pulled out his wallet and then handed me a cheque. It was made out in my name for $100,000 and drawn on an account called 'Key West Developments'. 'What's this? Nothing? I'm G. F. Benelli. I'm in comedy. You're dealing with somebody here. OK? You just calm down, Karl. Just relax and don't get so excited. I said I'd pay you for your time and I am, aren't I? So let's talk movies.'

I stared at the cheque for a long time. I counted the zeros three times and then put it delicately on my desk: I was worried it might fly away in a sudden breeze. My head was swimming.

Benelli stretched his arms in his sleeves and loosened his collar. His chest began to deflate. I decided to treat Benelli's behaviour as a private joke, and promised myself I would laugh about it after he'd left. The cheque made everything seem suddenly funny. I wanted to pretend that this was a European joke at the expense of a crazy, overwrought American. I even thought that I could use it one day in a script.

'OK, Karl, like I say, I got the perfect person to play Laura.'

I found myself transfixed by the cheque on my desk.

'You got any idea who?' Benelli asked. 'Go on, try and guess.'

I giggled and made a note in my mind that large sums of money make people childish.

'I don't know,' I said, 'Bette Midler.'

Benelli laughed dismissively and waved his hand.

'You think I'd work with her again?' he said.

'OK. Rosanna Arquette?'

'Too young.'

'Glenn Close?'

I was enjoying the game by now.

'Too serious. This is comedy, Karl.'

'OK, I give up. Who?'

Benelli got to his feet and put his head out of the door into the corridor. I heard him shout something and then I heard footsteps on the stairs. When Benelli stepped back inside the apartment, he was accompanied by Ms Lisson, barefoot, in a pink towelling dressing-gown.

'Scarlet Timberley,' Benelli said.

Ms Lisson was wearing no make-up and her hair was tied back in a pony-tail. She'd pulled the hair back tight so that it stretched the skin on her face. She had a faint smile on her face and she tilted her head to one side as a greeting. Her eyes were shining and they looked as hard as diamonds. It was not only a body that had entered the room, there was also a glowing presence that seemed to emanate from under her skin, a look of controlled vigour and total equilibrium. I'd seen it in young healthy heroin users who were only three or four months into their habit. I was momentarily convinced that this was a different woman from the one I'd seen on the stairs. She even had a different voice.

'Hello,' she said in a throaty whisper that could have been dubbed on to her lips by Lauren Bacall.

'Scarlet Timberley,' Benelli said again, as if waiting for a drum roll that had missed its cue. 'What do you say?'

'Miss Lisson,' I said, trying to conceal my total surprise.

'To hell with Miss Lisson, this is Scarlet Timberley. This is her. Scarlet Timberley *is* Laura Hopkins. Isn't she, though? Just look at her. She's Laura.'

Benelli ushered Miss Lisson into the room and she sat down on the bed. She had the look of a concubine being shown to her new master, a mixture of terror and coquettishness. I could see that she'd being worrying and fretting about this moment for days, maybe even weeks or months. For the first time, I began to glimpse the inner workings of some curious engine that had been operating around me ever since Benelli had called me up. I felt as if I'd been set up in some strange way. Cogs were turning. Wires were being pulled.

'We've met on the stairs,' I said, half to myself.

'Sure you have,' said Benelli. 'I'm a smart bastard, don't you think, Karl? Why do you think I put you here in this dump? I wanted you to see her for yourself. I hoped you'd put two and two together but you didn't and that's OK too. But now you see her like this, you've got to agree, Karl. She is, isn't she? She's Laura.'

The cheque for $100,000 was giving off a special kind of perfume on my desk. I couldn't think straight.

'Yes,' I said, almost entirely out of politeness, 'I see what you mean.'

'He sees what I mean! Listen to him, Scarlet! Look at his face! Put your eyes back in your head, Karl. You should see her on camera. Boom! Know what I mean, Karl! Boom.'

Scarlet was still staring at me with that tender smile. It was a look of hope and fear. Impossible to turn down or disappoint.

'So you two know each other?' I said.

Scarlet nodded her head and Benelli laughed out loud.

'Know each other? What do you think this is? A coincidence? You leave things to fate and fate'll fuck you over, if you'll forgive me, Scarlet. I wanted you to be the one to make the suggestion, Karl, but Scarlet tells me you're some kind of monk who doesn't talk to his neighbours so I thought what the hell. It's time to make it happen.'

It hadn't occurred to me that I could have directed a question to Miss Lisson herself. She was an exhibit. She was a curio who sat and smiled and had things happen to her. I thought about all those nights when I'd been irritated by the noise of her insane exercise routine. Benelli seemed to read my thoughts.

'She's been getting into shape for this moment,' Benelli said. 'Working out and staying off the booze. Isn't that right, Scarlet? She's coming back to the land of the living. Back from hell. She's lost sixty pounds and fifteen years off her age. Three months ago she looked fifty. Now she looks thirty. Guess how old she is really, Karl.'

I remembered that Crazy Jimmy had said she'd been a star in '71 or '72. If she'd been a starlet, a young nymph, that would make her around forty. She looked forty, but only sometimes, when she stopped smiling.

'She's forty years old,' Benelli said, triumphantly.

'Is that right?' I said, taking a little of Benelli's sense of mystery and wonder into my voice.

'But what a shape, huh, Karl? A body you'd kill for.'

I needed a cigarette but thought that Benelli might object.

Then I thought what the hell. I lit one anyway and studied Ms Lisson's face. Could this really be the grey lady on the stairs?

'Would you mind if I had one too?' she said in that treacly voice. I was in such a state, I almost gave her the cigarette I was smoking. I finally took the packet over to her and she stretched out her long, slender hand. She looked up at me with her deep, black eyes. It was the look Lauren Bacall gave to Bogart in *Key Largo*, in the bar of the hotel, just before the hurricane struck, when Edward G. Robinson was waving his pistol around. It was a look of total submission and of seduction. Ms Lisson put the cigarette between her lips and waited. I realized that I had my part to play in this scene. I took my lighter out of my pocket and lit the cigarette. She looked up at me again from the bed. Half a smile. A whispered 'Thanks'. This was even worse than anything I could write. Was she really offering herself to me with her eyes, just so she could get the part? This was too absurd. There *was* no part. For all I knew, there was no studio, no contract and no producer either. But there was a cheque, a cheque for $100,000. So maybe it was me who was absurd. Maybe this was how things worked here. Maybe that dull, damp, soporific half-life I'd been living in London was the fantasy. Maybe this was how things played in my new world.

I heard a cruel voice in my head saying, 'How much d'you get for writing "la, la, la"?'

'So I don't need to ask if you agree,' Benelli said, beaming. 'I can read it in your eyes. It says, "Yes please, Mama!"'

I sat down at my desk. The cheque and the pile of papers, side by side. The two things didn't balance. There was something crazy going on, $100,000, I worked out, was around £60,000. I'd written around eighty minutes' worth of dialogue, all of it creaky. Except for the final scene.

'Hey, baby,' Benelli said to Ms Lisson, as if he were talking to a small child, 'why don't you go back upstairs and workout some more. Me and the writer have got some business to discuss.'

Ms Lisson did as she was told. She gave me one last look before she left the room. It was a look of gratitude and total contentment. I suddenly felt immensely sorry for her, and afraid for her.

Benelli closed the door behind her, and then turned to me and clenched his fists, like an excited child. I shook my head and Benelli came over to me and slapped my back. From his side, this was a big adventure and we were the two adventurers. He was filled with the heartiness of the voyage in prospect and his slap hurt. I wanted to tell him to take his hands off me but maybe he thought for $100,000 he could do as he damn well pleased.

What I wanted most of all was a drink to sober me up. I suggested lunch and we walked downtown to Sloppy Joe's. I had the cheque in my pocket, and I could feel the heat of it against my leg. I didn't want to leave it in my room because I was sure that the wind would get up and come in through my window and blow it away. Walking down Duvall Street, I couldn't take my mind off the cheque, and I kept my hand on it as we walked through the crowds of tourists and vagrants and surfers that always gathered around Sloppy Joe's. That's the bar made famous by Hemingway. They say he used to get drunk there every night. There are line drawings of Hemingway on the beer coasters. There are Hemingway T-shirts for sale in the bar. There are stuffed tuna-fish in glass cases above the food area. Benelli said that he thought it would be appropriate to take me there for lunch since I was a great writer too. We walked through crowds of tourists to get to the bar, and found a table near to the window that looks out on to Duvall Street and the Mallory Docks. It was a beautiful bright day and the yachts that skimmed the water in the harbour looked like stranded butterflies.

'I need you to do some more research,' Benelli said, screwing his head around to attract a waitress. 'I need you to go see that cop again.'

'Baxter.'

'Sure. I told you if you want to write a killer you need a guy who knows killers. And I'd say that Baxter is the guy. Pump him on the technical stuff.'

A waitress came and stood at our table, but Benelli carried on talking.

'Tell him we got a guy who wants to murder his wife. I did some research of my own and I found out that, statistically, if a guy's going to murder someone, eight times out of ten it will be his wife. So Baxter'll know about guys who murder their wives. You want beer? Sure you do. Two beers.'

The waitress left the table to fetch the beers, not quite sure that she'd heard the conversation she'd just heard.

'Wait a minute,' I said. 'You want Max to murder Laura?'

'Sure.'

'But what about the other guy. The way I wrote it he murders the other guy. The copywriter guy.'

Benelli shook his head, as if what I had said belonged to a different age, a different movie altogether.

'Statistically, it's got to be the wife,' he said with supreme authority. 'And something else I found out. Seven times out of ten the guy'll kill her in the kitchen. Except in the movie, Max'll do it in the bedroom. Tell Baxter that. Tell him we want a murder in a bedroom and that we want it to look pretty. He'll know what you mean. Sure he will. Cops know that kind of thing. Cops know that murder is a dirty thing but movie people know that it can be pretty too. We want something clean. Strangulation maybe. Sure. Ask Baxter about strangulation.'

Benelli seemed to have lost himself in images of the murder. I didn't like the way Benelli had suddenly assumed total responsibility for the script, even though I had no faith or pride in what I had written myself, and even though interference was exactly what I had been waiting for for three weeks. I also didn't relish the idea of another meeting with Baxter. The beers arrived and I took a long drink.

'Does it have to be Baxter?' I said casually.

'Sure it has to be Baxter. He likes you. When I called him up this morning he wanted to know who you were. I said you were some big-shot writer who worked with Olivier. Dumb-ass policemen. He said he wanted to know who you were *really*. I told him that he should show you some respect because writers get hurt easily. You're going down the precinct tomorrow. Buy the cop a beer and pump him. He said he'd give you an hour. I said, wow, big favour, sure you can spare the time from fishing spiks out of the bay? Sure. I know how to deal with cops.'

Benelli took a swig of beer and grimaced. I got the feeling that he was drinking it just to please me. I drank my half pint down in two swallows and waved my arm for more.

'When we write the second draft,' Benelli said as the waitress brought us two mugs of beer and a Hemingway ashtray, 'we can open up a little. Now that we know that we've got Scarlet. Scarlet gives us opportunities. She's got range. She can do the hard stuff. We can maybe push Max into the background a little more. That way, when Scarlet gets murdered, boom.'

49

The beer had put a shine in my eyes. The air in Key West is freshened every evening by sea winds from the Gulf. At midday, it fizzes in the sunlight. Outside, a man with bare feet was playing a guitar on the street and singing a Bob Dylan song. I was thinking about my final scene, with Max and Laura splashing around in the bay by the shrimp docks, happy at last.

'What do you think, Karl? Huh? About Max?'

I thought for a long time. In the whole ramshackle, tumbled-down horror of the plot, the character of Max was the only thing I had been pleased with. I'd written him as a shambling figure. Not sure of which way to go.

'Sure,' I said, 'Max can go down a notch or two. Why not? If you really think Ms Lisson is that strong.'

My beer arrived. I took two quick swigs.

'Come on, Karl,' Benelli said. 'You saw her back there. She's high explosive. She's a racehorse. She's been kept off the track for too long and she's hungry. She's electricity. Look at her ass for Christ's sake.'

'Yes,' I said, thinking of bone and muscle and sleepless nights. 'Just look at it.'

Benelli's face dropped suddenly. His access to anger was impressive. His eyes died in his face.

'OK, Karl. Here's what you do,' he said. 'You take the cheque down to the First Florida Bank and you open an account. You wait exactly three hours and the cheque will be cleared. Then you'll know I'm for real, OK? You've been making wise-ass remarks all morning and I've let them go because you're a fucking European and Europeans are like that. But you take the cheque and you cash it and then maybe we can talk. I'll see you at your apartment tomorrow at nine. Here, you can pick up the tab. You can afford it.'

Benelli stood up and left the bar. I blushed and felt

suddenly foolish. I returned to the apartment, picked up the cheque and took it to the Chase Manhattan in Duvall Street. The teller made an express clearance call for me and told me that I now had a new account. A savings account with one hundred thousand real dollars in it.

CHAPTER FIVE

Baxter insisted that we meet in a café rather than in his office down at the precinct. He said that he was giving up his lunch hour for me but that he didn't want to give up his lunch too. I drove down to Smathers Beach and met him in a restaurant that had tables outside with thatched umbrellas and the finest bonefish on the island. Baxter ordered a burger and fries.

'So, Olivier, huh?' he said, deadpan, biting into a triple-decker burger with everything.

'Mr Benelli gets a little carried away,' I said. 'I think Olivier was the only English actor he'd ever heard of.'

Baxter wiped his chin. I felt uncomfortable watching him eat.

'If your Mr Benelli had spoken to anyone else at the precinct other than me, they wouldn't have known who Olivier was anyway,' he said. 'Stallone, yes. Sharon Stone, maybe. But, Olivier?'

I was afraid of Baxter. But I liked him at the same time. I liked the way he wore a plaid tie when it was ninety-five degrees. I liked his straight delivery. But I was afraid of what was going on behind those spectacles, behind the eyes. Afraid of what he could smell in the air around me. For the moment he seemed to be giving me the benefit of the doubt.

'Are you a movie lover yourself?' I asked, and he shrugged.

'Maybe you ought to tell me exactly what it is you want to know,' he said. I had a list of questions written in longhand and I got it out of my pocket.

'First,' I said, 'strangulation.'

'What about it?'

'Is there a term for it? A police term?'

'Yes, sir. We call it "strangulation". Next.'

I looked in vain for a flicker of a smile.

'OK, if say you get called to a house and there's a woman inside, dead, strangled, what do you do first?'

'Me? I scream and maybe go "Oh my God she's dead."'

'Oh. Right.'

At last a smile, or at least the ghost of one. He pushed his smeared plate away and fixed me with his unflickering stare.

'I'm sorry,' he said, as if he weren't. 'They told me I was supposed to go easy on you. If we find the body of a woman who has been strangled, that is, with obvious lacerations or marks around the neck, with eyes bulging, maybe blue or black in the face, odour of excrement, maybe urine, then the first thing we do is call in the forensic doctor who'll take the corpse's temperature.'

'Temperature, got it,' I said, writing furiously.

'Then, when we've ascertained time of death, taking into account the ambient temperature in the room, we go looking for the husband.'

'The husband?'

'Eighty per cent of all murders are committed by the spouse or a member of the immediate family.'

I told him that I knew that already and that seventy per cent of those murders took place in the kitchen. He paused and raised his eyebrows before he continued.

'Then, when we've dusted the place for fingerprints, spoken to the old man and the kids, checked the corpse for alcohol or other substances, we take the body to a cold place quick as we can before it starts to smell and fold up and fart all over the place. You not eating, Mr Stone?'

I told him that I wasn't hungry.

'Like I say, most times, the killer is right there in the house when we arrive. And if he's taken off, he's not so hard to find. But run-of-the-mill murder you've got a wife dead and you've got a husband puking up in the bathroom saying he don't know what came over him. You don't have to be Sherlock Holmes, Mr Stone. No, sir. Most times, you're something like a cross between a refuse collector and a marriage counsellor. Most times it's just some dumb family quarrel. Which movie to watch on the TV.'

'Has that ever happened?'

'Sure.'

'And who would you go looking for if there was no husband?' I asked. Baxter thought hard for a moment.

'Is there a husband in your movie?'

'Yes, there is.'

'Then I guess you don't need to worry yourself with that eventuality, do you, Mr Stone?'

Baxter looked at his watch and then looked around the restaurant. There were pelicans landing on the sea wall at the back of the restaurant, and people were throwing bits of fish to them, which they caught in their absurd leathery pouches and gulped down.

'Is the heat bothering you, Mr Stone?' Baxter said. As he said it, I realized that I had begun to sweat. Something about the image of the husband puking. Not knowing what came over him. I skipped several questions and went straight to the last one. It was the question I wanted to ask most of all and it wasn't on my list.

'Just out of interest, have you ever heard of a movie star called Scarlet Timberley?' I said.

'Scarlet who?'

'Timberley. She was in something called *The Last of Love* in the seventies.'

'No, Mr Stone, I can't say that I have. Why d'you ask?'

'It's nothing. I was just curious. I mean, I wondered how big she was over here in the States. I thought that maybe she was a household name, or used to be.'

Baxter couldn't have looked less interested.

'Are you through with the *professional* questions?' he said, and he left me in no doubt that there was only one answer he'd accept. He waved his hand for the bill and all the pelicans took off from the sea wall.

'Sounds like a heck of a movie, Mr Stone,' he said, counting out some bills. 'You find strangulation funny?'

His tone of voice was straight but I could tell from the look on his face that he was quite prepared to believe it. Perhaps, I thought, I should tell Baxter everything I knew about Benelli and Scarlet and the script and the movie house and say, 'There you are, Mr Baxter, you're the detective, you work it out.' Perhaps I could use Baxter to represent that part of me that was getting nervous about this whole project. It was a stupid idea. Baxter was a busy man, a serious man, and he was already itching to leave.

'I do have one other piece of expert advice for you though, Mr Stone,' he said finally. 'As a detective of eleven years standing, I'd make an educated guess that that lady over there, the blond lady – don't turn your head, Mr Stone – the blond lady two tables away to your left, I'd say that she's following you.'

He was talking softly and evenly in a monotone.

'She hasn't taken her eyes off you ever since you got here, and she arrived exactly six minutes after you arrived, just as I would if I didn't want to be noticed. Then she asked for that table specifically – I told you not to look round – she asked for that table so that she'd have a clear view. Now it could just be that she's got the hots for you, but I doubt it. You've got the look of a bad-news, heartbroken divorcee about you that turns women right off. They fix it to your face when you leave the divorce court like putting a bell around the neck of a cat. I'm keeping the conversation going like this, Mr Stone, because I've got the feeling that she's realized we're on to her. OK, you can look now.'

I looked around and saw that the blond lady was paying her bill and leaving. She hitched her shoulder-bag up on to her shoulder. Baxter stood up at the same time and shook my hand and said that he was glad have been of service.

'Be sure and call me up if you need me again,' he said. He waited for the blond lady to disappear down the wooden steps that led to Atlantic Boulevard from the restaurant deck. Then he said, 'Are you in some kind of trouble, Mr Stone?'

I was still staring at the empty table where the blond lady had been sitting. I turned to Baxter and said no, I wasn't in any kind of trouble. At least, not anything that I was aware of.

I drove back to the movie house and found a note in the kitchen from Benelli. It said he had checked into the Madagascar Hotel and that he was going to spend the day working up his ideas. The thought of it filled me with dread. It wasn't until I was back out in Duvall Street, walking down towards the Mallory Docks, that I wondered how the hell Benelli had got into my room to leave the note in the first place. This new anxiety took its place among all the others, a clutch of runners all going neck and neck, all heading for the same finishing line. Even the money, the hundred grand, wasn't like real money, not like a payment or a salary cheque. It was a weight in my mind. A question. If Benelli wasn't with S-Productions any more, where the hell did the hundred grand come from? As I reached the lime-white concrete of the dock area, my anxiety about the blond lady took the lead. The concrete reflected the sun and when I sat down on a bulbous iron docking hook, the metal was hot. Maybe Baxter had got it wrong. Maybe she wasn't following me at all. Think about it, why would anyone want to follow some guy who was writing a movie? A complete stranger in a strange town. Baxter was a cop and sometimes cops had one-track minds.

Key West harbour was dotted with yachts and pleasure craft and moored dinghies bobbing gently on the glassy ocean. The Pier House and the green island in the middle of the bay, with its swooping pelicans and gulls all made a hazy, panting picture of calm, of things happening the way they should. But projected on to the scene, like a transparency on an overhead projector, were all these crazy lines and possibilities, shooting out in every direction, with faces attached, and little pieces of conversation. I tried to put together all the possible reasons why the blond lady would be following me around the island. There weren't any. It was a pity that Baxter had dismissed the idea that she just simply had the hots for me. He had done it with such aplomb, with such assuredness, that the idea had instantly seemed ludicrous.

The only idea that made any kind of sense was that that shithead of the singing, dancing cows had persuaded Sarah to sue me for divorce. Maybe he had talked her into putting a private detective on my tail to come up with evidence of adultery, or something worse. It was bizarre, but it was the only explanation I had.

A large tug cruised across the bay, faster than was seemly on a day of perfect calm. It was high-hulled and brilliant in its blue and white livery. 'US Coastguard' it said, and there was a machine-gun mounted on the fore-deck, and some deck-hands in uniform preparing to dock. Tagging along behind it, pulled by a tow rope, was a tiny row boat, no bigger than ten foot by three, with the wash of the bigger boat almost flooding its gunwales. Inside the little row boat were around a dozen Cubans, all sitting facing inwards with their hands between their knees. They didn't want to turn around and look up at the smart Front Street restaurants, the shiny Pier House, the pretty lines of flags of all nations in front of the Harbour Lights restaurant, because that would just be too painful, because soon it was all going to be taken away. I felt like that too. The coastguard vessel carried on past the Mallory Dock, heading for the US Navy annexe at Garrison Bight, two miles further along the coast. There they would be unloaded, questioned, searched and then locked up in Baxter's tank until a boat could be fixed up to take them back down to Havana, or as near to Havana as was possible. Then they'd be cut loose, maybe to try it all over again.

'Say, Mr Stone,' said a wheezy voice behind me, 'how's the movie house?'

Crazy Jimmy had a long fishing-rod and a four-pack of beer. He was wearing shorts and sandals, and his legs looked warped and muscly from all that walking, carrying the mail. From being all alone on this island, it suddenly seemed that I had a whole crowd of people just dying to find out more about me. I told him that the movie house was just fine.

'Looks like they got some more spiks,' he said, looking out to sea. 'Those spik fishermen get the best hauls on the island. Better even than the shark fishermen. Me, I go for grunts and mackerel. Want to tag along?'

I said that I had some things I needed to take care of and he was about to set off for the quayside with his rod and his bucket of bait when he remembered something.

'By the way, Mr Stone,' he said. 'I had some lady this morning asking me all kinds of questions about who lived at the movie house. She said she wanted to know your name. She was kind of pretty, Mr Stone, and she didn't look like she had any harm in her. I hope you don't mind, Mr Stone. I only told her your name.'

I thanked Crazy Jimmy for letting me know and headed off, with some vague ideas in my head, for the café at the shrimp docks. After I had ordered my third brandy, I asked the Cuban bar owner if he could tell me exactly what it was that the blond lady had asked him about me. He looked down at me, anxious to get on to the next table where someone was waving their arm for service, and said, 'Say again?'

I realized that he had no idea what I was talking about, that he had forgotten who I was and that he had forgotten the conversation we'd had two days before. As I had suspected, he'd had a lot of gringo customers in his life, and Key West isn't the kind of place where you look too hard at people's faces.

'You want go fishing, sir?' he said at last. 'Good day for sharks. Nice and hot.'

CHAPTER SIX

Benelli came round at eight thirty. I was hung over,
draped like a spider over the back of a hard wooden chair,
staring out at the sunshine and sucking an indigestion
tablet. Benelli had said he would come round at nine,
and I wondered if he would still be angry from the day
before. But when he stumped into my room waving a wad
of tightly written script, I knew that yesterday was forgotten. Or maybe it was even that, as far as he was concerned,
what happened the day before was just routine. In his
eyes, there was nothing to forget.

'I got some ideas,' he said, his eyes brimming with
excitement. 'I stayed up till four. Saw the sun rise. I
looked at my watch and thought, Jesus Christ it's four in
the morning and I'm still writing. Like my pen had a life
of its own. Like a machine you can't switch off. Here.
Read it.'

Benelli handed me the wad of paper. There was no
uncertainty in his expression. He wasn't handing it to me
for my approval. He was showing me something he'd
found, a discovery that shouldn't be judged but accepted
with gratitude.

INTERIOR: THE HOPKINS' HOME. LAURA IS IN HER
DRESSING-GOWN . . .
LAURA: Max. I know it's hard.
MAX: Hard? Jesus Christ, Laura.
LAURA: Don't be mad at me, Max. I just can't help myself.

Benelli's handwriting was rounded and legible, like a

child's. I flicked through the pages and stopped at the places where he had underlined pieces of dialogue.

INTERIOR: MAX HOPKIN'S OFFICE. MAX IS SCREWING MARJORIE. HE LOOKS AT HIS WATCH.
MAX: Better finish up, Marj. Laura'll be home.
MARJ: Screw Laura.
MAX: I got to go, Marj. It's Steven's birthday . . .

I glanced at Benelli's wide brown face. He wanted to share my delight. I tried to look thoughtful.

MAX ENTERS THE BEDROOM. LAURA IS ASLEEP. SHE HAS AN EMPTY BOTTLE OF OLD CROW BOURBON IN HER RIGHT HAND. HER NEGLIGEE IS PULLED OPEN. HER HEAD IS BACK AND SHE IS BREATHING HEAVILY. MAX STARES AT HER. HE TURNS OFF THE LIGHT AND PULLS THE BLINDS. HE TAKES OFF HIS SPECTACLES. HE PICKS UP THE PILLOW FROM BESIDE LAURA'S HEAD. HE PUTS IT OVER HER FACE.
MAX: I'm sorry, Laura. I just can't take any more.
MAX HOLDS THE PILLOW DOWN HARD. LAURA STIRS A LITTLE, THEN RELAXES. HER BODY GETS LIMP . . .

My face must have registered some surprise because Benelli stood up and read the page over my shoulder. 'Which part are you reading?' he breathed. I held the script open for him. He smiled at his evening's work.

'I smothered her,' Benelli said softly, 'with a pillow.'

I thought about my research with Baxter. About the black face, the lacerations.

'What happened to the strangulation?' I said.

'That was yesterday. My pen had other ideas. The pillow thing came to me. Just as the sun was rising. Big scene, Karl. Really. The biggest.'

There was so much sober energy coming from Benelli that I had to move over to the window. He took the sheets of paper from my hand gently. He took his spectacles from the pocket of his shirt and began to flick through the pages. He stopped and handed me the last of the sheets and said, 'Here.'

'What?'

'Read.'

MAX IS STANDING IN THE DOCK. SCARED. PASPRAINN . . .

Benelli's handwriting had become illegible. I could feel the anxiety and pressure in it.

'Perspiring,' Benelli said, reading over my shoulder.

MAX BEGINS TO CRY LIKE A BABY.
MAX: I did it. I did it. OK, I did it. I did it for the insurance money.

The page ended there. I stared at Benelli and saw glints of sunlight in the lenses of his spectacles. He had an insane smile on his face.

'What?' I said again.

'Jees, Karl,' he said, 'for a writer you sure are a dumb ass. That's it. That's why he murders her. Max gets the missus insured and bumps her off. So he can go screw his secretary. But this cop finds him out. It's like half of it is building up to the murder, the other half is the court case. And in the end, Max cracks up in the dock. Gets what's coming to him.'

I couldn't help myself. I began to laugh in short spurts and took myself over to the window again to stare out at the ocean. In those few seconds, I had already begun to plan my flight home, the calls I'd need to make to the estate agent who had rented out my house in north London, the calls I'd have to make to some old clients to rustle up some work. I also contemplated how hard it might be to hand back $100,000.

'Pretty good huh?' Benelli said.

'Bloody inspired.'

'Sure. It was the pen you see. I just couldn't stop it working. This whole thing just wrote itself. It's still got some comedy in it too. I adapted some of the stuff you did and sort of polished it up a little. Adapted it for an American audience.'

I turned to him with a broad smile. He looked so full of childlike anticipation that, for the first time, I felt sorry for him.

'I didn't realize that you were a writer of such . . .'

I couldn't think of a word that wouldn't make me laugh out loud again. Things suddenly became clear all at once. I decided that Benelli had been fired from S-Productions shortly after commissioning my script. Maybe even *because* he'd commissioned my script. But he was too bumptious and arrogant to admit it and now he was making a desperate shot at becoming a writer. He was trying to use me and my flimsy idea as a life raft. Other things began to fall into place too. Scarlet Timberley, the washed-out actress. Maybe she was his lover. Maybe he'd promised her a part to get into her pants and now he was trying everything to make his fantasy come true. I wondered how I could ever have believed in it all. Even the house, the rotten, worm-eaten mass of it, suddenly looked unreal. I felt that at any moment I could fall through the floor-boards and find myself in a parking lot, or in the grip of that serpent beneath the floorboards. The only question that still bothered me was how Benelli had got hold of $100,000. The cheque was real. It was the only thing that was.

'I want you to look it over and write it up,' Benelli said.

'If you want to change things, you change them, you're the goddam writer. You're the one that's being paid all that money. We'll call it a second first draft. Call it first draft B. So I'll have to commission you all over again.'

I hardly heard what he said. Above our heads, Ms Lisson had begun to tramp lazily on the floorboards. That sounded funny too. But in a sad way. I had begun to feel something unusual for Ms Lisson. A kind of fatherly concern.

'Here,' Benelli said, handing me a cheque from the pocket of his shorts. 'This is the second commission fee. We'll call it payment for the first and second drafts. But I want results this time. No fucking around mooching. You've got to earn your corn from now on. This is going to go off like the Fourth of July.'

I took the cheque. It was made out in my name for $120,000 drawn from the same account, 'Key West Developments'.

'That makes it two hundred and twenty grand all in,' Benelli said. 'The other hundred and fifty on delivery of the finished piece. What shall we say? Three weeks? More?'

'Mr Benelli,' I said, and then stopped. I meant it to be the beginning of a sentence which would have gone something like 'Mr Benelli, I don't know who you are, or what's going on or where you're getting hold of this kind of money, or even what your exact mental condition is, but I cannot possibly take this cheque. I have never had any faith in this script, and I have even less faith in it now. What you have written is asinine, absurd and impossibly clichéed and to continue to work on the basis that you could function as some kind of co-writer would be dishonest and insane. I therefore return your cheque and terminate our contract.'

64

Instead, I just said 'Mr Benelli', and stared at the cheque.

'So, what do you say?' Benelli said. 'Three weeks, four weeks, five, what?'

'Oh, three,' I said with little hesitation and with great professionalism. 'If I use what you've given me as a framework and just sort of flesh it out ... then, yes. Three weeks.'

'That's fine, Karl. Just fucking fine a doody dandy.'

I had long known that the function of greed is not affected by solvency. Even if I had been solvent, I would have taken Benelli's cheque in the same way. The fact was, in the last few months with Sarah, when things had been bleak, my work had been falling off fast. Two of my shows had failed to get the expected re-commissions. There were some other guys, younger guys, who were wandering into my territory. Sometimes, when I really wanted to feel that exquisite joy of pain recollected in tranquillity, I imagined that it was the falling off of the commissions that had led to the falling off of Sarah's interest. It was, naturally, untrue, but sometimes, after enough beers, bitter accusations hurled at an empty room could be a great comfort. Me losing commissions while old shit-head was collecting some strange piece of burnished metallurgy, some industry award, for the singing, dancing cows.

Hot-shot shit-head and burnt-up Karl Stone.

Sober, I knew that Sarah was better than that. Drunk, she was the devil. And now, Benelli was handing me something other than a cheque. He was handing me justification, the second instalment of two hundred and twenty grand's worth of justification. Sarah didn't really care about money, sure, sure, sure, nobody cared about money, until it wasn't there any more. Sarah wouldn't be impressed by two hundred and twenty grand. Oh no?

The tramping of feet above our heads had stopped. Benelli was studying my face as I looked at the cheque, and I caught him studying my face, and he looked away quickly. Then there were footsteps on the creaking wooden stairs from the attic and a knock at the door. Right on cue.

Scarlet Timberley was wearing a low-cut cotton dress and she was barefoot. I still had the cheque in my hand as I opened the door, and the air around her smelt of lavender. Scarlet wore no make-up but I could tell that she'd put herself together with care. Her hair was up in a bundle on the top of her head, a style I'd never seen on her before. She looked twenty years younger this time and her eyes were shining.

'Baby!' Benelli exclaimed, and waddled across to give her a hug. She was looking embarrassed and sweet and childlike, all for my benefit. She didn't let her face touch Benelli's face when he hugged her. When he let her go, she stood in silence and looked at the floor, as good a rendition of nervous coquettishness as I'd ever seen.

'Baby,' Benelli said again, 'Karl and I have just been cooking up a hurricane. We got it, Scarlet! We've really got a movie! All Karl has to do is get off his ass and do some work for a change!'

Benelli laughed. I put the cheque into my pocket and Scarlet was smiling too. I smiled back at both of them. A pause that was way too long. At my back the sun was beginning to set, spilling its blood into the ocean. Benelli took Scarlet around the waist and he whispered in her ear. She pulled away, mock horrified. He nodded his head with his eyebrows raised, all phoney excitement and play-fulness. He whispered in her ear again and then said, 'Go ahead, baby, ask him. You don't ask, you don't get.'

Scarlet fixed me with a half a smile. I was in the middle of converting $220,000 into sterling when she said,

'Giorgio thinks it would be a good idea if you took me out to dinner.'

Benelli clapped his hands, a tiny explosion of happiness. Scarlet's look of innocence had changed to a phoney look of seduction. Something wasn't right.

'Sure,' Benelli yelped. 'Sure I think it's a good idea. Come on, Karl, be a gent about it, the lady just asked you for a date. Christ, these writers! Come on, Karl, what do you say?'

Benelli was looking from me to Scarlet and back again. Scarlet wasn't giving me any clues, but I knew this whole thing had been set up between them. Their performance wasn't good enough for me not to guess; maybe they wanted me to guess. Benelli was red in the face with enthusiasm.

'The lady wants you to show her a good time, Karl. So come on. You ain't a fag, are you, Karl?'

'No.'

'And you've got to say she is one beautiful lady, Karl.'

'Yes, yes, she really is,' I said. Scarlet and I were staring at each other over Benelli's head, as if Benelli were a fence between us. I imagined two Sicilian lovers staring at each other in the presence of a chaperone.

'So what are you waiting for, Karl?' Benelli said.

Another pause. Scarlet seemed filled with some obscure longing that I couldn't understand. Maybe even trying to tell me something with her eyes.

'But of course I'd love to take her to dinner,' I said, and Benelli slapped my back.

'Then that's settled,' he said. 'You two kids go out and enjoy yourselves . . .' (he really said that) '. . . and Karl, you can put it down as research. If you don't know the lady how are you supposed to put her on the page? You two kids go out and really get to know each other. Peek

67

into her soul, Karl. And, Karl, take her somewhere fancy. Somewhere really, you know . . .' He made some smooth movements with his hands, suggesting something only he understood. Then he said, 'Take her to the best restaurant on the island. She deserves it, and hey, Karl, you can sure afford it.'

Scarlet and Benelli left together, arm in arm, a curious double act, all cuddles and strange looks. After they had left me alone, I sat down at my typewriter and dutifully transcribed the script Benelli had written. It was easy enough to do, and my mind was free to wander. So as the sky grew dark over the Gulf of Mexico, I thought in circles about the cheque, about Benelli and about the script. Most of all I thought about Scarlet.

I knew that I'd just agreed to take her to dinner, but I was also almost sure I had agreed to something else as well. Something that I just wasn't smart enough to figure out.

CHAPTER SEVEN

The next morning I just drove and drove. Benelli had called me up before eight, angling for another 'script meeting' but I told him that I had to go and check out some locations. He hadn't been convinced until I'd told him that I needed to get 'the feeling'. He liked that. Before he hung up he told me that, during the night, he'd been thinking some more about the final scene and had figured that maybe it wasn't so clever to have Max get caught for Laura's murder. He said that courtroom confessions were '88. I wanted to ask whether he meant 1988 or 1888 but of course I didn't. So now, Benelli wanted Max to get away with it. He wanted Max to fool the dumb-ass cops and get clean away. That way, the audience would leave the theatre crying their eyes out for poor little Scarlet. I said that I would think about it.

I drove east along Highway One into the sun, through Big Pine, Marathon, Islamorada and Whale Harbor. The Keys are a string of islands and sand bars, all strung together like pearls on a necklace by a series of huge, ivory-white bridges that span the ocean in great bows of smooth concrete. East was the direction of home, back the way I came. The ocean was twinkling blue, the sand flats golden and livid green. The farther away from Key West I drove, the more a kind of animal joy began to well up inside me. I sang along to the radio and tapped time on the steering-wheel with my fingers.

I didn't stop driving until I reached Key Largo, a hundred miles along the highway and just thirty miles from the mainland. I parked outside the Sunset Motel, and felt the pleasurable slap of heat as I got out of the air-conditioned car. The sea was slopping lazily along the shore, behind the motels and bars and restaurants, and the pelicans were standing on the wooden roofs with their beaks open, cooling off as best they could. The Sunset had a bar area raised up above the beach on wooden stilts, and I took a seat in the shade. The waitress had bleached blond hair, and if the sun had been cooking her these past thirty-five years of her life, she looked just about ready to eat.

'You care to eat, sir?' she said.

'No, I'd just like a very cold beer.'

'We have Coors, Bud and imported. Imported we have . . .'

'Anything. Just cold.'

'Cold beer, sir, coming up.'

When she came back with the beer, I asked her about the huge sign that was hanging over the front of the motel, the sign that had made me pull up in the first place.

'Is this really the hotel where they shot the movie *Key Largo*,' I asked.

'Sure is, sir. Cold enough?'

I sipped the beer and said that it was.

'Of course there's old Sampson over the other side of the highway who claims they shot it in his place. And there's some little cantina another half-mile up the highway where they claim they've still got some of Bogey's cigarette butts so what more proof do you need, and there's Rick's café, he's got a great big neon sign outside saying that the movie was shot there. But heck, this place is the real thing. No question.'

We both looked out over the small inlet and mooring at

the back of the hotel. I thought that I recognized it, tried to imagine it in black and white, narrowed my eyes a little.

'But, on the other hand, if you'd asked me when I worked over at Rick's . . . well, the way I see it, if you believe it, it's true.'

We both laughed. I thanked her for her honesty and she said, 'You're real welcome.'

In the movie, the two brothers, the Seminole Indians who'd been accused of murder, poled their flat canoe into the hotel mooring from a mangrove swamp just a few hundred yards to the south. As they poled their canoe, a six-foot swamp alligator glided through the water, the only part of the movie that didn't quite work. You could see that the alligator was phoney, that it was made out of wood. And right here, where I was sitting, Lauren Bacall had rolled up the sleeves of her white cotton shirt and told Bogart about her Daddy. The hotel bar was behind me, in the shade. And Lauren Bacall and her Daddy said they just didn't believe that those two Indian boys were capable of murdering anybody. And they were right. And it wasn't Bogart who did it either. It was Edward G. Robinson.

I thought about Scarlet and Benelli, stuck together in that hotel bar, waiting for the hurricane to hit, Benelli waving his pistol around. And I thought about myself in there too. Bogart was a tough guy, a war hero, a guy who had medals for violence. A violent man who just wouldn't cut loose and face up to Edward G. because he was sick of fighting or because he was scared or because he didn't have the strength any more. And I thought about the way Bogart stood up to all that stuff, from the old man and from Bacall, not teasing exactly, more like people at a zoo poking sticks at a lion, trying to make him roar. I could roar too, I knew that, but I was scared just like Bogart. Scared of what would come out if I opened the door to the cage.

71

I knew that the waitress had been right. The only thing that mattered was if you believed it. I went and stood against the safety rail at the edge of the bar area and watched the ocean lazily licking at the wooden struts beneath. That was where Bogart had nearly been dragged away into the water by the rip current. I could see his black and white face looking up at me, inside a hurricane, the sea leaping the wooden barrier of the bar and soaking the tables. He only had one arm on the support of the pier, the water crashing over his head. The fury of the waves died in the blinking of an eye, and the water was calm again. I paid for my beer, walked back to my car and sat there for a long time.

That way along the highway was home. Tampa Bay airport, then London. The other way was everything else. I couldn't go home. I didn't *have* a home any more. The only home I had was back at the movie house. I began to think about London and thought that I finally knew what 'homesick' meant. Every time I thought about it, I felt this gnawing sickness inside. The car was hot but I didn't think to turn the air-conditioning on. Distance is context.

At this distance, a hundred miles from the movie house and three thousand miles from London, I could see both places in context. And myself inside them. I thought about the nights when I had cruised through the wet streets of London in taxi cabs, street lights splashing yellow on the pavement, the huddled figures holding their lapels together, the lines of dreary, exhausted shop fronts, and me with my head resting against the cold glass of the taxi window, always drunk or getting there. I remembered Sarah the way she was for the first three years, and the way I was for those same years. All my best memories of Sarah were in the rain or the snow, and when I closed my eyes I could feel the cold air around us. And between those memories, always the darkness of what had happened since, a kind of glue that held everything together but separate.

I thought about those nights in taxi cabs again, about my drinking, drinking even when I didn't want to drink, and I thought about jealousy. The beast that came between us. The sweat that was running down my face stung my eyes, and the sweat and the tears were the same thing. There were still a lot of things about London that I couldn't think about without the pain spilling out. I had my head on the steering-wheel, so I hardly noticed that there was someone inside the car twenty yards to my left. She was staring at me. I became aware of her slowly. She was blond and she had something in front of her face. She managed to fire off two shots before she put her camera down on the passenger seat and started her engine. She was reversing quickly into Highway One while I was still starting my engine. She set off west at full speed, and as I locked the wheels, there was a cloud of dust and gravel from under my tyres. By the time I was back on the highway, there was one car and a truck between us, all of us heading back in the direction of the movie house.

I didn't know much, but I knew now that the blond lady wasn't working for shit-head and Sarah. What use would a photograph like that be in a divorce court? A photograph of some guy sitting all alone in his car and thinking of home and crying like a baby.

But if not that, then what?

My Pontiac Firebird was a recent model and it took to the chase like a thoroughbred racehorse. I had overtaken the car and the truck before we reached the bridge off Key Largo, and I was a comfortable car's length behind her by the time we reached Tavernier Creek. We reached the first set of lights and I was able to see her clearly. I could even see her eyes in her rear-view mirror. They didn't tell me much, apart from the fact that she was looking at me and that she knew I was there, and that maybe she wasn't too concerned. We set off again, first slow and then fast and then slow and then fast, fast, fast. The speed made someone blow their horn, and then a truck blew its hooter like a cruise liner. She slowed again and we hit some more lights.

I probably had time to leap out of the car, but what would I say to her in the three seconds before the lights turned to green? That made me wonder what I would do anyway. What happened at the end of car chases in the movies? This wasn't so much a chase exactly as a kind of stalking manoeuvre. Car chases in the movies end with one car on its roof, or over the edge of a cliff. I thought about those big high bridges that spanned the ocean, the twinkling blue water below. We were moving fast again, eighty, then touching ninety, then back down to eighty. The limit was fifty-five and everyone stuck to it. Everyone. We were doing seventy-five and I was sweating hard. I tried to adjust the air-conditioning and the blond lady dodged in behind a car towing a speedboat. I had no choice but to move up alongside her, so that we were blocking both lanes. I turned my head and glanced at her. She was wearing sunglasses now, and she was staring straight ahead at the road. Her shoulders were bare. I glanced back at her again and someone behind was hooting their horn. She had slowed down to forty so I had slowed down too. She had her camera in her left hand and she was holding it up, pointing it at me without turning her head, firing off shots one after the other, the flash almost blinding me. I got mad. If I pulled in front of her, maybe . . .

Another hoot from behind. I was blocking the outside lane. This wasn't like a car chase in the movies at all. It was slow and the rules of the road still applied. They applied more than ever. I pulled in in front of her and slowed down to thirty.

The bottled-up traffic shot past. I glanced in my rear-view mirror to get a view of her face. I could just make out a snub nose and blond hair tied up in some way. Now the guy with the speedboat was hooting his horn because I had slowed down to twenty-five. Suddenly, the blond lady pulled out into the outside lane and cruised by. I could see her from the other side. I had now seen her from behind, from the front and from both sides, and still she hadn't once looked at me. She accelerated quickly and I knew that I would have to pull out quickly and get after her.

I didn't see the truck before I heard it. A great baleful moan, like the calling of a whale close to. The driver flashed his lights and I could see his silent fury in my rear-view mirror. My heart was pounding and the sweat was still getting in my eyes. Blondie was disappearing around a curve in the road, and when I accelerated, I saw the car towing the speedboat pull into the side of the highway.

We cruised at eighty on to the first bridge. Two miles of bolted concrete, dazzlingly white and effortlessly ugly. So ugly it was beautiful. Some of the fishermen along the side of the bridge turned to watch our progress. We were both doing ninety now, and they seemed to take our recklessness personally.

What would I do if I caught her? I didn't have the faintest idea. I just knew that I had to keep following her, because I had made a resolution to find out who she was and what she was doing. Somewhere between pulling out of the Sunset Motel and nearly being mashed into the road by the truck I had made a resolution. My resolution was fierce at first, but the higher up the spine of the bridge we got, the more I realized that it was phoney. My foot stuck at a hundred miles an hour. She was gaining ground. I thumped the steering-wheel and accelerated. If we were heading in this direction, back to the movie house, then maybe this should be a real car chase all the way. Perhaps this was what I wanted after all. We screamed off the bridge, me just two car lengths behind, the scrubby swamp to the left and right a dangerous blur.

Yeah, yeah, yeah, this was what I wanted. Maybe.

She took off at a speed I'd never even contemplated. The road was empty except for the grey Ford we'd just overtaken. She was a hundred yards ahead, the body of her car shining like silver armour, and I decided that I'd do that impossible speed too. I had my sun visor down and I was gripping the steering-wheel so hard my hands hurt. I became aware of some idiot trying to keep pace with me on the inside lane. That grey Ford.

Not just a grey Ford. A flashing light.

Not just a flashing light, a cop.

Not just a cop . . .

As soon as I stopped, the scrub at the side of the road came alive with sound, the sound of crickets and cicadas, and behind that, the crackle of a radio. The air died and became hot and still. Cars shot past as I took some deep breaths. Blondie was a flash of sunlight on the horizon.

'Hello, Mr Baxter,' I said.

'Hi,' said Baxter. 'Interesting piece of driving.'

'Are you the only policeman on the whole of the Keys?'

'No, sir.'

'Then I must just be unlucky.'

'Would you care to get out of the car, Mr Stone.'

Baxter explained in a quiet voice that he'd had a report of two vehicles exceeding the speed limit and driving in a reckless manner between Tavernier Creek and Islamorada. He said the word 'vehicles' with that formal little hiccup in the middle of the word, on the h. He said that he had been in the vicinity at the time, stopping off at a Mexican place to purchase some burritos for his lunch. However, he said, when the report had come through, since he was in the area and since his senior position didn't exclude him from mundane traffic duty, he had decided to get back on to the highway to see what all the fuss was about.

'Don't you want to write all of this down, Mr Stone,' he said. 'So you can put it in your movie.'

I didn't want to say anything but Baxter's silence made it inevitable. He was staring at me without blinking.

'It was her,' I said.

'Say again, Mr Stone.'

'The woman I was chasing. I mean following. It was the blond woman you pointed out to me in the restaurant. The woman who's following me.'

'You were following the woman who is following you. OK. I guess that makes sense.'

Baxter peered hard at me and sniffed the air.

'Have you been drinking, Mr Stone?'

'One beer. I mean it. You were right about the woman. She really is following me, but I don't know why. She took photographs.'

'Photographs?'

'Yes, bloody photographs. I thought she was a private investigator, but she's not. I think she might be a journalist. Or something. I don't know. Who else takes photographs of people from speeding cars?'

I hoped that my exasperation would set Baxter thinking. My theory that Blondie might be a journalist had only come to me after I had stopped the car. But it had no foundation. I wasn't exactly newspaper material. Baxter abandoned the puzzle.

'I'm sorry,' I said at last. 'For breaking the speed limit. I have my driver's licence here if you want to check it.'

I reached into my pocket. Baxter was accompanied by a uniformed officer, and as I reached for my wallet he made a move to get out of the car. Baxter waved his hand at him and he got back in.

'Mr Stone,' he said, and he put his arm around me. 'You have got me curious. I mean, real curious. Ever since I first saw you down at the tank, I've had this feeling. Do you know what I mean? I've had this feeling about you. Now, if I let my lieutenant back there get out of the car, he'll give you a ticket. If he gets close enough to give you a ticket, he'll smell your breath and he'll take you down to the tank for a blood and urine test. If he hears the reason you were doing one hundred and five miles per hour with alcohol in your blood was because you were taking part in a high-speed car chase through an urban area, then, well, I don't know, Mr Stone.'

I looked around at the cop in the car. Now *he* really was the man I would have cast in my movie.

'What do you say you get back in your car and drive, at no more than fifty-five miles per hour, back to Key West and have a good long think about your future here. Mmm? Why don't you go home and think seriously about packing up all your belongings and taking a flight home to London. I went to London once, Mr Stone. It's a very beautiful city. Here, all we've got is sharks and alligators. Why don't you spend some time thinking about that?'

Baxter gave me a smile. He smiled so rarely that I knew this was a significant moment. He was telling me that this was the last smile I'd get. This was the last time he'd give me the benefit of the doubt. I told him that he was quite right and that, yes, I really did have a lot of thinking to do.

I got into the driving seat and he came and stood in the way of the car door. He leant in so that his face was close to mine.

'I don't suppose you got her licence plate number did you, Mr Stone?'

'Her what?'

'If you'd taken her licence plate number I could have run a check on her.'

I shook my head. My hands were shaking and I was greasy with sweat. Why was I so dumb? I looked up at Baxter with a look of helplessness that made him shake his head too.

'Like I say, Mr Stone,' he said as he closed my door for me, 'you've got me real curious.'

Baxter followed me all the way back to Mallory Street. And when I parked outside 1131, he slowed for long enough to catch the number of the house and then pulled away.

CHAPTER EIGHT

When I got up to the landing outside my room, still damp with sweat from the highway, I heard the floorboards creaking inside, and the sound of someone shuffling papers. I opened the door, which was already unlocked, and found Clark standing over my desk.

'What the hell is this?' I said, and Clark blinked at me defiantly. He was wearing a tight T-shirt and cut-off jeans, and he exuded an air of raw energy. His muscles were pumped full of blood from years of working out, and the strength in his body was translated into an arrogance around the eyes that made me angry. More angry than I was before.

'Hi, Mr Stone.'

'Get away from my things.'

As I crouched to pick up the pages of script that had blown on to the floor, Clark explained to the top of my head that he had been checking the storm shutters. He said there had been a hurricane warning, just a blue one, not an orange one or a red one yet, and whenever there was a hurricane in the air, Sunset Realty made it their business to check all of the storm shutters on all of their properties. Especially the old ones like 1131. I straightened up and stared into his clear blue eyes. The arrogance was still there.

'You have no right to come into my room without my permission.'

He blinked lazily and said he'd tried to call first but I was out. I pushed past him (he was solidly rooted to the

floorboards) and closed the window. I hadn't heard anything about any hurricane warning, and I was pretty sure
some old guy in a bar some nights before had told me that
the hurricane season was over. What needled me most was
that when I had come into the room, Clark had been
standing at my desk, looking at my papers, maybe even
reading the awful script. Clark watched me struggling to
close the window for a while, swollen in its ancient frame,
and then leant over my desk and calmly jerked the thing
shut.

'If you came to check the shutters, what were you doing
at my desk?' I said, peeved at his display of strength.
Clark picked up an envelope and held it up in front of my
eyes. It had my name written on it and I recognized
Benelli's handwriting.

'I also came around to deliver this,' Clark said. 'Giorgio
asked me to give it to you.'

I took the envelope.

'You mean you know Benelli?'

Clark smiled at some private joke and said sure he knew
the sour old bastard. He explained that Benelli had been
renting places in the Keys for years, that he always used
Sunset Realty and that just lately he'd even started to buy
up some of the older property on the island. He said that
Benelli was a good cash customer and that if Giorgio asked
you to do something, you did it. That made him laugh and
slick back his wiry blond hair. He made for the door.

'I don't want you to come into my room again, ever,
unless I personally invite you,' I said to his broad back,
patterned with sweat. Clark mumbled something and I
added, 'Understood?' He opened the door, turned around
and smiled at me.

'What's wrong, Mr Stone?' he said. 'You got something
to hide?'

I was going to tell him to go to hell but he had already slipped out of the door, and I listened to his footsteps all the way down the stairs. I looked at the gnarled window frame and found myself wondering if I could take him on. He was strong, but if I was mad enough I could. I shook my head at my own stupidity, taking pride in something ugly in the way that Bogart never would have as he picked his teeth on the porch of the motel, waiting for the storm. After Clark had closed the front door behind him, I opened the letter from Benelli. It was one sheet, handwritten. It said that a limousine would be arriving at seven forty-five to collect Scarlet and me, and take us to the Benihana restaurant on South Roosevelt Boulevard. It said that a table for two had already been booked, overlooking the ocean. Benelli's handwriting to that point was rounded and legible, but it tightened up for the anxious PS at the bottom.

PS.
You've got to promise me two things:
1. You don't let Scarlet touch the booze. She's off it and she's staying off it.
2. Don't talk about the script. I don't want Scarlet getting any ideas about Laura until I've talked with her. Getting Scarlet juiced up is *my job*.

BENELLI

I put the note down on my desk and scanned the pages that Clark might have seen while he had been standing over my desk. To my horror, I saw a letter, badly spelt, with a rash of xxxxxs to cover up mistakes, rambling and wild and creased where I had finally screwed it up into a ball. Had I smoothed it out or had Clark done that? I didn't remember putting it back on top of my desk. The truth was, I didn't even remember writing it, but I knew

82

that I had done it on the night I had got drunk, the night after Benelli had given me my first cheque. I had come back from the Hog's Breath Saloon and Raw Bar after gallons of pale American beer, too drunk to focus. And I had sat down at my typewriter and I had written a drunken letter to Sarah. I picked it up and read it.

HEY SARAH,
xxxxxxxx
I wanted to write and let you know that Ive writen a bloddy good line. Hooray and hurrah Ive xxxxxxx
My hero, Max, is getting a divorce and someone says, 'Do you still see your wife?' And Max says, 'Only when I close my eyes.'
Get it? You fucking bitch. Youxxxxx Hows shit head of the cows fame. Your a fucking bitch did you know that? Well fuck you ive got this blond woman now and shes beautiful. She told me a xxxxxxx joke. How you stop a woman giving uyou a blow job. Marry her. Get it?

ALL MY LOVE, KARL

This time I tore the letter up into tiny pieces and dropped it like confetti into the metal bin beneath my desk. In London, when I had been drinking, I'd often found letters like this on my desk or in the waste-paper bin, or sometimes left on the stairs or strewn around the kitchen floor. I guess that the urge to write was never diverted by the effects of booze. So even when I was drunk I would sit myself in my hallowed chair in front of my typewriter and commit drunken sacrilege. I could never remember the next day what I had written, and when I found these letters, and read them as I always forced myself to do, it always felt as if I was reading something sent to me by an insane relative, a madman who had stolen into my house in the night. I had hoped that this madman hadn't got my new address three thousand miles away on this tiny island in the middle of the Gulf. But when I read the screwed-up letter on my desk, I realized that he'd caught up with me again, and that now he had my address, he might not be happy just to write to me. He might even start coming around to pay me a visit now and again. He might offer to take me out for a drink.

I still had two hours to wait before the limo arrived, and I spent some time staring out of the window at the sunset. Before the blond lady had almost run me off the road, I had been on the point of making a decision. I had almost decided to turn the car around and drive back to Tampa airport and go home. At least that's what I thought as I watched the sun turn into a scarlet bruise on the horizon. I really wasn't sure if I would ever be brave enough, or cowardly enough (I wasn't sure which), to go back. I realized that distance is only context for a while. After a certain amount of time, and a certain number of miles, distance becomes something else, and the strangeness of this place was beginning to make everything seem fictional. I needed now to grab hold of something solid, I needed to feel something familiar from my old life.

The letter on my desk had made me begin to wonder if I'd really come to this island to escape, or whether it wasn't maybe the exact opposite. Perhaps I'd deliberately put myself on this island as a kind of exile or imprisonment. Or even worse, as a kind of voluntary quarantine. Without making any conscious decision, I found myself on my feet, in the kitchen, with the telephone in the crook of my neck; soon I was listening to a telephone ringing in a flat in London.

'Richard?'

'Yep. Who's that?'

'Karl. Karl Stone.'

'Oh.'

The moment I heard Richard's voice, I knew it was too soon. My old life, all of it, even the best parts, were still too hot to touch. The desire to reach and grab some part of it disappeared in half a second and I would have put the phone down straight away if I hadn't already said my name. I'd worked with Richard for four years. He was a writer who'd co-written the series that first made my name. I'd been friends with him even before we began working together, and he had known Sarah long before he had met me. I suppose that begat a certain loyalty.

'This line is awful,' Richard said. 'Where are you calling from, Karl – Mars, the moon, where?'

'America.'

'America? Should I be impressed?'

'Impressed as hell, you slacker. How any writer with integrity and ambition can still be working in London defeats me. I mean, it's so provincial.'

'Yeah, yeah. Really, should I be impressed?'

'No, not really. Listen, I need some advice.'

I waited for the transatlantic delay and for Richard to make some smart remarks about Karl Stone actually asking someone for advice. Then I told him just about half of the truth of my situation. I dressed up the apartment a little, promoted Benelli, took ten years off Scarlet's age, but still managed to convey some of my unease. I told him the truth about the money I'd been paid and he whistled through his teeth. His flat, sardonic English accent made me feel homesick but also happy.

'Two hundred and twenty thousand dollars?' he said, and I repeated the figure. 'Karl, it's not me you should be asking for advice, you should be talking to a fucking stockbroker. Two hundred and twenty . . .'

'Yeah. I know how it seems.'

In the background, I could hear telephones ringing. Richard had moved into my old office, and I thought I could hear voices that I recognized. I might have been imagining it. I told him that I wasn't sure about the whole thing, even though the money was for real, and that I sure as hell wasn't sure about the quality of the movie I'd written. Richard said I had always been a second-rate writer anyway so why start worrying about it now. Then I told him that in one hour's time I would be taking the leading lady from my movie out on a date, and even that was making me uneasy.

'Just do it,' Richard said. 'Do it, live it, enjoy it, fuck it. What's the worst thing that can happen? The whole thing falls through and you wind up with a hole in your CV. So what? It's not like you to be so . . . I don't know, cautious.'

'Yeah, maybe you're right.'

I could hear more phones ringing and I imagined that maybe Richard might be anxious to get away and answer one of them. I wanted to talk some more because I wasn't sure I had really given him the full picture. The truth was, I didn't know how.

'And this Benelli guy,' I said with a laugh, 'you'll think this is insane but he's an Italian. He reminds me of some kind of Mafioso. I mean this is a lot of money. I've got the feeling that I'm getting involved in something that I shouldn't get involved in.'

Richard said, 'You've been watching too many movies, Karl,' in a singsong voice.

'Oh yes, and another thing. I think I'm being followed.'

'Too much booze, Karl' he said, in the same singsong voice. I laughed and told him that I was off the booze. There was a silence and I guessed that Richard thought he had accidentally stepped into dangerous territory. I knew he wanted to get off the line before the jokes dried up and we had to start really talking. I couldn't let him go without asking the question, the only question I had really wanted to ask.

'By the way, have you seen Sarah?'

'Mmm?'

'Sarah.'

'Yes, she's fine, Karl.'

'Fine?'

'She's better. She's getting better.'

There was a long pause, long enough for the sharks beneath the waves to take the line between their jaws and shake it around. My jaws were clenched tight too. Finally I said . . .

'I can't tell you how bad I've felt since . . .'

'Yeah.'

'Really.'

Richard and I had never talked deeply. Neither of us had ever wanted to. We were just too damn smart and funny to get tied up with saying anything we actually meant. I felt that I was breaking a holy taboo even stumbling into this area of conversation. But I did it anyway.

'What I mean, Richard, is, is she OK?'

'She's getting better. Time is a great healer and all that shit.'

'It is shit. It really is. From my side anyway.'

Richard paused, embarrassed.

'Well anyway, Richard, give her my love, won't you.'

So good that that word could be wrapped up in a pleasantry, the kind of thing you would say about anyone. Richard understood what I had really meant.

'Yeah, I will give her your love. Listen . . .'

'I know, you've got to go.'

'Hey, Karl, have a good time with your leading lady.'

'I will. When you see Sarah, tell her . . . well, tell her that I've written to her.'

'I will. Two hundred and twenty thousand dollars? Jesus, Karl, you lucky bastard.'

'That's me.'

'You deserve it. I'm happy for you.'

'Like fuck you are.'

'Yeah, like fuck I am.'

After I had put the phone down, and cursed myself for making the call in the first place, I put on my blue linen suit, the only suit I'd brought with me from London, a pair of real shoes, a tie, some aftershave, and I waited like a real hero for my leading lady to come down the stairs.

CHAPTER NINE

Scarlet Timberley knocked on my door at seven forty-five precisely and told me that a car was waiting for us in the street. It wasn't until we got out into the hallway that I saw her properly. She was wearing a white dress and pearls, her hair hung loose around her shoulders and her face was shining with oil. In fact her whole body seemed to have been oiled and it gave the naked skin of her neck and shoulders a golden sheen. Her make-up had been applied liberally but with taste, with particular emphasis on the eyes. It looked like stage make-up, which is always applied too thickly in order to give definition to the face in bright stage lights. I followed her down the stairs without a word, and she trailed a thick smell of oil and perfume. The limo driver whistled through his teeth when he saw her walk out into the street light and instinctively opened the door of the limousine and stood to attention. It wasn't until I sat beside her on the back seat that I saw the full glory of her face and felt the burning presence of her thighs beside me. This was a different Ms Lisson again. This wasn't Ms Lisson at all.

'I hope this isn't a bad time,' she breathed. 'I mean, Giorgio tells me that you are a busy man.'

The car pulled away and headed down towards the ocean. Duvall Street was already filled with its uneasy mix of wealthy Miami businessmen and their mistresses on vacation, barefoot minstrels, drunks, fishermen and illegal Cubans. There is a frontier feeling to downtown Key West. A constant hubbub of people at odds, the deafening sound of music systems blaring from open-fronted bars, the jangle of guitars. But inside the cab there was a bubble of silence and tension.

'I think it's a good idea,' I said stupidly. 'I mean, I'm happy. I'm looking forward to taking you to dinner.'

Neither of us spoke a word after that until we arrived at the restaurant. The driver pulled up at the bottom of a long wooden staircase with rope banisters that seemed to lead out into the ocean itself. At the top of the staircase (which I climbed a few feet behind Scarlet, illicitly breathing her perfume) there was a sea-deck that stretched out over the harbour and the ocean was visible through cracks between the planks, milky green in bright lamplight. The Benihana restaurant has a panoramic view of the ocean.

'If you believe in it, it's true,' said a voice in my head.

The head waiter caught Scarlet's arm as we entered and kissed her softly on the cheek. Then he shook my hand and smiled warmly before showing us to a seat by the huge ocean-front window, giving us an uninterrupted view of the moon and the ocean and the curve of the earth and the twinkling of lights on the horizon.

I felt that the silence between us had gone on too long and decided to launch into what I considered to be a bright conversation. I remarked that the finest place to witness American democracy at work is in a restaurant. I said that no matter how hard the Americans tried to create an atmosphere of exclusivity, they always let themselves down with their innate informality and hospitality. I said that if this restaurant were in Europe, the head waiter would have sniffed at my crumpled suit and my untidy hair and he would have launched into a complicated ritual of making me feel uncomfortable and unwelcome. I said that Europe, and particularly England, was a place where money meant less than class and appearance. Then I said that America was a true egalitarian society, and that I liked it here. Then I shut up.

'I'm sorry,' Scarlet said to excuse her silence, 'I'm very nervous.'

'Nervous? Whatever for?'

'This is my first time. I mean my first time back. I'm not sure I can make it.'

The waiter had lit candles on our table and in the candlelight I saw there were tears in her eyes. The tears made her eyes look enormous.

'Ms Lisson . . .'

'You'd better call me Scarlet.'

'Scarlet. I don't understand. First time back in what?'

'In the movies. I'm not sure that I can be what you all want me to be.'

Scarlet sniffed and threw back her head in a fine, theatrical gesture. The candlelight made her look younger, and her body looked more fragile and tender than I had ever seen it. It was as if the muscles she'd worked so hard to develop had turned into soft flesh.

'You mean the part?' I said, trying to laugh it off.

'Yes,' she said, 'I'm not sure that I can do it any more. I've been away from it for so long. I'm not so young as I was . . .'

The waiter took our order. We both took his advice and chose lobster. As Benelli had said, I could afford it. Then I ordered a bottle of Chablis and a bottle of mineral water. The moment I ordered the wine, my face reddened and I remembered Benelli's instructions. Scarlet didn't even notice my embarrassment.

'What I mean,' she said, 'is that I am grateful to you all for having faith in me. If it wasn't for Giorgio, then I don't know . . . I don't know that I'd even be able to carry on.'

Scarlet's hands were shaking as she lit a cigarette. When she blew the smoke out she narrowed her eyes, like Lauren Bacall. A cruel thought came into my head. I decided that Scarlet might be the weak link in the chain. If anyone was going to tell me what was really going on, it would be her. There was so much I needed to know that I didn't know where to begin.

'So how long have you known Mr Benelli?' I said with great delicacy. Scarlet waited for her anxiety to subside a little before answering. She reminded me of a nervous student at an entrance examination.

'Oh, I've known Giorgio since way back,' she said. 'He was my agent when I first broke into the movies. Back in '70. Then he went into production. He was the producer on my first movie. And my second, I think. I can't remember exactly. But he was always so good for me. Always made me do things that I didn't think I could do.'

'Yes,' I said, 'he sure knows how to get a person to do things.'

Scarlet laughed at the look of exasperation on my face.

'I think your hair looks fine,' she said, still laughing. 'I think it's awful that those waiters in London sniff at you.'

The head waiter brought us the bottle of Chablis and, in the American style, poured us both a glass without asking one of us to sample it. I felt momentary panic and then made myself believe that I didn't care. I waited for a while before raising my glass, but Scarlet took a drink first. She took a tiny sip, like a little girl with her father's beer. I decided that in this new world, in this world where people spoke plainly and weren't embarrassed at the consequences, I should explain to Scarlet about Benelli's note. In London, it would have been out of the question, but here it seemed ordinary.

'Scarlet, I have to tell you that before he left, Benelli

instructed me not to let you drink,' I said in one breath.

Scarlet nodded with resignation. 'I know,' she said.

'Well?'

Scarlet pushed the glass away and looked at her lap. To hell with Benelli, I thought.

'But I'm not Benelli,' I said.

'He's right, though. How am I supposed to get better if I keep on going back? Here, you drink it. You saw how I was the other night.'

I had hoped Scarlet had forgotten she had ever seen me on the stairs that night. The fact that she hadn't forgotten brought us closer together. Now we both had a secret to keep from Benelli.

'So you were smashed,' I said. 'So am I. A lot of the time. What right has Benelli got to tell you what you can and can't do?'

Scarlet looked shocked.

'Here,' I said, pushing the glass of wine back towards her, 'take it.' Scarlet took the glass in her hand and took another sip. She looked up at me as she sipped and grinned into the glass. Then she giggled and I giggled too. It was good wine, cold and crisp. And now that we had toasted ourselves and I had established that we were on the same side, maybe I could find out what I needed to find out. And the wine wouldn't hurt if I wanted her to open up a little.

'So Benelli is a pretty big guy in Hollywood?' I said airily. Scarlet shrugged.

'I mean, he seems pretty free with his money,' I said.

Scarlet became serious. I had hit on something. Maybe he hadn't put Scarlet on the payroll yet.

'He sure is throwing his money around,' I said, 'somebody's money. I'm not complaining, but, Jesus . . .'

I'd moved too quickly. Scarlet looked hurt and anxious.

93

Perhaps I should try a different tack. Maybe I should speak plainly and voice my anxieties about Benelli's credentials. Something told me that that would be even more cruel.

'How long is it since you made your last movie?' I asked, trying to change the subject, and I immediately realized I had said the wrong thing again.

'Twenty-one years,' she said quickly. 'But I started young. Too young, maybe. I always felt that . . . this is stupid, I guess, but I always felt that I hadn't done it all. I always felt that when I stopped, I still had a hundred movies left to do. I always thought that I could still . . .'

Scarlet took a long swig of wine. I had sounded like someone conducting a job interview. I didn't have the vocabulary or the eloquence to put her at her ease without making it sound as if I were trying to put her at her ease.

'I hope Giorgio didn't force me on to you,' Scarlet said, as if she had been rehearsing the line for hours.

'Well of course he didn't,' I said. 'You're perfect for the part. Really. You're just absolutely the right person. Really. Why do you think we're here? I'm writing the part for you.'

This was precisely what I hadn't wanted to happen. I was being forced to repeat the lies Benelli had given me. I should speak out now, while we still had the chance to get out. But I couldn't.

'Really,' I said. 'The moment I set eyes on you I knew you were her. Laura.'

Scarlet beamed at me.

'Laura? Is that her name?'

'Sure,' I said, proudly. 'And her husband is called Max. She's a therapist of some kind. We're not sure yet. And she's pretty and funny and she's got the most beautiful

94

eyes you've ever seen. And she's mysterious too. You don't really know who she is until near the end of the movie. And she's a kind of health freak. She's always exercising and running along the ocean and she knows all about diet and all those things and really she's just a fabulous person.'

Scarlet's face reminded me of a small child unwrapping a present at Christmas. I'd now broken both of my promises to Benelli. The booze and the script. I knew that I had done it and I didn't care. It was more important to feed the glee on the face in front of me.

'Really? A health freak?'

Scarlet drained her glass. I poured her another.

'I guess that rings a bell,' I said, with fatherly good humour, forgetting all those nights I had cursed at the ceiling of my apartment.

Scarlet laughed as she took a drink of wine. She waved her hand at me with her mouth full, as if she were anxious to speak but couldn't. Finally she swallowed.

'Gee, I'm so sorry, Karl,' she said, and my name rang like a clinked glass. 'I know I must have been a pain in the ass.'

I shook my head and smiled with disgusting magnanimity.

'But really, Karl, you should have seen me before Giorgio took me over. Really. Oh God, I shouldn't bore you with this, Karl, but really . . .'

Scarlet puffed out her cheeks and laughed. Her voice had a new raspiness from drinking wine.

'Two hundred pounds of whale meat. I mean really. I was so . . . Oh God, I used to stand in the bathroom and just . . . the hatred I had for myself. I wanted to take a knife and cut big pieces off my thighs and off my ass. I nearly did it too . . .'

Scarlet's laughter became a little bitter. I laughed to make it better again.

'Well, you look good now,' I said. 'What is it, ten hours a day? Twelve?'

Scarlet knew I was teasing and she liked it. She told me she had been working out for seven hours a day with three-hour respites in between. She said she was on a strict diet of fish and salad. She said she had been living like this for six months, ever since Benelli had told her that he had found the perfect part for her and put her into the apartment in Mallory Street.

'Six months?' I said.

'Sure. I moved in in spring. When I was still a whale.'

I made a fast calculation. I had been in the apartment in Key West for four weeks. I had written the first draft of the script for this movie eight weeks before. Benelli hadn't even known I existed when he moved Scarlet into the apartment. I was making these calculations when Scarlet said, 'So come on, Karl, tell me.'

'Tell you what?'

Scarlet giggled and took another tiny sip of wine. Her eyes were flickering, a look of stage-school seduction.

'Tell me what I really want to know. Tell me what happens to Laura. Tell me what happens to her in the end.'

I thought about Laura and Max, splashing around in the bay in front of the shrimp docks. I thought about how I'd wanted it to end, and I thought about lying. Luckily, I didn't have to. The waiter appeared from nowhere.

'Your lobsters!' he said, presenting us with two steel-blue lobsters on a silver platter. Scarlet put on her napkin and picked up her fork. The lobster on the left moved its antenna and rolled its eye and Scarlet shrieked.

'It's still alive!' she shouted, and the waiter almost leapt in the air.

'Of course it's still alive, Miss Timberley,' the waiter said, 'we haven't cooked it yet. I'm just showing it to you to make sure that it's OK.'

When Scarlet had calmed down, we both laughed about the live lobster all the way through the meal.

Scarlet told me why she had been away from the movies for so long. She said her last movie, *The Last of Love*, had been a moderate box-office success and that she herself had received good reviews. She told me some corny, over-rehearsed stories about working with Tony Curtis and someone called 'Jack T.', whoever he was. Six months after the movie was released, however, she had met a man who put an end to her career.

He was an admirer, or more than an admirer. He was one of those men who become obsessed with an image on the screen. And since he was a powerful, acquisitive man, he didn't find it strange that he should devote his life's energies to acquiring her. She said she had met James Lisson in Miami, and that he was a successful property tycoon who had made millions buying up swamp land in southern Florida and developing it as real estate. She said that James Lisson had fallen in love with her when he saw *The Last of Love* and had spent three months trying to get to meet her. He'd given everything else up in the attempt. Eventually he succeeded, at a party in Palm Beach which he had organized in her honour. She said that the tycoon had flown her in from New York in a private jet and had arranged for a company of set designers to erect an Arabian Palace on the beach, complete with fountains and mock dungeons and a harem stable. She said that James Lisson had spent half a million dollars on the party just to woo her. Scarlet became sad and said that he was stout and balding and fifty but that he had a sweet smile and he was kind and there was no question that he loved her. They were married in California in the spring of 1973, and James Lisson made her promise that, in return for her new life of ludicrous riches, she would give up her movie career. He had said that he wanted her all to himself.

Scarlet said that at the time it was no real hardship. She had grown tired of the struggle to move from co-star to star, the hardest struggle in the movie business. Harder even than the struggle from obscurity to co-star. She had lived with him in New York, Miami and Malibu for twenty years. He got sick but refused to die. 'I stay alive to be with you one more day,' he used to say. In the end, he looked like the soft part of a machine, hooked up to tubes and wires and weird-looking bellows that sucked and blew when he talked. Scarlet said that she had started to drink to pass the time while she waited for him to let go. She got fat and nervous and lonely and regretful. She used to drive down to the local movie theatre on her own and watch the movies that were passing her by. Slipping away. And all the time she knew that she could get back some day, that she *had* to get back some day. Then James Lisson died, and two days later, Giorgio Federico Benelli looked her up and saved her life.

'And what about before that?' I asked, as we walked east along Smathers Beach.

'Before the movies? Oh, normal stuff. Farm girl. Pretty poor. Over in Kansas. You know, where Dorothy got picked up by the hurricane and got dumped on the yellow brick road. I guess that's the story.'

'So you are poor little Dorothy?' I said.

'I suppose. Oh, I don't know. That sounds like a corny line, doesn't it?'

'Not at all, I think it's very appropriate,' I said. 'If you want to see corny lines . . .' I stopped myself. I wanted to

98

say something cynical about the script back in the apartment. The thought of it had been making me hot all
through the meal. If Scarlet knew what an awful shambles
this whole thing was, maybe she wouldn't be so sweet and
engaging with me. If she knew that this great venture in
which she had invested so much energy and hope was
nothing more than a few handwritten sheets written by a
producer with no talent, transcribed by a writer with little
more, then maybe she'd turn off like a light.

I broke off in mid sentence. For the first time since I'd
arrived on the island, the wind blew cold and strong and it
carried the scent of moist earth.

'Speaking of hurricanes . . .' I said, laughing and looking
in the direction of the wind. Scarlet shivered and took
hold of my arm.

'Don't joke, Karl,' she said, suddenly afraid. 'Don't
joke about that.'

'About what? About hurricanes?'

'They frighten me,' Scarlet said, and her voice was the
voice of a little girl. We walked on some more and the
wind blew so hard that Scarlet's hair was blown in my
face.

'I thought the hurricane season was over,' I said, but
Scarlet told me in a very serious voice that the hurricane
season had just begun. It wouldn't be over till late October.
Then she said she'd been afraid of hurricanes since she
was a child.

'In Kansas, we had typhoons. The movie got it wrong.
You get typhoons in Kansas. You see them across the
Plains, out on the horizon, six or seven of them together,
coming down from the sky like the fingers of a hand. A
big black hand. And you hear them too. Moaning and
moving real slow. When I was a little girl . . .'

She stopped and laughed, as if I wouldn't want to hear.

'Go on,' I said, teasing. 'Benelli wants us to get to know each other, let's get to know each other. What about when you were a little girl?'

'When I was little, around six or seven, we had a typhoon come straight down Main Street. We lived out on a dairy place a couple of miles out, but when it hit, it was just like midnight in the middle of the day. And it got cold and it lifted three of our old cows clean off the ground and dumped them in the next county. Vet said they died of fright.'

I said I wasn't surprised and then Scarlet said something that I didn't catch. The wind took her voice. The moonlight shivered on the ocean.

'I said the thing was, I thought it was all my fault,' she said.

'Your fault? How can a typhoon be your fault?'

'I'd been doing something crazy. I guess I was a little monster, and my Dad told me that if I didn't quit doing whatever it was, then the wind'd come and find me and blow me down to hell. So when it cut through Main Street, and cut the place all to pieces, I figured the wind had been looking for me. I figured the typhoon had thought I'd gone to school that day and it had been trying to find me. The school was smashed up all to pieces. Not even an eraser left. And for a long time I thought it was me that did it. That's crazy, isn't it?'

She said it as if it were a genuine question that needed an answer.

We were walking arm in arm now, and I was glad of the warmth from her oiled skin. We walked in step, just inches away from where the foam of the ocean was fizzing on the sand. I'd begun to speculate about James Lisson. I wanted us to keep on talking so that I didn't have to think what I was thinking, to stop myself putting two and two together.

'So why did you leave Kansas?' I said to distract myself. 'I mean, did you just run away to Hollywood to become a waitress like in the pictures?'

'Sort of like that,' she said. 'I guess I just wanted to get away from the cowboys. What about you? Why did you leave London?'

I told her I had left London to get away from a cowboy too, and when she asked me what I meant, I told her that it was a private joke.

'I don't like private jokes,' she said, a little hurt. 'I always think they're about me.'

'Well this one isn't about you,' I said, and when I turned to her, I could see that she had a serious expression, a look of anguish.

'Something else,' she said softly. 'That typhoon, the one that hit Main Street. A woman got killed. Broke her back.'

I didn't see the point. Then I did. I glanced at her to see if that look of crazy concentration had left her face. It hadn't.

'So?'

'So nothing,' she said. 'So a lady got killed and I thought it was my fault.'

'But you don't think that any more, do you?'

'No, of course I don't,' she said softly. 'What do you think? I'm crazy?'

The wind had dropped off into a steady breeze, still cool and still pungent. It wasn't like the smell of the ocean, more like the smell of land a long way away. I realized Scarlet was holding on to my arm tightly, and that her fingers were moving rhythmically to some beat in her own head.

'You didn't really answer my question,' I said, trying to sound playful, 'about why you ran away to Hollywood.'

Scarlet stopped walking and we both turned to look out to sea. The moonlight was doing what moonlight does. It was making us both retreat into ourselves, making us think huge thoughts, analyse regrets. It wasn't the place to be playful.

'I got pregnant when I was nineteen,' she said suddenly and without any emotion. 'I had a baby and gave her away. Then I ran off to Hollywood. That answer your question?'

I hadn't meant her to take my question so seriously. I hadn't meant it at all. Now I was embarrassed and I wanted to apologize but I couldn't think of anything to say other than whisper 'Sorry', so that maybe she wouldn't hear. We walked on in silence.

'So you gave up your movie career for love,' I said finally, purely as a light-hearted observation. Another attempt to be playful, another mistake. A mistake like walking along the beach and stepping on a land-mine.

'Ha, ha,' she said.

'What?'

'Nothing.'

I knew without her saying that she thought I was accusing her of giving it all up not for love, but for money. She put it into words.

'The papers gave me a hard time when I married James. They said I was double booking the church – our wedding and his funeral in the same day. Gold-digging bitch. Is that what you're saying, Karl?'

I said that I wasn't saying anything of the kind. There was an uneasy silence as we walked on, and in the distance, way in the distance, I could see the high wire fence and the searchlights and hear the dogs howling around Baxter's tank, another mile along the shoreline. A mile away, the blue area, the sounds of the jungle. And out here, peace and freedom and the smell of the wind. But along with the wind those uncomfortable thoughts still kept coming. Scarlet Timberley, faded movie star and now, it transpired, widow of James Lisson, a property tycoon. Two and two kept on adding up to four. I didn't want to put these thoughts into words but the thoughts wanted to get out anyway. The thoughts came as images. Scarlet at the altar, the cameras popping. Scarlet in a beach house in Malibu, wasting away. Scarlet in black at James Lisson's funeral. And finally, Scarlet at the reading of the will of the James Lisson estate.

If the guy had been a millionaire when she married him, what happened to all that money when he died?

Or did I already know the answer to that question? I couldn't think of anything to say that wasn't dangerous, anything that wasn't infected by what I was already thinking. I could have made a comment about the moon, about how it had turned yellow and looked as if it were made out of gold. Or I could have said nothing.

Instead, I said, 'You know, Scarlet, I've been wondering ever since I started on this project . . .'

'What?'

'If Benelli is working as an independent producer, I mean, if he's not with a studio any longer, where the hell is he getting all his money from?'

Scarlet stared at me for a long time as if she hadn't understood what I had said. Then she began to walk quickly towards the ocean. She reached the edge of the water and began to hurry towards the harbour, towards home.

'Scarlet, wait!' I shouted and ran after her. She began to run too but I finally managed to grab her shoulder and turn her round. I was already out of breath.

'Wait. Scarlet. Listen to me. It's none of my damn business . . .'

Scarlet broke away again and began to trot away from me into the darkness. I knew that there was no point in trying to catch her. The lazy water of the Gulf lapped and slurped at my feet and I felt an awfully long way from home. The moon looked big and clean and foreign. My hands still smelt of Scarlet's perfume. I thought about the cheque that was waiting for me on my desk. I thought about Scarlet's face when I had joked about how free and easy Benelli was being with his money. I had no way of knowing for sure, but I felt that I had just uncovered something ugly, like unwrapping the bandage from a wound, or lifting a rock. I had resolved to walk home along the beach alone, really alone, when Scarlet suddenly came back into view, running with long strides through the shallow water.

'Come on!' she shouted. 'Come in! It's beaoooootiful!'

She bent down and splashed her dress with water. I could hear that she was laughing.

'Scarlet. Your dress,' I said, and realized that I sounded unusually feeble.

'What about it?'

'Nothing.'

'You're right, Karl. I shouldn't get my dress in the ocean, should I? It cost me $2,000 in Rodeo Drive.'

By now I was standing by her, still retreating from the waves when they got near to my shoes. Scarlet took hold of her dress at the hem and lifted it over her head, then she threw it towards me. She stood in the moonlight almost naked, like a pillar of silver.

'And what about these pearls, Karl? What should I do with these?'

She wound her pearl necklace around her forefinger like a child with a string of bubble gum. Then she yanked the necklace and it snapped away from her neck.

'$6,000 from who cares where. What do you say, Karl? I think it's time the pearls went home, back to the ocean.'

Scarlet took the pearls in her hand and threw them as hard as she could into the water. The white rain of pearls seemed to hang in the air for a long time. As each pearl landed, beautiful droplets of pure white in the moonlight, I became more sure. She peeled off her pants and splashed her naked body with the water. I could almost feel the coldness on my own skin.

'Scarlet, I didn't mean anything,' I said. 'It's just I'd like to know the truth.' Scarlet splashed herself again, and I realized that the waves had covered my shoes. 'Or did Benelli ask you to make promises tonight too?'

Her body was firm and tight. Her skin was still shiny with oil. A feeling of desire came to me suddenly, a feeling of blood and heat and queasiness. I actually licked my lips like a dog and tasted the salt on them. She was standing with her back arched, making her breasts sit neatly in the air. I knew that if I moved closer to her, I would be able to feel the heat of her skin, and I wanted to feel that more than anything in the world. I felt as if I had been deprived of skin-warmth for years and years. For centuries. I welcomed old feelings of lust as if they were dearly loved friends. Old comrades in life.

'Scarlet,' I said, 'you've got to tell me the truth. It's your money Benelli is using, isn't it?'

Scarlet didn't hear.

'What is it, Karl?' she said. 'Don't you like my body? I made it like this for you. Don't you appreciate that? All for you, Karl.'

The wind had dropped completely and the evening was warm again. The smell of ocean came back and, from far away, the smell of bougainvillaea blossoms. Those thoughts about James Lisson and the money that before

105

had been so urgent were flooded out by warm blood. Why had I forgotten all this? Why had I let myself get so cold? It had been so long since I had had any shelter and Scarlet was shelter. I could go there and it would be easy. Lots of things could come out. Lots of things that had been waiting to happen would happen. I felt hard places grow soft, soft places grow hard.

Scarlet smiled. 'I've never seen a man get undressed so fast,' she said.

'It's been a long time,' I said, but I wanted to say something more.

CHAPTER TEN

The cold water made it hard. Or rather, it didn't. I found myself waiting for the next cold wave to come and submerge us, and it became a preoccupation. There was heat between us but the wind had got up again and my back and shoulders were cold. Scarlet pulled away from me and propped herself on an elbow.

'You know,' she said, in a joke Western accent, 'sumptn ain't right.'

Then she kissed me on the forehead.

'I talked to Deborah Kerr once, right after she'd starred in *From Here to Eternity*. She said it took her three days to get the sand out of her ass after they shot that love scene on the beach.'

I had been thinking about that scene ever since we had lain down on the sand. I had been seeing us both from the outside.

'How about we go home and do this thing properly,' she said. I liked her for the way she said it. It told me that this was a mechanical exercise for her as it was for me. We *had* to do it, so we might as well do it in the easiest possible way. An hour ago, this wouldn't have seemed possible. Now it was the most natural thing in the world. That was how I liked it. To come from nowhere. To fall out of the sky. The moonlight and the waves were an elaboration. We wanted to fuck, and that desire was sweet and considerate and romantic. This was how love starts, wanting to fuck somewhere warm, where you can do it right.

There was a nagging voice in my head telling me that Scarlet was only doing all this as an elaborate way of changing the subject. Another voice whispered back, cruel and stagy, 'Feel bad about it tomorrow. That's what tomorrow is for.'

We walked quickly back to the house in Mallory Street. We walked so quickly that it made us both laugh. Scarlet's dress was wet and it clung to her buttocks as she walked. I felt like a lion pursuing a nimble deer, except this deer wanted to be eaten. There was no question. She wanted it for real. This thing had to be done. We ran across Atlantic Boulevard barefoot, and felt the warmth of the tarmac, still radiating heat from the day's sun. We tiptoed up Mallory Street and then danced on our heels up the drive of 1131. The house wasn't in the mood for sharing our warm, kind lust. It glowered down at us as it always did, and when Scarlet opened the door, we were greeted by a breath of cool, damp air that smelt of turpentine and very old wood. None of it mattered. This was just someplace where this thing could be done properly and I felt triumphant that the gloom of the house couldn't chill me in the way it usually did. There was mail on the doormat and I remembered all the times that I had peeked at Ms Lisson's letters, like a masturbatory schoolboy. Now this was the real thing. I hadn't felt like this since Sarah, except all thoughts of Sarah were embargoed as of now. I had forgotten how violent this feeling could be. A violent desire. A violent desire to tear something open. And in that, there were the old secrets. We climbed the stairs with care, giggling every time a loose floorboard groaned and squeaked away our progress.

'Yours or mine?' she whispered with some urgency.

'Mine,' I said.

'OK,' she said. 'I've just got to get something from my room.'

108

I went into the apartment and quickly gathered up the scattered papers of the script. I patted them together and hid them in the cupboard under the sink. Then I took Benelli's handwritten script and hid it on top of the wardrobe. I felt deceitful but it was a small deceit. We could resume our conversation about the awful script, about the money, about Benelli after we'd done this thing properly. I took off my linen trousers, which were wet at the ankles, and my jacket and shirt, and lay down on the bed. My skin was tingling with the new warmth of the sheets. I could feel salt in the small of my back, and sand on the soles of my feet. The door was pushed open. It was G. F. Benelli.

'What the fuck are you doing here?' I hissed at the broad shape in the doorway.

'Hiya, Karl. Scarlet tells me you had a swell time.'

I sat up in bed and Benelli came nearer. I looked around for something to throw at him; then the urge subsided.

'Says you had lobster. Good lobster up there. Straight out the Bay. Oh, Mama, I love lobster.'

'Benelli, what the hell is this?'

Benelli sat down on the edge of the bed. I resented his closeness and the smell of sweat and sharp cologne after the dull, warm smells of oil and sand.

'I moved in,' Benelli said. 'Just across the hall. That guy Clark gave up his room for me. I thought it'd be easier if I moved out of my hotel and stayed here, where the action is.'

My face must have betrayed me. Benelli looked slightly offended.

'Hey, this is my place after all, Karl.'

I rubbed my eyes and pushed back my hair, which was matted with salt. I hadn't registered what he had said. But then, 'Your place? What do you mean, your place?'

'This house. It's mine. It belongs to Key West Developments. We bought it off Warner Brothers to use for locations. How do you think I got you an apartment so easy, huh? It'll look great in the murder scene, won't it, Karl? Right here. Right on this bed. Laura looking up at Max all wet from the ocean. Then the shit with the pillow. That reminds me, I need you to speak to that cop again . . .'

'You *bought* this place?' I said. Fast calculation, $300,000 minimum for the house. Those images of Lisson and Scarlet dressed in black returned. I was staring into Benelli's eyes, which were amber from the street light that was filtering through my blinds. The wind outside had begun to moan and I could hear the undergrowth out on the path scratching itself and clawing. Now Benelli had his hand on my shoulder, and some water dripped on to his hand from my hair.

'What have you kids been doing out there?' he said. 'Skinny dipping?'

I didn't answer and I thought that Benelli was too insensitive and unperceptive to realize that he had almost hit upon the truth. He slapped my bare shoulder. I hated him.

'I gotta go, Karl,' he said, standing up. 'You get some rest. We got an early start in the morning. I want to start going through the second act. Punch it up a little.'

Just then, I heard the familiar creak of floorboards above my head. The sound of frantic sit-ups followed by the thud of a body on to a bed. Something inside me wanted to scream.

'I told her she was getting a little fat,' Benelli said with a crazy smile. 'All that lobster! Too rich, Karl, too rich. The little baby said she'd see to it right away.'

Benelli half-closed the door but left his bald head hanging in the crack of light.

'Hey, and don't get any ideas about her, Karl,' he said. 'She's a racehorse. Nobody rides her except the jockey.'

It didn't take a genius to work it out.

I lay awake all night, listening to the wind gathering strength. The joints of old trees were creaking, and I could hear the branches and trunks whimpering with dread. The lids from trash cans were tossed on to the road and they skidded from place to place all night long. The street outside was restless, nervous, and I had to keep getting up to pace the room and smoke another cigarette. Most of the noises came from inside the house, the sound of the arthritic joists getting squeezed and pulled by the motion of the wind. And way down underneath the house, that fat, fifty-foot snake bedding itself down, blinking in the darkness, knowing just what to expect.

By the time the first streaks of grey light hit my window, I'd got the whole thing pieced together in my head, a jigsaw puzzle with big pieces, a child's jigsaw puzzle, not so hard to do if you just opened your eyes and used your head.

Benelli had worked with Scarlet in the early seventies. Then he'd lost her when she married James Lisson and that could have been the end of the story. But Benelli knew that when Lisson died, Scarlet would be worth a fortune. So when he heard about Lisson's death, Benelli had made his move, and he made it fast. His retirement pension had finally matured.

Benelli might act foolish sometimes, but he wasn't a fool. He would have known that a movie career like Scarlet's, cut short right at the start, would leave her with an unquenched desire. He knew that as soon as Lisson died, Scarlet would want to pick up the pieces and start all over again. He would also have known that no studio in

Hollywood would have touched her with surgical gloves on. Forty, faded, not much of a bombshell to begin with.

So Benelli said screw the studios, we'll make our own little movie. All we need, Scarlet, is x million dollars development money. The longer I thought, the more the metal lids scurried across the road outside, the more angry I got. And the more sure. I'd been told in London that the producer's hardest job was gathering development money, persuading the financiers. He would have been doing it all his life. All his life he would have been breaking his balls to raise vast sums of money to make movies, money that was spent on writers and directors and agents and stars and props and prints and studios. But then one day he thought, now wait a minute . . .

What would happen if, just once, G. F. Benelli raised x million dollars to make a movie and then the movie never got made? What would happen if Benelli set up his own little production company so that the development money was paid direct into his own account? What would happen if the person coming up with the x million dollars was so desperate to make a movie that they'd be prepared to keep it in development for ever? What would happen if it was the star who was writing the cheques, leaving Benelli to control the purse-strings? What would happen if there was no director and no cast and no crew and no designers and no one to use the money on? Maybe just some dumb, desperate writer, for the sake of appearances, someone from outside the business who wouldn't ask questions if you slipped him a few hundred grand?

It was simple. It was beautiful. It was even legal.

How do you prosecute a man for persuading someone to finance the development of a movie? Hold the script up in court and say, 'The script's no good, the plot stinks, the characters are all shallow, so the whole thing is a con'?

And if Benelli was prepared to pay me $220,000 to play the part of the writer in this scenario, then just how much money had he persuaded Scarlet to part with? One million? Ten? In Hollywood, they call it a low-budget movie if it costs any less than eighteen . . .

I even had time to fit the blond lady into my jigsaw puzzle too. Scarlet had said that her marriage to Lisson had attracted a lot of press interest. So it didn't take any kind of genius to work out in retrospect that the blond lady with the camera was a journalist who was doing a follow-up story. When James Lisson died, some features editor somewhere, reading through the obits. one morning over breakfast, would have seen that Lisson was dead and had decided that the gold-digging bitch from Hollywood had finally got what she'd waited so long for. It would be worth a spread, maybe even a cover. Especially if I was in the picture too.

'James Lisson is barely cold in his grave, and already former Hollywood starlet Scarlet Timberley has recovered from her grief sufficiently to roll around on Smathers Beach with . . .'

All night is a long time to be awake, and before dawn I realized that I was speaking my conclusions out loud, an old habit that I thought I'd beaten. I had time to write the whole story, *and* set the photographs on the pages of the magazine. Except that that story was nothing compared to the real story. Not if I was right about G. F. Benelli. Now that really would be worth a cover. Until I had some evidence this was all conjecture, and I thought that maybe the coming of the light in the morning might make me see things differently. It didn't. I resolved that I would confront Scarlet with my suspicions, and that I would confront Benelli. I wasn't afraid of him any more – at least not in the same way. When the sun came up, I decided that I needed to take a walk down to the shrimp docks to get my line of argument straight for when I saw Scarlet. I would apologize to her too, even though I wasn't sure what I would be apologizing for.

When I left the house, I ran into Crazy Jimmy. I was still wearing the jacket and trousers to my suit, which were dusted with salt. The moment I stepped outside, I noticed that the air felt heavy and that the sky was marbled with what looked like streaks of dark sand. Crazy Jimmy glanced up at the sky as he greeted me.

'Ah, Stone,' he wheezed. 'Looks like it's going to be a bad one.'

I didn't say anything. He had a white envelope in his hand which he was waving at me.

'Yes, sir, looks like that hurricane's going to look us up this time. News guy on the radio said it was eighty-five to ninety per cent. Looking at the sky, I'd say ninety-nine point nine.'

Crazy Jimmy was just about to shove the letter into the mailbox. I saw that it was addressed to Ms Lisson and that it was from the Chase Manhattan Bank. That didn't strike any chords for a few seconds. Crazy Jimmy was still talking.

'Yes, sir, Mr Stone, I guess they're going to want to evacuate the island like they did back in '75. Maybe not though. Maybe just get us all into our cellars like they did in '83. That was a bitch, Mr Stone, the '83. You ever been inside a hurricane?'

I shook my head, thinking a dark thought. The letter addressed to Ms Lisson was in the mailbox and the mailbox snapped shut.

'No, I haven't,' I said, 'we don't have them in England. We don't have anything in England.'

Crazy Jimmy chuckled. He liked the fact that I'd never been in a hurricane.

114

'I ain't lying, Mr Stone. It's like putting your head under a freight train. Like God's drunk and angry. Except I don't believe in God.'

I wanted Crazy Jimmy to go. I wanted him to disappear down the path and leave me to do what I now knew I was going to do. Instead he just smiled at me.

'You believe in God, Mr Stone?'

'No. No, I don't.'

Jimmy laughed and turned and finally set off down the path.

'Maybe you will,' he said as he turned into Mallory Street. 'Maybe you will after you've been inside the hurricane.'

When he had disappeared from sight, I took Ms Lisson's letter from the mailbox and set off with it down to the shrimp docks.

Front Street and Duvall Street were full of people packing up their belongings and preparing to leave Key West until this thing blew over.

'You want to go fishing, sir? Good day for fishing. Good day for sharks. Nice and hot.'

I didn't even answer the Cuban café owner. He stood at my table for a while with a look of resignation. This time, even he didn't believe it. The sky was getting greener, and on the horizon there was a long strip of black air.

'Are you trying to get me killed?' I said.

'Guess not,' he said.

After the owner of the café had left me alone with my coffee and my bowl of fish soup, I began to gingerly tear at the seal of Ms Lisson's envelope. I had figured if I needed proof, then maybe Crazy Jimmy had handed it to me right on cue. A chance to peek into Scarlet's bank account. I dipped my finger into the glass of water that the café owner had given to me, and tried to moisten the seal so that the paper wouldn't tear. After only a few tugs, it began to tear anyway, and I decided to just rip it open and what the hell. If anyone asked, I could always blame Crazy Jimmy.

Inside, there was a bank statement concerning a deposit account in the name of Mrs Caroline Lisson. There were four-transactions marked. Three of them were transfers of money from the deposit account into the Key West Developments account. The first was for $100,000, the second for $120,000, the third for $500,000: $720,000 in one week. Two twenty for me and, no doubt, five hundred thousand for Benelli.

The fourth transaction was another transfer of money into the account of the Mary Hope Foundation, $400. At the bottom there was a statement of interest accrued and a final balance on the deposit account. Scarlet had a little over seven million dollars in the account after the Key West Developments and Mary Hope money had been deducted.

'What do you think?' the Cuban café owner said, suddenly appearing at my side to collect my empty coffee-cup.

'About what?' I said.

He pointed with his nose at the horizon. I said that it looked bad. He grunted and said something in Spanish that sounded like a prayer. I folded up the bank statement and left some bills on the table.

'Does that blond lady still come around here,' I said as I stood up.

'What blond lady?' the café owner said. I added some more bills to the pile on the table.

'The blond lady who comes in here four mornings a week. The one who liked my ass.'

116

He didn't respond. I added another twenty.

'Sure,' he said, still looking out at the horizon. 'She comes around most days. Does a lot of writing.'

'Well, if she comes in this morning, I'd like you to pass on a message for me. Could you do that?'

He tilted his head, neither yes nor no.

'Tell her I need to speak to her. Tell her I want to meet her in Sloppy Joe's at midday. Tell her I've got a story for her.'

'A story?'

'If she's who I think she is, she'll know what I mean. If not, it won't matter anyway.'

The café owner picked up the bills from the table and I was about to go but he caught my arm.

'Hey, mister,' he said, 'you leave way too much here. I don't want a hundred bucks just to pass on a message.'

I smiled and said that it was OK because I could afford it.

CHAPTER ELEVEN

Just as I got back to the end of Mallory Street, normally a forum for six or seven barefooted beach bums, the rain started. It had been threatening all the way through my walk back from the shrimp docks, past the rusting hulk of the canning factory, along Eaton Street with its shell and sponge shops suddenly boarded up, and down Duvall Street, where the air tingled with distant electricity. On Duvall Street, I'd walked past an old Chevrolet with the doors open and three surfers strapping their blade to the roof. The radio in the car had been playing, and I could hear Highway One Radio broadcasting an interview about the hurricane. There was some deadpan, anti-hysteria advice crackling through and I recognized Baxter's laconic delivery. But when I reached Mallory Street, the rains really began.

I ran into the movie house with my jacket over my head, like some scurrying beach creature. Inside the air was dead and the rain beat the roof and the windows so hard the whole house seemed to vibrate. The wind was just tuning up, an orchestra gathering together, different winds all congregating in the pit, trying out their horns and drums and cymbals. Soon, there'd be a crashing chord. A wild symphony. I knocked on Scarlet's door and there was no reply.

'Scarlet,' I hissed, afraid that Benelli might be in the house somewhere. I knocked again and finally the door opened. It was dark in her room, her blinds were still drawn, and I could smell sleep in the air.

'Oh, Karl,' she said, and I could see that her face was screwed up with fear. I walked in and we embraced in the darkness.

'Karl, I've got to get out of here,' she said, and I said she was damn right about that. I knew that she was talking about the hurricane.

'Have you listened to the radio?' she said, and I told her that I'd heard bits.

'Karl, they're saying it's going to hit here or Marathon. I don't want . . .'

She was almost crying. I wanted to open the blinds but she wouldn't let me. The rain on the roof was like the roll of war drums and even in here, the air had a sickly, damp feel to it.

'Scarlet,' I said, after we had both sat down on the bed, 'I have some mail for you.'

She didn't hear me at first, and it wasn't until I held up the envelope, opened, that she realized what I'd done. She snatched it off me, torn between sudden anger and fear.

'You had no place . . .' she said.

'Scarlet, I know what's going on here.'

The rain and the wind dropped a little. Scarlet was listening to every change in pitch, listening intently and peering into my eyes, trying to see how I read it.

'Scarlet, for Christ's sake, forget the fucking hurricane for a minute. This is serious.'

I didn't mean that to sound funny but some part of me acknowledged the absurdity. But at least I had her attention. I also had my hand in her hair, stroking. She looked softened by sleep, and beautiful. The half-light in the room smoothed all the signs of age and I could see her in black and white.

'Benelli is ripping you off, Scarlet,' I said as softly as I could. I knew that she'd fight me but I hoped that if I said things plainly, simply and without emotion, she'd have to listen. I was wrong.

'Are you listening to me, Scarlet? This whole movie thing is a scam.'

She stood up and moved around the room, a shadow set against grey light. She took a cigarette from her dressing-table and lit it, illuminating her face. She looked scared. It wasn't until then that I realized that this was the first time I'd ever been inside her room. It was almost identical to my own, with an identical dressing-table and wardrobe, but the ceiling sloped with the gable of the roof, and there was no desk against the window. As she walked the floorboards creaked, a familiar sound – the sound of Ms Lisson in combat with the devil morning and night – but it was sharper up here. I wondered how we sounded from below, from my own room.

'What do you think the cellar is like in this place?' she said, chewing at a fingernail. 'Do you think it'll hold. That guy Clark said this place would hold up. I don't know. Do you think it might be rotten?'

Rotten? I wanted to tell her the whole thing was rotten, from the foundations up to the roof, the whole enterprise. The movie, the writer, the script. I wasn't angry but I decided that I would have to pretend to be.

'Will you fucking listen to me!' I shouted. 'You are not a child, Scarlet. You must have thought at some time, somewhere in the back of your mind that Benelli might just possibly, just possibly, be just a tiny bit interested in you for a reason other than your acting ability.'

It was crueller than I had meant. I had no idea how good an actress Scarlet was. At last Scarlet was engaged, or as close as she would get. Her face changed and I thought I recognized her from a movie I'd seen on TV some time long ago.

'You know what, Karl,' she said, quickly, 'you're obsessed . . .'

Her delivery made me uneasy. She'd flicked into a character, some character I wasn't familiar with. She was defending herself with it. This character was ugly and spoke fast and pointed her finger at me.

'You roll around with me in the sand and all of a sudden you think you have the goddam right to open my mail. Well, let me tell you something . . .'

She pointed again, and screwed her cigarette out. This character was slightly crazy in the dark.

'Let me tell you, Karl, that nobody owns me in that way any more. No man tells me what I can and can't do. No man opens my mail and tells me that I'm not a child. So you read my mail and you roll around in the sand with me. So that gives you the right to tell me what I can do with my life and my money! Is that how you see it? Is it, Karl?'

For the first time since I'd opened Scarlet's letter, I considered the possibility that I really had stepped over the line. Maybe getting mad and interfering like this was wrong. I'd been told before that whenever I met a woman, and liked her, then I almost immediately assumed I had some sort of authority over her. Scarlet had used almost exactly the same words that Sarah had once used, accusing me of believing I owned her. Sarah said it in a cool, even voice, English and flat, without cadence. Scarlet was vibrating with the indignity of it and I realized that I needed a crazy character too. I couldn't summon one yet. Not yet. I just said 'Scarlet' into my hands.

'So you've found out that it's me who's putting up the money for the movie . . .'

'You admit it.'

'Listen to yourself. Admit it? Admit what, Karl? It's

121

me who's paying the bills instead of Giorgio. Does that offend your sense of male pride? Don't you like to take money from a woman?'

'Jesus Christ, you know that's not the point.'

'I think it is.'

'Then you're crazy.'

She didn't like being called crazy. She bit on a word and turned to the window. The wind was getting up again. A sickness in the air. I thought briefly about the cellar.

'You know that that is *not* the point.'

'So what is the point?' she screamed.

'The point, Scarlet, is this. There is no movie. There is no fucking movie. This money you're giving to Benelli is not going to get you back into Hollywood again. Not ever. You want to see the script? I'll show you the fucking script! I'll go right downstairs now and get the fucking script and show you what you're spending your money on!'

I was going to go downstairs to fetch the script. I would have done it too, but Scarlet stopped me. Her face softened and that crazy character left her body. It was a physical transformation taking place before my eyes.

'Please, Karl . . .' Scarlet said, in her familiar voice.

The rain and the wind were easing off. I cursed myself for getting so angry. I needed to set this thing out in a straight line, in some kind of rational order. I was still uneasy about the way Scarlet had reopened old wounds. I had once overheard Sarah, using the telephone in the bathroom, describing me to someone as 'insane, so jealous'. I had wanted to kick the bathroom door down, but I didn't. I tried again to set this thing out in as cool and sober a way as I could.

'Scarlet, let me tell you how it is in the simplest way I

122

know,' I said, all reason. 'Benelli came to you six months ago and said he had the perfect part for you. Two days after your husband had died and left you God knows how many million dollars. Stop me if any of this is wrong, Scarlet . . .'

Scarlet had her back turned now, but I could tell from the angle of her head that she was listening.

'And he said, I don't know what his words might have been exactly, but he said something like, "We can make ourselves a movie if you'll put up the finance." Right?'

Nothing. Nothing meant yes.

'So then you and he set up a development company to make this movie with your money. But, Scarlet . . .'

Could I step on to this land-mine? Could I do it knowing that it was there and that it might blow us both to pieces?

'But, Scarlet, all that stuff I told you yesterday about the part and the script, it's all bullshit. The script stinks and Benelli knows it. And when it gets anywhere near to having some kind of shape, he changes it around again. How long did he say he'd need for development? A year? Two? Ten? Do you even look at the accounts he's keeping? Do you know how much money he's taken already? Have you spoken to a director, a locations man, a casting agent? Scarlet, you've written the guy a blank cheque to rip you off.'

'I think we should check out the cellar now,' Scarlet said, fretting at her fingernail again.

'Scarlet!'

'They said that it won't hit until after dark. If we check it out now . . .'

I had grabbed her by the elbows and I was staring into her eyes. I had realized she knew as well as I did what Benelli was doing to her. But I had also seen at last that

123

Scarlet didn't care. She wanted to believe it and so it was true. All that I was doing was saying to her things she'd already told herself a million times. And she was never going to listen. She was *choosing* not to listen because she needed to believe the lie so badly.

'What is it, Scarlet?' I said. 'Is it the fame you need? It sure as hell isn't the money. What is it? I need to know. What is there in the movies that you can't live without?'

At last, a question that meant something to her. At last something that she hadn't resolved herself.

'The cellar, Karl . . .'

'Tell me, for Christ's sake! Is it being young again? Is that what you want? You want it to be 1972 again, as if James Lisson had never happened?'

Scarlet softened in my arms and we embraced. I didn't want this to happen. I didn't want her to escape this easily, but I had no choice. I felt a tear on my neck and tried to look at her face but she was holding on to me too tightly.

'You don't understand, Karl,' she said. 'It's like having a snake in your belly, biting your insides. I lived with James for twenty years and I just watched it all slip by . . .'

She looked at me at last. Her tears were already beginning to dry and I wondered if they had been real. Couldn't actresses cry whenever they pleased? Where before I had craved her warmth and closeness, now I wanted to step away from her and shine a light in her eyes and make her see reason. I wanted to grip her more firmly and shake some sense into her, and the realization that that was what I might do made me let her go.

'It just slips by, Karl . . .' Scarlet said again.

The rain and wind had stopped. The sun was trying out a grin against the blinds. I looked over at the strips of sunlight, tiger stripes across the bare floor, but Scarlet shook her head, reading my thoughts.

'After the rain,' she said, 'there's calm for six or seven hours. Then it hits.'

I had an idea. I said that if we had six hours we could go outside right now and jump into my car and by the time the hurricane hit, we'd be in Miami, watching it all on the six o'clock news. I told her that distance was context. I told her that if we could just get out of the movie house until this thing blew over, we could maybe talk it through and check Benelli out and if we both agreed that he was being straight then we could start over. She shook her head again.

'Giorgio said to wait here till he got back. He told me to tell you. He said everything will be fine.'

There was a helplessness in Scarlet's voice that made me lose heart quickly. My will to carry on trying to make her see sense drained away. How many different ways were there of telling the truth? And the way Scarlet told me that Benelli had promised her everything would be fine reminded me of how I had felt just a few hours ago. Scarlet wanted this to happen because if she didn't have the movie, even a movie that was never going to get made, then she wouldn't have anything. Scarlet was saying that if I thought the cellar would hold out we could both hide out in the cellar, but if I didn't, we could go over to the Madagascar and hide out there. Whatever happened, she said she was waiting right there for Benelli to get back. She said she would do anything but she couldn't be alone in six hours' time. Not for anything.

'You know that you're going to need a new writer, don't you, Scarlet?' I said, and she lowered her eyes. 'Like you said, this is your money and your life and just because I rolled around in the sand with you I have no right to tell you what you should do. But I don't want to be a part of it.'

I asked her one more time if she was sure she was going to be OK and she said that she would. She smiled and said that I shouldn't tell Benelli but she had a bottle of sedatives in her drawer and she'd maybe take a couple to help get through the next twenty-four hours. What I wanted to do more than anything else was to get drunk. I needed to get drunk more than I had ever needed it. My fury needed a midwife. If I didn't get drunk, and just drove away now down Highway One with all the others who were fleeing the hurricane, then my fury might rattle around inside me and just blow me to pieces, just as it had before when I had let it slip out of the cage. I needed to get drunk in between this poorly lit scene in the darkness and the time when I would have to figure out what the hell I was going to do next. It would be best if I never set eyes on Benelli again. I would leave the movie house now, before he got back, and arrange to have all the money I'd been paid transferred back into Scarlet's account. That was the least I could do.

But on the way down the stairs, I bumped into him coming up. His face was filled with excitement and he was taking the steps two by two. I grabbed his collar and then hit him as hard as I could. He fell back down the stairs a little way and then straightened and held his chin, his eyes popping out of his head. When I got to Sloppy Joe's, my knuckles hurt like fury and I drank three brandies in quick succession.

Then I waited for the drink to take effect and, maybe, for the blond lady to join me at my table.

CHAPTER TWELVE

Sloppy Joe's was the kind of bar that prided itself on staying open right up to the last minute. What would Hemingway have said about a place that stops serving booze just because of some little bit of wind? They even had a special cocktail, made just for that day, called a 'Hurricane Mary', named after the hurricane that was even now wrapping itself around a cyclone somewhere fifty miles out to sea towards Cuba. It had three shots of brandy, two of tequila, a twist of lemon, a guzzle of Jamaican brandy and some weird-looking blue and green mixers that turned the whole concoction muddy brown. I switched from brandy to Hurricane Marys and I'd had two before I saw a familiar face in the doorway.

'Karl Stone,' the blond lady said as she sat down beside me. 'You like to cut it fine, don't you?'

I was smiling at nothing. A dumb Hurricane Mary smile. I hadn't really believed that the blond lady would make it, but here she was, as if summoned by the alcohol. After several strong ones, all things seemed possible, and her arrival proved that all things were possible. My sober self was just putting on his hat and getting ready to make for the door. I was still smiling, and for dramatic effect, running my finger around the rim of my glass.

'Can I get you a drink?' I said.

'Why not,' she said, 'it might be our last. What *is* that thing?'

I ordered her a special and tried to take in her features. She was better-looking close up, and scrubbed, and her nose was neat and her lips were full and her eyes were healthy-looking. She had a straw hat which she put on the seat beside her.

'My name is Azul,' she said, tired of waiting for me to ask. 'And I'm a journalist.'

I clicked my fingers.

'Ten points to me for being a clever boy.'

'I'm sorry?'

'Ah, nothing.'

The cocktail arrived and she took a sip through a straw. She coughed and patted her chest. Outside the sun was still shining, but it was like the sunlight in a dream. Bright but with no heat, and no body.

'For ten bonus points,' I said, acting more drunk than I really was, 'you're a journalist working on a story about Scarlet Timberley, correct?'

She opened her shoulder-bag and took out a notepad and a pencil. Even in my half drunkenness, I was already registering some surprise at how the blond lady had turned out. I'd known a few journalists who worked for the scandal sheets back in London, and I'd already assumed that Azul must have been working for some similar sort of paper here in the US. What other sort of journalist would go around tailing people and taking photographs of them from speeding cars? In London, the tabloid journalists I'd known all had an air of sourness and disappointment about them. They all seemed to me to be the kind of people whose hopes have been dashed and who are more sure than anyone else that they are downright awful people, but they don't really know how it happened. I sometimes found it touching. But Azul had a clearness about her which surprised me. Perhaps the American breed of this particular species lived a cleaner life.

'Well, am I right?'

She gave me a nervous smile and nodded.

'So you are working on a story about Scarlet Timberley?'

'Yes, yes, I am. The man at the café said you had something for me.'

She had her pencil poised. She was giving me a hopeful smile. She was in her early twenties, so it was possible that she had only just started out. After all, I didn't imagine that the Scarlet Timberley story was exactly the hottest news item. Maybe Azul was cutting her teeth.

'Well, aren't you going to apologize first?' I said.

She blinked with incomprehension.

'For nearly getting me killed on the highway. For taking pictures of me. For following me all over the island like some . . .'

She giggled nervously. I could have been talking about a dormitory prank that had worked out rather well.

'I thought it was all pretty neat,' she said, and giggled again.

I raised my eyebrows. 'Neat?'

'Exciting.'

'Oh.'

Her pencil was still poised. She reminded me of a high-school girl on an assignment, interviewing some local character.

'Well, it was certainly exciting,' I said. 'I nearly got killed by a truck and then I got stopped for speeding.'

She giggled again. I found myself smiling in spite of myself. Perhaps this calm sunlight was real sunlight after all. When I blinked heavily and looked out at the sky I saw that it had taken on the colour of burnished brass, like a huge brass shield held up in front of the sun. The ocean seemed to be changing colour every second, and the air pressure was making my ears buzz. Any other time, I would have been fascinated, or terrified, or something. Instead I found myself studying Azul's face, and she was studying mine. Any cars passing down Duvall Street were doing the speed limit and more. People were still walking outside but they were walking quickly, holding themselves in check, as if they knew that if one person started to run, everyone would start to run. Azul and I were on our own island, oblivious.

'Who do you work for, Azul?' I asked.

'Oh, just a little paper. You wouldn't know it.'

She put her pencil down at last, resigned to at least a minute of small talk.

'Try me.'

'The *Kansas City Mail*.'

'And do your superiors at the *Kansas City Mail* know that you drive around at a hundred miles an hour taking photos of innocent people?'

A giggle, a tossing back of the hair, a sly look that perhaps for the first time betrayed something behind the eyes. There was a cat up on the roof of the fast-food place across the street, arching its back at the sky and hissing, wondering whether or not it was crazy to jump.

'I'm pretty much free on this assignment,' she said. 'Free to do whatever is necessary.'

I drank some more Hurricane Mary, and Azul drank some too. We were smiling at each other with straws in our mouths. Some part of me was still angry, somewhere.

'So what is the story?' I asked.

She took up her pencil. 'Perhaps you could tell me that,' she said.

I was about to speak when she said, 'Your glass is empty, Mr Stone, would you like another Hurricane?' I said that I would. We were smiling cutely at each other again. I saw the cat falling through the air. It was crazy to

130

jump, but even crazier to stay up on that roof. Even a cat knew that time was short.

'You're doing a follow-up story to the stuff about her marriage to James Lisson, is that right?'

'Got it in one,' she said. Was there a hint of sarcasm there? Was I making this thing up as I went along and she was just following? She waited for my cocktail to be placed on the Hemingway coaster in front of me. When it came, I saw Hemingway's grizzled face sneering up at me and smiled down at him. There were only three other customers left in the bar, three tough guys with rock-and-roll haircuts and tattoos. They were draining their glasses with reckless abandon. One of them, a beard in a baseball cap, slapped his belly, opened his arms to the window and shouted, 'Do your worst, you son of a bitch.' Then they carefully loaded two dozen or more bottles of beer into boxes and shoved each other out into the street. That phoney sun was still shining.

'So what's your angle?' I said. 'That's what you journalists call it, isn't it? An angle?'

'Last I heard it was still called an angle, yes.'

'I don't like journalists as a rule,' I said. 'But at least I like them more than advertising copywriters.'

I thought this was quite a funny joke and felt rather superior when Azul didn't get it. I took a long drink. When I got into my car and drove away from this island, where would I be heading? Where was I going to sleep tonight, and for ever afterwards? I wanted to think things through and feel sorry for myself, but Azul's inquisitive silence was unnerving. I didn't like the way she was being so mysterious, making me do all the work. I became irritable for no reason and realized Hurricane Marys were even stronger than they seemed. They flowed directly into the brain blood.

131

'For a journalist, you don't say a lot,' I said, suddenly peeved at the way she seemed to be looking down her nose at me.

'I just listen,' she said, 'so perhaps you could tell me what you've got.'

I paused and thought. Thinking was taking a long time. This stuff was hotter and neater and fiercer than anything I had ever drunk, and I had drunk almost everything. When I'd ordered my first one, the barman (young, sober, probably American teetotal) had said, 'Here, this'll put a hurricane in your belly.' He'd been right, and now the hurricane was spreading to a place somewhere behind my eyes.

'Wait a minute,' I said, and sighed and chinked my glass with my thumbnail. Over and over. 'Wait a minute, you say you work for the *Kansas City Mail* but you're covering a story in Key West?' I said.

'Kind of.'

'What do you mean, kind of?'

'Well, I'm working freelance on this project. I took some time off. I picked up on it because Scarlet Timberley was a Kansas girl, but I guess that doesn't mean too much. I don't think the *Kansas City Mail* readers would really want to hear a story about some sleazy, boozed-up whore, do you, Mr Stone?'

She gave me that high-school smile again. This time it was maddening. The shadow of a shark beneath sunlit, calm waters.

'What did you say?'

'Say, Mr Stone?'

'You fucking sanctimonious bitch!'

'You want something more to drink, Mr Stone?'

Across the street, someone was nailing a huge wooden board across a plate-glass window, covering up a painting of a pig with a smile and a chef's hat. I smiled and waved the pig bye-bye. Azul turned to see what I was looking at and then turned back to me. There was no contempt in her eyes, just curiosity.

'Do you have something for me or not, Mr Stone?' Azul said.

'She is not a whore.'

'Whatever you say.'

'Fuck you.'

'Sure.'

My anger was beginning to spark. Back in London, this fury had become a dark companion to me, a creature that I summoned from a bottle like a genie from a lamp. Then, just as in the story, I couldn't get the damn thing back inside. That's when it had got out of hand. I was rapping the table with my knuckle, the knuckle that I had hurt punching Benelli. The pain reminded me of why I was here. I was here to blow Benelli's scam wide open. I looked at Azul and she was smiling cutely with a straw between her lips.

'Are you ready to tell me whatever it is you want to tell me?' she said, with no sign of impatience.

'Wait,' I said, looking around the bar, fuming, not knowing why. 'Take back what you said about Scarlet.'

My sober self peeked in through the window. 'Take it back? What the hell is the matter with you?' I closed the blinds on him.

'I take it back, Mr Stone,' she said evenly. 'Scarlet Timberley is not a whore.'

'Thank you.'

I was rapping my knuckles harder. The booze was a larger swell under my eyes. Rough seas. Azul was speaking softly.

'The fact that she screws pretty much every man she ever . . .'

I slammed my fist down on the table. She hardly blinked. This wasn't right at all. My ears were definitely hurting now, and the sounds from the street were muffled. I felt that I was wearing earplugs, or that I was hearing everything from inside a closet. The sudden softness of the sounds made everything seem remote and distant. I saw two cop cars flash by the bar with their lights rolling but I didn't hear any sirens.

'OK, OK,' she said, 'let's just both do what we came here to do. I've got a hurricane to catch.'

'You'll take pictures of that too, I suppose.'

'Please, Mr Stone, spare me the indignation. Two hundred and twenty grand, isn't it?'

'So you've done your homework.'

'Like a good little girl.'

No, this wasn't right at all. The air was as heavy as water. Then it changed suddenly and my ears popped. Everything was close up again and real, the sounds of cars and of people yelling to each other outside and the sounds of frantic hammering all had a sharp metallic edge to them. I realized that the birds had stopped singing. There were no gulls or pelicans in the air. I told Azul that all the birds had gone ... gone home. Home wherever that was. I began to think about where I would go when the storm hit. Then I remembered what Azul had just said.

'So you know about the money he paid me.'

She blinked to tell me that she knew everything. Every single thing.

'You're too clever by half to be working on the *Kansas City Mail*,' I said.

'You think so?'

'Yes, I think so.'

'Why, thank you. Now tell me all about this movie that you are writing for $220,000.'

'Tell me what your angle is.'

'My angle? OK, Mr Stone, but I don't think you'll like it. How about this for a headline: "Gold-digging Hollywood alcoholic gets stung for six million?"'

I smiled and shook my head. The world-weary wisdom of three Hurricane Marys. 'That's very pretty, Azul,' I said. She began to flick through her notepad.

'Now, as my story stands at the present moment,' she said, as if she were concluding a business meeting, 'I have two people who come out wearing black hats. That's you and Mr . . .'(she consulted her notebook)'. . . G. F. Benelli. Producer, Italian, possible mob connections, formerly of S-Productions. And in the story as it stands I have Scarlet Timberley coming across looking like a gullible, drunken tramp. Now I assume, Mr Stone, that the way you'd like it to be would be if I change it around so that you come out of the story looking like a hero. Isn't that right? The guy who blows the whistle.'

I didn't say anything. I took another long drink of Hurricane Mary. Azul watched me as if she'd just lifted a rock. That was exactly how I wanted the story to run. The guy who blows the whistle, Karl Stone, helluva guy.

'Got it in one, Azul,' I said. 'Go to the top of the class.'

'That's good. So what do you have for me? Do you have any evidence?'

I didn't want this conversation to continue. Even before I'd got drunk, part of me was looking forward to spilling the beans on Benelli. I thought that it would be a noble moment, the first moment of selfless nobility in my life for a year, maybe even ten years. Then the part about handing back the money. I would have enjoyed mentioning that in passing. Now she had stolen that moment away from me and I directed all my pointless anger at her.

'So can you tell me how you know so fucking much about me or is that a fucking secret?' I asked.

135

'It's not a fucking secret, Mr Stone. Like you said, I'm too clever by half to be working on the *Kansas City Mail*.'

For the first time a shadow of uncertainty on her face. How could anyone have found out what she had found out?

'You're not a cop, are you?' I said and lost my momentum. Azul turned to look out of the window. The sky was beginning to grow dark, and when I looked out, I saw what appeared to be the drawing of a set of mighty curtains across the sky. It felt like the end of a movie, when the curtains close and the light is turned off. The darkness was on the horizon, and some part of me, some part that hadn't been anaesthetized by the booze, contracted in terror. There were mighty curtains out on the horizon and they had just been closed by God.

'So you don't have any hard evidence for me,' Azul said.

'Go to hell. You talk like a cop.'

'Then perhaps you can confirm something about the plot of this movie you're supposed to be writing. She's murdered, isn't she?'

'Who is?'

'Laura. Scarlet Timberley.'

'You're the fucking expert.'

'She gets smothered with a pillow, isn't that right?'

I peered hard into her eyes. There was nothing to see but blue. She even knew the plot of the movie. She blinked again, telling me that if in doubt, I should just assume she knew everything, that she hadn't missed a single thing. If I had been sober, I would have been fascinated by her, I would have liked her mystery. But the alcohol had swelled my pride and made my ego tender, so I felt offended and righteous and indignant. She closed her notebook and put it back into her shoulder-bag.

136

'For all I know,' she said, 'this story won't even make the *Enquirer*. Maybe Scarlet Timberley is just old news, and maybe this scam of yours is just too plain stupid for anyone to believe it. But it's been an experience, Mr Stone. Pity you don't have any hard evidence.'

She stood up and I followed her with my eyes. My vision was becoming fuzzy.

'If I were you,' she said with great authority, 'I'd get to a safe place as quick as you can, Mr Stone. Do you have a safe place to go to?'

'Don't you worry your sweet . . . I'll go to . . . anyway I'm English, hurricanes can't get you if you're English.'

She was smiling down at me benignly. It was a look of pity that I'd seen so many times when I'd been in this condition and it always made me as mad as hell. Some voice inside my head instructed me to tell her that she was in danger if she didn't get away from me quickly. The moment passed.

'Your place does have a cellar, doesn't it?' Azul said, and I nodded at my glass, an ironic smile curled up with lots of phoney confidence.

'Then I suggest you go to your cellar,' Azul said. 'I'll mention that you came to me. In my story, I mean. I'll write about our little meeting. Who knows, you might come out of it as the hero after all. Or maybe an anti-hero. That's what you movie people call it, isn't it? Bad guy turned good, or bad guy with a conscience or something. And for what it's worth, I sort of admire you for what you've done. A lot of guys would have just taken the money.'

She was gone before any response could make its way through the sludge in my mind. A cocktail of drink and anger and regret and self-pity. Outside, there was some sort of cop car or ambulance cruising down the street, and

137

there was a voice coming through a PA system on top of the vehicle, but those words couldn't make it through either.

After Azul had gone, I smiled and winked at the line drawing of Hemingway on my beer coaster, and suggested out loud that he and I wait right here for the hurricane to come and seek us out.

CHAPTER THIRTEEN

The sunset was wrecked that day. By four, the air outside was thick and green, just as if the whole island had been sucked up into a cloud of heavy gas. Duvall Street was empty. Even the insects had found a place of safety, and I figured that in the whole of the island there were only two living creatures above sea level. Me and the young, sober barman at Sloppy Joe's.

'So anyway, this Benelli. This fat Benelli bastard. He's got her. He's got her like in a trap. In a hole. And he knows that whatever I say and whatever I try to do . . .'

The barman was closing and locking the wooden doors on the liquor cabinet behind the bar.

'Benelli's the director, right?' he said, without any apparent interest.

'Thassright,' I said, 'he's the fucking director. No, I mean producer. He's the producer. And he says . . . where did I get to . . .?'

The barman shrugged his shoulders. He glanced quickly out into the street and the sight of the first specks of rain on the glass front of the bar made him hurry with the last of his work, putting a box of glasses into a corner and covering them with a blanket.

'You'd got to the part where you said she'd have to choose. You or the movie.'

'Thassright. She'd have to choose. Shake us up another Hurricane, would you? And then she looks at me. And she's got a tear in her eye . . .'

The barman had his hands on his hips and a brave smile.

139

"Fraid the bar's closed as of right now,' he said. 'And if I were you I'd get back to wherever it is you're going and get under cover. You see that rain on the window?'

I turned slowly, blinking in slow motion, hardly seeing the large splashes of water that were starting to hit the window.

'Well, that ain't rain at all,' he said. 'That's the ocean. And if you look out at the sidewalk . . .'

I stood up on the crossbar of my stool to look at the sidewalk. I thought that perhaps I was beginning to hallucinate.

'Fish?' I said.

'Sure are, sir. Like I say, I think we'd better close.'

Out on Duvall Street there were maybe a dozen small red fish, still flapping and gasping for air. It was a jolt of primeval terror that for a moment cut through the alcohol. I saw a long wooden pole with some netting attached glide over Duvall Street in slow motion. It spun around as it moved, like a vision in a nightmare.

'I'd say we've got fifteen minutes left. Did you have a coat, sir?'

The barman had already skipped out from behind the bar and he was helping me to my feet. I shook him off and my knuckles hurt. He asked me where I was headed and I said that I didn't know. For a moment he was unsure whether he should invite me to go with him but the way I looked, I guess he decided against it. He escorted me to the door.

'I'll go back to the movie house,' I said, after a long pause.

'Where, sir?'

'Doesn't matter.'

'Has the place you're going got a cellar?'

The barman had his keys ready and he was anxious. He

took hold of the handle of the door like a parachutist about to leap out. I was thinking about the cellar, about the serpent and about Scarlet. By now, I guessed she'd be over at the Madagascar with Benelli. I also thought about Azul. Hell, I thought, I'd really liked her at first.

'When I open this door,' the barman was saying, 'you run like hell. Like I say, you'll be OK for fifteen minutes, but after that you'd better be under cover. Otherwise . . .'

'Otherwise what?'

'There is no otherwise.'

The barman braced himself. Then he yanked the door open and I heard a low moan. He stepped outside first and then I followed him. There were fish flapping around our feet and the light was as thick as treacle. When I stepped into the street, I felt a great heave against my back, like a huge body of water moving slowly against me. I couldn't get my breath and I found myself eye to eye with a red fish. The barman helped me to my feet again. The sound of the wind was like the sound of an infernal freight train, heard a mile away. Then the sound took on another tone, and it sounded exactly like the roar of an enormous crowd. There was an enormous crowd of people at my back, all 'oooohing' and 'aaahing' at me as I struggled to stand upright in the wind. And in the far distance, the torrential rain on the ocean sounded like a celestial round of applause. I took a drunken bow and turned my head and saw the great emptiness of the sky, thought even that I could see the sound, or see the mouth of something making the sound. The barman had hold of my arm and he managed to steady me, but then I heard a thick slapping sound and saw a dark, ragged shape thud into the wall that I was using for support. It wasn't until I saw the ragged feathers, the twisted beak broken and bloody, the dumb confusion in the eye, that I worked out

141

that it was a pelican, slung against the wall and pinned there, not even bleeding. Its leathery mouth gaped open, a silent question issuing from it. I had never been alone before. I had never been alone like this ever, and never at the mercy of the whole universe.

'Now you run like hell, sir,' I heard the barman saying, but his voice seemed to come from a long way away. I had stepped out of the bar, drunk, into a drunken dream. The light was the light of dreams, and the sounds were too mighty for my ears. Each house, street light, wall and tree had picked out its own note from the wind, and was vibrating at its own resonance. The wind had brought everything to life and the whole world had started to sing. I stumbled into a street sign that was screaming at high pitch, and the gable ends of the houses further down the street were all beginning to moan and mumble deep in their throats. My jacket and trousers were on fire, trying to tear themselves from my body, and every few seconds another mangled black body would whizz through the air a few feet above my head. The percussion of this symphony was being played all across the island, huge bangs and crashes of metal against metal, of whole buildings dancing in their foundations. I did believe in God now, or something, or fate or force or the devil. I was so scared that I thought that my legs were going to seize up. I hadn't realized it was going to be like this. I hadn't realized it would correspond on the outside with the worst thoughts on the inside. I hadn't realized the hurricane was going to be a personal thing, with me and my head inside it, or under it.

The barman waited a few precious seconds for me to get my legs working. I began to trot up Duvall Street and didn't look back. I was saying 'Jesus, Jesus, fucking, fucking, hell almighty . . .' and even my own voice was swallowed by the thousand voices. I imagined myself as a fish caught on a hook, being pulled fast through muddy water. The moan was getting thicker, and I suddenly realized how much air there was between the ground and the sky. A huge tank of air that was being sloshed around and tipped over. The world was getting insane. This was Duvall Street, and that was Mary's Bar and there was the Haitian Art Co. and over here the florist's, but all of it, all of us, had been transported to the bottom of the ocean, or the bottom of a dirty rusty tank where everything was green and sludgy. And everything, every single thing in the world had been given a voice. The air was so heavy it felt as if the sky had fallen in. I ran as fast as I could and found myself crashing into shop fronts when the wind, thoughtlessly, effortlessly, shoved me from the side.

'Jesus, Jesus, dear God almighty, fuck . . .'

The wind was taking my breath out of my mouth. I had a terrible desire to piss but I also had the crazy idea that it would have been sacrilegious. I didn't want to look up for fear that I might offend the deity of the hurricane, for fear that it would notice me and pick me up between its earthy fingers and toss me out into the Gulf of Mexico. I was pushed easily against the side of a pale blue Volkswagen Beetle that I had often walked past and which had been abandoned to the midnight wreckers. As I hit it with my hip, the car lifted a foot off the road, rearing up like a horse. An old, wrecked, rusted-up car suddenly taking life into itself, animated by the caress from up above. The rearing of the car and the way it clunked back on to the road, angry and alive, made me double my speed. I turned into Mallory Street and all the trees were bent in the same direction, bent almost in two and held there by the wind. Any wind I had ever known had blown in gusts and squalls. It had blown hard and then died or relented. This wind blew constant and even, as if it was being manufactured by a machine. The wind in the street was stronger but at least it was at my back now. The wind pushed me forwards so fast I fell over twice and gambolled forward like a tumbleweed. When I reached the gate of 1131, I had to hold on to a tree-trunk to stop myself being shoved past. The tangle of undergrowth along the drive was alive, scratching and writhing. But what was making my bowels twist in fear was the enormity, the sheer enormity of the sound.

Just as I reached the door and fumbled with my keys, I turned for half a second in the direction of the ocean. Down south towards Cuba and the darkness. There, on the horizon, the sickening black funnel, a ferocious twisting living creature stretching from the sky to the earth. And the thing had a voice of its own, a voice that seemed to contain an infinite number of harmonies. Even above the vibrations and the singing of the houses and the trees, this thing on the horizon had its own pure, deep note that held all the others together. I thought of a monastic choir, made up of a million voices of every pitch, all twisted together and magnified until the music was deafening. There was a hissing sound coming from the cellar too, the sound of the wind (please God) rushing through the cracks in the floorboards. The whole house seething. Just as I opened the door, something, I don't know what, hit me on the back of the neck and pushed me into the darkness.

After I had managed to heave the front door closed, I became dizzy and woke up still lying on the floor, maybe three or four seconds later. My neck hurt and I checked for blood but there wasn't any. In the darkness of the house, I felt drunk again, and my ears were buzzing. I heard a noise coming from the top of the house, from Scarlet's room, and I wondered . . .

What happened next I remember only as a series of images. Some of them are still images, in green and white, others have movement and sound. I must have dwelt on these images, like grainy, scratched film, only half-developed, a thousand times. I have run them back and forth over and over again. Always it is the same series of images. Always there is only darkness between the moments of flickering light. And the score to this nightmare is the million voices, the ooohing and the aaahing of an enormous crowd.

First, I was at the top of the stairs and a thought came to me that being inside the house was like being a mosquito inside the engine of a truck screaming down a highway. The pain in my neck had spread to the back of my head. I wanted to be sick.

The next image was of the ceiling of the house, buckling under a great weight. I was inside the dream now, fully inside it, and I could see myself moving slowly through it, lit by green light and deafened by the roar of the engine. I got up on to my knees and the house swayed and toppled. In my drunkenness, the world kept falling over on to its side, the floor kept rushing up to touch my face. I heard the sound of glass smashing inside Scarlet's room.

Next, there are two green and white still images.

In the first of them, the door to Scarlet's room is swinging on its hinges, falling outwards, a rectangular shadow that twisted across my eye line, blocking out the sickly green light from the skylight. I watched the door twist and thought that I could feel the handle of it in my damaged hand, as if somehow it was me who was pulling the thing out of its frame. As if I had the power of the hurricane in my arms.

After a period of darkness which could have lasted a few seconds or an hour, there is the second image. It is an image of myself, seen from outside, seen from somewhere above the skylight, and I am running down the staircase with my mouth open, letting out an almighty scream. But there is no sound. I can see myself clearly from outside, just as if I were looking at a green and white tinted photograph, acting out some scene in a drama, with my mouth open and my hand, my damaged hand, pouring with green blood. There is blood on my shirt too, and blood in my tangled hair. My shadow on the wall is enormous and the picture is accompanied by a deep groaning sound coming from outside, the hurricane itself opening its mouth and screaming for me. After that, there is more darkness.

I left the dream as I pulled open the door to the cellar, which was stiff and swollen and took an almighty effort to open. I used my damaged hand, and I remember the pain as a bolt of pure agony that filled my whole body. When the door opened, I saw the darkness of the cellar below, and smelt its rotten breath, just as if I had opened up a mouth filled with decay. I could smell turpentine too, and the smell of damp wood, a pure distillation of the faint odour that had always filled the house. I could hear the wind hammering against the front of the house, beating against the front door, and for just a few moments I was sure that the hurricane had a will of its own, that it had a purpose and that its purpose was to pursue me. I slithered down the broken wooden steps that led into the cellar, and after I had heaved the cellar door shut, I turned around to face the darkness. It was then that I found myself staring into the glinting, golden eye of the serpent.

PART TWO

CHAPTER FOURTEEN

Finally, the birds were singing. Blue jays and sparrows and black and yellow finches and some other birds, with throaty, tropical shrieks, most likely blown from Venezuela and blinking in the unfamiliar dawn of a Florida morning. Blown clear across the equator and waking up naked here, where they didn't belong. The grey light was filtering through the slats of the floorboards above my head like smoke and I could hear a voice outside in the street, a man's voice, broken up and trembling, calling out, 'Anybody seen my dog? Hey mister, you seen my dog? Little fella, red coat?'

The wind was still blowing too. An ironic moan through the cracks in the house. Gentle and soothing now but never the same again. Not now that my whole way of thinking had been broken up and twisted around. The whisper of the wind was a tease, saying 'Jesus, what happened here? I was drunk as a racoon last night. What did I do?'

The serpent in the cellar still had its ugly yellow mouth open, just as it had last night, when I had seen it in a crack of light that came from outside. The light had fizzed and sparked and I had figured that it was a power line hitting the ground and shorting out. In that light, I had seen the long snout and the brown, varnished rivulets along its back. I had fallen sideways on to a pile of boxes and stared into its golden eye, flashing in the light from the power cable. Now, in the grey, smoky morning, I could see that it was an alligator. A six-foot swamp

149

alligator made out of hardwood and painted and varnished, the varnish still shining through a thin coat of dust. The eye was open but sleeping now, the terror of it gone, and I could just make out the stencilled lettering on its yellow underbelly.

'Property of Warner Bros. Pictures and props. KL/ 142.'

More light, green and bilious, and more memories. I had crashed into something hard and sharp behind me. I was thrashing around down there among this unfathomable junk, this boneyard, but I couldn't make any sound. I had been screaming as loudly as I could but the sound was swallowed up by the great roar of the choir above the floorboards where the house had its own voice and where the wind was making the cavities and cracks howl with pleasure. I had slammed into a wall and I could even smell the ancient plaster that had crumbled as I hit it, but I couldn't make a sound. I couldn't make a sound big enough to be heard beneath the chorus of the hurricane and it had been that, amongst all the horror, that had made me most afraid. Last night, the cellar had had no shape, no up or down, no corners or angles, only sound and the pain it inflicted when I hit my body against a wall or floor joist. Now, I could just make out the geography of it, and feel the distilled decay in the air.

My hand hurt as I clenched my fists, and I cried out in pain to be sure that I could make a noise that I could hear. I cried out and the serpent still sat on its perch on top of an old wooden trunk, like a sea monster left behind by a retreating tide, belonging only to the visions of the night before. Outside, the dog owner's voice was more distant and more hopeless: 'Anybody seen him? Little fella. Red fur. He got out of the goddam cellar and I couldn't keep a hold of him.'

I tried to reach over to grab the wooden serpent and a pain shot up my arm like two thousand volts. 'Jesus, my hand,' I mumbled and I held my hand at the wrist as if it didn't belong to me. I wondered how it had got so bad and I thought that the sick air in the cellar had infected it.

'How the hell did it get like this?' I said out loud to myself.

The knuckles were swollen and I could see that a tendon had run out of its joint. Both my hands had dried blood on them, like a coating of rust, and I could also feel a dull ache in my head that was more than just the sour poison of last night's alcohol. I touched the back of my neck and found a damp swollen bruise and it felt like touching the inside of a water melon. I used my good hand to grab the throat of the serpent and as I turned it around its tail clunked against the cement floor. When I ran my finger along the wooden brow above its eye, lots of things suddenly began to fall into place.

All at once and in no order, I began to rerun the images from the night before and I watched them through a window misted up by alcohol. I stared into the glass eye of the alligator and it stared back into mine and I could see in its reflection a series of green and white images, some of them images from dreams, some of them real memories of what had happened after I had returned to the movie house from Sloppy Joe's. The real images were like frames of coloured film; a picture of Mallory Street with the trees whipping the air, a memory of how I had fallen in through the front door, a snapshot of the staircase, lit by the sickly green light of the hurricane as I climbed. The green light of the hurricane then becomes the green and white of my dreams, the dreams I had had after I had fallen, unconscious. And in amongst these images, lit like a jewel inside the eye of the serpent, there was one image

151

that stood out from all of the others. It was an image of Scarlet, lying on her bed, with her arms outstretched as if she were saying, 'Come to bed, Karl, I'm tired.'

The sound of sirens outside made me come to. I looked around at all that crazy junk, the alligator, the boxes of paper, a smock of some kind, or rather an ethnic cloak in an Indian design woven scarlet and black. And beside that there was a roughly carved oar from a boat, and then (emerging from the darkness that was shrinking into the corners) the up-ended belly of an Indian canoe. I could just make out the words 'Prop.' and 'Warner' written along its spine. I remembered how Crazy Jimmy had told me that this place used to belong to Warner Brothers and how I hadn't believed him.

I closed my eyes and the reel of images began to run again. I saw Scarlet on her bed, and this time I saw that there was green blood on her arms and around her face. Then another frame, then another and then the alligator (Jesus Christ!) falling with a crack on to the floor. Was that the wind getting up again outside or was it somebody crying out? Maybe the guy who'd lost his dog. Or maybe the sound was coming from up the stairs. I put my hurt hand deep into my armpit and squeezed it, as if the new pain would make the other pain go away. I was breathing hard, the way animals do when they are wounded. The pain in my hand and the pain in my head were both meeting up somewhere, sending out sharp flashes of electricity that made me flinch whenever I moved or thought too hard. I knew that the hurricane outside was probably over, but it struck me that a little piece of the hurricane had got into my head and was still swirling around in there, breaking open Scarlet's door, pushing me down the stairs, making me scream silently. I had an insane notion that it had got into my head through the wound in the back of my neck and I sat down on a cardboard box that farted and let me down all the way to the floor.

The sirens began to take over from all the other sounds. It was as if they had been summoned all at once, and I guessed that some kind of all-clear had been given. I took this as a signal to move, to try walking, to see if there was still a house above my head or just a bonfire of timber and wire.

Clark had been right. This old house had been built to last. When I pushed open the cellar door, the house was hollowed out and toothless but grinning back at me nevertheless.

All the windows had been broken and the door had gone, so that as soon as I walked out into the hall I could see into Mallory Street. The old oak banister on the stairs had held, but alongside it there was another length of timber, painted white, that lay up the full length of the lower staircase. It had rigging rope hanging from it, and a small red swallow-tail pennant. When I peered outside, I could see that there was a pleasure boat nosing up to the front of the house. The hull had been smashed at the front and I could see the remains of the cabin, gutted like a fish. As I made my way up the stairs, I saw a puddle of dried blood, and I had to step aside to avoid putting my foot into it. On the next stair there was some raw meat, and on the next one a mess of blue and green entrails and beside that a little bundle of red fur.

'Sure, mister, I've seen your dog,' I said.

I made the upper landing and the beating of my heart made my head hurt. Each pump of blood was more painful than the last. The door to Scarlet's room was a few feet along the landing, but I could see that it had twisted off, just as I remembered it. I made my way

153

forward towards the shadows and I heard the tinkling of a bell below me. The white mast on the stairs still had its little chrome bell attached and the wind through the open door was making it ring. Then the moment I had been dreading was already over and I was saying out loud, 'Well, what did you expect?' The curtains in Scarlet's room were billowing in the wind just as I remembered, but her bed was empty.

I stepped inside and crunched on broken glass. For no reason I had hoped to get into the room without making a noise, as if there was something inside the room that I didn't want to disturb. Scarlet's dressing-table was lying flat on its nose, and her wardrobe had tipped forward so that it was balancing precariously on the foot of the bed. Its doors had fallen open, enclosing a dark area of shadow within its embrace. The last thing Scarlet had said to me had been that she was going to wait right here in this room for Benelli, and then she'd go with him to the Madagascar Hotel. And that's where she'd be. Scarlet would be in the Madagascar, and this feeling I had, this chill, this odour in my nostrils, was just a product of the alcohol and the pain in my head. I said it out loud, but the image of Scarlet's bloody body in my dream was flashing on the wall, like the smudged image you get from an out of focus projector.

The wardrobe was lighter than it looked. I lifted its end like lifting a rock and beneath it, in the tent of darkness, I saw Scarlet's body, curled up and bloody inside the tomb that the hurricane had built for her. A sarcophagus made out of an old worm-eaten wardrobe and the rusting iron of a bed. The sight of her body had no effect on me. The moment I saw it, her twisted body (real enough, oh God, and grey) became a point of convergence. Her body was the place where my dreams and my memories met and became the same. I wanted to shake her, and talk to her, but instead I held the wardrobe up with my good hand and allowed myself to compare the sight of her body with the image in my dreams. Scarlet had never made it to the Madagascar. She had stayed here in this room and the hurricane had killed her. The hurricane which had been seeking her out since she was six years old had finally settled its account with her. It had come into the room and killed her and then built this tomb for her, to show its respect.

'Yes, yes,' I said out loud, 'the hurricane killed her.'

Then I whispered, 'OK, OK, come on, come on,' and I took a deep breath and even sighed as I exhaled as if this were a flat tyre on a rainy road. An inconvenience. I became calm and my own calmness was infuriating because Scarlet was witness to it and I wanted her to see (her eyes were open) that I wanted her to come back and to wake up. I remembered some of the more absurd farewells I had said to people in my life, cold and embarrassed when I was sober, tearful and embarrassed and sentimental when I was drunk. I may have said her name out loud then and my hand began to shake. I began to talk out loud but I can't remember what I said, only that it was some sort of prayer (probably for myself) and that it was the kind of prayer you would say if you don't believe that anyone is really listening. I let the wardrobe fall back and I was alone in the room again.

I thought about going back under the floorboards and staying there. I thought about going out to my car and driving as fast as I could to Tampa airport. Instead, I went out into the street, stood beside the wreck of the boat, which was called the *Santa Maria*, and began calling for help.

CHAPTER FIFTEEN

Since I was now inside my very own hurricane, a hurricane that had its own bizarre rules and meteorology, a sense of humour even, it was inevitable that Baxter would be called to the house at 1131 Mallory Street to look into the tomb beneath the wardrobe and take the case. But first, there were two paramedics in white overalls who introduced themselves solemnly as Sam and Nick. I had stopped an ambulance that was screaming past the end of the pathway and told them that I had something for them.

They whistled through their teeth when they saw the filleted body of the dog on the stairs, both silently making notes to add this one to their catalogue of stories. 'Little fucking thing had been split right down the middle . . .' They took hold of the boat's mast from the staircase and carried it with silent dignity outside to put it back on the deck of the boat, as if they were reassembling a body. They dusted their hands and asked me if that was all, the dog and the mast, and I said no, there was something else that they ought to see. Then they followed me upstairs to Scarlet's room.

'Jees,' said Sam, the older of the two, shoving the wardrobe back on to its feet and destroying the tomb for ever. Nick shook his head and cleared his throat, regaining his composure more quickly. He peered down at the body.

'You found her right here, Mr Stone?'

'Yes.'

'How comes she didn't go down to the cellar with you?'

I didn't say anything. Nick had Scarlet's head in his

hands and was rolling it around on the stiff joint of her neck.

'No,' he said firmly and the two men swapped glances. They hunched over the body and began a little dance, one at each end, to straighten her out on the floorboards. The older one began to massage her ribs and the younger one, the cooler one who looked puzzled, pushed his fingers into her throat. They didn't say anything and the fact that neither of them had said anything seemed to have great significance for them. Then Sam lifted her arm and peered at her wrist. It was caked in blood, a soft scab that looked like melted chocolate. He studied the other wrist, which was the same, and then he peered into Nick's eyes for a long time. Then they noticed the blood on the floorboards, on the doors of the wardrobe, on the mattress, and they saw the blood that was dried on my hands. They began to look around at all the black blood and I felt that the wind was taking my breath from the inside.

'OK, Mr Stone,' they both said, one after the other, and carefully laid the body back into the position in which they'd found it. Suddenly, without a word being spoken, the two men seemed to agree that the body shouldn't be touched any more. They leant over it with their hands behind their backs, hardly breathing, studying every inch of exposed flesh. I hadn't registered until then that Scarlet was still wearing her dressing-gown, but now, in the manhandling, it had gaped open and I could see the tops of her thighs, still firm and muscular. I looked down at the floor and the floorboards creaked beneath my feet. The two of them were whispering to each other softly and evenly.

'Looky here,' one of them murmured, and I looked up long enough to see that they were both peering up her nose. When I looked down again I heard the younger one saying something about her throat.

157

'Throat's full of vomit,' he said a little louder. They both straightened up and seemed to deliberately take a long time before regaining the breezy efficiency they'd had when they first stepped into the room.

'This your wife, Mr Stone?'

'No.'

'Girlfriend?'

I tried to speak but couldn't. I knew that I ought to look up and meet their eye, but for now, grief was a plausible explanation for the way I was standing in the corner of the room, tapping my toe rhythmically, staring down at the floor. When I did wipe my sleeve across my eyes and look up, I saw Sam pursing his lips and flicking his head, a silent but clearly understood instruction to the younger one who walked quickly out of the room. We listened to his footsteps all the way down the stairs and out on to the front drive.

'She didn't like hurricanes,' I said softly, purely to hear the sound of my own voice. The paramedic was peering out of the broken window, checking that his assistant was following instructions.

'What's that y'say?'

'I said she didn't like hurricanes. She was scared of them.'

This made Sam laugh. He turned to me.

'I guess nobody likes hurricanes, Mr Stone. Not man nor beast, fish nor fowl.'

He seemed to be deliberately using up time. He began to whistle under his breath without a tune to hold on to. I wanted to get his attention again because I needed to keep talking.

'No, Sam, what I mean is . . .'

'I'm Nick. The other guy's Sam. You got us the wrong way round.'

'Oh, OK. What I mean is, I should have stayed with her.'

'Or she should have gone to the cellar with you. That would have been preferable, Mr Stone. That's what you're supposed to do. Go underground. I guess that's where she's heading now though, Mr Stone. No offence intended.'

Now that they'd moved the body, I could see the violet slashes on Scarlet's wrists more clearly. All through the night and in the morning, in my delirium, I'd been having visions of blood. Now I could see clearly that the blood in my dreams had come from Scarlet's wrists, except that didn't make any sense at all. Not any sense at all. The cuts in her wrists, criss-crossed, angry as hell, made me want to try to reason this thing through. Maybe she'd argued with Benelli and he'd left her alone when the hurricane hit. Maybe she'd got scared. So scared that she'd . . .

'Are you OK, Mr Stone?'

I was leaping to conclusions. Except they weren't conclusions yet, they were leaps into darkness. I wanted to say every thought out loud to make sure that they were my own thoughts and not voices from inside the hurricane.

'I didn't realize that she was scared like that,' I said, running my bloody hands through my hair. 'I didn't think she'd do something like that.'

'Like what?'

I pointed with my nose at the body. The violet slashes on the soft flesh of her arm seemed to answer my question. But when I looked over to the paramedic I could see that he wasn't following my eye line but instead was staring directly at me. Something about the way he stared at me made the hurricane howl. I could hear a radio crackling out on the front lawn, and the younger paramedic's voice was being raised. An even but urgent monotone. I was holding my wrist and squeezing the bone to try to cut the pain that was spreading up my arm. The paramedic looked at my hand.

'Looks pretty bad, Mr Stone. How d'ya get it?'

'Mmm? Ah . . . I guess I don't know.'

'Let me see it.'

I jerked my hand away from him and he peered at the knuckle. He looked into my eyes to let me know that he'd seen hands broken like that before. Bar fights, wife-beaters. There was a dreary tick-tocking inside the room as he looked from Scarlet's body to my hand and back to Scarlet's body again. I wanted to stroke her hair and pull her dressing-gown together. Instead I rubbed my face with my good hand and this took the paramedic's interest because he glanced at me and then looked sharply out of the window. There were more sirens outside, in the distance and close up. Then there was a siren right outside and it sighed as it was shut off. There were car doors slamming and the paramedic shifted around on his feet. When we both heard footsteps coming up the stairs, he relaxed and moved out of the room. Then I saw two patrolmen appear at the top of the landing, and a few seconds later, I saw Baxter climbing the stairs and cleaning the lenses of his spectacles with his knitted tie.

After peering at the body for just a few seconds, Baxter told one of the patrolmen to fetch Dr Hesperez. The patrolman whispered to him ('with respect, Tom') that Hesperez was busy down at the basement of the pizza place on Rose Street helping out the regular doctors, but Baxter simply nodded twice. Which the patrolman took to mean 'Just do it.' Fifteen minutes later, an old Cuban doctor arrived with blood on his shirtsleeves and with a look of silent fury that never left his face throughout the

160

whole time he was examining Scarlet's body. I thought at first that he was angry with Baxter, but realized later that he was angry with God. As he was pushing a needle thermometer through the muscle of Scarlet's stomach and into her body cavity to ascertain her time of death, Baxter said, 'How many?' and Hesperez said, 'Three,' and I took that to mean the number of people dead in the basement of the pizza place on Rose Street.

Baxter and Hesperez spent some time standing at the bay window (jagged with glass) talking quietly to each other. I saw Hesperez clutch his throat, as if he were demonstrating something. He'd spent a lot of time peering into Scarlet's mouth and nostrils during his examination, and I had seen him pull a single white feather out of her mouth. The feather had been delicately put into a plastic bag and carried away with great solemnity by one of the patrolmen. After Hesperez had left, Scarlet's body was wrapped in a yellow blanket and carried out of the room by the two paramedics. One of them explained to Baxter that they had no stretchers to spare, and Baxter said, 'Sure, and, hey, you did well to call me.' After that, when Baxter and I were left alone, he turned to me and stared down on me as if he'd never set eyes on me before in his whole life.

'Hell of a night, wasn't it, Mr Stone?' he said, removing a tooth of glass from the broken window. I mumbled that it was.

'What was that, Mr Stone?'

'I said yes it was a hell of a night. Mr Baxter, perhaps you could tell me . . .'

'Yes, sir, Mr Stone, hell of a night. Five dead minimum. Three in the pizza place and two more somewhere over by the marina. Little kids. Two little twins. Little girls. Sucked right out of their mobile home like mussels from a shell. Cubans. Rosita and Carmelita. Guy who found them thought they were dolls underneath this pile of garbage. But no sir. They were two little Cuban girls. What time did you leave Sloppy Joe's last night, Karl?'

Baxter had never called me Karl before. I wasn't even sure if I had ever told him that it was my name. I certainly had never told him that I had been in Sloppy Joe's last night. There was something strange going on with the air pressure in the room. My ears were popping as if I were in an aeroplane that was descending too fast. Maybe crashing. I could hardly hear what Baxter was saying.

'Well, Karl?'

'I'm sorry. My ears.'

'Swallow,' Baxter said, and I did and my ears cleared. At least I knew now that Baxter could feel this pressure too.

'When, Karl? When did you leave the bar?'

'I don't know . . . it was just when the hurricane hit. Whenever that was, that was when I left the bar.'

'Five thirty-seven,' Baxter said and he walked across the room with great care, his hands pushing him forward in his pockets, even managing a little hop over a triangle of glass beside the bed. 'Five thirty-seven exactly. Then, you came back here to this house and went straight down into the cellar, that right?'

Baxter was staring down at the place where Scarlet's body had been. He turned around to me and raised his eyebrows.

'That's right,' I said.

'OK. And the fellas tell me you have a theory. About the death. Tell me that you think it was suicide.'

The word rang out like a bell. I hadn't said that I thought it was suicide, but I guess Nick had inferred it. I said, 'Her wrists were cut,' under my breath.

I felt that I was being led into a field of trip-wires and jagged teeth and broken glass. I felt sick but it felt like someone else feeling sick and describing it to me. Baxter could skip around in here all he liked. This was his country. I was from a different country altogether. Scarlet still wasn't dead in my own mind yet. Her death, like all deaths, was taking time. She was evaporating slowly, or the way I saw it, she was sinking inch by inch into a swamp. The passage of time was being marked by Baxter jumping from one conclusion to the next and by Scarlet sinking vertically into the green swamp. I could even see the muscles of her legs getting dirtied by the mud whenever I closed my eyes, which was often.

'Mmm? That right, Karl? You think it was suicide?'

'Yes,' I croaked.

'Wrong, Karl. Wrong. Not suicide.'

'Oh, OK.'

'What was that, Karl?'

'I said, oh, OK.'

'And it wasn't the hurricane either. You listening, Karl?'

'Yes. I'm just . . .'

For a moment the sun shone through the window and the room lit up and all the dust from beneath the floorboards that still hadn't settled became visible. The scene became grainy and brightly coloured and then went dark again.

'No, sir, not suicide,' Baxter said to his shoes. 'You see, Dr Hesperez tells me that her wrists were cut after she was dead; it looks like somebody cut her wrists after she was dead to make us think it was suicide. But that wasn't how she died at all . . .'

Baxter's voice was dreary and emotionless. Beneath the drone of his voice, I could hear someone sweeping up broken glass out in the street and realized that the rest of the world was already beginning the process of recovery. Only Baxter and I were left inside the hurricane.

'We can't be sure yet, Karl, but it looks to us like Ms Lisson died of suffocation. I'd guess that she was smothered on that bed. Maybe even with that pillow right there by your hand. Now tell me, Karl, you haven't touched that pillow since you came into the room, have you?'

I told him that I hadn't and in the long pause that followed, I heard the guy who had lost his dog sobbing like he'd lost his baby, somewhere out in the hall.

CHAPTER SIXTEEN

I should have thought about Benelli as soon as Baxter told me that Scarlet had been suffocated with a pillow, but I didn't. Not for the first few hours, which were still half nightmare. I should have remembered the way he'd changed the murder scene, the way his eyes had shone the night he'd told me that the murder would take place right there on Scarlet's bed, with Max holding the pillow over Laura's face and sobbing and saying he couldn't take any more. I should have thought about Benelli's handwritten script that I'd hidden on top of my wardrobe. Instead, I smoked a cigarette there in Scarlet's room and Baxter watched me like a doctor making a careful diagnosis. He asked me softly not to drop my ash anywhere and said that he was breaking all kinds of procedures letting me sit and smoke at the scene of the murder but that in this case he'd let it ride. He said that the hurricane had smashed all the evidence to hell anyway but I knew that he didn't mean it. I knew that what he was really saying was that it was more valuable to him to just stand and stare at me than to move me out of the room. He even steadied my good hand when I couldn't get the match to keep still to light my cigarette. Scarlet was dead in my own mind now. Really dead. When Baxter led me out to his car ('Let's take a little ride, Karl') he looked around at the wreckage of Mallory Street, and tapped the hull of the *Santa Maria* and said we were real lucky that the hurricane missed us this time.

'Missed us?' I said as Baxter helped me into the passenger seat of his car.

'Sure. Marathon took the eye.'

We crawled at five miles an hour down Mallory Street. It looked like something from a newsreel, blasted, broken, put into a sack and shaken around. Baxter rounded the corner gently, as if even the road were sore. Every moment passed slowly, the speed of the car slowing up the passage of time. The slowness of our progress was making me feel delirious. Both my hands were inside small Cellophane bags, fastened by elastic bands, and my right hand was throbbing. As we turned into Duvall Street, the air was grey as slate over the ocean, and the ocean itself was streaked pink and scarlet, as if it had been beaten up. My hand hurt so much that I wanted to squeeze it, but Baxter had told me I shouldn't remove the bags until he was through.

'Maybe you'd like to put that in your movie,' Baxter said without any humour in his voice. 'Murder suspect gets to wear Cellophane gloves.'

Every window in Duvall Street had been smashed, and the broken glass lay in drifts across the sidewalk and across the road. Baxter was driving at walking pace, and the slow procession of broken windows and splintered store fronts felt like a slow but unstoppable unravelling. I felt compelled to start talking, as if talking about what had happened would make it less real, the way talking sometimes can.

'I'm not really a suspect though, am I, Mr Baxter? I mean you don't really think . . .'

Baxter sniffed the air. I remembered what he'd told me once about people having a certain smell. I had to keep talking, brightly, as if we were discussing the weather. Except the weather here wasn't such a polite topic of conversation.

'I was unconscious for a while, Mr Baxter,' I said. 'I

166

mean, if you want a statement about what happened, I was out cold for maybe two minutes, more. I got hit here. Look, here on my head.'

Baxter slowed to round a concrete street light that had been snapped in two like a matchstick and it was bowing into the road. I saw the exposed wires from its guts, and they took an age to pass. The street looked like the set of a movie, and I saw a whole family, mom, dad, three kids, clambering out of an upstairs window, shinning down a porch roof and leaping down on to the street. They moved without making a noise.

'And then this morning when I found her . . . Jesus Christ . . . I've never seen a dead body before . . .'

'Mmm?'

'I've never seen a dead body before . . .'

'No?'

Baxter suddenly put his foot on the gas and we began to cruise at thirty. Maybe before Baxter had been looking for something. Now he had his eyes on the road as we approached the ocean and Atlantic Boulevard. I wondered if it would be better if I just shut my mouth but the silence, when it came, seemed to be full of accusations. I flexed my damaged hand and some droplets of blood fell into the Cellophane bag. Baxter looked down at my hand as we pulled up to let an ambulance go by and he sighed. The ambulance, speeding but quiet, was the first vehicle we'd seen.

'When I saw her lying there I thought she had killed herself,' I said and Baxter slowed again. He was looking all around. The road was strewn with dead fish, most of them red snappers but others the size of a baby, brightly coloured with fan wings and veiny underbellies. After he had slowed he wound down his window and sniffed the air.

'You smell gas, Mr Stone?'

I told him that I didn't and Baxter popped a mint in his mouth and rattled it against his teeth. I got angry quickly.

'For Christ's sake, Baxter, her wrists were cut. What did you *expect* me to think . . .?' I hissed and Baxter raised his eyebrows. On the corner of Atlantic Boulevard and Front Street, lying on a grass verge, there was a body. A black woman lying dead beside the road. She looked like some kind of stuffed effigy that had been torn apart by dogs. When I looked closer, I saw that she wasn't black. She had blond hair. She was just bruised all over. She had been twisted around and broken in places but there was no blood and the expression on her face, which I could see clearly as we crawled by, was the same expression I'd seen on Scarlet's face. I wondered if there was such a thing as a death expression, a look shared by all dead people. There was a priest kneeling by the body and two uniformed patrolmen with their hands on their hips.

'I guess that makes six,' Baxter said glancing at the priest and lifting his chin in acknowledgement. 'Worst thing is, if we don't get to the bodies first, then the birds get them. And the rats. I guess Mr Clinton'll come down here and say, "Shit, let's declare a state of emergency." I guess that'll make things OK again.'

Baxter peered out at the body on the side of the road being lifted on to a stretcher. The priest was getting up off his knees and dusting his trousers. We set off down the clear stretch of road and the silence in the car became unbearable. I wondered if I would be breaking some kind of police procedure to talk like this, without witnesses, without the conversation being recorded. Either that or Baxter was using silence as a trap. I decided to carry on talking anyway.

'When I saw her this morning I thought she had killed

168

herself because she was afraid of hurricanes. Did I tell you that?'

'Yes, sir, the President of the United States himself will be down here and do you know what he'll do, he'll call a press conference.'

'I know how this must look, Baxter . . .' I said and I forced a smile. I tried to rub my hand through my hair and felt the smooth plastic of the Cellophane glove. It made me angry again.

'Christ, are these things really necessary?' I said, but Baxter didn't seem to hear.

'Yes, sir, a press conference,' he said to the rear-view mirror. 'I guess the President'll want the whole department out there to keep his precious ass from harm. As if we don't have enough to do.'

'I can't even smoke with these fucking things on my hands . . .'

'Oh lord, those politician guys just make me so mad. Tell me, Karl, do you have a green slip?'

Silence. Was he talking to me at last?

'A what?'

'A green slip. A criminal history?'

There was a crowd of people blocking the road in front. Baxter switched on his siren and the muffled wail from the engine made me start. The crowd cleared. They were gathered around an upturned station wagon. A young guy ducked out of the upturned vehicle with a car stereo in his hands and he jumped over the barrier at the side of the road and ran down towards the beach. Baxter glanced at him quickly as he disappeared, and the crowd formed a line to watch us go by. Baxter's instinct may have been to go after the guy with the car stereo but he didn't. I realized that in his mind I was a greater priority.

'You do know that I didn't kill her, don't you, Baxter?'

Baxter finally turned to me and his spectacles hid everything from view.

'Mr Stone, I got a lot on my mind at the moment. Why don't you just shut the fuck up until we get to my office.'

Two patrolmen, bulging out of their khaki and chocolate uniforms, had a thin and frightened beach bum pinned to the wall, just inside the main entrance to the annexe of the tank.

'I swear to you it's my daddy's store,' the frightened kid said, his weather-beaten face losing blood and colour fast.

'So why d'ya take the TV set?'

'It's my daddy's store.'

'Ass-hole!'

The two cops wore reflector shades, and looked like honey-fed ants consuming a maggot.

'I have ID right here. Call my dad and ask him. It's my daddy's store.'

'Should have shot the sonofabitch for looting right there.'

'I wasn't fucking looting the store. It's my daddy's store. I was trying to save the stock.'

Baxter paused for a moment to look into the eyes of the thin white maggot. Then he put his hand on the shoulder of one of the patrolmen and whispered something. The two cops turned their heads and then loosened their grip. I guessed that Baxter had ascertained right there that the kid was telling the truth and that was good enough for the uniformed guys. He ushered me through a set of double doors made of wired glass, and we stepped into the carnival of rage and hysteria that the annexe had become.

The annexe reception area looked smaller than I remembered it, and was filled with two dozen excited matrons and their turtle-headed husbands, all sitting on benches and on the floor, wrapped in blankets. They looked like East European refugees, apart from their carefully coiffured blue and silver hair and their even teeth. The desk sergeant who had rolled my credentials through her IBM typewriter all those weeks ago was serving hot coffee. She stood beside a chrome urn amid a cloud of steam and was yelling out, 'Simmons. Mr Simmons. The diabetic gets served first . . .' and a dapper sixty-year-old leapt to his feet, casting off his blanket. The air was filled with delirious conversation, and the sound of the old people's voices echoed sharply against the tiled walls. Leaning against the left-hand wall of the annexe there were two female police officers, standing guard over a bedraggled Cuban guy who had spread himself out across four chairs to sleep. The old people eyed him nervously from inside their heady conversations. Baxter ran his hand through his hair and sighed deeply.

'We use the tank as a safe place for the old folks during hurricanes,' he breathed to me. 'They get to spend the night in the cells. I guess they think it's kinda fun.'

Baxter took my arm to lead me through the crowd, and heads turned to analyse the gesture. Was I being helped or was I being held? The old people eased off their conversations to figure it out. Was I one of the strange and exotic creatures that made a visit to the tank so much fun, or was I on their side of the line? A civilian. Some of them saw the blood on my hands and on the collar of my shirt and relaxed a little. I looked like a casualty. Baxter showed me to a seat beside the sleeping Cuban. He was about to walk across to the coffee urn but I took hold of his arm with my good hand.

'Mr Baxter, am I under arrest?'

I whispered it, but some of the turtle-heads heard, looked over, nudged the ones who hadn't heard.

171

'No, sir, you're not under arrest. But I need a statement and I need to take some samples. I need to take the blood from your hands, some hair and some body fluid . . .'

Someone was calling Baxter's name through the din that the old folks were making. A woman's voice. I saw that the desk sergeant had a telephone in her hand.

'. . . think of it as research, Mr Stone,' Baxter said as he acknowledged the call. 'But I wouldn't want you to think that this is how we normally proceed. These are unusual circumstances and I'll have to ask you to be patient.'

Baxter went to take his call before I had the chance to say anything. The old folks were trying to help, stepping out of Baxter's way, pouring their own coffee, getting under the desk sergeant's feet.

'Hey, my Momma always said I'd wind up in the clink,' one of the turtle-headed old men called out, and everyone laughed. I saw Baxter put his finger in his spare ear as he mumbled into the phone. The predominant accent among the old folks was New York. These were the people who came down to the Keys to retire, and who saw the annual insanity of the tropical weather as a price worth paying for the sun and the sand. They were the very backbone of the island. The men looked hard and the women looked in-domitable.

'Well, a prison cell sure as hell is where you belong,' the old guy's wife said, and there was more laughter. The old folks had turned into an irreverent, renegade band, like tourists on a cruise that has hit rough weather. The two uniformed guys we'd seen in the doorway came into the room, rubbed their necks and shook their heads and joined the queue for coffee. Their prey had been released. Baxter finished his call and came and stood over me. I'd never seen his face so tight with anxiety.

'We're ferrying these good people back to their homes.

Those that still have homes. We have to fingerprint them all before they leave for security and that takes a little time . . .'

Baxter wiped his mouth. He was speaking to himself as much as he was speaking to me, trying to get the whole procedure straight in his own mind.

'And I got to order some goddam taxis because we've run out of vehicles, so, Mr Stone, I'd be grateful if you could just wait right here for a while.'

I knew that, since I hadn't been charged with anything, I had the right to stand up and leave. A part of me had resolved that that was what I should do. I should get out into the air and try to get my story straight in my own head, before this insanity, this juggernaut of old folks and worn-out patrolmen and looters had a chance to roll over me. I felt that I was in danger of getting sucked into this whole thing before I had a chance to get my position set. But the way that Baxter was looking at me made me decide that I ought to stay. Baxter was a smart guy. Baxter was on my side. I said that I could wait for as long as it took. Before Baxter could answer, the wired-glass doors suddenly burst open and a three-man fight came into the room. A patrolman, a plain-clothes man and a black guy, bent double with his arms pulled up behind his back like wings. The three of them were silent and the room fell silent when they entered. The struggle between them was slow and delicate, but looked painful. The plain-clothes man loosened his grip and picked Baxter out of the crowd.

'Sergeant Ramirez has been shot,' the plain-clothes man said, his face turning pink. Baxter suddenly became calm, he even took off his spectacles and wiped the lenses on his shirt.

'Bad?' Baxter said softly. The old folks had all stopped breathing.

'Hit in the shoulder. We had to take him to the fucking veterinarian.'

Baxter put his spectacles back on and peered at the black guy, who was still bent double in a vice grip.

'This the guy?'

'No. But, Tom, look who it is.'

The uniformed patrolman straightened the black guy up so that Baxter could see his face. Baxter nodded. The plain-clothes man came and stood close by, taking half a second to check me out. Check if I was a good guy or a bad guy.

'Well?' Baxter said.

'It was this guy's kids,' the plain-clothes man said. 'He's the father. It was those two Haitian kids from the camp again. Tom, we know who they are. They were halfway out of Aaron's Boat Rentals with the stock computer when Ramirez tried to stop them.'

I looked at the black guy's face and saw that he had begun to weep. Baxter was still staring at him, nodding his head, sniffing the air.

'So why d'you pick up the old man?' Baxter said. The old folks were bursting with hissed conversations.

'Why? Jesus Christ, Tom, the kids had long gone. He was the only one still in the house.'

Baxter said in a quiet voice that the old man should be given a cup of coffee and then taken back home. He said that the bridges at Boca Chica Key and Summerland Key should be sealed and that Ramirez should be moved to the navy clinic at Garrison Bight the moment the doctors said he was well enough to be moved. Then he said in the same even tone that if those two Haitian boys turned up on a hurricane casualty list in two days' time, he'd take it real personal. The plain-clothes guy seemed to understand and ground his teeth a little; the old Haitian was offered a cup of coffee. Baxter then turned to me and asked me again if I would mind waiting a while for my samples to be taken, and I told him again that I would wait for as long as it took.

'It's getting pretty wild out there,' one of the uniformed officers said as he poured himself some coffee, and someone said, 'Amen to that.' When Baxter turned to go into his office, the patrolmen all glared at him, piercing him through with their eyes.

While I waited, I tried to piece my story together. It reminded me of working out a story line for a movie, but instead of taking it on as a marathon, this was a sprint. A mad, breathless sprint with my eyes closed. Even though I was still wearing my Cellophane mittens, I lit a cigarette. The sound of the old folks as they babbled and took turns to be printed had softened into a hum that I could ignore, like the sound of a train.

'. . . in Tennessee they call 'em snakes. Sidewinders that just rip up your house. No good getting inside a prison cell then, brother. Why a Tennessee snake'd just rip this whole place to pieces.'

I touched the back of my neck, wondering what the hell it had been that had made the wound. I guessed a piece of flying debris, maybe even a bird. Every time I thought about the stairs, about climbing up them, my memory drifted into dreams.

'Worst one I seen was in Java. I didn't mind fighting Japs but, Jesus, those typhoons . . .'

The Cuban guy, whose head was almost in my lap, stirred when I lit a cigarette. I guess he smelt the smoke and he peered up at me from his painful sleeping position. His hair was messed up and his eyes were bloodshot. He watched me smoke for a while, the cigarette slipping around awkwardly in my Cellophane mitten, and then slowly heaved himself upright.

175

'Hey, ma'am,' he croaked to one of the policewomen. 'OK, if I ask the gringo for a cigarette?'

The police officer stepped over to us and said sure, if the gringo didn't object. I offered the pack, trying to stay inside my story line, but the Cuban guy took an age to take one. He was handcuffed with a length of vicious-looking plastic, and he moved like a man under water. He chuckled hoarsely at his own lack of coordination and at the way the pack kept slipping in my gloves. He tried to take a light off my cigarette and the process of putting the end of my cigarette to the end of his was a delicate and difficult operation, like an orbital docking procedure. All the time, while he tried to light his cigarette, he stared deeply into my eyes. His eyes were shattered by heroin, two deep brown kaleidoscopes that looked without seeing.

'You have something harder?' the Cuban said and he laughed from deep inside the ruins of his chest. He put his cuffed hands on my shoulder and the lady police officer barked out something in Spanish. The Cuban guy let go and grinned at me, staring at the side of my face. The conversation from the other side of the room was getting louder and wilder, and I cursed myself as I stamped on my cigarette. The Cuban guy wouldn't stop staring at me, and the crazy thought entered my head that he was seeing right through into my insides. Seeing into the mechanics of my story, seeing things in there that even I couldn't see, things that I needed to shut off and button down. Maybe through the clouds of opium he could see right into those dark places between the green and white images. Maybe he could jump the edits in the film that was winding and rewinding in my head. I knew that it was crazy to think this way, but something clicked inside and I found myself shoving the Cuban guy's face away from mine with my good hand. I had grabbed his jaw and squeezed as I pushed, and he'd been lighter than I had expected. Like a frame made out of balsa-wood. He fell back a little way, and blinked slowly, not even surprised, and I thanked God that the two lady police officers hadn't seen what I had done. Some of the turtle-heads had seen it though. Three old men with eyes like raw eggs stared dumbly at me. Sure, they seemed to be saying, we know what kind of guy you are.

Finally, Baxter put his head round his office door and said, 'Mr Stone?' I almost ran into his office, because I had become pretty sure that if I had stayed out there in the waiting-room, with all those people, I would have remembered something from the darkness that I really didn't care to recall.

Inside Baxter's office, after he had closed the door, there was quiet at last. He pulled up a chair for me and offered me a cup of coffee that he had already poured. He spent some time thinking things through before he spoke.

'OK, procedure's this. I got to take some samples from your hands and I got to take some hair and body fluid. You agree to that, Mr Stone?'

I said that I did and he handed me a waiver form and a pen. I took the pen painfully in my damaged hand and managed to scrawl my signature. Baxter picked up the telephone and punched a number and said, 'OK, Melissa, he's agreed.' Less than ten seconds later, there was a knock at the door and a sweet-looking young girl in a white uniform came into Baxter's office carrying a small bag with a flowery pattern, like an overnight wash-bag. She was moving fast, just like everything was moving fast. And things were getting faster. Without speaking to me or Baxter, she knelt down at my feet and gently took hold of my hands.

'Trying for a blood and spit match?' she asked softly and Baxter said, 'Uh huh.'

'Rape?'

'Nah.'

Melissa carefully tugged the Cellophane gloves off my hand and whistled at the bloody swelling on my right knuckle. The tender way in which she turned my hand around made me want to weep. I could see the black roots of her blond hair as she knelt at my feet, and she smelt of sweet perfume and ordinary life. She was humming a tune under her breath as she unzipped her wash-bag. Then she took out a silver blade and began to scrape under my fingernails. I screamed with pain. Neither Baxter nor Melissa seemed to hear.

'I just heard from Marathon,' Melissa said casually, 'that Farmer is on his way over.'

The pain eased until she started on the next finger. The torture was made worse by the boredom in her voice as she spoke to Baxter, and by the lilacs in the air around her.

'I heard that the National Guard have already taken over in Marathon,' she said, teasing a quick of fingernail on to her scalpel and into a sterile bag, 'and so Farmer has been sent to take over here.' She looked up at Baxter and smiled. 'Sorry, Tom, didn't mean to spoil your day.'

Melissa rummaged in her bag and found a tiny rectangle of glass inside a Cellophane wrapper. She carefully broke the seal and then started to torture my knuckle with a second scalpel, adding skin and dried blood and some fresh blood to her samples. She was smiling furtively at Baxter's reaction to the news she'd given him. He was shaking his head and he asked her if she could possibly be serious and she laughed and said that unfortunately she was dead serious. Baxter said the name Farmer to himself a few times, like it was the name of a disease. The lady was now picking dried blood off my injured palm, and

178

scraping skin from the back of my broken hand. I had stopped crying out because it didn't seem to have any effect.

'Looks like we're in for a hell of a week,' she said, and then, for the first time, she looked up at me. She looked at me as if I were an exhibit, or a difficult pet.

'You think Farmer will want to take this guy's case?'

I turned to Baxter, and Baxter shrugged. The lady took a small plastic flask from her wash-bag and peered into it. Then she pushed it against my lips and said, 'Spit.'

'What?'

'Spit.'

I stared deep into her eyes and spat. She stood up, and in one deft movement took a snip of hair from just above my ear. My blood and my spit and my hair all went into the flowery wash-bag, which the lady zipped up and put under her arm.

'Did they say what time Farmer would get here?' Baxter asked as she made for the door.

'Who can tell?' she said. 'You just got to pray that the bridge at Islamorada is down again. But I wouldn't hold out much hope. It's not like the old days, Tom. Farmer'll get here by hook or by crook. See y'all in hell.'

Baxter was thinking hard, looking out of the window. Then he remembered something.

'Melissa,' he said, 'I want those samples analysed by Harry S. Rose, no one else.'

'You got it,' Melissa said.

'They got some new guy down there now,' Baxter said, suddenly irritated, 'but tell them that this stuff is for Harry.'

'You know he's sick,' Melissa said.

'I know he's sick. But Harry sick is better than the new guy healthy.'

Melissa smiled to herself, some private joke at Baxter's expense. I thought I knew what the joke was. Baxter might be young but he was old too. Old in the head. Melissa shook the bag of samples in her hand.

'For Harry's eyes only. Orders of Tom Baxter. Hey and, Tom, give my love to Farmer for me, won't you.'

Baxter grunted. The smell of lilacs began to disappear and so did the fresh pain in my hand. Baxter had turned to sit back down at his desk but Melissa put her head round the door again.

'By the way, Tom,' she said, looking down at me, 'the guy's hand has been broken before. Recent. He's got some calcium deposits between third and fourth finger. I guess he's some kind of street fighter.'

Before Baxter could take in what she had said, and before I could open my mouth to ask her what the hell did she mean I was some kind of street fighter, a patrolman burst through the door, pushing Melissa aside. He was moving fast too.

'Tom, you'd better come. We got two kids taken over the Marine Hardware. There's enough guns and ammunition in there to last them till Fourth of July . . .'

The patrolman paused to catch his breath and he dug his fists deep into his sides. Melissa had disappeared.

'Guess it's the same two kids who shot Ramirez,' the patrolman said. 'We still got the old man in custody?'

Baxter shook his head. The patrolman frowned and took a deep breath.

'Pity. Maybe he could have helped us talk them round. We'll have a heck of a task finding the old guy now that . . .'

'Yeah, OK, bring a car around the front,' Baxter said, then he turned to me. 'Mr Stone . . .'

Baxter paused and ran through a list under his breath. He could have been a student revising his study notes a few moments before the start of an examination. Halfway through his list he dismissed the patrolman and then carried on with his revision. Finally, he said, 'Mr Stone, do you have a cigarette?'

I gave him a cigarette and he smoked like a beginner, or a man who hadn't smoked for a long time. I couldn't believe that for the past thirty seconds I hadn't thought about Scarlet once. I guessed that maybe Baxter hadn't thought about her in the past two hours. He tried to nail the situation as quickly as he could. Trying to get the correct form of words.

'OK, procedure's this,' he said at last. 'We have your samples and we will run forensic tests overnight. That is if the bridge is still up and we can get the stuff over to . . . whatever. We'll run the tests tonight and then I'll need you to call back in here. Let's say tomorrow at ten. Make it ten thirty. I already have your passport and your car has been impounded. It would be a bad idea for you to try to leave the island before we've had a chance to talk. But I guess you know that already. In the meantime, go back to your house. I don't have to tell you that you should stay out of the room where the murder took place . . .'

Baxter's phone rang. He picked it up and replaced it without pausing for breath.

'And perhaps, Mr Stone, you'd take one of these . . .' He handed me another form. 'Write out a statement including everything that happened from around noon yesterday until the time I arrived. Everything. And bring the statement with you tomorrow morning . . .'

His revision continued, a learned mind, an agile mind, working at full stretch. I wanted to speak but there was no point in interrupting. Somewhere above our heads, the air had begun to throb. The sound reminded me of the horror of the night before, the sound of the hurricane.

181

'You understand, Mr Stone?'

I said that I did. The throbbing above our heads got louder, and my head throbbed in unison. I could hear a furious wind howling just outside the window and I wondered for half a second if the hurricane had escaped from inside me. Then I saw that Baxter could hear it too. It sounded like the beating of mighty wings, a sound that made the room seem small and fragile. Baxter twisted open the blinds and we both saw the gleaming blue and gold hull of a police rescue helicopter. It was delicately easing its tail on to the ground, the sand and gravel of the parking lot whipping up around it in a whirlwind. After the engine had been cut, and the blades had stopped rotating, a fat, yellow-haired guy jumped out of the passenger seat and waddled with great purpose towards the rear entrance of the annexe. His face was glowing and his head was bowed down with fierce intent. Baxter closed the blinds and turned to me. He stubbed out his cigarette.

'I guess this is my lucky day,' he said softly.

'Is that Farmer?' I asked, and almost allowed myself a smile.

'That's Farmer,' Baxter said. 'If I were you, Mr Stone, I'd get out of here right away. Mr Farmer doesn't have a lot of time for guys like you.'

'What do you mean guys like me?'

'For murderers, Mr Stone. See you at ten thirty tomorrow.'

CHAPTER SEVENTEEN

All along the way back to the movie house, I watched crowds of children and teenagers who'd swarmed on to the beach, picking at the booty that the hurricane had washed ashore. There were thousands of ladies' shoes strewn across the sand, like the shells of bizarre sea creatures, and the kids were racing around with the shoes in their hands, trying to match up pairs for size and colour. I guessed that a cargo ship had run aground somewhere out in the Gulf. Further west along the beach, there were hundreds of wooden crates, some of which had been split open, spilling their cargo of brown sugar. There were six or seven Cuban ladies, scooping up the sugar with plastic bowls and loading it into sacks, not working too hard to separate the brown sugar from the white sand. And further still, there were bananas, salty and water-logged, and typewriters and more shoes and street signs and torn pieces of sail and rigging. And everywhere along the beach there were the bodies of pelicans and black-backed gulls, all twisted around and broken up, and beside them the bodies of fish which had just begun to dry in the burning hot sun. Crowds of black flies were starting to dine on all this rotting flesh, and I thought about Scarlet. It was right here, among the sugar and the flies and the bananas, that she had taken off her white silk dress and thrown away her pearls.

The looters on the beach were filled with a raw energy that seemed to be coming direct from the sun. A feeling of renewal and of recovery which I couldn't share. The sand was getting into my shoes, making my feet hurt, and my hand was still throbbing. I hadn't slept properly for two nights and my eyes were silting up. But I knew that I had to keep my mind clear. I had to keep my mind on what was happening to me, inch by inch, second by second, or else this hurricane inside would just blow me away to hell. Blow me right into the blue area and maybe even beyond. The state of Florida still had the chair. I'd read that somewhere, in one of those guidebooks, and it had made me laugh when I read it. The same guidebook that told me that once you've been to Key West, you'll never find home again. Most of all, I had to keep my mind on Benelli, shine it on him like a searchlight, and piece together this whole conspiracy from the beginning. Benelli was in my mind now, buzzing around with all the black flies. And I had figured that Benelli had had this whole thing planned right from the beginning.

The only real comfort I had as I strolled along the beach, casting shoes and pebbles into the water, was that Baxter was smart. Sure he was. Baxter was smart and when I managed to get this whole thing into one piece he'd figure it out for himself. I walked close to the ocean, and thought that I could see a white silk dress floating there in the white foam. When I rubbed my eyes, the white silk dress turned into something else, and I decided that I needed to get away from the beach quickly, and get back home.

When I finally reached the empty doorway of what was left of the house at 1131 Mallory Street, I heard the sound of floorboards creaking from inside. Then I heard the sound of glass being swept up, and a voice singing off-key somewhere up on the landing. A woman's voice. I stepped inside, into the darkness, and saw a silhouette in front of me.

'Well, hello, Karl. How's your head?'

For a moment I thought that I recognized Scarlet's voice and was on the point of fleeing in terror. But as the silhouette came closer, I saw that it was Azul. She was wearing jeans and a T-shirt and she looked like a different person altogether from the woman I remembered in Sloppy Joe's. She had a scarf wrapped around her head like a turban and she was wearing rubber gloves. She turned to me with a confident smile.

'The cops left an hour ago,' she said. 'I told them I was your cleaning lady ... Hey Karl, don't look at me like that. You look like you've just seen a ghost.'

Now that I was sober, I could appreciate the perfect composure with which Azul delivered her lines, her sweet smile and the 'only putting you on' curl to her lips when she told me that before Scarlet's death this story was destined for the editorial waste-paper bin but now it was going to be front page. She was as delicate and pretty and deadly as tropical nightshade. A bizarre concoction, almost a freak, where just this once nature didn't give you any clues on the outside as to what you would find on the inside. She followed me up to my room and said that this old house really was full of the most exciting damn little things.

'You go back down the stairs and you leave me the fuck alone,' I said when I got to the door of my room, which was still in one piece but open. 'I have nothing to say to you and no comment for your magazine.'

'Ah, come on, Karl, we can start again. We can surprise each other. Yesterday I was just playing the hard bitch for some crappy little story. But this is different. This is fun.'

My room had been spared the worst fury of the wind, and the wardrobe was still standing. I stood on a chair and ran my hand along the top of it. I knew that I'd left

Benelli's handwritten version of the suffocation scene on top of the wardrobe, and I figured that those sheets of paper would be the first piece in the jigsaw puzzle I would hand to Baxter the next day. But the papers had gone. I cursed them.

'What have you lost, Karl?'

'What have I lost? Well, Azul, if I tell you, do you promise me that you'll keep it a secret and not tell anyone in the whole wide world?'

Azul smiled. 'You might think it's a joke but you'll find out that you can trust me.'

'Sure I can. Talking to you is like picking toadstools blindfold.'

'That's a bizarre thing to say.'

'I feel bizarre today. Why? Hell, I can't imagine.'

Azul was sitting on my bed and scanning the furniture. She said that under the circumstances she understood I might be a little cranky, as I checked inside and underneath the wardrobe. The same make, the same wood, the same iron handles as the one in Scarlet's room.

'Not much of a room, Karl, for a man who's just made two hundred and twenty grand,' Azul said.

'If you don't like my room, Azul . . .' I was searching through the drawers in my desk. I thought that maybe I might have put Benelli's handwritten script in there but I could only find my own typewritten version. One of the drawers was open and some of the sheets had fallen on to the floor. The wind had blown them around a little. Apart from that, and apart from the broken window in the kitchen, the hurricane seemed to have deliberately gone out of its way to leave my room intact. I had thought that when I got back to my room, and had a chance to think things through, the roar of the wind inside my head might die down a little, but it didn't. There was a buzzing in my ears that kept taking my attention.

'If you don't like my room, why don't you leave it?' I said, to calm myself down. I had discovered that the sound of my own voice was the only thing that made everything real. 'Better still, why don't you leave the island? Why don't you just hop on a bus back to Kansas?'

Azul clenched her fists and thumped her knees like a little girl.

'Oh, Karl, just when the fun is starting.'

'There's that word again. "Fun." Like before when you thought that running me off the road was "neat". You're some kind of monster, Azul.'

I gathered up some of the sheets of script that had fallen on the floor. Azul was angling her head, trying to read one of them.

'So come on, tell me. I come around to say thank you for last night and there are cops and forensics and Baxter no less. Did you do it, Karl?'

I grabbed her arm and pulled her up from the bed.

'The cops think you did it,' she said with a smile. 'The one I talked to, the one who thought I was your cleaning lady, he said that the woman had been suffocated and that they'd got the guy who did it. I guess he meant you.'

'That's right, Azul. I killed her. It was fun. Last night, the whole thing, it was real fun. Now get out or I'll call the police.'

Azul hitched up her shoulder-bag and said, 'You can let go of my arm now, Karl.' I realized that I was squeezing it a little too hard and she looked genuinely afraid for just half a second. The look of fear on her face, the intrusion of that ugly expression into our conversation, was as painful as biting on a rotten tooth.

'I didn't kill anybody,' I said as softly as I could.

'I believe you, Karl. Tell me all about it.'

'And I don't want my name in your magazine.'

'Promise.'

'Please, Azul, I mean it. I need some time. I need some time to rest.'

'Tomorrow. Sloppy Joe's at noon. If Sloppy Joe's is still there.'

'I've told you, Azul, I have nothing to say to you.'

'Well, I'll be there anyway. You want me to write it down?'

Azul didn't want to leave and I pushed her more gently towards the door. This armour of hers, this disguise, was so perfect that I could forget who she really was and what she really wanted after just a few seconds of looking at her smile. She stood in the doorway and pretended to search for a cigarette but I told her that she could get a cigarette outside. She insisted that she find her cigarettes and I leant in the doorway while she found her pack and her lighter in the hallway. When she flicked her lighter, the hallway was illuminated and I felt the shadows flickering inside my head. She turned to me, her eyes lighting up.

'Ten grand for the exclusive,' she said and then thought for a moment. 'That's if you did it. If you killed her. If not, maybe five. But if you did it, it's ten grand and the money goes to your next of kin. You married, Karl? Kids?'

I dared to look up the stairs. The door to Scarlet's room had been sealed with an iron brace and there was a blue and white sign nailed to the door. I only managed to look up briefly before the brightness from Azul's lighter died. I told Azul to go to hell.

'You don't believe I can get ten grand? Sure I can. One phone call. OK, two.'

I thought that she would be happy to babble like this for hours, and I knew that I had to get inside my room and close the door quickly before I dared myself to look up the stairs again. I knew that the shadows of leaves and branches would be playing on the landing the way they always did, and I half imagined I could hear the sound of floorboards creaking above my head. I told Azul again as I closed the door that she was wasting her time and she called out that she'd be at Sloppy Joe's at noon tomorrow and if I changed my mind, she'd be waiting. After I heard her footsteps going down the stairs, I sat down at my desk and put the TV on. I figured that Scarlet Timberley's death would have made the local bulletins by now, but I was wrong. There was a 'hurricane desk', with lots of footage of last night's wind lashing the islands, of trees bent over and breakers breaking through the sea walls and cars flipping over like kids' toys. Mostly it was about Marathon, and I didn't recognize any of it. Trapped inside my tiny black and white TV, the whole thing was a puny fiction, and it was a fiction that didn't even come close to how things had really been.

Then they cut from the hurricane desk to a scene outside the Key West Marine Hardware store, where two black kids were being led in handcuffs out into the street, and where Tom Baxter was being given a hard time by three TV reporters who looked like high-school kids and all wanted to know how come those two psychotic Haitians had been paroled in the first place. Baxter looked fictional too, inside the TV set, but he made a reasonable job of quietening everyone down. Just before I turned the thing off, the hurricane desk lady read out a statement from chief of police Farmer which contradicted everything that Baxter had said and which admitted that, 'Yes, mistakes have been made.'

When I set off on writing my statement, in agony from holding the pen in my damaged hand, I began to feel that maybe Baxter and I had something in common, and I

189

found myself writing the whole story, from the day back in London when Benelli had called me up, as a kind of personal letter addressed just to him.

I arrived at Baxter's tank at ten thirty the next morning. I walked all the way and it seemed that the whole of the island had come alive with the sound of hammering and sawing and mending and making good, like the heartbeats of a thousand tiny animals coming back to life after a hibernation. For the time that it took for me to walk from the movie house to the tank, I shared in some of the spirit of hope and renewal that had taken over the island. I'd spent most of the previous night writing, my hand itching and finally going numb, and I thought that at last I'd got this whole thing figured in my own mind.

When I walked into the annexe, I was surprised to see Baxter sitting uncomfortably behind a desk that was too small for him and which had been placed beside the reception desk. The place was calm now, with the desk sergeant at her typewriter and uniformed guys wandering in and out with slips of paper and curious pieces of debris. Baxter was sitting at his desk with his head down, poring over some paperwork. He looked vaguely ridiculous squeezed behind his makeshift desk and he knew it.

'Ah, Mr Stone,' he said, 'take a seat.'

'What happened to your office?'

'Farmer's taken it. Needs it. Something. That your statement?'

I pulled up a plastic chair and handed him the statement. It ran to seven pages, and the first three had brown bloodstains on them from my hand. I thought that it was true, you couldn't keep your life off the page no matter what. I waited while Baxter retrieved an envelope from a pile of paperwork. The envelope was marked 'Caroline

Lisson'. He sifted through it while the telephones all around chirruped and the uniformed guys drank coffee and swore they'd never seen any hell like the hell they'd seen over at Marathon. Baxter and I looked tiny in our chairs beside them.

'OK, Mr Stone. I have the results of the forensic analysis,' he said and he sifted through some papers.

'According to Harry S. Rose,' he said, finding the page he was looking for, 'there were no prints on the body. Time of death between 5.00 p.m. and 6.00 p.m. Harry guesses most likely 5.00 p.m., so I'd say we can discount anything after 5.30. Cause of death suffocation, probably with a pillow. The body was moved after death, but it was probably the hurricane that moved her. There were traces of blood all over the room, so I guess the wind picked up her body after she was dead and threw her around a little. Then she wound up under the wardrobe.'

Baxter turned the page over and read from the back.

'Ms Lisson was sedated before she died but that was probably self-administered. The cuts on her arms were made shortly after she'd died. Razor-blade. Not found.'

Baxter studied the forensic report over again in silence. He read the whole thing through. He rubbed his eyes often, and swept his black fringe back from his forehead. He looked tired, but he was fighting it with breezy efficiency. We could have been discussing a real-estate deal.

'Did you tell me, Mr Stone, that you touched the body when you found it?' he said, still staring at his papers.

'No, I didn't. At least I don't think I did.'

Baxter looked up at me and his eyes flickered. I suddenly realized that I had been ushered into a trap. A siren blew in my head. Baxter wasn't tired at all. At least not in the way I had thought he was.

'So you didn't touch Ms Lisson's body after you found it?'

191

'Like I say. When I lifted the wardrobe I guess I was shocked. I can't remember whether I touched her or . . .'

The stare grew cold. Cold enough to chill the Florida air.

'Because you see, Mr Stone, Harry says that there were two blood types on your hand. Yours and Ms Lisson's. You had her blood on your left hand. Do you have any idea how Ms Lisson's blood could have gotten on to your hand?'

I leant back in my chair. The sounds inside the office were the same sounds as ten seconds before, but now the clicking of the word processor, the whirring of the ceiling fan, were the sounds of hell. I tried to remember, second by second, what had happened when I had lifted the wardrobe and found Scarlet's body. I had still been half-concussed. I had wanted to pull her dressing-gown together . . .

'Like you said, there was blood all over the room,' I said at last. 'Maybe I picked up some blood from the floor, or from the sheets when I went inside.'

Baxter returned to his papers.

'Good answer,' he said, half to himself. 'You didn't touch the body but you maybe touched something in the room that had her blood on it. Like maybe the wardrobe.'

'Yes,' I said.

'Because you see, Mr Stone, if you'd told me that you'd touched the body when you found it, then I would have wanted to know why in that case there weren't any of your fingerprints on her skin. See what I'm saying? Good answer, Mr Stone.'

Baxter took my statement and leant back in his chair too. He started to read, and I felt that my face, my calm expression, was made of iron. That it was an iron wall holding in a great tide of anxiety. I had to keep the wall in one piece while Baxter read my statement. I kept it in one piece by remembering that there had been a lot of blood on the wardrobe when I lifted it. I hadn't seen it it at first because the wardrobe was made of dark wood, but after I had found the body, and after the two paramedics had come into the room, I had noticed that there was dried blood all over the floor and all over the wardrobe.

Baxter only read the first two pages of my statement before he stopped reading and smiled at me.

'What's wrong?' I said.

'For a writer, you sure don't make a lot of sense,' he said.

Baxter placed the statement down on the desk, as if I had failed some kind of script test.

'Which part doesn't make sense?' I said.

'Oh, pretty much all of it. You see, Mr Stone, when I ask for a statement, I want a series of facts. I want what actually happened, I want your experience of what happened. I don't want a lot of conjecture. I don't need a lot of theory.'

Now that the time had come to spill the whole thing to Baxter, I didn't know where to begin. I was about to launch into my full explanation of what had been going on at the movie house when a phone began to ring. The ringing came from beneath Baxter's desk. He looked acutely embarrassed for a moment and reached awkwardly under his desk to retrieve the phone. He grunted several times and took down a name and address. Then he carefully placed the phone back under his desk.

'I got the job of tracking down the next of kin of the victims of the hurricane,' he said by way of explanation, and then he glanced venomously at the door of his old office. I sensed that Farmer had given Baxter the job of tracing next of kin as some kind of insult, and the insult had hurt. Then Baxter's eyes flickered again and he returned to the business that interested him more. The business of traps and puzzles.

'I got to trace Ms Lisson's next of kin too,' he said. 'I guess someone is going to get very rich very quick. Ms Lisson had quite an estate to leave to somebody.'

I was relieved to hear that Baxter was at least aware that Scarlet had been a rich woman. Now perhaps we really could get somewhere. If he'd found out about her estate, then perhaps this thing wouldn't be so difficult to explain. I decided to act cute and smiled at him.

'Yes, sir, she had quite an estate,' I said. Baxter raised his eyebrows at me.

'Well, come on, Mr Baxter, you're the detective. Read my statement. Don't you think that a rich lady like that might attract interest from a certain kind of person. Attract the occasional freeloader and con artist. Attract a man like G. F. Benelli. That's G for Giorgio and F for Federico. He's Italian. From Naples.'

Baxter nodded and sniffed, all indifference. His dismissal of the name made me angry. I wanted him to ask me to tell him everything I knew about Benelli but instead he just stared at me, or looked through me. I had to get his attention.

'Look, Mr Baxter, this guy Benelli . . .'

'Hold it right there, Mr Stone. I'm not here to discuss Mr Benelli or anyone else with you. For the moment I'm only interested in you. And I am also interested in your relationship with the deceased. Were you her lover?'

I remembered what Baxter had told me about the eighty per cent of murders where all he had to do was go find the husband, or the lover. About the guy in the bathroom throwing up and saying he doesn't know what came over him. I guess I fitted that description. Almost.

194

'No, I wasn't her lover,' I said. 'That is, I almost was.'

'Almost?'

'The night before. We almost . . . we got interrupted. By Benelli. That's G. F. Benelli. He's Italian. From Naples.'

Baxter took a pen out of his jacket pocket and made a note. I decided that he was trying to irritate me on purpose. He spoke out loud as he wrote.

'"You almost made love but you were interrupted,"' he repeated. 'Did that make you angry, Mr Stone?'

'Oh come on, Baxter, spare me the sexual psychology.'

Baxter glared at me. Behind his carefully manufactured indifference, he really was tired.

'No, Mr Baxter, we weren't lovers but we almost were. None of which is the point . . .'

Baxter suddenly slammed his hand down hard on the desk. The uniformed guys all turned their heads. The reception lady peered at us over her spectacles.

'You don't tell me what is and what isn't the point, Mr Stone,' he hissed. 'You just tell me about your relationship with Ms Lisson.'

The hurricane twisted inside my head. Baxter was staring me down and I knew I had to look away. I told Baxter in a calm and even voice that Ms Lisson had been introduced to me as Benelli's choice for leading lady in the movie we were supposed to be working on, that we'd got to know each other through the project, that I'd taken her out on a date, and that afterwards we had almost made love. I tried to drift on to the topic of Scarlet's finances but Baxter stopped me.

'You didn't put any of this in your statement.'

'It's not relevant.'

'Jesus Christ, Mr Stone. Not relevant?'

'Baxter, it's Benelli you should be talking to.'

Just at that moment, the door to what had been Baxter's office opened. I heard voices and saw that Baxter was staring anxiously over. I turned to see Farmer shaking hands with two men. I recognized them instantly. It was Clark, the realtor, and G. F. Benelli. It was as if I had summoned him when I mentioned his name. He had his back to us, but I could see the broad grin on Farmer's face, and the warmth of the handshake. Farmer was calling him 'Freddy' and Benelli was calling Farmer 'Seth'. Benelli turned to leave the office and saw my face. I was staring at him with my mouth open. Farmer closed his office door. Clark saw me too and the two of them waited for a moment. Benelli began to smile and whispered something funny to Clark. Clark laughed.

'It's him,' I said, turning sharply to Baxter. Baxter shook his head, maybe a clue that I should keep my mouth shut. I turned back to see Benelli and Clark making for the door.

'Benelli!' I yelled. 'Jesus Christ, Baxter, that's him!'

Baxter tried to stop me from getting out of my chair. He skipped around the desk but I was already on my feet and on my way over to cut off their escape. Benelli and Clark backed away a little but I could see the amusement in Benelli's eyes. I could see the taunt in his expression: 'Yeah, that's right, Limey, make an ass-hole of yourself.' I reached the door at the same time as they did.

'Fucking nut,' I heard Benelli mumble. Baxter had caught up with me and had his hand on my shoulder, gently urging me to back away. I was about to reach out and grab Benelli around the throat, but that crazy notion was suppressed fast. Benelli made the most of my uncertainty.

'That's right, you fucking Limey screwball. Take another whack. You see this lip, you fucking screwball? You split it right open. And then you go and take it out on Scarlet. Big guy. Big tough guy, taking it out on a lady.'

I knew now that he wanted me to hit him. He had spoken as loudly as he could, announcing it to the whole room. The uniformed guys by the coffee machine had joined Baxter in holding me back. Farmer opened his door.

'What the fuck's this?' Farmer said.

'The Limey screwball wants to take another whack,' Benelli said with a venomous smile. Farmer came to join the fray. He was big close up, his blond hair stained by nicotine at the front, and his face was deeply tanned. He took hold of my shoulder and shoved me back towards Baxter's desk.

'Tom,' he said, waving his finger, 'who the hell is this?'

'Karl Stone,' Baxter said, pushing his spectacles up the bridge of his nose. He was as close to blushing as I would ever see him. A huge humourless grin spread across Farmer's face. Benelli basked in it.

'So this is your friend from the movies,' Farmer said, trying to load his voice with irony. 'The one who wanted to know all there was to know about how to commit a murder.'

Farmer's eyes glistened as he looked at me. I felt there was a huge reservoir of this sarcasm that for the moment he was holding back. I knew I had stumbled upon an office joke. The uniformed guys were trying not to smile.

'What is it, Mr Stone?' Farmer said. 'You come for some more information? Will you get me this guy's autograph, Tom?' Farmer laughed. 'Maybe have him sign a pink sheet, huh?'

Farmer's eyes swivelled from me to Baxter and back to me again. I didn't dare to look at Benelli because I knew that if I did, I'd have to go for him. I knew he'd be beaming at me.

'You try to keep your friend there under control,' Farmer said. 'You try to keep him on the leash. Now, Giorgio, you get away from here too. Haven't I got enough on my plate with a fucking hurricane?'

Benelli backed out of the door, his face purple with rage but still smiling. Baxter sighed and shook his head and showed me back to my seat. The uniformed guys all eyed me up and down and went back to their coffee and their horror stories. I demanded to know from Baxter what the hell was going on. He answered me in a half whisper.

'Mr Benelli owns a lot of real estate on these islands,' Baxter said. 'He's . . . what should I say, he's prominent . . .'

I was about to speak, but Baxter shushed me with his hand.

'Now that doesn't mean anything at all, Mr Stone. Not in my book. Not any damn thing. You've got to believe that.'

Baxter's face was deadly serious. He looked swamped sitting there behind his tiny desk, surrounded by the big guys who now all seemed to be trying to prise a way into our conversation. His seriousness dissipated some of my anger.

'We have taken Mr Benelli's statement and we are making our investigation,' Baxter said, and I grunted and shook my head. This whole thing suddenly seemed sick and funny and absurd. I had got myself tangled up in this thing, I was fighting it like an animal, and the wires stretched a long, long way. The wires stretched right here into Farmer's office and soon the wires would stretch all the way back to London. I knew that.

'We are aware that Mr Benelli was an associate of Ms

198

Lisson and we are making our investigation,' Baxter was saying. He would have sounded feeble if it hadn't been for the look on his face. He seemed to be trying to communicate with me in some silent way.

'But I guess he's not a suspect,' I said, turning back to Farmer's office. Baxter shrugged his shoulders.

'The fact is, Mr Stone, he's not a suspect.'

'Why not?'

'Well, because at the time of the murder, between five and six on the day of the hurricane, he was sitting right here in that chair. He was sitting right here, filing a complaint of assault. A complaint against you. He came down to the tank and made a statement that you had punched him in the mouth and he was still here when the hurricane hit. He was right here and half a dozen officers are witnesses including Rose and me. So I guess you'd say that's why he's not a suspect.'

The hurricane blew some more. Baxter was giving nothing more away and it took a long time for what he had said to sink in. After it had, Baxter asked me if I would object to answering a few more questions and I said that yes I did object. I stood up and said I needed to get some air. The clock on the wall of the annexe said it was already eleven thirty, and so I knew that I would have to move fast. Baxter followed me to the door and said, in a soft and confidential voice, that if I was to have any hope of getting through this investigation, I should in future try to keep a hold of my temper.

It was then, for the first time, that I sensed maybe Baxter was on my side in all this. I wondered if it was something to do with his sense of smell, his ability to detect innocence and guilt instinctively, or whether it was simpler than that. I remembered how Farmer had smiled when he heard that I was the guy who Baxter had briefed on how to commit a murder. If I were to be convicted of this thing, I imagined that Baxter would look pretty foolish and he wasn't the kind of guy who would enjoy looking foolish.

CHAPTER EIGHTEEN

Sloppy Joe's was boarded up and closed. The wind had got inside through a back door, and now there was a seven-foot stuffed tuna-fish tangled up in the cat's cradle of telephone wires down towards the harbour. The barman who I remembered from the night of the hurricane was up on the roof, throwing tiles and sheets of corrugated iron down into a truck parked in the street. The noise of the iron scraping across the roof sounded like a scream of anger. And the barman really was angry. So were the two Cubans prising chipboard away from their broken windows, cursing the nails that they themselves had hammered in only a day before. At the end of the street, towards the harbour, there was a low-loader reversing into an alleyway that was too narrow for it, and a little black dog was yelping at its chunky rear tyres. Somewhere inside one of the smashed-up stores, someone was playing a radio at full volume, and the frantic salsa rhythm made everyone madder than ever. The seagulls were back now too, and even they were angry, hanging in the air above the twisted telephone lines and occasionally swooping to peck at the varnished flanks of the stuffed tuna-fish, getting mouthfuls of paint and wire and screaming about it. Azul was standing on the other side of the street, all blond serenity, smoking a cigarette. It was noon.

'Hey, Karl,' she yelled, as she dodged between the parked truck and the low-loader to cross the street, 'I didn't think you were going to make it.'

I looked at her wide open smile as she swung her bag

on to her shoulder and she could have been anything. She could have been a high-school girl, a beauty queen or a doctor of philosophy. She looked at me as if I were her brand-new date and she even offered her hand to shake.

'Come with me,' I said, 'but before you agree to come, I'm only doing this because I need your help.'

We walked down Duvall Street towards the docks, heading for the café on Salt Pond Key. It was a familiar walk for me but I guess all the familiar things had been blown away. I didn't see any of it, except at the end of Rose Street, where I saw a seven-foot statue of Poseidon made out of plaster and painted blue and gold being winched into an upright position. I saw it but even that couldn't break my train of thought, which had set off in Baxter's office and which hadn't stopped since. The faster I thought, the faster I walked, and Azul trotted along behind, trying to keep up and occasionally trying to break in with conversation. I didn't stop walking or thinking hard until we had taken our seats at the table overlooking the harbour that I always used.

'I need your help,' I said again, 'and I can't give you anything in return. Not yet. What do you say?'

'Wait a minute,' Azul said, regaining her breath. 'Do you always talk to yourself like that? When you're walking in the street?'

'Talk to myself?'

'I think you need a drink, Karl.'

Azul put her sunglasses on and a young Cuban boy I'd never seen before came over to take our order. I ordered two coffees and Azul ordered two brandies. I told her I would pass on the brandy and she peeked at me over the brim of her sunglasses. The Cuban boy was grinning down at me and I asked him what had happened to the guy who usually served at the tables. The boy became very serious, his smile disappearing like the sun going behind a cloud, and he shook his head. He pointed back towards the café, and it was then I saw for the first time that the roof had been torn off and that there were steel support rods sticking up out of it like strands of fabric. I couldn't imagine how I could possibly have failed to notice when I had walked by.

'You mean he's dead?' I said to the boy, and his grin came back again.

'Dead? Shit, no. He's just in a bad mood about his roof. He says he ain't serving tables because God don't want him to run a restaurant. This is Dad's third time. The wind's had his roof twice and his mains water once. He says God wants him to be a farmer so he says I can serve the tables today.'

The boy walked back towards the shell of the bar, and he turned round once to laugh at me and wave his hand.

'You should never ask a Cuban that kind of question after a hurricane,' Azul said with irritating authority. 'They think hurricanes take people for a reason. They think it's God doing a little housekeeping.'

'So do I,' I said, and Azul laughed as if I were joking. The chair I was sitting on was buckled, and the table had been creased in the middle, and all around our feet there were little piles of broken glass where the Cuban boy had started to clear up. There was a small fishing skip ploughing through the still water of the ocean, the first boat I'd seen since the hurricane. The sight of it made me angry because I didn't want things to get back to normal before I'd had a chance to sort this out, get clear, get things straightened up in my own head. I wanted the boat to sink but it cruised on by and Azul stared at me, fascinated, as I watched it. I knew I had to hurry and get on to business quickly before Azul started to irritate me so much I'd forget what I wanted her to do.

'I need information,' I said. 'That is, I need verification . . .'

Azul was about to speak but I shushed her by raising my hand.

'. . . I need you to verify what Benelli was doing to Scarlet. And in return, if what you give me convinces the police, I'll give you an exclusive for your magazine. I'll give you the whole story.'

Azul stared at me for a long time. Then she took off her sunglasses and her eyes were full of mischief. What kind of mischief I didn't know yet, but I knew that she was going to say something or do something that would make me want to push her backwards off her chair. Instead she just gave me a blank smile, like an opponent who had just put me into checkmate.

'If you want to listen to what I have to say, then fine,' I said, with as little emotion as possible. 'On the other hand, if you want to sit there with that stupid fucking grin on your face then we can forget the whole thing.'

'Suits me,' she said, her face clouding a little, and she even went so far as to stand up. I took hold of her arm and eased her back into her seat as gently as I could.

'Forgive me,' I said, and rubbed my face. 'Let me try this another way. When we talked before, in Sloppy Joe's, you said you had the whole Benelli thing figured out. You said you knew that Benelli was ripping Scarlet off with the phoney movie thing. Right or wrong?'

Azul put her sunglasses back on and rested her chin demurely on a little temple of fingers.

'OK, so you knew about Benelli. You even knew how much I had been paid to write the script. How did you know that?'

Azul didn't move a muscle. Her sunglasses hid her eyes

from view but I could feel that smouldering, indifferent stare through them.

'OK, so I'm talking to myself. But let's just assume that you knew. Let's just accept that you're going to be a pain in the ass. But I'm the one that's dangling on the hook so I'll just have to accept that. Somehow you knew about Benelli's plan to relieve Scarlet of her money. Now we're coming to the hard part . . .'

Azul sighed, like a sassy teenage girl being told the facts of life two years too late. I began to explain how Baxter told me that Benelli had been down at the tank at the time of the murder, filing an assault charge against me. So I figured that since Benelli hadn't actually murdered Scarlet himself, he must have hired someone to do the killing for him. I mentioned the fact that Benelli might have connections with organized crime, I even reminded Azul that when we'd met in Sloppy Joe's she'd said 'possible mob connections' in reference to Benelli. This made Azul spurt with laughter. I told Azul this was probably all very fucking amusing from her side of the table, but from where I was sitting it wasn't at all funny. Not at all. Then I remembered I really did need to get Azul on my side, or at least to see reason, and asked her again if she could just tell me or tell Baxter everything she knew about Benelli and the movie deal, and anything else she might have turned up in her investigation.

'That all?' she said, and raised her eyebrows and giggled at her own private little joke. I wasn't sure which part of what I had said had made her laugh but I figured it was probably the part about Benelli hiring someone to kill Scarlet. The way she laughed made me think that perhaps I was crazy. It was a brief moment of uncertainty when I saw everything from a new perspective, as if I were watching someone acting crazy in the street and feeling

205

sorry for them. Then I figured that Azul was just laughing to make me angry.

'OK, forget the part about Benelli hiring someone to kill Scarlet,' I said. 'Let's just talk about the movie scam. If I can't show Baxter that Benelli was ripping her off, the police will take the easy route and pin the whole thing on me. And I didn't do it. Except, God help me, they'll have reason to believe I did soon enough. So I need to be ready for them. I've got to hand them Benelli on a plate and you've got to help me.'

Azul said nothing. I had been talking so quickly I was out of breath and the sea breeze was stinging my eyes so they had begun to water. Two coffees arrived. I was staring hard into the lenses of Azul's sunglasses. I looked up as the coffees appeared and I saw the familiar face of the Cuban bar owner. He was smiling at me.

'Hey, you want to go fish today? Good day for sharks. Nice and hot.'

He put his hands on both of our shoulders and squeezed us gently together. The proprietor of our romance. When he put two glasses of brandy down on the table I told him I thought that God didn't want him to wait on tables any more. He said 'screw God' and skipped back towards the café, where the boy had begun to kick a football around in the twisted debris. The owner slapped the back of his head, proof that he was officially back in his shit bad mood. Azul spoiled it all by crinkling her nose at me and cuddling her glass of brandy, a spiteful parody of 'Now, isn't that just the sweetest thing.'

'I come here a lot,' I said, to explain myself. 'He always asks me if I want to fish and I always say no.'

'I know,' she said, feigning boredom, 'I've got it all written down in my notebook. Following you around this island really was a riveting experience.'

'Azul, are you going to help me or not?'

Azul sipped her brandy and then pushed the second glass over towards me. I pushed it back. She said, 'Serious?' and I said that I was.

'I mean all this, Azul. As far as I know, you are the only other person in the world who knew about Benelli's phoney movie deal.'

'Oh goody.'

She smiled. Her smile was a little softer. Maybe I was getting somewhere, drilling into the magma with a broken toothpick.

'Think about it, Azul. Who else apart from Benelli would want Scarlet dead?'

'You.'

'Why?'

'Because you were her lover. True or false?'

'Not true,' I said, with a deep breath. Then I said, 'Almost.'

'"Almost"? What does "almost" mean?'

'It means it's none of your business.'

'Sure it's my business,' she said; 'that's exactly what it is. Give me details.' I thought that she was parodying herself but I couldn't be sure. I couldn't be sure of anything about her. I said again softly that I didn't fucking kill anyone.

'Oh no? You were drunk that afternoon. I should know, Karl, I had to sit there and take it. And you were banging the table like some kind of maniac and staring around the place like you could have murdered everyone in the bar.'

I remembered how I had acted in Sloppy Joe's. All that alcohol and sloppy pride and disgusting vanity. I remembered how I had started out that afternoon hoping to do something noble, and should have, but instead I had ended up beating the table like a monkey while the world outside was getting ready to tear itself to pieces. The memory of it made me grunt. And there was something else too. I realized as Azul smiled to herself about the crazy way I had acted that I liked looking at her face. I liked it when she leant across the table and I could feel the warmth coming from her. Even though I hated it too.

'I was angry with Benelli,' I said, not really hoping to explain my behaviour in Sloppy Joe's.

'And with Scarlet.'

'Yes, I was angry with Scarlet. But only because she was letting herself get ripped off. Only because she was choosing to be a victim. Like a lot of women.'

Azul narrowed her eyes at me. I knew that I'd let her win a hundred points in our game and I'd done it for no reason. She began to nod her head as if she suddenly knew everything about me.

'Is that how women are, Karl?' she said, with almost medical concern. 'Is this some kind of psychological theory of yours?'

I said, 'Fuck you,' and shook my head and tried to take a sip of coffee.

'You see, you even talk like a killer,' she said, analysing me. 'Look at the way you're squeezing your coffee-cup.'

'I don't need you to give me a breakdown of how I hold my cup. I need you to tell me how you found out about Benelli.'

How was it that, when I tried to interrogate Azul, I always ended up by being interrogated myself? Or was that true of the way I was with everyone? I asked her again how she knew about Benelli, trying this time to make the question sound harmless, already answered.

'I'm smart,' she said and smiled triumphantly.

'Oh Jesus, come *on*, Azul. If you've got anything, any

208

little piece of paper, that would help. If not, then just go to Baxter and tell him what you know. It might be enough. If I don't have one other person to back up my story he'll think I'm just crazy. He already thinks I'm crazy. But if you go and see Baxter . . .'

'I already did.'

Azul used the moment to tip her glass of brandy theatrically into her mouth. She washed it around and gulped it down. She looked like someone who wasn't used to drinking but who was trying hard to pretend she was. Sometimes Azul's mask slipped, but I couldn't be sure if she wasn't letting it slip on purpose. Or if beneath the mask there was another, and another. I could see the brandy was burning her throat.

'You did what?' I said.

'I went to Baxter. Or should I say, Baxter came to me. He's smart, you know, Karl. For a hick cop. He came up to my hotel this morning. Asked me where I was at 5.15 when the hurricane hit. The son of a bitch took a piece of my hair. He wanted blood samples too but I told him to go to hell . . .'

Azul did a passable imitation of Baxter's dead-eyed stare, a look that had become so familiar to me. She had his voice worked out too. She growled in Baxter's clipped East Coast accent.

'"Ma'am, we are only trying to eliminate you from our inquiries."' Azul laughed at her own impression. She picked up my brandy and took a sip. 'I told him there was no need because I was in my hotel room at the Flamingo Key when the hurricane hit. Me and two cleaning ladies, hiding out in the john. I told him to go speak to them if he didn't believe me. I thought those ladies were going to pee in their pants when . . .'

'Azul, did you tell him about Benelli?'

'Benelli? Nah. He wasn't interested in Benelli. Left a hole in my hair, look, right here. Took an inch . . .'

Azul was showing me the place where a lock of hair had been cut away. I knew that she was teasing me on purpose, that she got some kind of pleasure out of stoking my anxiety. She began to ramble about the two cleaning ladies, about how it was those two ladies who had told her that Cubans believe hurricanes take people for a reason. I stopped her.

'Azul, you know what I'm saying. Did you tell him anything about the movie scam? About Benelli's involvement?'

'Like I said, he wasn't interested in Benelli. But he sure was interested in you.'

'What did you tell him about me?' I said, grabbing her hand.

'I told him that I left you in the bar at a quarter to four. That you were drunk. That you were hitting the table like a maniac and talking on and on about Scarlet.'

'Thank you, Azul. Thank you. Great to have you on my team.'

I wanted to stand up and walk over to the ocean. I wanted to jump into the bay and join those two ghosts who always swam there and laughed and shouted out that they loved each other.

Azul had taken her notebook out of her bag and was searching for a pencil.

'So, come on, Karl,' she said, 'how long had you "almost" been screwing Scarlet?'

Her pencil was poised, waiting for me to start talking.

'How long, Karl? This is the interesting part. Did she almost seduce you or did you almost seduce her. How often did you almost do it? Once, twice or often . . .' I didn't want to listen to what Azul was saying, but I

210

listened anyway. Her voice had a new urgency, and she had adopted the delivery of a TV news reporter, which one day I guessed she might become . . . 'When you say "almost" do you mean she pulled out at the last moment? Is that why you killed her? Now if you want to talk to me about your love affair with Scarlet Timberley, in detail, then maybe we can help each other.'

When I looked back at Azul from staring out at the ocean, I expected to see her sneering, or smiling, that cute high-school girl on a project smile. But she wasn't. Her face was expressionless. There was something dead about it altogether. Like Scarlet's face lying on the bare floor-boards.

'You asked me if I would help you,' Azul said with a smile. 'Well sure, Karl, I can help you. We can help each other. What exactly do you want me to do?'

Like bedding down with a serpent, this thing made me uneasy.

Azul and I walked back to the movie house, and on the way I delivered my side of the bargain by telling her everything I could about my 'sexual liaison brackets almost' (Azul's phrase) with Scarlet. It was like eating bones with broken teeth. I told her about the night on the beach and about how she'd talked to Deborah Kerr and how she'd thrown her pearls into the ocean. I told her about how Scarlet was afraid of hurricanes and about the typhoon in Kansas and about how Scarlet used to work out above my head for seven hours a day to keep in shape. This time, Azul was silent as we walked, but as I spoke, she wrote furiously in her notepad. When we got back into my room, I closed the door and told her that it was her turn.

'OK, ask me some questions,' she said airily.

'How did you know that Benelli was ripping Scarlet off?'

'I'll pass on that one. You almost did it on the beach? Really?'

'Do you have anything that I can show to Baxter to get him interested?'

'No. Not anything on paper. Do you have any coffee, Karl?'

I stared at her for a long time. She was sitting on my bed and leaning back on her elbows. I had convinced myself that she was enjoying her position of absolute power over me and I had always hated the cruelty of power. I used to tell myself that I had had plenty of opportunities in my life to wield power over other people but I had always refused them. I liked to think that if I had been more cruel in this way I would have got further, made some better choices, maybe had a decent life. And it seemed that I never had been able to meet anyone who wasn't prepared to leap up and down at the chance to use their power over me. It seemed unfair. All of this in one deep breath and a look of incredulity. Looking down on her, feeling the strength in my arms and comparing it to her weakness.

'You don't have anything at all?' I said, moving towards her. 'You knew about Benelli but you can't tell me how. You even knew how much I was being paid but you never saw it written down on a piece of paper? You had the whole thing worked out before but now you know nothing. Don't you understand the position I'm in? Can't you fucking comprehend that they're not kidding, those guys, and they're talking about a murder?'

'You frighten me, Karl.'

'I tell you everything about Scarlet and me, you cut it out of me, and when I turn around and ask you for something you just blank me off? Is that right or wrong?'

Azul edged away from me on the bed. I wanted to slap her, hard.

'I don't mean to make you mad,' Azul said, in a small voice. 'There are some things I don't know and there are some things that I don't think I should tell you because it's my work.'

'Your work!'

'I'm a journalist. I have my sources, but I'd like to not have to tell you about them. Don't look at me like that, please . . .'

Another Azul again. Soft and afraid. I wondered how she could keep changing like this, right in front of my eyes, and then that other possibility struck me again. A different perspective, seen from outside the window. I saw myself hanging over her, Azul caught in my shadow and frightened.

Maybe it was me who kept changing. Maybe I was getting sick again. I hadn't had a drink for a day and a half and this fury that kept coming up from the pit of my stomach was only half circumstance. The other half was chemical. Now Azul had stood up and she had her hand on my shoulder. She was as close to me as anyone had been since Scarlet on the beach. I was breathing hard, as if I'd just been submerged in water.

'It doesn't mean that I don't want to help you, Karl,' she said softly. 'I *do* want to help you. But if you want me to help you then you have to tell me everything. The whole thing. Sometimes I can't keep up with what you're saying. Why don't we start from the beginning and then I can help you. I'm good at this kind of work. But you have to try to keep yourself in one piece.'

We looked into each other's eyes and I wanted her to tell me there and then whether or not she thought I was crazy. I wanted to explain that I had no one else to ask. Since I assumed that she didn't even know the question, she didn't give me an answer. She just looked into my

213

eyes and I made myself concentrate on the fact that I needed her more than she needed me. To her, I was just a story. For me, she could be the difference between a ticket home (wherever) and ten, maybe twenty years inside Baxter's tank. I told her that sure I had coffee and that I would make us both some coffee and then we'd go through the whole thing from the beginning. I said that I was pretty good at this kind of work too. When I went into the kitchen, I found that there was broken glass in the kettle. This made me laugh at first and then I began to cry a little and laugh at the same time. Azul was kind about it and pretended she thought I was only laughing. Then Azul poured us two glasses of brandy from a bottle I kept behind the television instead.

CHAPTER NINETEEN

We sat in my room and talked and worked this thing through for three hours as the sun went down pleasantly on our backs. The fading light made us talk softly, and there was a breeze blowing through the broken windows that smelt of bougainvillaea blossom. When it was dark outside, and the wind carried a chill, we spent an hour putting cardboard up at the windows and Azul took some sheets from beneath the bed and pinned them up over the broken glass. I wanted to turn on the light but Azul said she preferred to think in the dark. We drank two glasses of brandy each and the alcohol soothed us both. At least I knew for sure that it soothed me. Azul explained that she had found out about Benelli's scam through some pretty illegitimate channels and that she didn't want the police asking questions about them unless it became absolutely necessary. I said that I could understand that. I thought we had, in effect, started all over again with each other; it was easier to listen to her voice when she was just a silhouette against the boarded-up window.

'For what it's worth,' Azul said, as a kind of conclusion, 'I'll speak to Baxter.'

'Thank you, Azul.'

'No details but just the bones. Tell him that he should go through the Key West Developments accounts and find out what happens to the money now that Scarlet is dead.'

I wasn't listening too hard to what Azul was saying but instead I was concentrating on the timbre of her voice.

She had a lazy Midwestern accent. I even thought about asking her to talk about something else, to tell me about her life, but I thought that if I did, I might have to tell her about mine. And that would have destroyed everything.

'Agreed, Karl?'

'Agreed.'

'Because if Benelli stands to keep all the money in the event of Scarlet's death, then we've got ourselves a pretty cute motive. Did you love her, Karl?'

I wanted to answer every question with the truth and so I said that I hadn't loved her. Then I tried a long and inconsequential explanation of what I thought love really was. I could hear my voice in the darkness, telling Azul that I had only been in love once and that I couldn't really talk about it yet, and that sometimes I was romantic with people and felt a lot of longings but that that was a different thing altogether. She listened patiently for a while and then said softly, 'Jesus, you sure talk some crap sometimes, Karl.'

'Yes, don't I? So do you.'

'Thank you. What crap do I talk?'

'All this stuff about things being "fun" and "neat". All this hard stuff that you try to pull. Nobody is like that, Azul, nobody in the whole world. Now, sitting here, you're OK. But then other times . . . and don't tell me it's part of your work. Don't tell me that it's because you're a journalist. I've known lots of journalists. The very worst kind in all the world. And they weren't like that. They were just people who were afraid of being fired.'

'Maybe that's what I am.'

'Fired by whom? I don't even know who you work for.'

'Associated Press,' she said, and sniggered, 'mostly anyway. I sort of freelance for everybody. At least, that's

216

kind of true. You see, this is my first real assignment since I left the *Courier*. I guess I'm afraid of fucking up. I said when I left that I would do whatever was necessary. It was a motto. I said I would do whatever was necessary to make it with a story and this is my first time out. And I resent the way you try to tell me how I should do my job.'

Azul poured me another brandy and I asked her how she'd latched on to the Scarlet Timberley story in the first place. She told me she had a cousin in Hollywood. Some kind of gossip columnist who'd agreed to throw Azul some scraps. There'd been talk around town about Scarlet ever since James Lisson had died, but Azul had been told by her cousin that no other journalist had thought it worth following up. It had been the perfect first case for Azul. A clear field and no need to fight against any of the other 'painted bitches' (her phrase) for an exclusive. More than that, she'd been told that Scarlet lived in Florida and Azul liked the sunshine. She had thought it would be some kind of recreational assignment, a chance to get a tan and start working on a reputation. Instead, she'd got a hurricane and a murder. She said the word 'murder' softly, I thought for my benefit, and I thanked her for her concern without saying anything. I just nodded at her and smiled.

We were quiet for a few moments and I heard footsteps on the path outside. Azul had told me earlier she had been talking to some of the other press people who'd swarmed on to the island since the hurricane. She said they were all busy with the wreckage and the bodies floating in the bay and psychotic Haitians and no one had spoken about the Scarlet Timberley story yet, but that soon those painted bitches who'd given her a clear field would be circling like vultures. And not just the gossip girls, but the real thing from real newspapers. There were journalists hanging out at the hospital, at the morgue, at the tank, everywhere, and any time now one of them would read the name Lisson in some list somewhere and start to put two and two together. When we heard the footsteps outside, we both thought the same thing.

'Don't answer the door,' Azul hissed when we heard the footsteps stop.

'We don't have a door,' I said and we both giggled, listening intently for the next move from downstairs. We heard the footsteps inside now, creaking in the hallway, looking for a light. Then the footsteps were on the stairs and we both stood up at the same time. We stood close to each other and I could feel she was smiling in the darkness.

'Bogeyman coming,' she whispered in a ludicrous voice, and I shook my head to stop myself from laughing out loud at her. Then there was the beam of a flashlight under the crack of the door and then the handle turning. In the wash of light from beneath the door, I could see that Azul had her eyes tightly closed and her shoulders hunched, like a little girl waiting for the bogeyman. This really was a stupid way to be behaving. The brandy was a pleasant vapour in my head. The door opened and I saw Baxter blinking into the darkness.

'Mr Stone?'

Azul sniggered and I saw the shadow of Baxter's hand as he reached for his gun in the inside pocket of his jacket. An instinctive movement.

'Mr Baxter. Hello,' I said, as reasonably as I could manage.

He shone the torch on my face and then on Azul's face. I thanked God that Azul wasn't giggling any more and I wondered how I should adjust my voice to make this thing seem ordinary.

'You lost power, Mr Stone?' Baxter said, flashing the light around the walls.

'No, Mr Baxter. We were just talking. The light switch is just there, right beside you.'

Baxter turned on the light and I silently cursed myself and cursed Azul and cursed Baxter for his sense of timing. We were now all three standing, and Baxter had that infuriating look of weary confusion on his face.

'I was hoping we could talk,' Baxter said and he looked sharply at Azul.

'This is Azul,' I said.

'I'm his cleaning lady.'

'She's a journalist.'

'I know,' Baxter said. 'We met.'

I sensed that Baxter hadn't liked her, and right now, I knew how he felt. He glanced around the room, saw the bed against the wall, maybe even, somewhere in the laboratory behind his eyes, analysed it for signs of action.

'Azul, perhaps you could go now,' I said, and Azul looked theatrically confused.

'Go where, Karl?' she said. 'I don't have anywhere to go. My hotel closed this morning for repairs. I told you that already, didn't I?'

Baxter stroked his eyebrow with his ring finger, the flashlight by his side. I gestured to Azul and hoped that she'd get the message but she didn't move. There was a half-smile on her face.

'If you two guys want to talk, go ahead. I'll make the coffee. That's what girls do in situations like this. Girls who choose to be victims.'

'Please, Azul. Go somewhere.'

'Like to hell maybe?'

'Just let Mr Baxter and me talk for a while. That's all.'

'Then I can come back, Karl?'

Baxter was rubbing his chin now, staring up at the blank wall. I couldn't believe Baxter had caught me in a darkened room with Azul and I couldn't believe Azul was doing this to me. I could tell she had no intention of leaving the room and in a flash of inspiration I decided to try to make her presence work in my favour.

'We were discussing the case,' I said and Azul giggled. She actually giggled. I wanted to punch her.

'You were discussing the case with a journalist. That's not very smart, Mr Stone.'

'She's not a journalist, she's involved. She has something to tell you. Tell him, Azul.'

Azul smiled at me and then at Baxter.

'Are you sure you two boys don't want coffee?' she said, and went into the kitchen. I didn't know whether to chase after her and grab her around the throat and ask her what the fucking hell she thought she was doing, or try to appease Baxter. I knew that Baxter had to come first. I began to explain that Azul had something very important that she needed to tell him but he raised his hand to stop me.

'I already have her statement,' he said.

'You mean about me being in the bar. About me being drunk and . . .'

'Drunk?'

'That's what she told you, isn't it? That I was in Sloppy Joe's and that . . .'

Azul was singing loudly in the kitchen and I figured she was singing for a reason. Baxter had that sharp look of puzzlement again, intensified so as to be almost funny.

'She didn't say anything about you being drunk, Mr Stone. She said you were drinking iced tea and that you seemed to be concerned about Ms Lisson's welfare.'

My silence was agonizing. Baxter and I listened to Azul's terrible singing from the kitchen for a few moments and then she arrived with two cups of coffee.

'Coffee for the boys,' she said sweetly. 'Do be careful of broken glass, won't you?'

In the next hour, Azul was perfection. Together, we told Baxter all about Benelli's movie scam. We explained that we didn't have anything on paper that we could show him but that it wouldn't take much effort to trace Benelli's accounts and confirm the story. I told Baxter all about Scarlet's late husband, and about her desire to get back into the movies, and Azul made a plausible attempt at explaining that her journalistic integrity would be at stake if she revealed her sources. I smiled at her throughout her explanation, as if yes, I understood and, hey, I even admired her for it. We finished each other's sentences and apologized when we interrupted. Baxter fidgeted in his seat and often removed his glasses to wipe the lenses, and I thought maybe he couldn't believe his eyes. He waited for us to finish and gulped the last of his coffee. He suddenly looked puzzled and held the coffee in his mouth, puffing out his cheeks. He walked to the kitchen and I heard him spit the coffee out. When he returned he looked sombre and he raised his eyebrows at Azul.

'You weren't kidding about the broken glass, were you?' he said.

'No, sir,' Azul said flatly, and she blinked at Baxter and then at me like an owl or a pussycat. The broken glass seemed to have put Baxter off his stride for a moment and he took off his spectacles again and held them up to the electric light.

'What do you say, Mr Baxter?' I said, glancing at Azul. 'Are you going to at least pick up Benelli? Or check his accounts?'

Baxter didn't like to be prompted or questioned. And he didn't like the fact that Azul was in the room. But I could also see that our strange relationship interested him. He had listened to us both speaking and half the time he had been looking at whichever one of us wasn't speaking at the time. Judging reactions, looking for secrets. It struck me then that Baxter liked to look for secrets more than anything else in the world. Finally, he'd finished with his glasses and he put them back on and crossed his legs.

'The reason I came here tonight, Mr Stone, wasn't anything to do with Benelli,' he said. He looked tired. 'No, sir. Nothing to do with Mr Benelli at all. It was to do with you, Mr Stone. It was to do with something I found out at around six o'clock this evening. And maybe it's something that you'd prefer to talk about alone. Do you understand what I'm saying, Mr Stone?'

I said that I did understand what he was saying. This was a moment that I had known had been coming ever since the murder, maybe even before that, and now it had arrived I almost welcomed it.

I was suddenly as hot as a furnace and my skin was burning. I didn't want to look at Azul and I didn't want to take my eyes off Baxter. I wanted Baxter to start talking, to spill the whole thing, evenly and if possible (please God) without any kind of recrimination. I had learned to shave the edges off this thing, to make it not hurt so much, and I prayed that Baxter, being a cop, could do the same. Maybe put it into technical language. He had already started to say that it was up to me whether Azul stayed in the room for this and I had already nodded my head at him. Baxter waited a long time for me to say something, and he shushed Azul when she tried to speak. He asked me again if I knew what he was talking about and I said softly that I did, that he should go ahead, that I really had no choice but to listen.

'I want to ask you again, Mr Stone, if you want this journalist in the room.'

'Yes, Mr Baxter. She can stay. You called London?'

'Yes, Mr Stone.'

'And you found out about Sarah.'

Baxter nodded. Was that some sort of concern twinkling in his eyes, or was it utter contempt? I wanted it to be contempt. I felt myself shrinking away into nothing, the way I always did whenever I thought about that night with Sarah in London. It had been a physical sensation inside me ever since it had happened and now I felt it more powerfully than I had ever felt it. I could feel myself disappearing into an empty place where Baxter's voice echoed.

He began by announcing flatly that he had checked out my name with the police in London and discovered that six months before I had been convicted of assaulting my wife. He called it a 'serious physical assault'. He said that the police in London called it 'grievous bodily harm' but that they had told him that it corresponded to the American term 'assault and battery'. Then he took out a piece of paper from his pocket (I was watching from my small empty place inside) and he read aloud the list of injuries which I had inflicted. The broken jaw ('Ah, Jesus, Karl, please . . .!'), the broken ribs ('You fucking little bitch!' and then I stamp on her side with my heel as she rolls over), the bruised face, the cuts to the wrists, the knee which she twisted when she tried to get out of my grip on the bathroom floor ('It was wet; she slipped'). Even down to the torn dress, the broken necklace, the earring that was almost pulled out of her pierced ear. Each detail was a step down, a step on a long dark staircase that led into some place like the cellar beneath our feet. The small empty place where I had lived for six months.

The room was quiet. Outside, the blue jays and orioles were calling to each other. I could hear Azul taking deep breaths, and I didn't dare to look at her. Now the moment was here, almost passed, I could begin to talk. I began by saying the worst thing I could have said.

'Are you married, Mr Baxter?' I said, and couldn't believe that I had said it. I was going to say that if he was married, then maybe he might be able to understand how it feels. I was going to say that if he was married to a woman who he loved, he might be able to understand how it feels when you see her with another man. I wanted to ask him to picture it in his mind. Picture the Great Room of the Grosvenor House Hotel in London, some phoney advertising-awards ceremony, where the men dress in penguin suits and the wild boys, the really crazy wild outrageous boys, they dress in white suits and they have their hair in pony-tails. I wanted him to picture that great cavernous room, with its phoney chandeliers and its disgusting sumptuousness, and I wanted him to see it from the other side of a whole bottle of brandy, the way I had that night. It was December, I'd already been to two parties, and I had been drunk since noon. By the time I joined Sarah at her agency table (nearest the kitchen door) I was red-eyed and mean and just about the smartest arse in the whole world. I sat and sneered and drank through the whole ceremony, the chandelier lights getting closer and brighter, the penguin suits getting more and more absurd. A challenge, an affront. And then the deafening applause for the guy who wrote that master work with the singing, dancing cows. He's younger than me, and he has a buccaneer smile, and when he steps up on to the platform, Sarah doesn't even join in the clapping. She just squeezes her hands together in her lap, and even through the whole day's booze I knew for certain. I had known already of course, that was the only reason I'd shown up in the first place, to know for certain and to suffer. Then I wanted Baxter to picture Sarah fleeing up the absurd spiral staircase of the Great Room, sobbing. (I'd picked a fight with her about nothing, about the role of advertising in society, or something worse and she had run away from me. And old shit-head had followed, still clutching his award, his bizarre piece of metallurgy. So I had followed them both up the spiral staircase too, and then a blackness descends.)

Between the acres of blackness, there are the images of what happened in the cloakroom. Like pictures you'd see in the flash of a camera. I see Sarah and shit-head embracing, him touching her tears and smiling. Then its shit-head doubled over, and then shit-head sailing across the counter of the cloakroom like he had wings. Then it's Sarah in the doorway of the ladies' toilet with me in pursuit. Then I'm in there. The Muzak is playing 'Strangers in the Night'. The air smells of ersatz lilacs and farts. I am inside the ladies' toilets with Sarah in my hands and then the bolts begin to fly inside me and there is a buckling of iron bars as this thing (it has no name) is released. A thing that has been inside a cage for a long time and now siezes it's chance to swap places with me. This thing gets outside the cage and pushes me inside and I watch while it kicks and punches and bites and hurts the woman that I love. And I am stuck with my head between the bars, trying to shout out that it should stop but I find that I am not able to make any noise. Until finally the cage is opened again and the beast goes back inside and I slam the door and I swear that I'll throw away the key while I sit and cry on the cold, tiled floor of the ladies' toilet and wait for the police to arrive. But I know that I never can throw away the key. Not even if I really want to. I wanted to say all that to Baxter but when I asked him if he was married, he came as close as I ever saw him come to looking disgusted.

'None of your damn business, Mr Stone,' he hissed. I nodded my head, and because this hurricane that I was living in had a sense of humour, it was right at that moment that the floorboards above our heads creaked. The wind shifting the house on its foundations. We were all silent for a long time and it was Baxter, who had managed to restore his calm, who finally spoke.

'You're quite a guy, aren't you, Mr Stone?' he said.

'I was in love with her,' I said, and the dryness of my voice came as a surprise. Now that this moment was over, even now, a few seconds later, I felt more assured than I had for a long time.

'You were what, Mr Stone?' Baxter said, trying to mock me. I felt contemptuous of him. Another new feeling.

'I was in love with her. That's why I hurt her. You find that hard to believe, Mr Baxter? You shouldn't. Wasn't it you who said that all you have to do is find the husband when there's been a murder. Or the wife, or the lover? I loved her and I found out one night that she had been sleeping with another man . . .'

I couldn't continue but it didn't matter. I felt that it didn't matter if Baxter didn't understand. I knew what he thought of me now because I felt the same way about myself. Ever since that night I had been trying to throw myself away. That was how I saw it. I had decided back in London that I wasn't worth keeping and that I should throw myself away. I had thrown myself on to this island, hoping that the bridges wouldn't stretch all the way back to where I'd come from. Somehow, in London, I'd escaped a prison sentence. The hotel security guys had finally pulled me off her, and by then someone had already called the police. I was taken to West End Central Police Station where I was held overnight and charged. The next morning I had walked all the way home in my dinner suit that was rusted up with blood. Mine and hers and his. And two months later, after I had agreed to plead guilty to the charge, they gave me a suspended sentence. I was bound over for two years. I sentenced myself to life and then set about the process of throwing myself away. I hadn't been brave enough to actually throw myself off a bridge, and so I had thrown myself across the ocean to see how long it would take for this thing (like a body drifting across the Atlantic) to wash up on my shore again. And now here it was before my eyes. I was staring at myself, my real self, for the first time since I had left London. And instead of making me fall apart as I had feared it might, I felt dry and calm and contemptuous. It wasn't until I turned to Azul that I made a decision about what I was going to do next. She was smiling that high-school smile at me, and I decided it was time to haul myself ashore and get myself into one piece again, just as she had said I should.

'. . . I took her into the bathroom, Mr Baxter, and did all those things that you have written on your piece of paper. I did it because I loved her. But I didn't love Scarlet. I won't love anyone ever again. I didn't love Scarlet and I didn't kill her. No matter what I did to Sarah, I didn't kill Scarlet.'

Baxter stared at me through his microscope lenses and, for the first time, I managed to meet his eye and stare back. I wondered if his love of puzzles included puzzles of motive as well as puzzles of circumstance. I wondered if he was as careful in his analysis of the human heart as he was in his analysis of blood and semen and tissue. I doubted it but I couldn't be sure. Finally, Azul said, 'He really didn't love Scarlet, you know, Mr Baxter. He told me so himself.'

Baxter got to his feet without even looking at Azul. I guessed that he'd heard the word 'love' once too often and needed some air. I understood that. I'd been practical and decent in that way myself once. I didn't bother to get up to show him out, but as he opened the door Azul said, 'Are you going to check out Benelli's accounts or not, Mr Baxter?'

Baxter didn't even bother to turn around to say, 'Ma'am, I already have.'

CHAPTER TWENTY

'Benelli's still on the island,' Azul announced with an apple-blossom smile and a little rebel yell. She caught me as I was loading groceries into bags at the checkout of the Sunbeam Market on Kennedy Drive. I'd bought ice cream, potatoes, pasta, oil and fresh grunt fish, as well as some Mexican herbs. Azul helped me to fill the bags and kept whispering, 'Hurry, hurry,' to the checkout lady, some kind of irritating personal habit. Finally we were out in the street, and the sun was starting to burn.

'He's still staying at the Madagascar,' Azul said, nosing through one of the bags for something to eat. 'The concierge said he'd checked out yesterday but he'd checked right back in again the same afternoon. I said, "Why was that?" and the guy said he didn't know. One of the cleaning ladies said, "Oh, sure, the little Italian guy," and she screwed up her face like he was being a pain in the ass. So I guess Benelli is getting nervous. I talked to one of the girls on the telephones and she said he'd made three calls to New York on the afternoon he checked back in, thirty minutes, twenty-five and ten, so I guess those are calls to his legal people. And here's the best part, the guy in the elevator said that the cops had been up to his room three times already. Here, hold this while I unwrap the ice cream.'

I took Azul's bag of groceries and she opened two ice cream bars for us. Kennedy Street had a carnival atmosphere, with all the anger dissipated, and there were lots of people doing things they didn't normally do. Guys in suits hammering chipboard, little kids sombrely sweeping up glass and acting grown up, beach bums in frayed shorts skipping up ladders with tubs of bitumen to mend roofs. The smell of the ocean was consumed by the smell of industry.

'Tomorrow I'll get to see Benelli himself,' Azul said, slurping her ice cream. 'He wasn't in his room when I called, but I've had this really neat card printed that says I'm an IRS investigator. And some documents too. He'll see me, sure he will. And I went to see the realtors too . . .'

A dollop of ice cream fell on to my shirt and I stopped walking. Azul laughed and said that in Florida you had to eat ice cream so fast it made your teeth hurt, otherwise it would melt all over you.

'Azul,' I said, scooping some of the ice cream off my shirt and licking my fingers, 'you shouldn't be doing any of this.'

'Sure I shouldn't,' she said, as if she were saying, 'Sure I should.'

'I mean, it's OK checking out his hotel, but you shouldn't go and see Benelli himself. You mustn't. I won't let you.'

This didn't even make Azul laugh. She just ignored me and carried on talking.

'Don't you see, Karl, this means that Baxter is taking Benelli seriously? He's on to him. Baxter's smart, you know, Karl. He'll have this whole thing figured. Hey, and wait till you hear what happened at the realtor's.'

There was suddenly a huge roar, like a bomb exploding two blocks away, and I saw that, on the corner of Rose Street and Duvall Street, a brick and plaster shop front was being heaved away from its joists by chains attached to an earth mover, and that all the debris was falling in a huge white cloud into the belly of a truck. There was an obscene crash that seemed to tear the whole street apart for half a second, then only dust and the sound of some construction workers yelling and clapping their hands. They were demolishing the remains of the pizza parlour where Dr Hesperez had got blood on his hands. Azul carried on talking, as if she hadn't heard a thing.

'I told them I wanted to rent the attic room at 1131 Mallory Street, and the guy's eyes, Karl, you should have seen them. Like they were popping right out of his head.'

'You did what?'

'I went to the realtors. Some guy called Clark. And I told him that I wanted the room at 1131, and you know, the son of a bitch wasn't even going to say anything, but then I guess his conscience got the better of him. He went serious and said, "Ma'am, I have to tell you that there have been some unfortunate incidents in that house and I would prefer to rent you a room someplace else."'

'You tried to rent Scarlet's room?'

'Sure. Succeeded too. I'm your new neighbour.'

We were forced to cross over the road around a make-shift steel barrier that separated the pizza parlour from the street. Now that the shop front had been pulled away, it was possible to see inside to where the restaurant had once been. The place had been cut to pieces, just as if someone with a thirty-foot knife had dug into its insides. There was still a neon menu board and the doors to the washrooms were in place. The stairs down to the basement were sealed off.

'You went and rented Scarlet's room?'

'Like I said.'

'Wait a minute.'

Azul didn't get it. I figured that either she was dumb, or playing a game, or maybe she was insane. She was laughing at the way I was staring at her. I said, 'Wait a minute, wait a minute,' to myself as well as to her.

'Wait for what?' she said. 'You said yourself that if I help you with the investigation you'll give me an exclusive. And I need this exclusive real bad. So I'm going to help. Hey, and it'll look great for the story, won't it? I mean the fact that I wrote it in the same room where it happened. Sure it will. That'll probably swing it for me. Sure.'

Azul had been like this ever since Baxter left the night before. She'd become so breezy I thought she might blow away. Now she really was the high-school girl I thought she was when I first met her in Sloppy Joe's. After Baxter had gone, she'd poured me another brandy and talked on and on about Benelli and about the scam and about how she was going to get this thing worked out. I'd hardly said anything at all, and I figured that maybe she had started to talk like this because she was afraid. Even more afraid than before, and afraid specifically of me. With good reason. She'd heard what Baxter had said. She knew now what I had done. But she stayed with me all night, talking till 3 a.m., when she finally lay down on the bed and fell asleep. I slept too, for an hour or so, and then I'd left her to walk out along the ocean and pick up some groceries.

I stopped in the street, choking on the clouds of white dust from the pizza parlour, and told her she could not possibly move into Scarlet's room, that it was absurd and dangerous and that Baxter would hit the roof and I didn't want her there and the whole thing was ghoulish and sick. And besides, I said, Scarlet's room was still sealed.

'Not any more,' she said. 'They take the seal off today. The place has been stripped. Baxter has finished with it. He told me so himself.'

'You spoke to Baxter as well?'

'I called him at home. Told him again about Benelli. He sounded kind of . . . sleepy.'

I had forgotten to go in any particular direction, and soon we were walking aimlessly towards the ocean. On Key West, when there's nowhere to walk, you always walk towards the ocean. I could see a glinting triangle of blue at the end of the street, and there were even yachts skimming the surface. I couldn't think of anything to say to Azul because I wasn't sure which Azul I was speaking to. She took my arm and told me again she really believed now that Baxter was being harder on Benelli than he was on me, and that that was a good sign. Then she said I should hurry up and finish my ice cream because there was someone she wanted me to meet.

The house was on South Roosevelt Boulevard and looked out on to the Sigsby-US navy base. It was a hunched up little one-storey wooden bungalow, painted white and with the paint corroded and flaked at the edges as if it had been gnawed at by a giant rodent. We were quite a way out of downtown Key West, and the boulevard was crammed with trucks bringing supplies from the mainland. There had been some sort of appeal, a lot of donations from other states, mostly things that no one needed, like biscuits and blankets. Some of the vehicles were military, and the soldiers hung half out of their cabs, panting in the heat and smoking and cursing the traffic. On the other side of the boulevard, there was a slab of concrete military buildings, but on this side of the highway, there was just this exhausted-looking line of whitewashed bungalows. Azul led me up the path of number 2033 and said she had to get her hair straight because this guy only liked girls who looked like prostitutes.

After she had tidied her hair, she rang the doorbell and

a dog began to bark. Then the door opened a little way and I saw the grizzled white hair of Crazy Jimmy.

'Jimmy?'

'Hey, Christina.'

Jimmy opened the door all the way, and saw me and looked confused.

'This is Karl Stone. He's a Limey. Can we come in?'

Azul didn't wait for an answer but walked straight into the dark interior. Crazy Jimmy scratched his head and mumbled something about not having his shoes on, and then a small dog came up and began to grizzle at me as I tried to get inside. Crazy Jimmy scooped the dog off the floor and took it out into the kitchen. The house was dark because all the shutters were closed, and the air inside smelt of dirty sheets and bad feet and very old cooking grease. When Jimmy reappeared, Azul kissed him chastely on the forehead and Jimmy's wicked blue eyes began to twinkle.

'So, so so, hey, hey hey,' he said, and he shook his head, in just the way his dog had shaken its head when he picked it up. I could smell the dog too, and the air was too hot to breathe. The TV was on but the sound was turned down. 'So, hey, hey, hell, I wasn't expecting no visitors.'

Azul gave me a conspiratorial smile. I was still too shocked at seeing Crazy Jimmy to say anything, but in my own vague way I was beginning to follow a train of thought. Maybe this explained how Azul had known so much about Benelli and Scarlet and me. Jimmy was getting excited and he stood on tiptoe to kiss Azul on the cheek. Azul yelped and hit him playfully on the shoulder.

'Sorry to call so unexpected,' Azul said, with a broader Western accent than I had heard before, 'but we're here on business. You understand, Jimmy?'

'Sure, Christina,' he said, and he gave me an anxious look.

'Don't worry about Mr Stone,' she said, 'you see, he's . . .'

'We've met,' I said. 'Jimmy is our postman. How are you, Jimmy?'

Jimmy looked down at his stockinged feet. Here, in his house, away from his beat, he looked smaller and more feeble. He was as embarrassed as hell about something.

'I'm OK, Mr Stone. Say, sure was bad news about . . .'

He suddenly became choked and looked down again. I was searching Azul's face for some clues. She was busy putting her arm around Jimmy's shoulder.

'About Scarlet? That what you mean, Jimmy? Yes it sure was bad news, wasn't it, Jimmy? Wasn't it, Karl?'

I said that it was bad news. Azul was talking to Jimmy as if he were six years old, and I found myself talking the same way. Jimmy regained his composure but his eyes were swimming in tears.

'Why did the Lord have to do a thing like that?' he said. 'A fine and beautiful woman like her? When there's all these spiks and greasers and niggers all over the island he could have taken. Don't make sense, does it, Mr Stone?'

I said that it didn't make any sense at all. Azul was starting to move around him now, standing in front of him and then behind him as she talked.

'Like I say, Jimmy, it's this business about Scarlet that brung us here.' Her accent had become ludicrous. 'You see, Mr Stone here has some things that he needs to find out. You know what I'm saying, don't you, Jimmy? Sure you do. You understand.'

Jimmy was becoming more nervous by the second, and I could see he wanted to whisper something to Azul, but she wouldn't let herself get close enough. He shifted from foot to foot for a while and then chuckled and tried to get close to Azul, who stepped effortlessly out of reach. The house stank so much that my eyes were beginning to water.

'Christina, I'm not sure that maybe Mr Stone should be here when we're discussing this business,' he said at last. Azul said nothing. For the first time, I registered he was calling her 'Christina'. I would have asked but Azul was giving me all kinds of crazy signals in the dark.

'You don't have to be concerned about Mr Stone,' Azul said, now with her arms behind her back and peering up at the ceiling. 'He's in on our little secret too. You see I told him about the mail.'

Crazy Jimmy shook his right hand in his left and his mouth became crooked. I thought that he was about to run out of the room but he stayed where he was and began to whisper, 'So, so, so, hey, hey, hey,' again.

'Yes, Jimmy, I told him all about our little arrangement with the mail. He won't squeal on you, will you, Karl?'

I said that I wouldn't and tried to mouth something to Azul to tell her to tell me what the hell was going on. 'You see, Karl, Jimmy and I made a little arrangement with the mail for 1131 a while back, didn't we, Jimmy? Old Jimmy here, well, he got a kind of kick out of reading Scarlet's mail. He used to bring it here to his home and read it before he delivered it. Didn't do no one any harm, did it, Jimmy? Just that he got a kind of thrill out of it. Something, I don't know. I don't know what turns you fellas on. But that was what he was doing. And I made a little arrangement that I'd have a peek at it too. You understand now, Karl?'

I said that I understood now. Azul smiled at me from inside this crazy part she was playing with its twanging vowels and its curled-up intonation. I had almost worked it out already and I realized how simple it had been for her. All she had to do was read the bank statements that came through to Scarlet every Wednesday from the Chase Manhattan bank and the rest would be simple. That was how she knew how much had been transferred into my account and how much Benelli was creaming off. The only mystery now was how Azul had conceived this plan, and why. Even in the darkness I could see that Crazy Jimmy was blushing and that he wasn't sure this wasn't an unravelling he had been dreading for months. Azul didn't give him time to settle.

'Thing is, Jimmy, I figured with this being Thursday then maybe you might have something for us. Understand, Jimmy?'

Jimmy looked at me for the first time, and I did a reasonable job of smiling at him. He smiled back, reassured that I wouldn't squeal on him. He began to fuss among a chaotic pile of papers and envelopes that were squeezed behind an old clock on the mantelpiece, and as he did it he mumbled something about how the mail of dead folks gets redirected back to the sender and that he put a redirection order on Scarlet's mail the day before yesterday, just like regulations said. He said that all Scarlet's mail would go straight back into the system from now on, and it sounded as if he was trying to explain he didn't actually have anything for us, but he continued to sift through the pile of papers anyway. Finally he found an envelope which he held up to the light from the kitchen window before pushing it under his arm.

'That it, Jimmy?' Azul said, not looking at him.

Jimmy said that it was, and he began to whisper something and glance at me as if he were more embarrassed now than ever.

'That a letter for Scarlet from the Chase Manhattan?' Azul said, and Crazy Jimmy grinned at her.

'Sure is, Christina.'

'Can I have it?'

'You'll have to come and get it,' Jimmy said, and then he wiped his mouth. Azul turned and walked slowly over towards him and stood directly in front of him. As she reached out for the envelope under his arm, I saw Jimmy's grey arm curl around her waist and then slip down on to her behind where it rested for a few seconds. My mouth fell open. Jimmy squeezed her ass a couple of times and I could hear him gurgling in the darkness. Azul took the envelope slowly from under Jimmy's arm and waited for a few seconds before moving away. Jimmy's hand was shaking when Azul finally took the envelope and slipped it into her bag. I wanted to get out now and throw up. They'd made such a repulsive statue locked together. I could feel the bile rising inside me. Azul had turned to me and winked. My mouth was still open.

'OK, Karl, I guess we've all got what we wanted,' she said in her normal voice. I couldn't say anything. Azul was already heading for the door, and as she walked by me she said, 'Hey, and you should see some of the videos that old Jimmy keeps here. I guess he's got every movie Scarlet Timberley ever made right here in this room. Like I say, I don't know what turns you guys on.'

We were a long way down North Roosevelt Boulevard, following the line of choked-up traffic, before I spoke to Azul. She was nursing her shoulder-bag like a kid with contraband. The traffic was getting throaty and the big military vehicles were making enough noise to force me to shout when I finally spoke.

'So that's how you get your information,' I said, trying not to sound as furious as I really was.

'Like I said, Karl,' she called back, 'I decided back in Kansas to do whatever was necessary.'

238

'So you let an old cunt like that screw you. Is that what was necessary?'

'Don't get so fancy,' she said, watching a twenty-ton amphibious landing vehicle rumble past. 'He just gets what you saw. Nothing more. I guess you think I'm crazy, don't you?'

'No, Azul. I think it's me that's crazy. There are other words for what you are.'

This made Azul laugh silently under the roar of the traffic. I hated her now more than I had ever done, but only because, well, I didn't know because. I just hated her. And I couldn't get that image out of my mind, the image of Crazy Jimmy's hand on her ass. The long silence between them. The ugliness of it.

I began to shout at her that there was no fucking need to go through all of that to get the bank statement because Baxter would be checking Benelli's accounts anyway and besides we could have waited for Jimmy to deliver the mail. She shouted something back at me and I waved my hand and tried to walk away from her but she followed me. She followed me all the way down the boulevard and into First Street where it was quieter and there was some shade. I tried to reason with myself that I didn't give a fuck how Azul got her information and I didn't give a fuck about Azul. I was only going through all of this with her because I needed her help. I was going to tell her that too, but instead, I found myself saying, 'How old are you, Azul?'

She said she was twenty-eight and I said bullshit. Then she said that she was twenty-one.

'Twenty-one. You're twenty-one. Jesus Christ, don't you understand how dangerous this stupid game is you're playing? Don't you understand what a man like that can do to a woman?'

239

'I'm not afraid of men like that,' she said. 'If I was going to be afraid of anyone, I should be afraid of you, isn't that right, Karl?'

Azul had a way of taking away all my momentum, of turning me around like a ball hitting a concrete wall. Of course she was right. She was smiling at the ease with which she did this thing that she did.

'If I was the kind of girl who was afraid of men like that, then what the hell would I be doing hanging out with a guy like you? Besides, I have a friend. I carry protection.'

I had looked away from her in disgust, but turned back to see that she was holding something in the neck of her shoulder-bag. She pulled the black butt out of the bag so that I could see it clearly. She had an insane, mischievous grin on her face, like a child showing you a pet she wasn't supposed to have. She opened the bag further and the barrel gleamed dull and oily in the shadows.

'Smith and Wesson .38,' she said softly. I looked at it in horror and she yelped with delight at the look on my face.

'Loaded too,' she said as she hid it away amongst her notebooks. 'Come on, Karl, let's go back home and take a look at the letter.'

I told her to go to hell and sat down on the kerb. The sidewalk was hot and I was shaking my head at my ankles and cursing the way this hurricane just wouldn't spare me from every lunatic and screwball in the whole of Florida. It had them lined up for me, one by one, starting with Benelli and Scarlet and now Crazy Jimmy and Azul and maybe even Baxter. And of course myself. Azul sat down beside me on the kerb and I edged away a few inches which made her laugh. She took the letter out of her bag and began to read it. I refused to look in her direction. She whistled through her teeth as she read the letter and I found myself shaking my head again at her feeble attempts to get my interest. Then she whistled again and I *was* interested.

I peeked over her shoulder at the letter. We both read it over and over and after we had both taken in what it said Azul made me admit that it had been worth it after all.

CHAPTER TWENTY-ONE

The letter was from Karl Weingartner, head of business affairs at the Chase Manhattan Bank on 5th Avenue.

Dear Caroline,

You are the only client on my roll who begins her business letters with an inquiry as to the welfare of the stray kittens we found in our summer place. Well, they're just fine!

As to the freeze on your account, consider it in place. No further transactions will be authorized without your signature in triplicate. The payments into the Mary Hope Foundation will of course continue and will be upgraded to $1,000.00 per month as per our annual agreement.

As the manager of your account, I have no place whatever passing comment on how you use your money, but if I were your financial adviser (which thank the Lord I am not!) I would tell you that I am mightily relieved these payments have been frozen. I would also tell you that as a friend.

Best wishes, Karl Weingartner

Baxter handed the letter back to me and his face was without expression. Twice he had tried to wave me away and twice I had forced the letter under his nose. I had caught up with him in the car park at the back of the tank, which had once been surrounded by a high wire fence, like a basketball court, but now all the fences were down. On one side of the car park, the fence had fallen on top of a line of cars and all the cars had been shifted around by the hurricane so that they were parked nose to tail. Most of them were write-offs, but no one had got round to moving them yet. The heat on this slab of concrete was intense, and all the cars appeared to be shiny with sweat. Baxter had a small Honda, and we were standing either side of it. He had read the letter while leaning on the roof of the car.

'Look at the date on the top of the letter, Mr Baxter,' I said and Baxter said, 'Go home.'

'Scarlet must have written to him on the day she was murdered. She must have written to him right after I had told her that Benelli was ripping her off. And she must have posted it then too. She'd got cold feet, Mr Baxter. She froze the account. That's why Benelli had her killed. Notice that I say "had her killed". I'm not saying that he actually killed her himself. He's Italian. From Naples.'

Baxter unlocked the driver's door and got in. The car had central locking, so the passenger door flicked open too. I took my chance and jumped inside. The heat inside the car was intense, as hot as a pizza oven, and it almost took my breath away. Baxter switched on the A/C and we both waited for it to take effect.

'You've got to admit,' I said at last and with great seriousness, 'it does look pretty suspicious.'

Baxter leant forward on his steering-wheel and began to rub his eyes under his spectacles. I realized after a moment that he was laughing in short spurts.

'What's funny?' I said.

Baxter tried to stop himself from laughing but failed. 'Ah, nothing,' he said.

'Come on, what's so funny?'

'Nothing . . . it's just . . .'

He laughed again and then sighed and shook his head.

Then he laughed some more. I was more than a little put out.

'That's right, Mr Baxter, you laugh. You will forgive me though if I don't see the funny side.'

Baxter got a hold of himself and started the engine.

'Where are you going?' I said.

'I don't know,' he said, swivelling in his seat to reverse the car, 'that's what's so funny.'

We drove in silence along South Roosevelt Boulevard, which was free of traffic. Here and there were the odd smudges that the hurricane had left. Wooden colonials reduced to splinters, cars on their roofs, helpless, like upturned beetles, power lines dragged into the branches of trees, the ragged sail of a yacht draped over the neon sign of a gas station. Neither of us noticed any of it much. Baxter only slowed and peered out of the window when we passed the junction with Bertha Street, where the National Guard had set up some kind of road block.

'Ass-holes,' he whispered as he waved and smiled at one of the guardsmen. 'They get here two days too late and they find that it's all over. So they get jerked off and start trying to make something happen. I had some guy in my office, some surgeon, a black guy, giving up his vacation to help out down at the hospital, and he says that one of these ass-holes from Alabama called him a nigger.'

The National Guardsman was waving us on furiously. We drove on. Now it was my turn to laugh. Baxter didn't ask me why I was laughing so I told him anyway.

'You really couldn't give a shit about Scarlet and me, could you, Mr Baxter?' I said. He slowed for a set of lights which were on red. We waited for a long time, and then Baxter seemed to remember something and we drove through the red lights anyway.

'I mean, I understand that you've got a lot on your

244

mind at the moment, but for me, this is everything. You still think I killed her, don't you?'

Baxter braked hard. We had stopped outside a set of dilapidated wooden gates at the end of a drive that were held together by a piece of rope tied in a sailor's knot. Baxter told me to get out of the car.

'No,' I said, 'I need to talk.'

'Get out of the car and open the gates.'

He pointed at the wooden gates with his nose. Above the gates, I could see the masts of yachts moored some way away in the Garrison Bight Marina. Baxter waited while I got out into the furious heat and untied the rope that held the gates closed. I swung them open and saw that behind them there was a dirt track leading down to a piece of waste-land and scrub that sloped down on to the harbour. There were six or seven trailer homes on the waste-ground which were upright, and half a dozen more lying on their sides or on their roofs. It was like opening the doors on to another world. The sun was still shining here but the light was sharper and uglier. As Baxter cruised through the gates and stopped for me to get back in the car, I felt the silence behind the gates with my skin. There were some children squatting underneath a tarpaulin and picking at the dirt, but they didn't make any noise. Even the gulls didn't make a noise as we bumped down the dirt track towards the middle of the waste-ground. There was an old woman who looked Cuban or mestizo, sitting on the steps of one of the trailers. When she saw Baxter's car, she stood up and straightened her hair and brushed down her clothes. I felt that we had driven into a depression of some kind; the air was still, like in a basin. Baxter got out of the car, took some packages from the boot and took them over to the old lady.

I opened the window of the car and breathed in the

245

deathly salt air. I could hear Baxter talking to the old lady and I could hear that he was speaking in Spanish. He spoke softly and fluently. I saw him hand the packages to her and then he walked back to the car and got inside.

'They were her grandchildren's clothes,' Baxter said, peering out towards the ocean.

'Yes, OK, Mr Baxter,' I said, 'point taken.'

'What point is that, Mr Stone?'

'Ah, nothing. Nothing at all.'

We sat and listened to the murmur of the ocean, under the heavy air in this basin. I could smell the death that the hurricane had left behind. I wondered how I could break the impasse and get Baxter on to the subject of Benelli again, but it was Baxter himself who started talking.

'You know, Mr Stone,' he said, without looking at me, 'my father sells peanuts outside ball games up in Orlando. Makes a damn good living.'

I nodded my head. He turned and looked at me and maybe remembered who I was, what I had done, what I might have done, and I could see him withdraw behind his spectacles again. He started his engine.

'Yes, Mr Stone,' he said as the engine fired, 'a damn good living. He has a franchise deal with Disney too. My wife sometimes says maybe we could go up there. He's getting pretty old, you see, Mr Stone . . .'

'I didn't kill her, Mr Baxter.'

'She's Cuban you see, my wife, and she has family up there. She says I should leave this island to the fishes and the alligators.'

'You've got to believe me. I know I hurt my wife but I didn't kill Scarlet.'

We were reversing slowly, out of respect for the silence of the place. Baxter turned the car around and we began to bump up the dirt track towards the wooden gates and back to the broad, sunlit highway. When we reached the gateway he pulled up, leant across me and opened my door.

'I'm heading west,' he said. 'You'll have to walk.'

I unfastened my seat-belt, prepared to leave Baxter to his thoughts about peanuts and Orlando. I was almost out of the car when Baxter took me by surprise again. He took hold of my arm and pulled me back into the seat.

'Mr Stone, you should forget about Benelli,' he said, stretching his neck, mumbling. 'I checked the Key West Developments stuff. Went through the whole thing over three days and three nights. You were right about the scam. He was ripping her off for two million, maybe even more. But there was a clause . . .'

Baxter was blushing. I couldn't even guess what was making him tell me this, and I could tell that he didn't know why he was doing it either. Maybe it was something to do with the place we had just left, or his wife, or the heat.

'There was a clause. A termination agreement. If Scarlet Timberley died, the movie deal was off and all monies would be taken out of the Key West Developments account and returned to the Lisson estate for distribution to the heirs. It was a clause her attorney had drawn up on day one. I already spoke to Weingartner at the Chase Manhattan and he told me Ms Lisson's attorney was suspicious about Benelli and had a death contract drawn up. And Benelli signed it. I've got a copy of it on my desk. What I'm saying is that Benelli knew that, if Scarlet died, he would lose everything. He's a con artist, OK that's true, but if anyone on this island wanted Scarlet Timberley alive, it was him. Benelli didn't have a motive, Mr Stone. In fact, just the opposite.'

Baxter didn't look at me at all as he spoke. I got out of the car and walked back to the movie house, where Azul was waiting with more bad news.

CHAPTER TWENTY-TWO

When I walked through the overgrowth of the drive to the movie house, I saw that there was a brand new shiny black door with a brass handle fitted into the doorway. The windows at the front at ground level had been replaced too, and when I looked up to my own room and Azul's room, I could see all the windows in the house had been reglazed. There was an envelope pinned to the door with my name written on it. It contained a key that fitted the chunky new Banham lock.

Inside the air smelt sweeter than I had ever known it. I could smell fresh-cut flowers and also the sickly sweet smell of putty. The stairs had been swept and all the debris from the hurricane had disappeared. From way up on the top landing, I could hear the floorboards creaking and Azul singing softly to herself, off-key but with great tenderness. I stood in the hallway for a long time, thinking about Baxter. Then I remembered to close the door behind me, and when it was closed, the house was dark again.

I started up the stairs and Azul called down, 'Karl, that you?' and I heard her skipping down the top flight of stairs. We met on the landing outside my room, which was always in shadow, and Azul took hold of my arm.

'Well?' she said, letting her long blond hair fall across her face. I grunted something at her and fumbled for the key to my room. When I walked inside I thought Azul was going to follow but she stayed out on the landing.

'What did Baxter say?'

'Azul, I need some time on my own.'

I took the tumbler that was stuck to the top of the television and poured myself a large brandy. Not so large but large for daylight. I took the first swig staring out of the window, hardly registering that there were now curtains hanging there with bright flowers printed on them. Azul still hadn't come into the room.

'Come on, Karl,' she said, 'tell me what Baxter said about the letter.'

I was silent for long enough to finish the brandy. I poured myself another tiny one, just enough to colour the bottom of the glass but enough to know that I still had some left. The bottle was almost empty and I thought about going to buy some more. Azul had ventured into the doorway now and when she spoke I noticed her voice was uneven. Different.

'Karl, can you even hear me?'

'Baxter didn't say anything at all about the letter,' I said, half amused. 'But he did have some real interesting news for us. That is, it's real interesting news for me. For you, it's just another detail.'

When I turned to Azul, I saw that her hair was still hanging down over her right eye, and I thought maybe she was trying to look seductive. She sniffed hard and the picture changed in an instant. She was holding on to the door frame as if she were about to pass out or fall over. Then when I moved closer, I saw that, beneath the strands of blond hair, her right eye was swollen. She'd put cream on it and foundation and maybe even some powder, but I caught a glimpse of purple around the eyelid and red beneath the eye, and black around the side of her face. She tried to turn her head away but I was already close enough to see the bruising clearly.

'What the hell is that?' I said.

'Ah, this? Nothing. I walked into the door. Forgot it was there. I'd got so used to not having doors around the place . . .'

She sniffed and sighed and then turned to me and flicked the hair away from her face.

'Kind of pretty, isn't it?' she said with a smile.

At first I thought about Crazy Jimmy, but then I remembered what Azul had told me about her plans for the day. She'd had that stupid card printed giving her name as 'Christina Fontainbleu', an IRS investigator. They made up joke business cards in some tattoo place near the docks and the one that Azul had had made wouldn't have fooled a blind man. But she'd told me she was going to use it to get to see Benelli. She'd set off that morning for the Madagascar saying that she was going to get this thing sorted out and I hadn't bothered to try to stop her. I knew that I wouldn't have been able to anyway.

'Benelli?' I said, reaching out to touch her face beneath the bruise. Azul didn't say anything but flinched when I touched her. I knew it was true. I was calm for long enough to pour another brandy, and this time it was a shot that would have been large even for night-time.

'I guess he didn't buy my story about the IRS,' she said, covering her eye with her hair again. I shook my head and swallowed my brandy whole. There was enough left in the bottle for one last big shot and I went ahead and drank it.

'He didn't buy it, huh?' I said. 'Well now, isn't that the damnedest thing. You go to all the trouble of having some dumb two-dollar card printed and he doesn't buy your story. So tell me, just what happened exactly? You know, Azul, blow by blow.'

The brandy was like water thrown on to hot iron. I

could feel the steam and the pressure building, but I was also getting colder and harder. Things were getting clear through the clouds of steam. I knew things I hadn't known before, I saw a long line of possibilities stretching out on to the horizon, stretching back to the night of the hurricane and the murder. Things I hadn't wanted to see before were showing themselves, appearing from the mist. Sure, I got Scarlet's blood on my hand when I lifted the wardrobe. Sure, Mr Baxter, that's just how it happened. Sure, Mr Baxter, I was drinking iced tea. No, Mr Baxter, I wasn't in love with Scarlet and you see this blood on my hands, it got there when I lifted the wardrobe. You believe me, Mr Baxter? Mmm? Tell me about your daddy who sells peanuts at the ball game.

'Tell me, Azul, just exactly how did Benelli react when he realized why you really wanted to talk to him?'

'Do you like the curtains, Karl?'

'No, Azul, as a matter of fact I hate the fucking curtains. Tell me what happened with Benelli.'

Azul tried to laugh but it didn't work out. I had my own picture of what had happened and I really didn't need Azul to fill in the details. She'd gone up to his room with the card in her hand and he'd invited her in and after ten seconds flat he'd realized who she was and what she wanted and he'd tried to throw her out of his room and Azul had started to act tough the way she would when she was frightened and then Benelli had started to act tough too. I wondered about the Smith and Wesson .38 in her bag, and imagined how much worse things might have been. I didn't like the pictures in my mind and when Azul confirmed what I had imagined I got even angrier. Except it wasn't anger neat, it was anger and fear mixed. I was scared of what Baxter had told me, that Benelli had no motive, and by implication that no one had a motive except maybe me. I was afraid of that so much that I drank through clenched jaws. I was like Azul. When I was scared I started to act tough.

'Where are you going?' Azul said when I pushed my way past her out of the room.

'To get some more brandy,' I said, and I gave her what I thought was a good imitation of a crazy smile.

Out in the street the air was hot and sullen and the colonial houses of Mallory Street were panting like old dogs. There was still the background noise of buzz saws and hammering but it wasn't so frantic any more. This island had been bruised and wounded so often that it healed quickly. I thought maybe Key West wouldn't have been the same without its annual beating. Maybe the island needed the hurricane to keep it sassy and wild. That thought made me smile because in the vapour of the brandy I thought I saw some kind of analogy with lots of things. My knuckle had healed pretty quickly too, but it hurt when I punched it into the palm of my hand.

There was a taxi place on Duvall Street, and outside I saw a cab with its green sign wedged under the windscreen saying 'Free'. The driver was twenty stone, sucked into the driving seat and apparently a permanent fixture. He was tossing pistachio nuts into his mouth and piling up the shells on the sidewalk. When I ducked my head into the car and asked him to take me to the Madagascar Hotel, he dusted the salt off his trousers and said, 'Madagascar Hotel comin' right up.' We drove fast through the streets of downtown Key West and out along Highway One, and the twenty-stone driver told me some stories about fishing for bonefish and sharks out on the sand flats, and whenever he turned his head to look at me I whistled through my teeth and said, 'That must really have been something.'

The more I liked his stories, the faster he drove, until he screwed the car around a tight bend to take the exit that led down to the Madagascar. We drove through a shaded cypress grove for a quarter of a mile, with the ocean either side of us, until the pink façade of the hotel became visible, like a ghastly American wedding cake floating on the water. The brandy was making the Madagascar look funny, perched on the end of its sand spit, all turrets and towers and badly remembered images from French châteaux. When I paid the driver, I was laughing at the ugliness of it, set against the beauty of the sunset which was just beginning to bleed into the ocean on the horizon. As the driver started to pull away I said, 'You people don't deserve this island,' and he gave me a sharp look. But I guess he'd smelt my breath and he let it pass.

The cool air inside the lobby sobered me up a little. I wasn't really drunk but I'd drunk enough to stir memories of being drunk, and I knew that I was sitting on the pivot of some kind of seesaw. The air-conditioning smelt of damp earth, and there was soft music playing from vents in the ceiling. Everything inside was pink, even the face of the lady who was working the reception.

'Benelli, Benelli, Benelli,' she murmured as she checked her computer screen. Then she said, 'He's a pretty popular guy.' I said sure, he was popular OK. When she found his room number and picked up the phone she asked who she should say wanted him.

'A friend,' I said.

'Just that?'

'It's kind of a surprise.'

She held the phone away from her ear to make sure she didn't spoil her hair, which looked to be stiff with spray. I could hear the phone ringing softly and, as it rang, some part of me began to catch up. I took some deep breaths and asked myself what the hell I was doing here. The only answer I had was that I was here to sort this thing out. I asked myself if I was drunk and I answered that I wasn't drunk but that I just couldn't stand to sit around any longer in that house and let all of this happen to me.

'What did you say?' the lady on reception said, and she gave me a puzzled look.

'Nothing, nothing,' I said. 'Just thinking out loud.'

I wandered away from the reception desk and peeked out through the pink dining-room (the Sunset Lounge) towards the ocean. Between the lounge and the ocean there was a swimming-pool which was shimmering in the last full sunlight of the day. I wasn't really seeing the pool or the lounge as I continued to ask myself what the hell I was doing here and what the hell I was going to do if I caught up with Benelli. I just knew that I had to ask Benelli some questions otherwise I might explode. It was then that I saw his tanned bald head appearing from beneath the water. Then the bulge of his belly and finally his hairy brown legs shivering uneasily on the steps at the side of the pool.

When I set off at a run for the doors of the Sunset Lounge, the receptionist tried to call out to me and I heard her saying that the lounge and the pool were reserved for residents only and that it wasn't permitted to go through to the patio in street shoes. I was already into the lounge and I had to force the doors of the fire exit to get out on to the patio. The air outside was still hot, and Benelli was shaking water out of his ears and drying his belly with a hotel towel. He froze when he saw me walking towards him. There was no one else in the pool or any of the sun loungers, but when he saw me, Benelli instinctively looked around for help. He was afraid at first and then he began to smile.

'Well, look at what the fucking cat . . .'

I grabbed his arm and eased him down into the chair behind him. I pulled up a chair of my own, without letting go of his arm, and stared into his eyes. The Hobgoblin at Bay. The mythical creature blinking nervously under my gaze.

'Hello, Mr Benelli,' I said softly. 'I'd like to ask you some questions.'

He shook his arm free from my grip and carried on rubbing his legs with his towel. He was shaking his head gently, smiling, tut-tutting.

'I told them you were crazy,' he said flatly; 'now it's confirmed. Get the fuck off my arm.'

'Question number one . . .'

'Fucking fruit cake.'

'. . . who else was involved in the Scarlet Timberley scam? Just you or is there someone with brains somewhere who thought the whole thing up for you?'

Benelli was now drying himself frantically, shaking me off whenever I took hold of him. He was still managing to smile between shakes of the head.

'Oh boy, I sure know how to pick 'em, that's for sure.'

'Why did you do it, Giorgio?'

'Get off my fucking arm or I'll call security.'

'Why did you kill Scarlet?'

Benelli stopped drying himself and stared at me. His big brown eyes were filled with wonder. Phoney wonder. Behind the eyes there was something evil.

'You should be in a cage, you know that, Karl?'

I took hold of his throat, or at least, something inside me took hold of his throat. His head twisted awkwardly and he began to gurgle, more for effect than out of pain. I still had an image of Azul's swollen eye somewhere in my mind. Benelli thrashed his arms around for a few seconds and I tightened my grip. He stopped struggling and I loosened it again.

'Why the huck would I hant to hill Scarly?' he choked and his face turned pink.

'I don't know,' I said, 'that's what I want you to tell me.'

Benelli looked at me from the corner of his eye. I had his face turned away and he had to struggle to see me. He needed to see my face. He needed to know if I was going to kill him. The look of terror in his eyes told me something, something that I didn't want to know. I knew from the way he looked at me that he really did think I was capable of killing him, and that he really did believe I had killed Scarlet. But if he believed that I had killed her, then he hadn't, and who did that leave? I loosened my grip enough to let him talk.

'Jesus, Karl . . .'

'Tell me about the two million dollars. Tell me about the scam.'

He didn't have to say anything for me to know that this had all been said a hundred times. The scam was old news. There was no remorse and I didn't expect any.

'The whole thing was her idea in the first place,' he said, trying to get comfortable in my grip. His skin was slippery with sweat and greasy with sun oil. 'It was Scarlet who came to me. Didn't she tell you that? Sure. She came to me. Maybe we even would have made a movie. I don't know. But when someone comes to you and hands you two million dollars, well, I ain't no saint, Karl.'

I let him go and expected a few moments to think things through. Instead Benelli grabbed me around the neck and heaved me out of the seat. Half a second later, I was immersed in water and gasping for air. He was stronger than I had imagined, powered by fury. I came up for air standing in the shallow end of the pool.

'The guy's a fucking nut!' he screamed.

The chlorinated water stung my eyes and I was gasping for breath. The cool of the water cleared the last vapours of the brandy and the sun had gone behind a cloud. Benelli was standing above me in the grey light.

'I've got friends, you know,' he hissed. 'Don't just think that you've got twenty years in the can to look forward to. You won't even do six months. You're going home to England in a box.'

The lady receptionist appeared from the Sunset Lounge, tottering on her heels, and she hurried to Benelli's side. Behind her, there was a hotel security guard in a kind of fancy-dress police uniform. He had his hand on the holster of his revolver, and his revolver was real. All three of them were looking down on me as I dragged myself towards the side of the pool. I heard Benelli say, 'Call the cops, this guy's a nut,' and the lady receptionist hurried back towards the hotel. The shallow end of the pool had some shelved steps that led up to the patio, and my shoes slid on them as I tried to get out. I could see that the security guard was getting nervous, and Benelli was still taking huge breaths to calm himself down. I got out on to the patio and sloshed and splashed my way over towards them.

'Just tell me one thing, Benelli,' I said, as both he and the security guard backed away from me, 'how come you left the house without Scarlet that afternoon? How come she was alone waiting for the hurricane?'

Benelli turned to the security guard and mumbled something about me being a fucking nut.

'Scarlet would never have stayed in that house alone,' I hissed. 'Scarlet said she wouldn't be on her own in the

257

house for anything in the world when the hurricane hit. But that afternoon you left the house without her. How come?'

Benelli had backed away far enough to feel brave.

'For what it's worth, screwball, that was down to you,' Benelli said and he danced a little closer to me. He was jabbing the air with his fist. 'Down to you, ass-hole. She said you'd made her see the light. Like some kind of goddam saviour. She said you'd made her see that she didn't need the movies any more and she wasn't scared of hurricanes any more either. So she popped some pills and said she was staying in the house and waiting for you. She said she knew you'd come back for her. And you did, didn't you, Karl?'

The sun was setting fast and the wind was cold when it blew on my wet clothes. Benelli and the security guard stared at me like I was some kind of wild dog they had to keep on the leash. I saw myself through their eyes and the images from the night of the hurricane were swinging around in my head like horses on a carousel. Among all the horses there was one black horse that kept on coming around and around.

Then two Florida patrolmen arrived to take me away from the hotel. They put a plastic sheet down on the back seat to stop me from ruining the upholstery of their car.

CHAPTER TWENTY-THREE

I had dried out by the time I arrived at the tank. Farmer came to fetch me from the reception area, and in the echoes of the annexe it sounded as if the uniformed officers who greeted him were calling him 'tenant farmer'. This made me laugh somewhere down at the bottom of that empty place where I was prowling. Baxter's desk had gone.

'Sumptn funny, Mr Stone?' Farmer said softly as he showed me through the door to his office. There was a photograph of a Cuban lady, young and pretty, on his desk and I figured that it was Baxter's wife. When I sat down in the seat he pulled out for me, I realized how comfortable I had been with Baxter. With Baxter, all of this had seemed less real. Baxter had always been a fictional cop in my own mind. I'd shaped him, built him out of the scraps of conversation we'd had before the murder, the way writers do. Farmer was the real thing and I didn't like it. He swivelled in his chair and closed the blinds behind him.

'I asked you a question, Mr Stone.'

'No. Nothing funny. Nothing funny at all. Serious.'

'Yep. It's serious, OK.'

He still had his back to me and I could see the rhino skin on the back of his neck, burnt orange from years in the Florida sunshine. This animal belonged here. He was as much a part of the island as the alligators and the hurricanes. A patrolman came into the room and handed Farmer an envelope. As he left, he looked down at me and said, 'This him?' and Farmer nodded.

'Did you really write for Laurence Olivier?' the patrol-man said, mangling the name in the threshing machine of his island accent. I shook my head and Farmer sniggered.

'Guess this guy's just full of bullshit,' he said. 'From day one.'

The patrolman left.

'OK, Mr Stone,' Farmer said, 'why don't we get down to it like grown-ups, mmm? Why don't you let me have the whole thing.'

I had thought when the cops had brought me in that Farmer was going to process me for an assault charge against Benelli. No one had said a word to me since I had got into the patrol car. The two cops had talked about some ball game they'd both seen on TV for the whole journey from the Madagascar to the tank. But now that I saw Farmer with an envelope in his hands labelled 'Caroline Lisson' I began to entertain other possibilities. The possibilities made me burn.

'Where's Baxter?' I said quickly, with panic in my voice.

'Tom's had to take a little vacation,' Farmer said. 'Left me a whole trunk full of shit to handle. So come on, Mr Stone, what do you say? Let's talk like grown-ups.'

He swivelled around to look at me. His face was dull and weary but menacing nevertheless. More menacing for the weariness and dullness of it. He looked at me the way another man would look at a notice-board or a letter from the bank. There was none of the curiosity which I'd seen in Baxter's eyes and which had made me so afraid. There was only boredom and resentment at having to have this conversation in the first place. I knew that he was an ordinary man, a man not troubled by too much imagina-tion, the kind of man who would have a stock of irritating catch-phrases which he'd use over and over again because he couldn't think of anything else to say. 'Let's talk like grown-ups' was obviously one of them. He said it again and stared at me.

'I don't know what you mean.'

He humphed and rubbed his mouth as if I'd been holding out for hours and hours. He wanted a straight line, the shortest distance between me and the blue area so that he could get back to luring bonefish, or drinking beer, or whatever it was that Farmer did. Finally he said, 'Look, Mr Stone, I spent a half-hour looking over the file and well, it's like this.' He smiled at some private joke. 'Ole Tom, he can get pretty fancy sometimes. He can get pretty high and mighty. But me, I'm different. I like to talk like a grown-up with people. Talk straight. I like to get things off the green sheet and on to the pink sheet. That's a conviction, you understand.'

He left a long pause to make sure that I understood. I was racing a long way ahead of him.

'The way I read the file, they find the lady in the bedroom, and they find you down in the hall with your hand all beaten up and with her type O all over your hands. And well, that's good enough for old Frank. You following me, Mr Stone.'

I said that I did follow him. Most of my attention was taken up with thoughts about Baxter. Just how long a vacation had he taken? Had he really handed me over to this? I knew deep down that this hadn't been Baxter's choice at all. I knew that the vacation had been Farmer's idea and that maybe I had been the cause of it. Farmer was carrying on with his little speech about talking like grown-ups, a speech he'd made a hundred times to men who by now were up in Miami or Tampa or in the tank here on the island, and maybe even some who'd been fried in their own juices. It would all be the same to Farmer.

261

He said he'd read the stuff about Mr Benelli and that well, he was just a plain kind of a guy who didn't understand the movie business. Maybe ole Freddy was pushing the line a little, but maybe not. Farmer said he'd looked at the stuff about some account somewhere and about how Benelli was doing this and doing that to the Lisson woman but hell, the way Frank Farmer looked at it, Benelli was right here in the tank when the murder happened so all that stuff was just so much ass-wipe. Did I understand? I said that I did.

'That's good, Mr Stone. So come on. Let's talk like grown-ups.'

I felt the danger in the air now like a thick gas that made me breathe hard. Every word would have to be considered. I could maybe say nothing. If I said nothing then maybe he'd grow tired because he was so lazy and let me get out into the air again. The thought struck me that at any moment he was going to begin that mantra I'd heard so often in the movies and on TV. The reading of my rights. I was almost curious as to how it would sound for real. If he read me my rights, then I would have to change everything. I would have to call Azul and get her to get me an attorney. I'd have to stay silent while this animal slumped in front of me, needling me with his eyes. Then I figured that if he was going to charge me with the murder he would have done it the moment I stepped into his office. I realized that Farmer still needed more evidence to make a case, and I was the only person in the world who could give it to him.

'What do you say, Mr Stone? You tell me all about what you did to Mrs Lisson and we'll forget the assault charge on that fella Benelli. Deal?'

I said nothing. Finally, after half a minute of listening to the rigging bells clanking in the harbour, Farmer asked me if I wanted coffee and I nodded my head. He left the room and as he walked by, he put his hot meaty hand on my shoulder and squeezed it, maybe to let me know that he was a pretty strong guy and that I should remember that.

'So, you're from London,' Farmer said as he handed me the coffee, an almost comical attempt to sound bright and interested. I nodded my head.

'Never been to Europe, Mr Stone. Nope. Never have. The way I see it, I ain't going nowhere where I ain't welcome. Oh sure, they like your Yankee dollars but that's the end of the story. Yes, sir. That's the end of the story. Is it true that you Limeys eat chips with your fish?'

I nodded, nursing a fingernail that I'd bitten to the quick on the way to see Benelli. Farmer was staring at my face and I was staring at my finger.

'Ever had tea with the Queen, Mr Stone?'

I looked up at him and he laughed. He didn't laugh with his eyes. Maybe he never did.

'You don't say much, do you, Mr Stone?'

'I want to see Baxter.'

'Sure.' A long pause and then softer, 'Sure you do.'

Farmer found something amusing somewhere in the thicket of his mind. He breathed 'sure, sure' and smiled and tried to let me know he was way ahead of me.

'I can understand why you'd want to see your old buddy, Mr Baxter.' Farmer ran his hands through his hair, deciding in his own slow way whether or not it would be OK to be indiscreet with me. 'I can understand that. The way he put his ass on the line for you.'

Farmer finally had my attention, and he knew it. He reminded me of a school kid with a secret he just couldn't wait to spill. He peered out of the crack between the blinds, talking casually to the window.

263

'Yes, sir, he sure had a candle for you, Mr Stone. Me, I just couldn't figure it. Maybe he thought he'd look kind of foolish if it turned out he'd helped a guy commit murder. Given him all the inside information. Maybe he was right. He sure will look foolish. But I guess he's got his own way of going about things and I've got mine. Nothing wrong in that. Free country, Mr Stone.' He turned to me and then looked at the photograph on the desk. 'Did you know he was married to a Cuban lady?'

'Yes.'

'Sure. I guess that figures.'

Farmer was pretending to find something interesting out in the parking lot at the back of the tank. He widened the gap between the blinds and peered this way and that. I could hear the gulls screaming out over the harbour, and the rigging bells were still clanking in the breeze. Farmer studied the yard for a full minute before he let the blind close, shutting out the blade of sunlight.

'But you see, Mr Stone,' Farmer said, 'I don't have a degree from Penn State. I'm just a good cop. So come on. Let's you and me talk.'

'Like grown-ups?'

This reckless beast, the beast in the cage, rattling its cup along the bars. Did I really want to make this guy beat me senseless by making smart remarks? Farmer either didn't notice or pretended not to. He took a long time to register what I had said. He wasn't sure yet about the way I talked, he wasn't sure about my accent – the accent or the way I looked at him. He changed gear from casual to mad like a truck lumbering up a steep gradient.

'You get a kick out of hurting women, Mr Stone?' he said.

'Say again?'

'Women. You feel good when you hurt them?'

In that dark and empty place I heard a deep groan and I imagined the serpent with its yellow eye glinting at me. I realized that I had my eyes closed and I opened them to find Farmer standing directly at my side. He put his hand on my shoulder again and squeezed it hard.

'In ole Frank Farmer's book there are two ways of cracking a nut,' he said softly. 'You take a sharp knife and you squeeze it into the crack and you kind of work the thing open. That's Baxter's way. The other way is to take a hammer and . . . well, you understand what I'm saying, Mr Stone?'

'I didn't kill her.'

'Now you shush.'

'Either charge me or let me go.'

'Shush your mouth.'

'If you're not charging me I am free to leave.'

Farmer backed away. He circled his desk and I could see that he was thinking about trying the blind again but he was bored with those theatricals. He leant on his desk on his fists.

'Do you think this is a smart way to behave, Mr Stone?'

I didn't say anything. Silence hurt but it was better than anything else. He picked up the envelope labelled 'Caroline Lisson' and began to take out the sheets of paper inside. I glimpsed a Chase Manhattan bank statement, and some files and letters. Farmer whistled softly as he sifted through the papers and removed paper-clips. Finally he found the piece of paper he had been looking for.

'The reason I ask you about you getting your kicks from hurting women is because of this.'

He handed me a sheet of paper. At first I thought it was going to be some kind of duplicate of my charge sheet from London. Then I saw that it was a typewritten sheet

265

from my own Singer manual typewriter. An original. The a and the r both faint. I didn't have to read much to realize which page it was. It was the murder scene. With the echo of Benelli's voice running all through it ... I read the line 'I'm sorry, Laura, I just can't take any more,' and froze. Baxter was talking over my head.

'What do you do, write it first and then do it?'

'Where did you get this?'

'Well, that's none of your damn business, Mr Stone. What is it, you jerk off at the typewriter? Jerk off about how it's gonna feel?'

When I had gone back to my room, I had found most of my original script intact. A few of the pages had been missing, and some of them were strewn around the broken window in the kitchen, so I figured that some of the pages had blown out in the storm. This page had a dried brown stain along the top, as if it had landed in mud. There was half a footprint on the back.

I read the directions, typed in capitals on the page. The part about Max taking a pillow and holding it over Laura's face. Max and Laura, me and Scarlet.

'We already checked it against the keys of the typewriter we found in your room. Now come on, Mr Stone. You want to talk like grown-ups *now*?'

Lots of possibilities presented themselves all at once, and for no reason I could fathom, the most absurd possibility presented itself most urgently. It was that the hurricane had done this to me. The hurricane had deliberately stolen into my room that night and with its earthy fingers had rifled my desk and selected this one page to carry away. Almost as if the rest of the carnage that the hurricane had wreaked had been a diversion, just so that the eye of the storm could quietly peer into my desk and read my script. Farmer was suddenly filled with confidence, feeding off the look of horror on my face. And he knew that he still had his ace to play.

'Something else,' he said, peering at a handwritten note that he had taken off his desk. 'I got the boys round at your place, just kind of mooching around, and one of them just called. Real interesting piece of news.'

He put the handwritten note back on the desk. Max was still speaking to me from inside the page of the script . . . 'I'm sorry, Laura, I just can't take any more.'

'You listening to me, Mr Stone.'

I tried to get a hold of myself. Farmer was laying a trap for me with all the stealth of a quarterback.

'I said I just got some real interesting news from your home.'

'Are you charging me or not?'

'Tell me, Mr Stone, where exactly were you for the duration of the hurricane?'

I knew that I didn't need to answer. Farmer had read my statement. I had decided that silence was my best defence until I could work out how the hell a page of my script had got into the hands of the police. I knew that the door to the house had been wide open for at least a day and a half after the murder and it seemed that people were moving in and out as freely as the warm summer breeze. I'd even seen Crazy Jimmy peeking around the hall, scratching his head and saying, 'Well, Lord almighty.'

'Because, you see, Mr Stone, according to your statement, you went straight down to the cellar after you found Miss Timberley's body. That correct?'

I didn't even nod my head. Farmer's eyes were shining.

'And one of the boys just called to say that he took a little peek down the cellar this afternoon, and down there among all the junk, found this razor-blade.'

I stood up. I still hadn't been charged and I knew that

I had the right to leave. I didn't want to hear what Farmer had to say, but he said it anyway.

'Found this razor-blade down there and we got it over to the forensic lady straight away. It matches, Mr Stone. That is to say, it is feasible that it's the same razor-blade that was used to cut the lady's wrists. Right down there in the cellar. Guess no one's been down in that cellar for twenty years except you.'

I already had the door open and Farmer was breathing deeply behind me. The sigh of a man contented.

'She says there are no prints on the blade, and that is unfortunate, but hell, Mr Stone, I guess that now old Frank Farmer's on the case, we're starting to get somewhere.'

CHAPTER TWENTY-FOUR

When I got back to Mallory Street, there were six patrol cars, nose to tail, outside 1131. Some of the neighbours were peeking out of their curtains, and a group of kids had gathered across the street to watch the commotion. As I walked by them I heard a little girl of eleven or twelve lecturing the others with great authority about what had happened in the murder house.

'. . . And then, the man and the lady took turns to kiss the sword, and there was blood all over . . .'

Inside the house, the cellar door was open and there was a bright light shining up from inside and up through the cracks in the floorboards. The light through the floorboards looked like strands of silver. When I got to my room, the place was occupied by a dozen cops, all loading my things into Cellophane bags. I saw that my script had been laid out on the floorboards and a bored-looking plain-clothes guy was on his knees, shuffling from one page to the next. The cops all worked in silence. One of them had had the good taste to take down Azul's ghastly flowered curtains, and they were draped over my desk like shrouds.

I tried to skip past the door to get up to Azul's room, but as I walked by Clark appeared in the doorway.

'Ah, Mr Stone. I wonder if I might . . .'

'No, Clark, you might not.'

I wanted to push by, but he grabbed my arm. He squeezed hard and then relented. Sure he was a big guy, and sure he had muscles like marrows, but I had a

269

reputation now for being crazy, and I guess my reputation gave me some kind of authority. He swallowed hard and I shook myself out of his grip.

'You see, Mr Stone, all this . . .' he nodded in at my room, '. . . all this, it ain't good for Sunset Realty. It ain't good at all.'

Two cops walked by with a box of papers. I wondered how many drunken letters I had written. How many had survived the hurricane.

'And you see, Mr Stone, I just had a call from Giorgio. Mr Benelli. And as the owner of this place, he wants you to . . .'

'Tell Benelli to go to hell. My rent is paid till the end of the month.'

I began to climb the stairs, up towards Azul's room.

'Yes, but, Mr Stone, it was Mr Benelli who paid your rent.'

'Then tell Mr Benelli to take it up with Mr Benelli.'

I knocked on Azul's door and waited. Clark was peering up at me, up into the shadows, still not sure how far he could push me, handling me like gelignite.

'Mr Stone, I have to warn you that if you don't vacate the property after we've given you notice, you could be in a whole lot of trouble.'

Just at that moment, two more cops shouldered their way out of the room, big guys, laughing and smoking. I thought they made my point. 'What will you do, Clark, call the police?'

When Azul answered the door, I grabbed her by the hand and led her down the stairs and into the street. I heard one of the kids hiss, 'That's the guy,' and as we walked by the last of the patrol cars the engine fired. The car set off behind us and crawled at our heels. I hadn't said anything to Azul, and I guess I didn't need to. My

270

face was enough to make her realize that I needed her to come with me. She started to tell me that she'd heard some real interesting news from one of the cops, but I shook my head at her. After that she didn't say a word as I led her down Mallory Street and across Duvall Street.

Ever since I had left Farmer's office, I had heard a loud voice in my head, telling me that I should get myself into one piece. It was a woman's voice. Sometimes it was Scarlet's voice, but mostly it was Azul's voice. It said that I should get myself into one piece and that what Farmer had told me was good news because it meant that Baxter was on my side, that Baxter had put his ass on the line for me, and that Baxter was a smart guy. Sure he was. The voice was like a voice calling down from the top of a mine shaft, or through the cellar door.

'Karl, you're hurting my arm,' Azul said as we crossed over into Truman Avenue. I loosened my grip and she turned to eye the patrol car that had been caught by a red light and had accelerated to catch up with us. It slowed down at our heels like an attentive dog. From now on, Farmer was going to do things his way. A little way down Truman Avenue there was a set of ornate scrolled gates, the gates to the city cemetery. There was a footpath that wound its way through the lines of tombstones, and its course had been almost swallowed whole by the lush island undergrowth. I pushed open the gates and pulled Azul inside. The cypress trees behind the gates gave us some cover and I quickened the pace so that by the time we had disappeared into the trees, the patrol car had already overshot the cemetery gates. The air under the trees was cooler but the mosquitoes hung in clouds. We half walked and half ran towards a stand of trees swirled around with thick laurel. I almost had to drag Azul into the undergrowth and finally we found a place to sit on the bony root of one of the trees. The mosquitoes were biting but I didn't feel them.

'Azul, I think it's possible that I killed Scarlet,' I said.

The mosquitoes droned. The air hung heavy and above us there were huge spiders' webs hanging from the branches of the tree like silk drapes. The sunlight sparkled on them. In amongst the thick branches all around us, I could see the curved edges of very old tombstones, wrinkled and pockmarked by rain and wind. They circled us, stuck into the earth at crazy angles. Azul stared at me without expression.

'Well?' I said. Azul still didn't say anything. Suddenly she yelped and leapt to her feet. She began to shake her head frantically and ruffle her hair.

'Goddam you!' she shouted and finally slapped the mosquito that had bitten her on the back of the neck. 'Jesus Christ, I hate these little bitty bugs!'

I held my head in my hands. Azul finally got a hold of herself and sat down beside me again. She brushed off a few imaginary bugs before she asked me what I had said.

'I said I think I might have killed Scarlet.' Azul scratched her head frantically and spat something out of her mouth. I shook my head at her.

'I forgot to put on my protector,' she said meekly. 'I hate bugs.'

I had been intending to ask Azul if she thought it might be possible that I was crazy. It struck me then that there would be no point asking Azul since she was almost certainly crazy herself. The thought made me laugh.

'What's so funny?'

'Everything. It's all funny. Did you know, Azul, I used to actually write comedy? Before I came here into hell. And this whole thing would make a damn good comedy if I could only arrange it right.'

Azul smiled because I was smiling. She looked sweet

272

and innocent and twenty-one. Her swollen eye had turned blue and orange, the colour of a sunset, and the sight of it hurt me. She didn't belong in this graveyard. I knew that she was reckless and probably crazy and that she had no conception of the danger she sometimes put herself in, and I knew also that being with me was one of the things she really shouldn't do. If I had any nobility at all I would have told her to get the hell away from me and find herself another story. I had even begun to believe that there was no story. In the days since the murder I hadn't heard a single radio or TV news bulletin which had mentioned Scarlet Timberley, and I had worked out that Scarlet just hadn't been that famous any more. Baxter had told me himself he had never heard of her. I thought Azul was knocking herself out for an exclusive that was going to be read exclusively by her.

'Azul, you heard what I said just now, you're just pretending not to hear.'

'I know,' she said softly.

'So tell me what you think.'

'I think it's not true.'

'More please.'

'More what?'

'Tell me that you think the whole idea is absurd and that if I had killed Scarlet I would remember it.'

'All of that.'

Azul smiled at me, trying to end the conversation there. She was tapping her foot rhythmically, and that told me she was nervous beneath the smile. I wanted her to speak next but she just let the mosquitoes drone in the hot air.

'You saw how I was that afternoon,' I said finally. 'You saw how drunk I was. And how angry. I could have . . .'

'Nah. No way.'

'Come on, Azul. Think about it.'

Azul pretended to think about it. She started to hum
and brushed her hair away from her face. I knew she had
thought about it already. She had thought about it a lot.
Maybe she was even scared. Maybe she had been terrified
when I dragged her into the undergrowth and now she
was just ticking over on fear that she was trying to
conquer. I needed to do something to put her at her ease.
I didn't mean to do it but I reached over and brushed her
hair back across her face to cover her swollen eye and she
gave me that nervous smile that could have meant anything.

'Think about it, Azul,' I whispered. 'It's not as if I've
never done anything like it before. And half of what
happened when I got back to the house is gone. Just
holes. Just darkness.'

I left a long pause for Azul to tell me that the whole
idea was crazy and it had never even entered her head I
might have killed Scarlet. Instead she brushed away a
couple of mosquitoes and said again that she hated the
bitty little bugs. In the distance I heard the gates to the
cemetery opening and the sound of footsteps. The patrolmen would find us soon enough, but for now, we had
silence, and cover, and our own world here among the
tombstones. Azul trapped here for God knows what
reason. Me trapped here by the weight of God knows
what conspiracy. In this world, in these few moments,
Azul was the only person who could help me. She was the
only other person on my island. It was my fate that my
only companion here was a twenty-one-year-old girl with
some pretty twisted ideas of morality and duty and the
truth. And to make it even harder, I was beginning to feel
the same way about her as I had about Scarlet.

Did that mean she was in some kind of danger?

The thought hit me as a blue jay took flight with a

piercing alarm call over towards the cemetery gates. The patrolmen had disturbed it, and I could hear them stomping around in the undergrowth, calling out to each other. What I wanted was to put all the arguments that had been revolving inside my head to Azul and have her dismiss them, or at least see them from a different angle.

'Azul, I know now that it wasn't Benelli who killed Scarlet. So who does that leave?'

'Plenty of people.'

'Name one.'

Azul reached into her shoulder-bag with great purpose. I hoped she was reaching for some new clue or piece of evidence that would help, but instead she produced a pack of cigarettes. We both took one. She tried to ease the situation by telling me that, whenever she needed to think things through, there was always something in her shoulder-bag that would help. Even if it was just a cigarette. She said she'd had this old bag since she was nine years old, and that she kept her entire life in there. She said she still had stuff in the bottom of her bag from grade school, and that, when she died, she wanted her ashes buried inside her dumb little shoulder-bag. We both blew our smoke up at the mosquitoes. I knew the smoke would show our position to the patrolmen but it didn't matter. They would find us soon enough, and besides, their brief was only to follow. We could sit and smoke and talk all afternoon if that was what we wanted. Azul blew some of her smoke purposefully and then said, 'Baxter will know.'

'Know what?'

'He'll know who really killed her. Sure he will. Smart guy. Sure.'

The blue jay landed in the branches above our head and began to skittle around the leaves, clicking and clacking. All three of us, me and Azul and the blue jay, hiding

275

from the cops in this little pool of shadow. Our cigarette smoke hung beautifully in the sunlight, and the mosquitoes vanished. I told Azul it was fine, Baxter being smart, but that I'd just found out Baxter was no longer dealing with the case. I was about to tell her that Farmer had put him on vacation when she told me she knew that already. She said that he'd been given twenty-two days' compulsory leave.

'Azul, how the hell do you find out these things?' I asked.

Azul tapped her nose and smiled and said she was smart too, but the crazy gesture didn't work any more. It was poisoned by fear. The blue jay took off and left us alone again. Azul said she'd found out about Baxter from one of the cops who came to break up my apartment. Suddenly the fear disappeared and she warmed to her subject.

'I gave him a cup of coffee in my room. He was up there for two whole hours. He said Baxter was a pretty unpopular guy. He called him a smart ass and said that he'd never once played in the big pool game down at Flamingo Key. He said everybody played in that game because it was for sick kids and because it was sociable. But Baxter wasn't that kind of guy and they all thought he was pretty weird because he didn't joke around like the other guys. Some of the cops had a kind of vendetta against him. He said that everybody knew the Limey killed the movie star and it was just like Baxter to hold out and act smart. He said I was cute too.'

'Who?'

'The cop who I pumped for the information. He said I was pretty and that we should go out together some day.'

A terrible vision entered my head of a cop with his hand on Azul's ass, squeezing it as she pumped him for information. The voices of the patrolmen were getting close and I got the feeling that Azul was enjoying this game of hide and seek. And maybe enjoying the game of toying with my concern for her, igniting my jealousy, or whatever it was I felt. She enjoyed it like a kid throwing twigs at a lion in a cage and watching it roar. I decided to dismiss the image of the cop with his hand on her ass quickly. Azul was rummaging through her bag again. She produced her tiny grey and pink address book and a pen.

'Hey, what did I tell you about always having something in my bag,' she said, suddenly delighted. 'Remember I called Baxter at home once? And you got mad. Well, I still have his number. You can call Baxter at home.' Azul began to flick through the address book, mumbling, 'Owl, owl, owl.'

'Owl?'

'I filed Baxter under "owl", because he looks like an owl.'

Finally she found Baxter's number. 'Here,' Azul said, 'write the number on your hand. I'll keep the cops busy and you call him from a phone booth. The phone in your room'll be bugged by now.'

Before I could take the pen from her, or even begin to think through the idea of calling Baxter at home, Azul had grabbed my hand (still stiff from the night of the murder) and was writing Baxter's number across my knuckles. She wrote fast and pressed hard, and my injured knuckles still hurt a little. She had just finished the last digit when the red face of a Florida patrolman peeped in through the bushes.

'Mind if we join the party?' the patrolman said, and Azul immediately stood up, dusted off her ass and introduced herself to the patrolman and his partner. They both shook my hand, introduced themselves as Carlos and

John, and told me that they'd be sticking pretty close to me from now on.

Carlos and John cruised at our heels all the way from the cemetery gates and all the way down Simonton Street, a pleasant and quiet suburban street lined with lime trees. Azul said there was a call-box I could use at the back of the Inside-out Natural Food and Bodycare store. She said it was hidden from the street by a big street sign, and that she'd keep Carlos and John busy while I made the call. I wasn't sure yet that calling Baxter would be a good idea, wasn't sure that he'd be there and wondered what the hell I would say to him anyway. But I was sure that I needed to hear Baxter say he didn't believe that I had killed Scarlet. I needed to hear him say it in that cool, emotionless voice, making it sound like the most obvious thing in the world. Just ten seconds would be enough. Just enough time for him to say, 'No sir, Mr Stone, I don't see how anyone in their right mind could believe that you killed her.' I wanted Baxter to be the voice of my own reason, in the same way that I needed Azul to be the voice at the top of the mine shaft, telling me to sit tight.

Azul had all kinds of schemes for distracting Carlos and Jimmy while I made the call, and she went through them as we strolled down Simonton Street.

'No, Azul,' I hissed at her, 'you cannot take off your shirt.'

'Oh, Karl.'

'I mean it.'

Azul giggled. When we reached the store, she went across to the patrol car, which braked at our heels, and Carlos wound down the window. She said she was going to ask for directions to the Club Nautico, and tell them that she wanted to taking scuba-diving lessons. She had a theory that Carlos and John would be real interested in

278

scuba-diving, and she said she'd only flirt a little bit with them, so I'd better be quick. I had already suggested this whole thing would be easier if I called from the phone in my room, but she had told me again that my phone would be bugged. She said that one of the guys who had come to break up my room had worn blue overalls, like the overalls that telephone engineers wear, and that that was all the proof I needed. I figured, knowing Farmer, she was probably right. When Azul bent down to put her head into the patrol car, I slipped around the corner of the store and found the call-box.

'*Aló! Digame,*' said the voice on the other end of the line. The call-box had a perspex cover that focused the sunlight and made my skin burn. I knew I had to get this thing done quickly.

'Mrs Baxter?'

'*Sí.*'

'I'm looking for Tom. Tom Baxter.'

'Who is this?'

Mrs Baxter had a strong Cuban accent. She sounded nervous and I could see from the corner of my eye that Carlos and John had spotted me and were getting out of the car. Azul was still talking, all animation and coquettish gestures, but the boys had seen through her straight away. I felt sorry for her, and ashamed of myself for letting her do this.

'I need to speak to him urgently. I'm a friend of his. I wonder if you could give me a number where I could call him.'

Mrs Baxter was silent. The line chirruped in my ear and I could see Carlos and John both hitching up their trousers as they strolled over towards the call-box.

'He's busy right now,' Mrs Baxter said.

'Tell him it is very urgent.'

I heard Mrs Baxter calling out to someone in Spanish. I heard a child making a noise like a machine-gun and Mrs Baxter hissed at the child to be quiet.

'Maybe you should call another day.'

'I can't, Mrs Baxter. I need to speak . . .'

The line went dead. John's hand was on the button and he looked almost guilty. He sighed and said, 'Now come on, Mr Stone . . .' and took the receiver out of my hand. I asked him if he had any idea how pissed off I was becoming with this and he said that he had a pretty good idea.

'You mean I am not allowed to make telephone calls?'

'No, sir. Not from call-boxes. Farmer's orders.'

'Does he have any legal authority to . . .'

I didn't need to say any more. John just smiled and put on his reflector shades, a neat gesture I thought, to let me know that Farmer had the authority to do whatever the hell he pleased. I looked around for Azul but she had already disappeared. I wanted to find her but John told me she'd gone off to the Club Nautico to go scuba-diving and that it might be best for all of us if I just went on back to the house. He said he and his partner were getting kind of tired of crawling all over the island at five miles an hour in the midday heat. He said that their engine was starting to overheat.

'We'll even give you a ride back to Mallory Street,' John said, and I got into the car. We drove back slowly to the house, and we talked about the difference between soccer and football while I wiped the phone number off my hand with the sweat from my forehead.

CHAPTER TWENTY-FIVE

The next morning, the rising sun filled my room with hot winter light and hope. I dressed quickly on the arthritic floorboards and went up the stairs to rouse Azul. She was already awake and when I put my ear to the door I thought I could hear her dancing to some awful tune she was singing under her breath. I listened for longer than I should, imagining her floating in the early light from the sunrise, maybe clutching something to her chest, maybe dreaming of someone.

'Azul, you've got to go down and talk to the boys,' I said when she came to the door. I discovered that Azul hadn't been dancing at all. The sounds of creaking floor-boards and movement had come from the vigorous way she brushed her teeth. She was wearing an ancient-looking silk dressing-gown and her injured eye looked darker without make-up.

'You trust me to distract them after yesterday?' she said, and spat white foam from her mouth.

'You take them some coffee, anything, breakfast. Wear that dressing-gown. You have my permission.'

'You're going to see Baxter?' she said. She nodded her approval. After Azul had returned the night before, she said that if Carlos and John wouldn't allow me to call Baxter, and if his wife refused to put him on the line when I did call, then I should go and see him in person. I had assumed she was joking, but she'd taken out the Key West, Marathon and Islamorada telephone book from my kitchen cupboard and looked up Baxter's address. She

281

circled it with green ink and left the book open on my desk, saying that Flagler Avenue (where Baxter lived) was a five-minute drive, or a half-hour walk. And if I was any kind of a man I'd find a way of getting over there to see him. Then she had left me alone. At the time, the idea seemed crazy.

'Hey, I have another dressing-gown even shorter,' she said, reaching into her wardrobe. I told her that the one she was wearing would probably do the job, and that she should try to position herself so that she cut off the eye line from the car to the house. My plan was to use the overgrowth on the front drive to cover me down to the street, and then to crouch and run while Azul dazzled the boys with her coffee and her beauty. The plan still seemed pretty crazy but in the morning light, even brighter in Azul's room, it seemed to have innocence and ambition on its side. During the night I had been buoyed by half-dreams of resourcefulness and initiative. I had decided to shift the furniture around in this situation. I had decided to look at my incarceration in a new light, look at it as a kind of challenge. I had even begun to think of it in terms of plot and story line, imagining myself as a character who suddenly decides it's time to strap on his intellectual guns and go shooting for the truth. Something awful like that. My first decision had been that Azul was right, that I had to speak to Baxter no matter what. I had to speak to him because I was sure that he believed in me, and he would be able to give me some kind of direction.

'I'm going to investigate this thing for myself,' I said, half out loud, but Azul leapt on the phrase. She clapped her hands together as if she'd been waiting for this moment for a long time, as if I'd passed some kind of test. She went into the kitchen and cursed the kettle when it took its own time to boil. When she had poured two big mugs of black coffee, I followed her down the stairs.

'I'll tip one of the cups over Carlos,' she said to the shadows. Her voice echoed and I thought I had misheard, but she said it again and added darkly, 'This coffee's real hot. That'll distract him OK.'

Azul opened the front door and adopted a ludicrously prim posture as she walked barefoot down the front drive. I crept a few feet behind her, catching my shirt on thistles, wrapping my feet around suckers and vines and cursing them. It was hot out in the sun and I began to sweat straight away.

From the end of the drive I saw Azul rapping on the window of Carlos and John's patrol car. I hadn't thought too much about whether Azul had been serious about pouring scalding hot coffee over a Florida patrolman, but the moment Carlos wound down his window, I saw that she had meant what she said. I heard Carlos shout 'Jesus' as Azul stepped back from the car and then I ran on all fours until I reached a line of three garbage cans which had been left for collection halfway down the street. I crouched behind them for a few moments, and I heard a car engine firing. Then I heard the car coming down the street, moving fast. I sank down into the sidewalk and closed my eyes, and then opened them to see an old Subaru with a surfboard strapped to the roof cruising by. When I glanced back up the road, I could see that Carlos was out of the car and tugging his dark blue shirt to keep the hot coffee off his chest. I was sweating hard now, knowing that I was in this thing, that I was inside the mechanism of it, and that for the first time I was beginning to tug back at it, to dispute its inexorable motion. I began the long walk to Flagler Avenue with my chin tucked into my chest, trying hard to look like some Miami businessman out for a stroll.

The regular grid layout of the roads, streets and avenues

on Key West made Flagler easy to find. It ran parallel with Atlantic Boulevard on the east of the island. By the time I reached the corner of Flagler and Reynolds, my shirt had a dark bib of sweat all down the front and hoops of sweat around the armpits. I straightened my hair and tried to cool myself down in the shade of the old colonials that lined both sides of the road. It would be bad enough taking Baxter by surprise like this without looking like a man who is just about to pass out with exertion or anxiety. I guessed that the temperature had exceeded a hundred degrees twenty blocks ago. Number 204 Flagler was as neat and scrubbed and private as Baxter himself. Even if I hadn't known the number, I would have known the house.

I slicked back my hair again and wafted some air into my shirt. I felt like a distant relative dropping by unexpectedly to borrow money. At the worst possible moment.

There was no reply from the doorbell but I could hear a commotion round the back of the house: children screaming and the sound of frightened laughter. I walked across the spongy lawn and ducked under a clothes-line to get round to the yard. This was even worse than I'd feared. I realized that if Baxter wasn't here I'd terrify his family half to death, but I needn't have worried. Baxter was there and his family were already terrified half to death anyway.

Baxter was standing at the end of the yard, which was bigger than I had expected, training a garden hose with great purpose at the foot of a magnolia bush. He was wearing shorts and a flowery shirt and I wouldn't have recognized him if it hadn't been for his spectacles and his immaculately groomed hair. Near the house Baxter's wife and two kids were huddled by the open door, the children yelling and their mother (ten years younger than Baxter, Cuban, square-jawed) holding on to them and trying to make them be quiet. All attention was fixed on the roots of the bush and on the spray from the hose, and that meant that no one saw me for a few moments. Then Baxter turned to speak to his wife and saw me out of the corner of his eye. He let the hose droop and peered at me as I emerged from the shadows.

'Carmelita, take the kids into the house,' he said softly.

Carmelita and the kids all turned to look at me. The excited fear that had made them scream out disappeared and they fell silent. Carmelita hissed at them in Spanish and they all went into the house. I heard the door being shut as Baxter resumed his spraying of the magnolia bush. I walked over to him, bouncing on the lawn, formulating what I was about to say and trying to compress it into as few words as possible.

'Stay back,' Baxter said and peered into the magnolia bush. 'There's a snake. A cottonmouth. One of the kids nearly picked the damn thing up.'

Baxter put his finger over the end of the hose to make the jet of spray sharper. I heard something skittering around in the shadow beneath the bush, and finally Baxter let the hose fall to the ground. The water flooded the grass around our feet.

'You sure pick your times, don't you, Mr Stone,' Baxter said to the bushes, 'or maybe the snake was an omen.'

'I had to talk to you.'

'Wrong. You get the hell off my property.'

Baxter said it without conviction. He looked nervous and I guessed that the sight of the snake, the sight of one of his kids crouching to pick the thing up in the beautiful early morning sun, had shaken him up a little. I could feel the water from the abandoned hose flooding my rope sandals.

'Five minutes,' I said.

'You don't hear too well, do you, Mr Stone?'

'Tom, you've got to help me.'

Baxter looked at me hard. Calling him Tom was worse than walking uninvited into his backyard. Worse than frightening his kids. Maybe even worse than the presence of the cottonmouth lurking in the shadows. I had wanted it to sound informal; instead it had sounded incongruous.

'Let me get to the point,' I said quickly. 'Farmer tells me that you've been taken off the case because you don't believe I murdered . . .'

'Jesus Christ, Mr Stone. Jesus *Christ*!' His face was contorted with controlled anger.

'I'm sorry I have to intrude like this,' I said flatly and Baxter shook his head. 'All I need is that you tell me that you don't believe I killed Scarlet and that you tell me which direction your investigation was going. I'll take it from there.'

Suddenly, in this beautiful sunlit garden, everything I had to say sounded absurd. It wouldn't have been so bad if Baxter had been in his heavy woollen suit, his knitted tie and his black leather brogues. But his khaki shorts and flowery shirt made me feel that I was violating a sanctum, that I was dragging a great darkness into the garden with Maybe the snake had been an omen. I would have felt the absurdity if I hadn't known that so much depended on carrying on, ploughing through the impropriety. The sweat was pouring from my face and I could just see Baxter's wife and children peeking at me through the shutters on the kitchen window. Baxter folded his arms and stared into the bushes like a statue.

'Mr Stone, if you don't get out of my yard in ten seconds I'll . . .'

'You'll what? Call Farmer and have me arrested?'

Baxter picked up the hose and for one moment I

thought he was going to train it on me. Instead he tightened a screw on the nozzle and the flow stopped. Water dripped from the end of it.

'Very smart, Mr Stone.'

'The way I see it, we are on the same side, Tom. I know that's putting it rather bluntly . . .'

'Rather bluntly?' he said, imitating my accent, and I felt alien, even to myself. Just at that moment, I thought I heard a dry-throated hiss coming from the bushes. The damp, leathery leaves at the base of the magnolia began to shake.

'You and I are not on the same side of anything,' Baxter said, and we both instinctively edged away from the magnolia bush. I thought I saw dull diamonds and glistening skin shifting among the shadows.

'You know damn well that that isn't true,' I said. 'If Farmer nails me for Scarlet Timberley's murder, then how will that look for you? As far as Farmer is concerned I used you as a stooge. He's turning this investigation into a contest. You against him. If he nails me, he wins. That puts us on the same side of the fence and you know it.'

Baxter hooked the hose around his elbow and began to wind it, reeling it in as he walked towards the house. I assumed he was going to walk inside the house and bolt the door and wait until the heat in the garden drove me away. But he took me by surprise.

'You'd better come inside,' he said, with great sadness. 'I've made that cottonmouth as mad as hell' – he turned to me to make sure I was following – 'and knowing your luck, Mr Stone, it'll be you who'll get bitten.'

Baxter's living-room reminded me of the inside of a Spanish hacienda. After the brilliant light of the garden, the darkness inside blinded me for a few moments, but then the furniture and the whitewashed walls and the

287

scrubbed wooden floor began to take shape and colour. There was a birdcage on a chrome stand over by the shuttered windows, covered with a black shawl, and the walls were decorated with dozens of silk fans, embroidered with flowers. The air inside was cool and smelt of orange blossom and I couldn't pick out one single feature of the house that would have told me that this was a house inhabited by Baxter. Maybe Baxter took care of the outside of the house and Carmelita took care of the inside. She'd constructed it like an island of old Andalucia, right here in the blankness of a Florida suburb. Baxter seemed as remotely charmed by it as I did as we both sat down at the dining-table.

'Do you want coffee, Mr Stone?' Baxter mumbled, embarrassed at the enforced formalities of host and guest. I told him that I was fine.

'Then maybe you should get to the point.'

I figured that I'd already told him most of what I had to say, but I needed to use the invitation to speak to try to pump Baxter for information. I told him again that Farmer had told me why he'd been taken off the case, and that I appreciated his concern for me and that as much as anything else I had come here to thank him for having faith in me. I said the word 'faith' several times. Baxter smiled and shook his head and finally rested his head in his hand.

'Were you followed here, Mr Stone?'

'No, I wasn't. I gave them the slip.'

'I doubt that,' Baxter said softly. 'But what the hell. What the hell. You sure you don't want coffee? Carmel! Carmel, do we have any fresh coffee?'

The door that led to the kitchen suddenly sprang open. Carmelita must have been listening, and when she appeared in the gloom, she smiled at me nervously.

'This is Karl Stone,' Baxter said to her. 'I told you about him.'

'Hello, Mr Stone,' she said, extending her hand. She peered into my eyes for a long time before we shook hands and suddenly a lot of barriers seemed to break down by themselves. I felt that Baxter had finally let me in, that he had been waiting for his wife's approval. She was bony beneath her cotton dress, and her eyes were the colour of dark honey. Languid and soft. She appeared to be staring at me for a reason, then she glanced at Baxter. I thought that maybe she had the same keen sense of smell as Baxter, maybe she could detect innocence in the same way he could. I thought all these things as Carmelita shook my hand, and as Baxter sighed, suddenly relaxed. I said that yes I did want coffee now, and Carmelita went back into the kitchen and began to sing to herself, an old Spanish lullaby, as Baxter drummed his fingers on the table.

'So am I right?' I said at last.

'Right about what?' Baxter said. His voice came over as indifferent, solemnly playful, and I knew it meant he was as anxious as hell.

'About me being a piece of rope between you and Farmer. About this case turning into a contest.'

Baxter nodded his head and told me that I should be real flattered. His willingness to speak took me by surprise. It seemed that he was being urged into conversation by the brightness of Carmelita's lullaby.

'My friend Farmer is from the old school,' Baxter said, without emotion, 'and do you know what they teach you in that old school?'

He raised his eyebrows as if it were a genuine question. I shrugged.

'They teach you that all you need to be right about

something is a uniform and a service revolver. You pull your gun, you're right. No questions.'

'And you don't believe that?'

'Ah, I don't know that there's anything to believe or disbelieve, is there? Anyway . . .'

Baxter picked at a fingernail, narrowing his eyes in the semi-darkness. What he could see in the shadows I had no idea. Suddenly there was a loud rasping squawk from the corner of the room. The sound of a parakeet or a hornbill. I turned and looked at the covered birdcage, but Baxter didn't seem to hear it. The noise was as loud as a car horn.

'So, yeah, I guess you're right, Mr Stone,' Baxter said with quiet contempt, 'me and Farmer aren't exactly *simpático*.' In the kitchen his wife was warbling like a songbird. 'You understand, Mr Stone?'

'Yes, I think so.'

'I wonder if you do.'

Carmelita finished her lullaby with a flourish. One of the kids crept down the stairs, smiling coyly, and he fired off a pistol-shot with his finger, taking careful aim right between my eyes.

'You go back upstairs,' Baxter said, and then called out, 'and if you're going to use that thing you hold a gun with both your hands.'

Carmelita opened the kitchen door with her ass and laid a tray of coffee, cups, milk and sugar on the dining-table. She and Baxter spoke in Spanish briefly and then Carmelita sighed and put her hands on her hips.

'You know, Mr Stone,' she said, 'those cottonmouths get all over this island.' I nodded and she left us alone again. When the kitchen door closed, the darkness in the shuttered room seemed deeper.

'So I guess I've got you into a lot of trouble,' I said, to

break the silence, to lighten the atmosphere. Baxter seemed to remember suddenly that it was OK to talk.

'It's not just you, Mr Stone,' Baxter drawled, trying to put me at my ease. 'There's the Cacique brothers too. The two Haitians. That's the nail in my right hand. You are going to be the nail in my left hand. All they need now is a nail for my feet and I'll be crucified for sure.'

His analogy made him smile. In the darkness of the Spanish room, Baxter seemed almost vulnerable. The flowers on his shirt matched the scrolls and roses on the walls and I guessed that this was the inside of Baxter. Right here in this room, Carmelita had built a soft interior for her husband, like the inside of a sea shell. I still wasn't sure that Baxter was happy to have me inside there with him, and he wasn't sure about it either. He spoke between long pauses, but when he did, he sounded relieved to have the chance to unburden himself. An image entered my mind of a priest and a penitent, though I wasn't sure which one of us was which. Among the silk fans, beside a leather wine flask hanging on the wall, there was a pink and grey crucifix, delicately painted.

'Problem is,' Baxter said, 'down here I'm kind of a tail gunner. You know about tail gunners? Take all the flak. Sitting there in a ball of glass just waiting to get shot up. It's kind of a hobby of mine. World War Two fighters. You take sugar?'

I spooned my own sugar into my cup. I thought about brandy, about the bottle that I could see glinting on the drinks cabinet beneath the crucifix. Carlos Tercero, all the way from Spain. My favourite brand. Baxter slipped into another long pause and I knew that I needed to prod the conversation along. Baxter was in a bad way. Worse than I had imagined. I figured he was the kind of guy who defined himself through his work, and that if his work was

291

taken away he'd be filleted. It wasn't easy to be with him like this. I helped myself to milk.

'So you're the tail gunner?' I said.

'Sure. And Key West is the tail. The tail end of the state of Florida. The bridges to civilization get pretty thin sometimes you know, Mr Stone. At least in my line of work.'

I heard a deep throbbing from up above. The same sound I'd heard in Baxter's tank. I recognized it this time as the sound of a helicopter. Baxter heard it too and he allowed himself to glance upwards. His jaws tightened at the sound and the throbbing air made the parakeet squawk again in its darkened cage. I paid no attention to the helicopter, to what it might mean, until Baxter sighed and said, 'That's a Sea King. Tell by the engine noise. Zero zero nine.'

The throbbing of the air got louder and we both fell silent, hunching slightly as the throb turned into an angry roar that made the room vibrate. The line of ceramic ornaments lining the shelves above Baxter's tiled fireplace rattled and tinkled until the helicopter had flown by. Then the sound faded, until it was a distant buzz.

'We use them for surveillance,' Baxter said when the drone had almost disappeared.

'Who do?'

'Police department.'

Baxter stared at me and forced a smile. He didn't need to make the point any more clearly.

'You mean the helicopter is for your benefit?' I said.

'Four, five times a day. I get buzzed. Just to keep me on my toes. Just to let me know that old Farmer's eye in the sky is watching.'

Baxter lifted his coffee-cup to his lips and I thought I saw a tremor in his hand. His cup shook in just the way the ornaments had shaken when the helicopter had flown over. If it had been anyone else who'd said that the helicopter was for their benefit, I would have suspected incipient paranoia, but not Baxter. The sight of Baxter trembling, even so slightly, filled me with terror. Suddenly the inside of Baxter's shell didn't seem so safe or invulnerable.

'What do you think of the coffee?' Baxter said.

'Tom, what the hell is going on here?'

I wanted to go to the shutters and look up at the sky. The drone of the chopper got louder again. It seemed to be circling the house in a big and lazy lasso.

'It's Cuban,' Baxter said, 'the coffee I mean. We're not supposed to get it up here in the States but some of the guys bring it in. Some of the guys who we fish out of the water. They give it to me as a gift. They give it to me because I'm a good guy. Because I'm a good gringo. That's why I get to drink such good coffee.'

Baxter seemed to be talking about the coffee for a reason. He was talking right into my look of horror. The helicopter was making another sweep over the house. This time it was approaching fast.

'Do you understand what it means to be the recipient of such good coffee?' Baxter said and, as he said it, the helicopter swooped and the sound of its engine was momentarily deafening. I ducked, Baxter didn't. I thought that he was talking in riddles, or making small talk to take my mind off the helicopter above our heads.

'It means that you have to cover your ass with brass or get it shot off,' he said.

Baxter took another sip of coffee and I did the same. He nodded his head and suddenly things began to fall into place. I remembered the tank, the sorry collection of Cuban refugees who were imprisoned there in their darkened cages.

'This isn't just about me and those Haitian brothers, is it?' I said as the buzz of the chopper began to fade again. I had a sick feeling that I had stepped deep into a tropical jungle, blind, without any paths to follow.

'No sir, Mr Stone, it's not,' he said, 'it's not just about you or the Caciques.' He seemed to be relieved that I had finally put two and two together for myself, even though I hadn't. Baxter spent a few seconds figuring out whether he should continue. Carmelita had begun to sing again and Baxter glanced at the door to the kitchen. The sound of his wife's voice seemed to help him make up his mind.

'No, sir, it's not about you and the Cacique brothers at all. You see, before I took over here, before they gave me the county, the Key West PD and the harbour patrol had a kind of cosy arrangement.'

He nodded his head, mock-impressed at the cosiness of it.

'The law states that any illegals picked up in United States territorial waters have to be brought in to be processed. And that takes time. And manpower. So I guess sticking to the law can be a pain in the ass. But I'm from the new school and we kind of like being a pain in the ass. In the old days, before they gave me the county, well, you see . . .'

Baxter sighed and rubbed his face, aware of the depth of his indiscretion but unable to stop himself.

'. . . In the old days some of those illegals in their cracker tins and oil drums, they never really made it to the shore to be processed. Sometimes the harbour patrol would just turn them around right there in the ocean. And sometimes they'd just blow them out of the water. It was the good guys who blew them out of the water. That was the kindest thing to do. Because if you turn them around, well they'd just die of thirst. Or hunger. Or sometimes

294

they'd cut their own throats and throw their little ones to the sharks. It's a long way back to Cuba, Mr Stone.'

Baxter began to whistle between his teeth, still picking at a fingernail. He glanced up at me sharply and then looked down at his hands again. Being in the presence of Baxter in this mood made breathing difficult. I felt I was peeking through a tiny crack at ancient relics.

'And sometimes, Mr Stone,' he said, 'round about early fall, if the boys from the harbour patrol picked up a boat full of Cubans or Haitians, and if there was a fair proportion of strong-looking guys, then they'd take them on up to a little harbour east of Pensacola. Little sandy bay there. And the harbour patrol guys would hand the Haitians or the Cubans over to the chargehands working for a couple of the big cotton plantations up there. Tell the refugees that they'd got lucky, that they'd got themselves real jobs. So the refugees would work their butts off through the fall taking in the harvest for these big plantation guys, and then, when the harvest was over, and the refugees had busted their backs, the harbour patrol guys would call the Pensacola PD and all the refugees would be picked up and arrested and put on boats back to Cuba. So the plantations got their harvest taken in for free, and the harbour patrol guys got a few hundred bucks apiece for the service. Like I say, it was a pretty cosy arrangement.'

We were quiet for a long time. I could feel the weight on Baxter's back. The darkness that had been pursuing him. And I understood now why this room had the feeling of a refuge, the feeling of sanctuary, and I understood why it had been so painful when the buzzing of the helicopter had made the ornaments rattle, right here, deep inside Carmelita's Spanish sanctuary. Farmer was smarter than I had imagined. He knew how to play games.

'So you put a stop to all that,' I said.

'Most of it,' he said and he shrugged. 'But worse than that, Jees, I am a pain in the ass, Mr Stone, worse than that, I asked some of the guys up in Miami to start an investigation, going right back to seventy-eight. That's why they need me out of the way so bad. They want to bring negligence charges against me for the Cacique brothers, and on the Lisson case they want to start a whole damn circus. There's a couple of press people around, *Miami Herald*, *Tampa Courier*, maybe even the *National Enquirer*, and those guys would just feed out of the hand of anyone who offered them a story about a cop who taught some writer how to commit the perfect murder and then had the writer go ahead and do it. That would look real pretty, wouldn't it, Mr Stone? And just to sweeten it, the story's got a movie star in it too. If the papers got a hold of a story like that, I'd be finished for sure. And Farmer's going to feed it to them like candy.'

I wanted to apologize, or to tell Baxter that things would turn out OK, or just say something that would comfort him, but that kind of thing wasn't possible with a man like Baxter. To express sympathy would have been crueller than to sit in silence. Baxter peered hard at me, perhaps to stop me from saying anything at all.

'What I'm saying is, if they nail you, they nail me too. So save your gratitude, Mr Stone. Save your fucking gratitude for someone who deserves it. And please don't thank me for having "faith" in you because I don't. I don't have faith in you at all.'

At that moment Carmelita breezed through the room and lifted the black shawl off the birdcage. Baxter had used the word 'faith' as if it were an obscenity, and the word hung in the air. In the half-light, I saw a large orange and blue parakeet in the birdcage, with a horny, curved bill and eyes that shone gold. Carmelita said,

'*Buenos días*' to the bird as she drifted by. '*Buenos días, Senora*,' the parakeet said. Then Carmelita disappeared up the stairs. Baxter tapped his coffee-cup with his thumbnail and then looked up at me. His face had lost all expression.

'The reason I'm telling you all this,' he said quietly, 'is that Carmelita and I have decided you can help me. You can help me and you can help yourself.'

I wondered when Baxter and Carmelita could possibly have decided something like that. Maybe that little exchange in Spanish over the coffee-cups. It wasn't like Baxter to act in such an unconsidered way. Maybe inside, here in the interior, it was Carmelita who called the shots. I didn't like it when Baxter, the voice of my reason, acted this way. The parakeet gurgled to itself and then cried, '*Madre mia, madre mia!*' Baxter stood up and reached over to the bookshelf behind his head. He took out a large hard-backed atlas from the shelves and opened it on the dining-table. Inside, there was a yellow folder. As he opened the folder, I began to picture the story about me and Baxter in the *Miami Herald* or the *Enquirer*. I began to think dark thoughts.

'I took most of the Lisson case file with me when Farmer canned me,' Baxter said. 'Didn't want him destroying all my work in his enthusiam to get to you.'

He sifted through the pages of lined foolscap, all covered in tightly written notes. There were business cards attached to some of the sheets, along with bank statements and business letters. It was too dark in the room for me to read any of it. Baxter found the page he was looking for.

'The way I saw it, there were three possibilities,' he said, matter of factly. The business of sifting papers had restored some of his customary dry efficiency and that made me feel a little better. 'There were three lines of inquiry,' he said. 'If Farmer hadn't taken me off the case, possibility number one would have been this guy.'

Baxter handed me a sheet of paper. It was hard to read in the gloom and I held it up to a shaft of light from the shutters. I read the name Jimmy Ford and an address on the South Roosevelt Boulevard.

'The lady in the house next door to 1131 Mallory Street came forward and said she'd seen this guy in the backyard of Mrs Lisson's house two or three times in the weeks previous to the murder. She said he had been masturbating right there in the yard. She said the third time it happened it had been light enough for her to recognize his face. She said she realized that he was the mailman who delivers the mail to Mallory Street.'

I had already recognized the address. Crazy Jimmy's place. Baxter was about to start sifting through his papers again but I guess his attention was taken by the way my mouth fell open as I read and reread the name and the address.

'Crazy Jimmy?' I said.

'You know this guy?'

I told Baxter quickly about how I'd been taken to his house by Azul, about how he'd been intercepting Scarlet's mail. I told him that, according to Azul, he had a copy of every single movie that Scarlet Timberley had made. I was going to tell him how he'd put his hand on Azul's ass, but he stopped me.

'The lady journalist took you there?' he said, with a look of puzzlement.

'Yes. Four days ago. She'd been using him to find out about the movie scam.'

Baxter thought for a long time. I could almost hear the wires and circuits buzzing inside his head. He tried to disguise his puzzlement and his anxiety by burying his head in the file. I thought that he was being deliberately obtuse.

298

'For Christ's sake, Tom, this is it!' I declared.

'This is what?'

'Crazy Jimmy. If I hadn't been so dumb I would have figured it out for myself. Jesus, Baxter, you're a genius, do you know that?'

I had raised my voice and this inspired the parakeet to greet the darkness in Spanish again. He bid good day to the invisible señora. Baxter looked up at me, perplexed.

'I may be a genius, Mr Stone,' he said, 'but the way I see it, Jimmy Ford is a long shot. Maybe five per cent possibility. That's how I like to work. On percentages. I'd say he was a five per cent possibility because in my experience masturbators are rarely killers. Take a look at this. This is possibility number two.'

Baxter handed me a business card. I tried to read it but I couldn't take in what it said. My head was filled with visions of Crazy Jimmy. I remembered the first morning when I had met him on the drive of 1131. How he'd told me I was the lucky one, living in the same house as Scarlet. How Scarlet Timberley was a weird name for a kike.

'What did you say?'

Baxter nodded at the card in my hand. I wanted to reach over the table and kiss him. Baxter was the cavalry. Baxter was the light of my reason shining bright through the gloom. But hell, I thought, I'm a writer, not a detective, so how the hell should I have been expected to work this thing out for myself.

'Crazy Jimmy,' I whispered.

'Maybe,' Baxter said, 'but like I say, probably not. Jimmy Ford is just a routine follow-up. I wouldn't get too excited about him. Look at the name on the card.'

I read the card. Harry S. Rose, medical doctor.

'Harry S. Rose is the forensics guy over at Marathon,'

Baxter said to get my attention. 'He was running some tests for me when Farmer canned me. He's an old guy but he's kind of on my side. He said he'd get the results of his tests to me anyway, even though I've been taken off the case. Possibility number two is ten per cent. Another long shot.'

I had hardly heard what Baxter had said. I studied the card again and Baxter told me that I should remember the name. Then he took the card out of my hand and clipped it back in the yellow folder.

'Wait a minute,' I said, excited as a kid at Christmas, 'I didn't catch that. What's this about Harry S. Rose?'

'He's head of forensics over at Marathon and like I say he's on my side. He's running some tests for me on the second possibility and I need to get my hands on them. That's where you come in.'

'So what is the second possibility?'

'I can't tell you.'

'Why not?'

'Because I can't trust you not to fuck up.'

There was a silence but it was a happy silence. I hadn't yet done my mathematics on Baxter's system of percentages and possibilities. All that I knew was that Crazy Jimmy was in the picture now, that he had emerged from beneath the water like the dark shadow of a shark and that Baxter had unravelled this thing effortlessly, casually, almost without thinking. Baxter was unimpressed with my excitement.

'Are you listening to me, Mr Stone?'

'Loud and clear.'

'Harry's going to be through with his tests the day after tomorrow. He'll be in touch with you. Somehow, I don't know. And whatever he gives you, I want you to get it over to me straight away. Do you understand that? He can't get it to me direct because I'm being watched, but between us, me and Harry will find a way of getting the results to you and then you can get them to me. Without being followed.'

I nodded. I hesitated. I asked him to say again what he'd said about Harry. Baxter sighed and rubbed his eyes under his spectacles. I knew that he was disgusted with himself for having to trust me.

'He's an old guy. He's sick. He's up for retirement and I guess he's got nothing to lose so he's agreed to help. If he comes up with something, then maybe we'll both have a chance.'

'You mean he'll help us nail Crazy Jimmy?'

'Will you forget about Jimmy. This is another possibility altogether. Like I say it's a long shot. It's a ten percenter.'

I was almost panting by now, like a dog waiting for more treats. Baxter closed the yellow folder in his atlas and replaced it in his bookshelf. When he sat down again, the dark intimacy we had been sharing had dissipated. He looked like the old Baxter again. No more treats. In fact, just the opposite.

'So you understand, Mr Stone. I need you to act as a go-between for me and Harry.'

'And what should I do about Jimmy?'

'You do nothing about Jimmy. You stay away from him. I told you, Jimmy Ford is just a routine follow-up. If there's anything to be done about Jimmy Ford, I'll do it in my own way.'

Baxter stood up quickly and made for the door. At last I was doing my calculations. The two possibilities that Baxter had told me about were a ten per cent and a five per cent. That still left the third possibility.

'Tom, tell me about the third possibility,' I said and he stopped still with his back to me.

'You already know who that is,' he said.

'So it's eighty-five per cent that it was me who killed her. Is that what you're saying? That I'm the third possibility?'

'I think it's time that you left, Mr Stone.'

Baxter turned to me. I could hear the kids chanting along to a Spanish nursery rhyme in the kitchen. On the other side of the door, there was a bright sunlit kitchen and a sweet suburban family scene. On this side, there was darkness, a return of darkness where a few moments before there had been wild hope.

'Now you listen to me, Mr Stone,' he hissed into my face, 'if I could do this any other way I would. Do you think I enjoy having my number one suspect running my errands for me? Do you think I like having you here in my house, with my wife and my kids? The way I see it it's not a possibility that you killed her, it's a probability. Let's stop talking in riddles here. But while there are other options then I have to try to make them work. For my own sake. For the sake of a lot of other people too.'

He stepped back, a little shocked at his own outburst. The parakeet squawked '*Madre mia!*' in the darkness.

'So you're saying ... that you still think it was me?' I said.

Baxter leant back against the door. I didn't want to endure his look of passionless contempt.

'Reasonably and rationally,' Baxter said, 'I'd say that eighty-five per cent is doing you a favour. Now I told you to get out of my house, Mr Stone.'

Baxter opened the door to the kitchen suddenly. The two kids were sitting on a work surface, their hands covered in flour. They were patting hands with Carmelita, who smiled shyly at Baxter and me. Baxter lifted the youngest of the two kids high up in the air and nuzzled his belly, saying that the big old snake was coming and he ate little children like this one for breakfast. Everyone laughed except me, and Carmelita caught my eye and stopped laughing for my benefit.

Baxter pushed me gently out into the sunlit garden. I hesitated for a moment but when I turned around he had already closed the kitchen door and bolted it. It wasn't until I reached the shrubbery at the end of the lawn that I remembered that the angry cottonmouth was probably still lurking in the shadows. The sound of the helicopter whining through a 180 degree turn somewhere out on the horizon made me decide I would have to take my chances. I scurried through the magnolia bushes and then climbed Baxter's picket fence to get out on to Vernon Avenue. It took me half an hour to walk back to the movie house, and the whole time I spent trying to decide whether or not I had finally remembered how Scarlet Timberley's blood had got on to my hands.

PART THREE

CHAPTER TWENTY-SIX

I woke up lying on my bed, soaked in sweat. The window was open and the cool wind made the sweat freeze on my body. It was already dark outside and those ghastly curtains were billowing outwards, giving glimpses of the street light outside. I'd been having a dream which I'd had a dozen times since the murder. A dream in green and white. In my dream, I was trapped inside an engine, the motor of some huge machine that roared and bellowed and smelt of turpentine and kerosene. I was stuck inside this engine not seeing any of the mechanism but occasionally seeing a glint of green metal or a flash of green light from one of the pistons, each piston the size of a train compartment. I could feel the vibration of the machine all around me, and feel the heat and smell the grease that was burning on the hot metal, but most of all I could hear the roar of it. And then I was climbing a set of stairs inside it towards Scarlet's room. I climbed the stairs for a long time, talking to myself all of the time but not being able to hear my own voice. Then I opened Scarlet's door and I saw the serpent lying down on the bed. Then the door blew off its hinges and the room was dark and the smouldering eye of the serpent became the street light outside winking at me every time the curtain blew. I had had this dream since the murder every time I drank too much brandy.

I had spent the afternoon thinking about Crazy Jimmy and sipping from the bottle, careful not to drink too much but sipping quickly nevertheless. When I hadn't been thinking about Crazy Jimmy, I'd been thinking about Baxter's eighty-five per cent. It was just like Baxter to reduce this whole thing to mathematics. By the time the brandy bottle was halfway empty, Crazy Jimmy and Sarah and Benelli and Scarlet had all started a crazy dialogue with each other, a dialogue all about that guy Karl Stone and what a nut he was. Their voices had made me tired, and it was that which had made me fall asleep just as the sun went down. I realized I had been woken by the sound of footfalls on the floorboards above me. The floorboards were creaking to an incessant rhythm. As I came to, I realized that I was still pretty drunk.

When I got up to the door of Azul's room, I rubbed my eyes and felt a pain at the core of my head where the brandy was still doing its work. I could hear Azul inside, counting softly under her breath, counting and then falling, counting and then straining and then falling. I could hear her body creaking on the floorboards and whatever she was doing, she had got up to forty-five. I listened to forty-six, forty-seven, forty-eight, forty-nine and then fifty, and a sigh of relief. She was taking some deep breaths. The creaking stopped and I knocked on the door. Before she'd even had a chance to answer it, I called out 'Azul' and my voice sounded mean and croaky.

When she opened the door I tried to make a joke about Azul keeping herself in shape and she looked puzzled.

'I didn't know you were a health freak,' I slurred. Azul didn't seem to understand what I meant and let it pass.

'Jesus, you look awful,' Azul said and showed me into the brightness of her room. I hadn't stepped inside there since I had found Scarlet's body, and I expected it to look different. It didn't. The wardrobe was back on its feet and the dressing-table was in one piece but the rest was the same. Azul had the same curtains at her window as the curtains in my room, and the bed looked the same too. I wasn't even sure if the sheets had been changed but I guessed that they must have been. Azul was wearing a thin cotton T-shirt and baggy pants and there was a cigarette burning in the ashtray.

I told her I had been drinking and thinking, and the rhyme made me laugh. I sat down on the bed and I guess that and the way I looked around the room made Azul feel nervous. She asked me if I needed anything to drink and I asked for water. I listened as she poured me a glass of water in the kitchen, humming under her breath, out of tune and shaky. I hoped she was shaky because of the exercise. I called out to her that I'd been to see Baxter, and she waited until I'd had some sips of water before she asked what Baxter had said.

'He's a smart guy,' I said, finishing the water, the brandy sharpening my thirst. 'He said before he got canned, he was following up a lead. Guess who, Azul. Take a guess.'

Azul shrugged her shoulders and backed away from me. Was that fear in her eyes, or maybe just disgust at the way I looked.

'Crazy Jimmy,' I said triumphantly. 'What d'you say to that? Baxter said if it was down to percentages he'd say it was a fifty per cent chance it was Crazy Jimmy. Maybe higher. Maybe sixty per cent.'

Azul didn't seem to have heard me. She hadn't heard my lie and that made me mad for a few seconds.

'Well, Azul, what d'you say to that? He's been right under our noses all along. Should have worked it out for ourselves.'

Azul didn't seem to be convinced. She nodded and smiled at me, as if she were trying to pacify me. Those dark thoughts that I'd had in Baxter's house came back to me. The image of the story that Farmer would feed to the press like candy. The story about Tom Baxter and me, the cop who teaches the writer how to commit a murder. Was it possible that Azul had been working for Farmer all along? I wanted to shut that idea down, so I asked her again what she thought about Crazy Jimmy. I realized that I had raised my voice.

'Please don't get angry with me, Karl,' Azul said, in her little girl's voice.

She looked pretty against the brightly coloured curtains. She looked pretty and afraid. I realized as I looked at her that I was playing a game with myself. I was playing the game of 'Just how crazy are you, Karl Stone?' I was tempting myself to think crazy thoughts just to see if those thoughts had a direction to go in, to see if they were familiar to me. I was still just drunk enough to play this game the way a drunk plays poker. I was taking risks because I wanted to hit the jackpot. I wanted to prove something. I looked at her and I challenged myself to think about the night Scarlet had died, right here in this room. 'Anything familiar here, Mr Stone?' said a voice inside. 'Recognize this feeling, OK, and how about this one, and this one.' Ugly pictures came and went, all of them transposed on to Azul's face. I didn't recognize any of them. I wanted to stop playing and I thought that maybe I had won this hand. There was no reflex inside me that was being triggered by the way Azul was staring back at me. I pushed it some more. 'Just how crazy are you, Karl Stone?' whispered the voice. It was the voice of the wolf from some fairy-tale cartoon I had stored somewhere in my head. I searched myself for a feeling that would maybe come from beneath my eyes, a feeling that would crash over me, tell me something, make me say something. Nothing came. The hurricane blew over.

310

'Karl, don't look at me like that,' Azul said, and I realized I had been staring for a long time. Something snapped and I felt embarrassed. The brandy pain was easing. I was glad I'd played that game because I thought that I had won.

'Azul, I'm sorry,' I said, and I smiled at her. 'I guess you really know how to pick guys, don't you?'

'It's been said before,' she said, perhaps relieved at my familiar tone of voice. Then I decided that, since she was the only other person on my island, I should tell her everything, even the crazy parts.

'Do you know what I was doing just then, Azul?' I said and I shook my head in disbelief. 'I was seeing if I could make myself want to hurt you. Can you believe that? I was testing myself. Seeing if I could call out the monster.'

Azul peeped out between the curtains. I imagined that she was checking to see if the cops were still in the street outside, maybe thinking that it might be possible she would need their help. I got angry about it for half a second, and then I felt more sorry for her than I had ever done. I didn't want her to have to entertain me any longer, not like this. She whistled as she looked down into the street at Carlos and John or whoever had taken their shift. She said, 'Those poor guys.'

'Maybe you'd like to invite them inside for a party,' I said, and I wondered if the game was really over, because I hadn't meant my voice to sound so bitter. She smiled, and that made it OK again.

'Sure, why not,' she said and as she walked over to the bed the floorboards creaked beneath her feet. 'I guess you still think I'm some sort of whore, don't you, Karl?'

'No,' I said. 'But you think I'm some sort of lunatic.'

Azul said nothing.

'Well?'

311

'No, Karl, I don't think that at all.'

'Then that's good,' I said and she sat down beside me on the bed. 'You're not a whore and I'm not crazy. We're just plain ordinary folks, aren't we, Azul?'

'I guess that's what we are.'

'Then let's just sit here like plain ordinary folks and talk about something just plain and ordinary.'

We were both silent and then we both laughed. The game was over and the monster hadn't come and maybe the monster didn't exist and so I could put my hand on her hair and stroke it awkwardly, like a schoolboy on his first date. If this was wrong, if I'd misread things, then I knew Azul would tell me and if she did that would be fine too. I had no place doing this and I wasn't even sure this was what I wanted. I only knew I wanted to stroke her hair and for her to tell me again that she didn't think I was crazy. I had never known the street outside so silent and I realized the light bulb in her room actually made a noise. It hissed.

'Should I go now, Azul?'

Azul shrugged her shoulders. She was going to be mysterious to the last. That shrug could have meant anything, including get the hell away from me. I couldn't take a chance on it so I put my hands between my knees and nodded to some conclusion in my head.

'Or maybe we can just sit here and talk about the murder,' I said. 'I mean, if you can bear to talk about it any more.'

'Sure. That's why I'm here, isn't it?'

'I don't know. Is it?'

'Sure it is, Karl.'

'I don't know, Azul. It doesn't make sense. You should get out of this place and pick up some story about something decent. Like incest or tax evasion or some movie star who screws his dogs. Or maybe you're working on a different story altogether, Azul. That's something else crazy I've been thinking. Baxter told me that . . .'

I could feel the heat of Azul's stare on my cheek. I looked into her eyes and the noises from outside were switched on again. I could hear some music playing in a bar somewhere down by the harbour. It was a loud salsa beat and I could hear some people drunk and screaming.

'Baxter told you what?'

'Nothing. It's not important.'

Now there were sirens outside but the sound of the sirens was soft and velvety. Azul had left the window open a little way and the air that blew through the crack was coloured with the sounds from Duvall Street.

'But what is important,' I whispered, 'is that, according to Baxter, Crazy Jimmy is in the frame.'

A long pause. I thought Azul was thinking about Crazy Jimmy but then she whispered, 'Were you making a pass at me just now?'

I said that I wasn't sure. She put her hand on my shoulder, the way you put your hand on the shoulder of a blind man.

'Because if you were, Karl, that would be OK.'

'Just OK?'

'It would be fine.'

I stood up and walked across the room. I had the insane thought that I had suddenly become successful with women, just when I least needed it. First Scarlet and now Azul. I wasn't laughing but I found the idea that I had suddenly found the formula for attracting women very funny. I sat back down on the bed beside Azul and laid my hand on her knee. She looked at my hand and I looked at her face. We could have both been twelve years old.

'It would be a pretty strange thing to do at a time like this, wouldn't it?' I said.

313

'Yes, I guess it would.'

'OK. Then let's talk. What do you think about Crazy Jimmy?'

Azul was looking at my hand, which I removed. She stroked my hair.

'I think it's possible,' she whispered. 'I mean, Crazy Jimmy is something we should both think about.'

'Sure it is.'

We were talking with our faces three inches apart. Her breath smelt of sweet caramel. I guessed that mine smelt of stale brandy and cigarettes, but she was breathing it like a child eating honey. I said that she had told me herself that Jimmy kept all of Scarlet's videos in his house and she said sure he did and that he was a creepy kind of old guy. I kissed her on the lips and told her she should have been more careful when she let him do those things to her and she said she was sorry. We kissed each other again and I asked her if she had ever told Crazy Jimmy anything about the movie scam and she said that she couldn't remember but that she would think about it.

'That's good, Azul. You must think about it. Because if he knew about the scam and if he knew . . .'

We kissed again and lay back on the bed.

'. . . if he knew about the plot of the movie, then there's a chance that he knew about the suffocation scene. So if he was smart . . .'

She took hold of me around the shoulders and squeezed hard and that feeling of being held so tight made me close my eyes. It felt as if she were squeezing tears out of me. If she never said that she trusted me, that she didn't think I was crazy, that she didn't believe I had killed Scarlet, then she said it just by holding me like that. We were lying awkwardly on the bed, and my legs had got twisted when we lay back. I could smell the dampness of the sheets and the caramel of her breath and she kissed me hard on the face and I wanted to scream at her that she shouldn't do this. I wanted to tell her that I wasn't the kind of man who you should do this to and that I didn't deserve it. Just like I'd once wanted to tell Scarlet. Scarlet and Azul became the same person for a moment as I fed off the warmth of their bodies. That same feeling of release, of the door to the cage flying open and finding that inside was the same as outside. I could have been lying on Smathers Beach with Scarlet, except this time the room was warm and there was no ocean to come between us. I pulled away from her and leant up on my elbows and said, 'Ah, Jesus.'

'What is it, Karl?'

'Talk to me, Azul. Talk about Crazy Jimmy. Or make some coffee.'

'You want coffee?'

'Of course I don't want fucking coffee.'

'What are you afraid of?'

'I'm afraid of myself.'

Azul went across to the light switch and turned the light off. The fizzing of the light bulb stopped. In the darkness she looked bigger and I couldn't make out what her face was doing. She came and sat beside me on the bed and leant on her elbows.

'You don't want to hurt me, do you, Karl?'

'Don't say that, Azul.'

'Because if you do . . .'

I turned to see if she was laughing but I couldn't tell. I knew that I should get out of the room now before Azul had a chance to say anything more. I had ugly visons in my head now, of Azul and Crazy Jimmy locked together. I wanted to think about the case and about Crazy Jimmy, but I couldn't untangle him from Azul. I had to remember

315

that I had been OK once. Before the business with Sarah I had been a straight, regular sort of guy who drank too much. All of these things were games that I was playing with myself and I should explain to Azul she shouldn't be afraid because I was a victim of circumstance. Except she wasn't afraid. I could see glints of light coming off her teeth. She was grinning at me.

'Don't be so hard on yourself, Karl,' she whispered. 'Just let it go.'

'Make some coffee, Azul.'

'Why?'

'Because I'm not sure.'

'About what?'

'You know what. I'm not sure what kind of man I've become.'

'I can take it, Karl. I mean if you want to . . .'

'Don't you ever talk like that . . .'

I was breathing hard and Azul reached out and stroked my head. I was sweating so much that the warm breeze blew cold. I thought that a moment of truth had arrived, I thought that things would go one way or the other right now. Instead, the moment drifted into silence while Azul stroked my head and told me I should just let it go. I began to recover a little and I was filled with awe at the extent of this game I was playing. Azul kissed me softly and I kissed her softly back. I touched her face as gently as I could and she pulled me down on to the bed to lie awkwardly on top of her. She had to shift around to take my weight off her arm, and she eased me to one side when I tried to kiss her neck. We wrestled for a position, inelegant and silent like adolescents, and all the time I was letting something go. Letting it ease out of me. Then I lost the feeling in my foot because I'd had my leg twisted and I had to beat it against the floor.

'What are you doing, Karl?' Azul whispered.

'Foot's gone to sleep,' I grunted and she laughed. I laughed too and she said she had heebies in her hand. I asked her what the hell were heebies and she said that it was her own private word for that tingle when the blood gets cut off. We laughed about that too.

'God, I wish I'd met you in Covent Garden on an autumn morning,' I suddenly declared, and she laughed at the seriousness of my voice. 'I wish you were a tourist who was lost and I was showing you the way to the station. That's what I wish. I wish it was ten years ago.'

'I would have been eleven, Karl.'

'You know what I mean.'

She pulled me down from my declaration and suddenly a simple thought cleared a way through my mind. The simple thought was that we had the whole night together on this island and that nothing could happen to us while we were in this room and that the distance between us and the sunrise was as wide as the ocean. And so what the fuck did any of it matter?

We made love and she laughed at me because I seemed to take the whole thing so seriously. And because I seemed so pleased with myself when it was over.

CHAPTER TWENTY-SEVEN

I woke up before dawn to the sound of glass smashing and the deep belly-punch thud of my wardrobe being turned over in my room below. I guessed that Farmer's boys must have a warrant and that it wouldn't be such a good idea to go down now and challenge them. Azul grabbed hold of my arm and my leg and began to hum softly to herself as we both listened to the heavy tread of what sounded like a dozen cops all angry as hell with my furniture. I hoped in some dark part of my mind that this time they'd take the curtains with them.

After the cops had left, I got dressed and kissed Azul goodbye. Then I crept down the stairs to the cellar and pulled open the door. The dawn light was just turning the air milky grey down there and I didn't dare to turn my head to look at the junk that I had found on the night of the hurricane. Before I had fallen asleep I had decided that if Baxter had still been on the case he would have gone down to Crazy Jimmy's place and paid him a visit. Baxter would have sniffed around, talked to the guy, taken a look at his video collection, asked some questions. But since Baxter was no longer on the case, I figured that it was down to me. Azul had tried to talk me out of it but I imagined she was only trying to stop me because she was concerned for my safety. Which was more than I was. I decided I couldn't just sit and wait for Baxter or Farmer or anyone else. I knew that it would be tough to get out of the house a second time using Azul as a distraction, but I remembered from the chaos of the night of the hurricane that there was an old wooden grille at the back of the cellar which would be just wide enough for a man to squeeze through. The grille was as flimsy as I remembered it and it didn't take much effort to ease it out of its frame. When I had pulled the grille away, a breath of sharp morning air and birdsong came into the cellar and I briefly turned my head, a dumb challenge to myself, to see if the serpent was still on its perch over by the Indian smock. It was still half dark, but I could see the blurred images of the serpent and the Indian smock and the canoe, all of them in black and white. I realized then, suddenly, that I recognized them, that I knew which movie they were from, that they had been lying around in my memory for years and years before I had ever set eyes on them in the cellar. I didn't have time to dwell on it. I eased my way out through the grille and into the yard.

I'd only ever seen the yard at the back of the house through the grimy round window on the landing, and it had looked like some primeval wilderness, boxed in by a rectangular wooden fence. Now that I was down there, I discovered it was even more wild than it had looked, with weeds that had become trees, flowers that had grown wild, terracotta pots in the twenties style all swallowed by hybrids of the plants they had once contained. This would have been where Bogart and Bacall and Edward G. and Marilyn would have lounged in the sunshine on their days off from shooting. I found what had once been a stepping-stone path and pushed my way through the undergrowth to the fence. I climbed it and leapt down into the alley at the back that led through to Rose Street. I'd instructed Azul to go down and open the curtains in my room (if they were still there) at around this time to keep Carlos and John occupied. I ran down Rose Street and through the sleeping streets of downtown Key West until I was on the South Roosevelt Boulevard, heading towards the Sigsby naval base.

The hurricane might never have hit. The houses which had been smashed were reglazed and the debris had been cleared from the streets. The gulls were wheeling above the harbour and calling out to each other, but the highway itself was empty. As I walked past Salt Pond Key I could hear the engines of motor boats being fired by hand, revving and then dying and then firing. The air was cool and the coolness distilled the smell of the ocean so I could gulp down the air and make myself dizzy as I walked. Azul was a sweet baby and if I thought about it I could just punch the air and say that I loved her, and as I did it I could despise myself at the same time for being such a fool. I could hold those two feelings at the same time and it didn't matter because the morning was so beautiful and because I could feel something rising inside me, a kind of phoney strength, which made me believe that at last I was going to get this thing resolved.

'I'll take her to the theatre in London and then we'll eat in Mon Plaisir,' I said out loud to myself as I scurried along the grass verge of the highway, a strange-looking creature, hunched up with hands in pockets, grinning at his feet.

I walked quickly and it didn't take long to get to Crazy Jimmy's. The white concrete of the naval buildings across the highway shone in the dawn sun like ivory teeth. Crazy Jimmy's house was basking in the blue light and looked almost pretty. In the night I had put lots of things together, lots of pieces of the jigsaw. It had been Crazy Jimmy who had handed the page of script to Farmer. He'd got into the house when the front door was off its hinges and he'd searched through my papers until he found the page that would incriminate me. Sure, that's

320

what he'd done. Crazy Jimmy had been right under my nose all along and I hadn't realized it. When the hurricane was about to hit, he'd walked down the path at 1131 Mallory Street as crazy as a wild cat. He'd knocked on the door and maybe Scarlet had leant her head out of the window to see who was calling. And when she saw that it was Jimmy, maybe with a parcel in his hand, she had come down the stairs and let him in. Then he'd forced her up to her room and he'd murdered her. I said all of this out loud to myself as I walked down the path to his home. I'd catch him before he left for his delivery round, I'd get him out of bed and I'd be smart. I'd talk him around. I'd make him talk and it would be easy because Crazy Jimmy was even crazier than me.

I knew that this jigsaw puzzle was full of holes. The pieces didn't quite fit together. But I'd shaved the edges off the pieces, buckled them and forced them until I had a kind of cracked-up picture that wasn't pretty but it was all that I had.

I knocked on Crazy Jimmy's door and waited. The first of the morning traffic was beginning to use the highway and suddenly I felt exposed. I knocked four times and waited, and then I tried the handle to his door. Some of the older people on the island still claimed that you didn't need to lock your door on Key West because it was that kind of place. The handle turned and the door opened. Crazy Jimmy was crazy enough to believe what the old people said.

I stepped into the darkness and smelt that same smell of ammonia and old cooking grease. I called his name and waited in the doorway; then I closed the door behind me and the air stultified. There was a new smell in the house, too, a smell like sweet rotten meat. I groped in the darkness for a while and then found a lamp which I turned on. When the light came on I called Jimmy's name out loud three times and all I could hear was the ticking of his clock. If he had gone to make his deliveries, he'd taken his dog with him. I peered into the kitchen and saw a sink full of dirty dishes and a tap that was dripping in time with the ticking of the clock. When I was sure that he was gone, I cursed him out loud.

Jimmy kept his videos in a neat pile on top of an old fifties drinks cabinet with a Formica top and gold legs. I scanned the spines of them and saw that he had three copies of *The Last of Love* and two copies of a movie called *Price Pretty Good*. Two of *The Last of Love* videos had '71 written on them, the other was labelled '72. The *Price Pretty Good* video was labelled '87. I took the first of *The Last of Love* videos, slipped it into the video player, turned on the power and sat down in Jimmy's bulbous armchair to watch.

The picture came to life in gold and blue. Jimmy had the thing set at a certain place. I saw the ocean and the white sand of a beach, and Tony Curtis was spread out on a hotel towel reading a book. There was no sound and the volume control didn't work. Then there was a shot of the ocean and a shot of a woman drying herself with a towel that had the same name on it as the one that Tony Curtis was lying on. The woman had long blond hair and her body was plump and rounded and not quite firm. Her skin was the colour of toffee. She dried her back for a few seconds and then the picture cut to Tony Curtis who looked up from his book (which I could see now was *The Beautiful and Damned*) and he smiled. Then he called out and tossed a little pinch of sand in the air. Cut back to the woman drying herself with the towel. She turns around and it is Scarlet, looking young and more flimsy with her hair blond. It looked as if blond was her natural colour.

She turns and she looks mad, spitting something that looks like 'go to hell'. The shot was carefully done but it didn't cut away in time to lose the cellulite on her thighs, the beginnings of fat, and the way the flesh on her arms shook a little as she set off across the sand. Cut back to Tony, wise-ass, smirking, expecting what comes next and not really caring. Scarlet's shadow covers his face and we see her, just an inch too broad, just three pounds too heavy, as she whacks him across the face. Tony falls back into the sand, mock injured, and Scarlet's face looks beautiful as she screams with well-crafted rage. Her eyes were the same as I remembered them. That look of craziness and vulnerabiltity that reminded me of the night on Smathers Beach and the night I'd just spent with Azul. I froze the frame and her expression changed. The picture flickered on the pause, and her face suddenly seemed to be filled with terror. I saw the expression change in the freeze frame, and I saw Azul's eyes frozen there too, looking up at me from the pillow while I made love to her. The expression that before had looked like cute feminine anger was transformed by the freeze into a look of terror, a look that haunted the whole room and chilled it. The ocean behind was bright electric blue and the sand was shimmering white but Scarlet's face peered out like the face of a furious ghost. I began to play the game again with myself, stacking the cards one on top of the other.

'Remember that expression, Karl?' said the voice inside my head. 'Remember how she looked up at you when you went into her room?'

The pause didn't want to hold. The video was an old model and the electronic scratches just made Scarlet's face look more afraid. The ocean was smudging into her thighs.

'Remember how she looked in green and white?' said

the voice, the hiss of a wolf. 'And remember how you shook her to wake her up and then you took the pillow . . .'

I pressed the play button in panic and Scarlet stomped back across the sand to where her towel was lying. Tony Curtis was laughing and slapping his belly while poor Scarlet dried herself with her hotel towel. I thought about Baxter's eighty-five per cent.

'Sure,' I said out loud, 'I remember that.'

Then the picture cut to the inside of a hotel room, and some fat guy talking on the phone. I pressed rewind and quickly scanned Jimmy's dark cabinet to see if he kept any booze in the house. You can't play poker without a drink and a cigarette I told myself. But Jimmy used his cabinet for records and for papers and for piles and piles of letters. I put the video of *The Last of Love* back in its sleeve and then put *Price Pretty Good* into the video player. Jimmy had this movie set on a certain place too.

Scarlet was fat and naked. She was lying on the deck of a yacht that was moored in a lagoon. It looked like a lagoon somewhere in the Aegean, with shimmering green forest surrounding the sea. She was lying on her back and she was wearing sunglasses and reading a book. Her hair was dyed auburn this time, and her body was brown but her ass was white and spreading. Her thighs were flattened against the deck and the camera lingered to catch the crease of her buttocks and then swooped when she opened her legs a little. The camera shook and rocked in the swell of the ocean and there was no compensation for the brilliant sea light so the colours all bled and flared. Scarlet put down her book and laid her head on it. Then some old guy with white hair and white whiskers in a jaunty captain's cap appeared from below the deck. He called out something and Scarlet raised her head and smiled at him.

When she lifted her head I could see she was wearing a silver chain around her neck and I could feel the pain of her smile. The captain, in his little white shorts and his blue sailor's cap, steered himself across the deck against the swell of the ocean and knelt down beside Scarlet's body. Scarlet handed him a bottle of sun oil, colours flaring and bleeding all around her, and the captain, grinning through his white whiskers, took the bottle of oil and squirted some of it into his hand. Then he slapped it hard on to Scarlet's white ass and he began to rub.

I pressed stop and the screen was black for a few seconds, before the bright blue and gold lights of a silent game show on the regular channel began to flicker in the room. The label on the video said '87. I could either press 'Play' now and watch some more and see what kind of devils *Price Pretty Good* could conjure up, or I could press 'Rewind' and put the video back in its sleeve. I hesitated for a long time, long enough for Marilyn from North Carolina to win ten thousand dollars in silence on the TV. Marilyn hugged the game-show host and she waved out at me in the darkness.

'Sure, I remember that,' I said again, and sat back in the musty armchair, like a loser watching the pot being swept from the table. Or maybe the game wasn't over yet. I couldn't think clearly but I knew that there was a double exposure in my memory. There were two sets of memories bleeding into each other, and Scarlet's face was dead in one of them, and in the other she was waking up when I knelt on the bed. Her eyes flickered for a moment, like blue paraffin flames, only to be extinguished by the white pillow that I held in my hands. I was squeezing 'Rewind' so hard that my finger hurt. Then I ejected the tape and fumbled it back into its sleeve and then back into the pile on top of Crazy Jimmy's table. From the table I went to

325

the cabinet and began to pull the papers off the shelves. At the top there were bills out of their envelopes, and below there were torn envelopes and packages and letters that scattered around my feet as I clawed them out of their filing system. The cabinet had flimsy glass doors and I broke one of them with my arm as I dug into the back of the pile and heaved the whole lot of letters and envelopes out on to the carpet. Somewhere in here I would find something that would make me believe, something that would make the second exposure go away. I wasn't reading the letters or any of the addresses on the envelopes, I was searching in the way a man searches in his dreams. A compulsion to get everything out of the darkness and into the light. The second glass door cracked and a sliver of glass fell out on to the carpet, and by now the dark cabinet was empty. All of the envelopes and papers were at my feet and I began to run my hands through them, digging like a dog for meat. And when I stopped digging, I saw that one of the folders at my feet, a dog-eared brown folder bound with string, had the word 'Scarlet' written in pencil on the cover.

The folder was bulging with letters, all in chronological order. The first two dozen were photocopies of the same standard reply from a theatrical agency called Levant and Levine. The letters all thanked Jimmy for his kind comments and said that the photograph enclosed had been signed by Scarlet Timberley herself. The letters had all been sent between 1971 and 1972, and were spaced exactly one month apart.

The next letter (a dozen copies) was dated 1973 and explained that Scarlet Timberley was no longer being managed by Levant and Levine, and that she had given them no authority to pass on a forwarding address. Then there were two letters from Lisson Property Services, stating that the commercial manager had no dealings with Mr Lisson's immediate family and that it was company policy not to pass on home addresses. Then there was a gap of ten years before a badly printed mail shot from a company called Olympus Films of Santa Monica, offering a selection of twelve of the hottest videos allowed by the state for the price of just six. *Price Pretty Good* was one of them and was circled. After that, from 1984 on, there were half a dozen letters from an attorney in Los Angeles, stating that, if the letters and telephone calls to their client Mrs Caroline Lisson didn't stop immediately, legal action would be taken and constraints applied. It was stiff and formal and written in legal language, but it did stoop to calling the letters 'racist and obscene' and the telephone calls 'disgusting and acutely distressing'.

There were press cuttings too. Some were from *USA Today* and the *Miami Herald*, others were from *Stage*. I didn't have to read them to know what they were about. They were mostly reviews of *The Last of Love*, but there were also accounts of Scarlet's wedding to James Lisson. One in particular, a gossip piece from the *Herald*, had the headline 'The Man Who Bought a Movie Star'. I caught the first few lines which read 'Some rich men buy islands. Some buy yachts. Some even buy a seat in the Senate. But James Lisson, a Florida realtor, bought himself a real live movie star. And that's not just our opinion. The lady herself thinks it too . . .'

Finally, there was another letter from Lisson Property Services, edged in black, thanking Jimmy for his kind comments about the good work that the late James Lisson had done, and promising to pass his condolences on to his wife and family.

At the back of the folder, there were a dozen publicity shots of Scarlet when she was young and blond. All of them were signed. I sat back on my heels and read the whole thing over and over again, and I felt as if a huge cylinder full of white-hot steam was being slowly released from inside my head. Suddenly, all the terror was gone out of the room. The TV screen flickered but it had no power any more. I felt for the first time in days that the tide of insanity which had submerged me was beginning to recede. That broken, buckled-up jigsaw puzzle that I'd put together in my head suddenly didn't seem so crazy.

I'd come across obsessive fans when I worked in TV in London. Some stars, not always even the best-looking ones, attracted guys like Jimmy in the way that a lamp attracts moths. The TV people I had known had all been spooked whenever they received letters from these people. And everyone always told them the same thing. The guy who writes you a dirty letter will never be the guy who attacks you. Ask any cop. Writers and phoners are always harmless. They don't have the balls to actually try anything. Except the truth was that there were sometimes exceptions. As I looked through Jimmy's neatly compiled dossier, I decided, with cool and rational deliberation, that Crazy Jimmy had been one of those exceptions.

The double exposure in my head suddenly seemed as remote and fictional as the images I'd seen on the TV screen. There would still be a lot of talking to do, but not even Farmer could ignore what I had found.

I carefully placed the folder to one side, and began to sort through the other letters. Mostly they were bills and bank statements, all of them addressed to Caroline Lisson, or Ms Lisson, or Mrs Lisson. It appeared that Jimmy had stolen Scarlet's mail at random, picking out certain letters to keep for no reason, and letting others through. He'd even stolen standard mail shots from the publishers of *Workout* magazine. It didn't seem to matter what the mail was, just so long as it was addressed to Scarlet. I put all the letters into the brown folder and squeezed it tight. I held on to it like it was a little baby. At last the sun outside, the bright, brilliant Florida sunshine, was shining for me too. And I had earned this feeling of euphoria that picked me up off Crazy Jimmy's floor and had me spring over to the door. If Baxter had been around, this folder alone would have been enough. James Lisson hadn't been the only guy who'd seen the image of Scarlet Timberley on the screen and fallen in love with it. Crazy Jimmy had done it too, except Jimmy was just some low-rent working guy who couldn't afford palaces on the beach and helicopter flights from New York. So he'd lived out his fantasy in the only way he'd known how. I even had room in my chiming heart for a little sympathy for him. There was no difference between James Lisson and Crazy Jimmy, except for maybe a couple of hundred million dollars. And the fact that, while James Lisson's obsession had almost killed Scarlet, Crazy Jimmy's obsession really had killed her. I was sure of that now. And as sure as I could be that the faces on the TV screen, the double exposures in my head, were all just part of the game I had been playing with myself. 'Mr Farmer,' I said out loud to the ticking clock and the dripping tap, 'I think you might be interested in taking a look at this.'

I began to laugh out loud when I imagined the look on Farmer's face. I was still laughing when the door suddenly burst open. I turned and expected to see Crazy Jimmy standing in the doorway, but instead saw flashes of silver and blue, the dark silhouettes of two patrolmen, the orange light of a patrol car flashing behind them in the street. Carlos and John came and took me by the arms, and then Farmer appeared from the glaring sunshine and slapped me hard across the face.

'Mr Stone,' he said, his eyes flashing in the TV light, 'I am arresting you for violating private property and for unlawful entry of the home of a private individual, Florida statutes five zero five and six.'

I smiled at him. A mistake. He slapped me hard again and flicked his head at Carlos and John. They took me by both arms and led me towards the door. As John grabbed my elbow, the folder slipped from under my arm and I bent down to pick it up. Farmer turned round.

'That your property, Mr Stone?' he asked. I said calmly that it was not, that it belonged to the guy who lived here. A guy named Crazy Jimmy.

'Here, Mr Farmer, take a look at it,' I said, 'I think you might find it interesting.'

When I said it for real, the look on Farmer's face didn't make me laugh at all.

CHAPTER TWENTY-EIGHT

Carlos and John drove me to the tank with Farmer following on behind in an unmarked car. He'd taken the folder, and the knowledge that he had it in his hand, that maybe he'd even peeked at it and begun to put two and two together in his own way was making me see the island in a whole new way. The ocean sparkled and the clear blue sky was a delightful canvas for the brushstrokes of gulls and pelicans and F111 fighters, leaving vapour trails over towards Cuba. I asked Carlos and John how Farmer had found out that I was at Jimmy's house and they said that Azul had told them.

'She did what?'

'Farmer came to pay you a visit just after nine. When he found you weren't there, he made Azul tell him where you'd gone.'

'What do you mean he made her?'

Carlos and John glanced at each other. Suddenly the air didn't seem so light. A part of me ached for what might have happened, but John said that I shouldn't worry, she wasn't hurt. They glanced at each other again.

Before we reached the tank, I explained to Carlos and John why I had gone to Crazy Jimmy's house and what I had found. They both said in a distant way that they were real pleased for me. I knew they were a little angry with me for skipping the house, for getting them into trouble with Farmer, but I was also sure that they both wanted me to be innocent. I babbled in the back of the car for the rest of the journey about the cuttings and the letters and photographs and about the videos that Jimmy kept.

'Farmer will have to listen,' I said and they were both silent. 'What do you think, guys, he'll have to pay attention to that, won't he?'

When we reached the annexe, Carlos and John stood over me while we waited for Farmer. He went into his office with the folder under his arm and came back out a few minutes later. He looked glum and bored. He took John to one side and I strained to hear what he said. He whispered and I couldn't make out any of it. Then he went back into his office and John winked at me.

'I got to go pick up Jimmy Ford. Find out where he was at the time of the murder. Just informal but, hell, it's something. Good luck, Mr Stone.'

John left the annexe with great purpose and I prayed through a hot sweat, prayed up through the strip lights and the tiled ceiling that he would do his work swiftly and that the Lord would smile on his endeavours. There was a kind of euphoria building inside me, the feeling a marathon runner gets when he enters the stadium at last after all those hills and valleys, and feels a new strength kick into his limbs. At last, I thought, I'm running on level ground. I knew there was still a way to go yet, but maybe the door to Farmer's office, still ajar, was the finishing line. When Farmer came back out of his office and instructed me and Carlos to follow, he looked angry. I decided that what was making him most angry was the idea that maybe Baxter had been right.

When we had reached the tank, and passed through the chunky wired door and walked into the third cell on the south wall of the blue area, Farmer explained to me in a delightfully theatrical tone of voice that there were three areas of the human body which could take punishment without squealing. What he meant was, there were three places on the human body that you could hurt and not leave any marks. Of course you avoided the face and also the arms and any part where there was enough bone to support a bruise. You had to aim instead for the solar plexus (he tapped my upper belly playfully), the kidneys or the spleen. He said that I needn't worry because he knew as much about how much punishment a kidney could take without rupturing as any medical doctor, it was just that he approached the problem from a different angle.

The first punch to the belly hurt like hell.

'You see, Mr Stone, that's area number one,' he said. 'Just thought I'd like to point it out to you.'

I regained my wind quickly and looked up at Farmer and shook my head.

'For Christ's sake, Mr Farmer, is this necessary?' I said and Farmer sniffed hard, winding himself up. 'You saw the folder, can't you at least wait until John gets back. Until you've heard what Crazy Jimmy has to say?'

He hit me in the stomach again, harder.

'Mr Stone,' he said, 'I guess you could say that I have run out of patience. I don't have any more time for your bullshit. And I guess you could say that half the reason I am doing this is because I just plain want to. Because I've wanted to for a long time.'

He hit me again. I spluttered 'Jesus' in a huge exhalation of breath and phlegm, and I was about to say again that it was insane to do this before John got back but Farmer spoke first.

'What's the matter, Carlos?' Farmer said. 'You have wind or something?'

Carlos, who was standing to attention in the corner of the cell, had winced with the power of the blow. I was doubled up with pain but the pain was a glorious pain. It was an easy pain. Trickling through my body there was a fizzy chemical that killed the pain and restored my breath in just a few seconds. The chemical had been distilled by what I had found at Crazy Jimmy's house and I told myself that it was stronger even than Farmer's adrenalin. I decided that Farmer was doing this because he knew somewhere in his head that it was possible I was right about Jimmy. And if I was, then he'd miss his opportunity to give me a beating. He wasn't doing this in spite of what I'd found, he was doing it *because* of what I'd found. This was the last pain, the last agony of the final few yards before I reached the finishing tape. And I could take it. Farmer was getting angry.

'Speaking to you, Carlos,' Farmer growled. 'You getting soft on this guy?'

'No, sir,' Carlos said.

The cell was warm and the thick door that Farmer had closed behind us shut out the jungle noises from the rest of the cells. As we had come through the door that spoke and let civilians pass, I had heard the same soundtrack coming from deep within the blue air-conditioned menagerie that I had heard when Baxter had shown me around. I had seen Baxter's face all around me as Farmer had shoved me along the blue corridor. I had heard his voice in every Spanish prayer and exclamation in the air.

'Then give me a hand to hold him.'

Carlos took off his cap and took me gently by the arm, helping me to straighten up. Farmer caught me in his indifferent stare.

'I enjoy this, Mr Stone,' he mumbled. 'So you take all the time you need. Huh? What do you say?' He took my wrist and began to twist it. His voice turned into a sneer. 'What do you say, huh? Huh?'

It struck me that Farmer wasn't good at this kind of work and that surprised me. He twisted my wrist without

334

conviction, even though it hurt, and he reminded me of a man without rhythm trying to dance. He punched me again in the solar plexus and this time I thought I felt something split inside. The fizzy chemical of hope took longer to make the repairs, and I stayed doubled up for a few moments. Carlos eased me back into an upright position.

'This is just for starters,' Farmer said and he eased his neck around in his collar, trying to sustain his anger. I thought that maybe Farmer was too lazy even to stay mad with anyone for too long. He was doing this out of a sense of duty.

'Yes, sir, just a little appetizer. So come on. Let's talk.'

I gasped for air and the split in my belly felt to be getting wider, like torn rubber. I looked at Carlos and I thought I saw a trace of embarrassment there.

'For Christ's sake wait,' I said. 'Wait until . . .'

'Are you a fag, Mr Stone?' Farmer said to the wall of the cell. 'Because in my experience, men who get their kicks out of hurting women are usually faggots. That true in this case? Mmm? That why you beat up your wife back in London, England? Not speaking to me, faggot? Twist his arm a little, Carlos . . .'

Carlos, who still had hold of my arm, pretended not to hear. Farmer jerked his head, a final order. I felt Carlos's grip tighten and he began to ease my arm up my back until it hurt a little. Farmer saw the reluctance in Carlos's eyes but let it pass.

'Oooh boy, I hate faggots,' Farmer was saying. 'You see Mr Stone, I have a family. A little boy of eleven years old. So you understand why I hate your kind.'

'This is all unnecessary and you know it,' I said, and I saw a spark of genuine anger in Farmer's face. I knew instinctively that the thing that had made him angry had been the way I had said 'unnecessary'. I thought that Farmer didn't like words that were longer than his attention span and that thought made me smile under the covers.

'You think I'm a dumb-ass hick cop, don't you, Mr Faggot,' Farmer said and he came near me. 'Your friend Tom Baxter wouldn't do something like this to you, would he? Hell no. But I'm not Tom Baxter.' I could smell coffee on his breath, and also some sweet cologne. I didn't dare to answer him and he took my silence as defiance. Carlos braced himself for another punch, which landed heavily in the same place. The torn rubber inside was split open a little further. This time the fizzy chemical that had been so pure and strong when I had walked into the cell didn't do its work for a long time. And a terrible thought came to me.

Farmer didn't hit me again for another hour. In that time he simply droned interminably like a troubled mosquito about faggots and hurting women and about the blood on my hands. His mantra was punctuated by his absurd catch-phrases: 'That's the end of the story', 'talking like grown-ups', 'this is a free country, Mr Stone'. I stayed silent except to say that I didn't kill anyone, and Carlos looked on with puzzlement. I had been allowed to sit down on the bench bolted to the wall of the cell while Farmer hovered above me. All the time I was praying that John would find Jimmy quickly. Finally, when the hour had passed, Farmer ordered Carlos to stand me up, and when I was straight, Farmer stepped behind me and hit me hard in the kidneys.

The hour without pain hadn't been good to me. The folder wouldn't mean a damn thing to anyone if there wasn't some kind of corroborative proof that Jimmy did it. I pinned my hopes on the fact that since Jimmy was

336

crazy, he'd crack at the first sign of pressure. I prayed that John would hurry up, that maybe Jimmy would confess the moment he saw a police uniform. But it was possible that the old devil was smarter than he looked, that he'd covered his tracks. Or perhaps that the hurricane had covered his tracks for him. And there was that other possibility. Maybe Jimmy hadn't killed her at all.

'I didn't kill her,' I said again to reassure myself and was rewarded by another punch to the kidneys. I figured that, if Farmer had been right about his expertise on the punishment the human body could take, there were only a certain number of punches he could deliver to each place. It had been six for the stomach and so I guessed it would also be six to the kidneys. The dreary calculation dulled the pain a little.

'Hey, Mr Stone,' Carlos whispered, 'why don't you just tell him what he wants to hear. He's getting mad. Just tell him and maybe we can fix you up . . .'

I turned to look into Carlos's eyes and thought I saw a great tide of compassion behind them. My back was burning inside and the rubber in my belly was ripped to shreds. Six punches and already the machinery inside was acting crazy. Carlos was speaking softly in my ear, and I believed that he really did want to see an end to my suffering.

Farmer had delivered seven blows to my kidneys, so my calculation had been wrong. His line of inquiry had turned into a singsong repetition of the same facts, always ending with the same chorus: 'So why don't you and me talk like grown-ups, Mr Stone.'

And beneath the melody of the song, there was the occasional whispered interjection from Carlos: 'Just tell him what he wants to hear, Mr Stone. Then we can get you cleaned up.'

The last two punches had hurt like fat needles being pushed through my flesh. And now I could taste blood in the back of my throat and I cursed Farmer for lying to me about knowing how much a body could take. The dumb bastard had split something inside me and now I could taste the blood that was seeping into my belly. I still felt that I was outside this thing, that at any moment John would walk through the door of the cell and offer me deliverance. It was only that thought that was holding my insides together, making me strong, making me look Farmer in the eye when he stared at me. I wanted to tell him again that this whole thing was unnecessary, but each time I did, the blows got harder.

'You don't look so good, Mr Stone,' Carlos whispered. 'Why don't you just talk to Mr Farmer and tell him what he wants to hear?'

Carlos held me softly by the arm. He nodded at the mental calculations he thought I was making.

'OK, Mr Farmer,' I said, sitting down uneasily on the bench. 'I do have something to tell you.'

Carlos and Farmer exchanged glances. Their masks slipping for just a moment.

'Shoot,' Farmer said, resuming his cover.

'I want to tell you that the smell of your cologne is making me feel sick.'

This beast that I sometimes couldn't control was going to get me killed. I saw Carlos shaking his head with disbelief as Farmer yanked me up off the bench and threw me against the wall of the cell. My belly hurt and I felt that a grain sack had split open inside. Farmer was about to hit me hard in the belly when there was a rapping on the door of the cell. Farmer hesitated and Carlos helped heave the heavy cell door open. It was John. He had his cap in his hands and his face was made of stone. He twirled his cap around in his hands a few times, fretting.

'Well,' Farmer said, 'd'you speak to the mailman?'

'Yes, sir.'

I couldn't breathe. Neither could Farmer. He wanted it to be me so badly.

'So?'

'Well, I caught up with the old guy over at the dock. He'd gone fishing. Told me that at the time of the murder between five and six on the day of the hurricane, he was down here at the tank with the other old folks.'

I felt the blood draining from my face, the pain intensifying.

'So, I checked him out with the desk . . .' John looked at me for the first time. 'We keep a record of what time they arrive and leave. Fingerprint 'em and all. And, well, his story checks.'

'It what!' I hissed.

'True, Mr Stone,' John said. 'Can't be a mistake because we print them all when they arrive and when they leave. We have to keep a real careful record in case one of the prisoners tries to get out with the old folks. He was here alright. He was here at the tank from two p.m. until six a.m. the next day when he went to do his rounds.'

John couldn't look at me any more. My face had cracked into a thousand pieces. Carlos had turned away from me. Only Farmer's face was alive, and for the first time, I saw him smile with his eyes.

Step by step, I walked by myself down into the dark and empty place. I told Farmer again that I hadn't killed her and he got mad and hit me again in the solar plexus. There was no maximum number, and no ceiling to the pain I was feeling. The pain in my belly and my back was superseded by the pain in my head. A real, searing pain at the centre of my head, as if something in there had turned rotten.

'Talk to me, Mr Stone!' Farmer yelled.

Another blow to the kidneys, then another. I fell to the floor and the walls of the cell began to spin. There was a deep buzzing sound that seemed to be coming from my stomach, and Carlos helped me to my feet with great care. He seemed anxious not to hurt me and he put his lips close to my ear when he whispered, 'You just stop acting crazy and tell Mr Farmer what he wants to hear.'

I shook my head and Farmer approached and then backed off, responding to a look from Carlos. It seemed in the dizzy sickness of the room that Carlos was protecting me from him.

'Hey, Mr Stone,' Carlos whispered, 'you promise me that you'll stop acting crazy! You promise me!'

The light in the cell seemed to be suddenly intense. It hurt my eyes and shone straight through to the inside of my skull. Carlos was smiling and asking me to promise. I said that I did promise and that made Carlos smile even more. He looked across to Farmer, and I could see that he was asking with his eyes if he had done well to make me promise.

'Fuck you!' I shouted as I straightened up, my belly full of acid and blood. 'Fuck you both!'

I pulled myself out of Carlos's grip. I decided that they were playing a game with me, that the whole thing had been choreographed. The oldest game in the movies, the nice cop and the nasty cop.

'I didn't kill her. You understand that, you fucking dumb animal?'

Farmer looked suddenly tired. For a moment, their roles were abandoned and they both relaxed.

'What time is it?' Farmer asked.

'Noon,' Carlos said.

'OK, what do you say we go eat and leave this fucking nut to crawl up the wall?'

Carlos nodded and rapped on the door of the cell.

'Jesus, what's that smell?' Farmer said as they waited for the cell door to be opened.

'I guess he's shit himself,' Carlos said, glancing at me and shaking his head at what he saw.

The pain made time pass slowly, as pain always does. I couldn't taste the blood in my mouth any more but the shit in my pants made me uncomfortable. The smell was unbearable. I had stared at the same spot on the wall of the cell for what seemed like three hours, praying all the time. Praying not to God but to Baxter. Baxter who was good and who was all-powerful and who I believed in. While I had been taking my beating, after John had said that Crazy Jimmy's story checked, I had remembered the final ten per cent. The second possibility which was the only other possibility left. I had no faith in it but I did have faith in Baxter, even though I had no reason to have faith. I felt like a priest praying out loud into the hurricane of his own doubts. All these images painted painstakingly on the wall of the cell.

I heard the key turn in the lock of the cell door and Farmer and Carlos returned. They were laughing and talking about some woman. Some woman who . . .

'. . . just dropped her drawers right there and peed in his fucking coffee. Ah, Jesus, we got to get this boy cleaned up.'

Farmer and Carlos both grimaced at the smell as they walked into the cell. They talked about it for a few moments as if I didn't exist. I peered up at their contented, newly fed faces.

'What do you say, Carlo, we get someone down here to wipe his ass?'

'Maybe. Maybe we don't need to. Maybe he's ready to talk to us.' Carlos looked down on me. 'What do you say, Mr Stone, you ready to talk yet?'

I shook my head.

Farmer and Carlos continued to discuss whether or not it would be worth while getting me cleaned up, or whether they should wait until I had made my confession. They spoke loudly, all for my benefit. I was making my own calculations.

'I need to speak to Baxter,' I said.

Farmer took no notice of me and I said it again louder, trying to stand up and feeling a deep, searing pain in my stomach that was all the more acute for being a well-established pain. I could no longer control my insides, and I hoped that there was nothing more from inside that could come out. There were all kinds of adjustments being made deep inside my belly. And I was sure that I was bleeding.

'Sure, Mr Stone,' Farmer said, 'we'll get Tom back from Fairyland and I'm the King of England.'

Farmer carried on with his discussion about getting me cleaned up and I sat back down on the bench, holding my head in my hands. Finally, a few moments later, Farmer helped me to my feet and hit me with all his strength in the seat of my worst pain. I fell back against the wall, and hit my head. I passed out for a few seconds, and when I came to, Carlos and Farmer were studying the back of my scalp.

'Getting careless,' Farmer said softly, twisting my head into his chest. 'But I guess it's nothing that'll show. I'll say you hit your head getting out of the patrol car. Sound good to you, Carlo?'

'Good to me, sir.'

I asked them in a dreary, drunken voice if it were possible that they could let me rest for a few moments. I said in a slobber that I believed that I had split inside. Farmer said that he was getting sick of my whiny faggot voice and then he said that he'd had an idea that it might be better if they took me out for a ride.

'What do you say, Carlo, we go dump this Limey fag in the swamp. Let the alligators take care of him. You think we don't do that kind of thing, Mr Stone? Sure we do. When we get real irritated with a guy, we take him down to the swamp and we feed him to the alligators.'

Farmer and Carlos laughed. I didn't like the way he'd said the word 'alligator'. An image of the serpent entered my head.

When I tried to raise myself up on the bench, something snapped inside. I lunged forward towards the orange smudge that was Farmer's face and I felt the door to the cage fly open. I felt the beast inside ripping its way out of my belly, tearing through the split that Farmer had made in my abdomen. The pain of its release was white hot and searing, and then the white light changed to black and there was only darkness. I felt a pain in both my hands and in my elbows, and when the darkness cleared, and the ordinary light of the cell returned, I saw that Farmer was lying on his back, like an up-ended truck with the wheels still spinning, and Carlos was sliding slowly down the far wall of the cell. Farmer was holding his fist against his nose and there was blood on his arm. Carlos had his eyes closed, and I could see that he was already unconscious. Then there was darkness again and I guess that it was Farmer who suffered the most at the hands of the creature. After this second period of darkness, I remember a huge commotion, the sound of a jungle in flames out in the blue area, and I remember three heavy guys in uniform coming into the cell.

After that, there was darkness again. And images in green and white.

When I woke up, I was lying on the bench in the cell and someone was wiping the corner of my mouth. I sat up with a jolt and spilled a silver tray of blood and spittle that was lying on my chest. The blood oozed on to my shirt. I narrowed my eyes to focus and saw the face of the black desk sergeant. She was smiling and tut-tutting as she tried to wipe the last of the blood from my mouth.

'What happened?'

'You're quite a guy, aren't you, Mr Stone?'

I sat up on the bed and my head cracked open. The air whooshed around me, thick and full of eddies, like troubled sea water.

'How many fingers am I holding up, Mr Stone?' the lady said and I counted two.

'Two's right. Guess you ain't concussed. Think you can walk?'

I said that I'd try, and I did try, and I could. She helped me to the door of the cell.

'Am I free to go?' I asked and she said that I was free to go. I tried to piece together the fragments of what had happened in the cell before I had fallen unconscious, and my first thought was a kind of prayer that Farmer wasn't dead. The beast was safely back inside its cage now, but I was free to go. Had she really said that?

'Are you serious? You're letting me go?' I said.

The desk sergeant nodded her head sadly. Then she sighed and in the sigh there was an ancient grief.

'Sure, Mr Stone, you're free to go. Free to go outside and meet with your destiny. Do you understand what I'm saying?'

I said that I didn't. The desk sergeant hesitated in the doorway. She whispered at me.

'If Tom was here things would be different. But he ain't here so I guess . . .'

She sighed again. I felt a deep fear inside, beneath the pain in my belly.

'What I'm saying, Mr Stone, is that when you leave this place you will have to be real careful. Please understand without me having to put my job on the line. I guess they're planning for you to have an accident and so you should be real careful. Do you believe in God, Mr Stone?'

I said that I didn't.

'Well, pray to him anyway,' she said. She held me gently and we walked down the chirruping air-conditioned blue corridor.

'I've got to see Baxter,' I said out loud to myself as the desk sergeant spoke into the automatic lock on the chunky sealed door. She heard me and I thought I saw some sort of message in her eyes.

'Do you know where he is?' I said sharply and she shushed me. After the door had clicked open, she said that where Baxter was was a secret, but that I'd find out soon enough.

CHAPTER TWENTY-NINE

When I got back to the movie house, I climbed the stairs slowly, singing 'Streets of Laredo' to myself as if I were drunk. I broke up the phrases of the song in time with each step, taking it carefully so as not to split anything inside. The bleeding had stopped, and I'd managed to clean myself up, but I felt that the membranes and valves in my stomach were all on the point of bursting, and that any sudden movement could cause them to rupture. I was singing 'Streets of Laredo' to keep myself company in my agony, and I had discovered, almost as an aside, that this condition of agony, of guilt, of torment, was the same as the condition of being drunk. I had freed myself of recrimination, I had let myself go like a helium balloon, because tugging on the string down there on the ground had become too painful. Now I was floating up the stairs, one clumping step at a time, singing instead of talking, counting the steps instead of thinking.

I walked automatically right to the top of the house, to Azul's room, to what had once been Scarlet's room, because, I told myself, a ghost always goes back to the scene of his crime.

(And maybe, some wicked part of me still imagined that Azul still believed in me. That there would be some comfort there. That if Azul had faith then I could restore my own.)

I knocked on Azul's door and when I knocked, the door opened. The room was empty and I figured that Azul had forgotten to lock it, as she often did. Instead of turning around and going back to my room, I went in and I sat on the bed, still singing my song to myself, my despair imitating heady indifference.

'So I guess it must be me,' I said brightly, and I lay down on the bed. The bed felt soft and comfortable, and I didn't even try to tease myself with memories. Had the bed sunk down like this when Scarlet had been on it? Was this the pillow I had used? How different it all looked when it was in green and white. None of those thoughts troubled me as I lay on the bed, smiling up at the ceiling. Crazy Jimmy had been with the old folks, Benelli had been at the tank and so it had to be me. And back there in the blue area, back inside the wired-up, sealed and bolted cell, the beast which I'd been teasing this past week, the beast which I had been pursuing through the wilderness, stalking it, calling to it, baiting traps, that beast that had refused to come out for Azul or for the videos in Crazy Jimmy's house, had leapt right on my back. It had leapt out of nowhere and put Farmer and Carlos on the floor like they were children. Was there any pride in me for what the beast had done? Maybe a little. This beast was inside me and always would be inside me so maybe it would be entertaining to come to some kind of agreement with it. The thing was trying to get me killed, and I had been trying to kill it ever since that night with Sarah, so now maybe we could both come out on to clear ground and make a deal. And if I sat down with this beast on this piece of clear ground I could ask it the question out loud.

'It was you who murdered Scarlet, wasn't it, my friend?'

'Yes, Karl, I'm afraid that it was me. It was both of us.'

'A process,' I said out loud in a ludicrous accent, 'of elimination.' And then I began to sing again.

After a while I grew tired of my own indifference, and decided (with a smile and a mental flourish) that it would be wise to become drunk. I was sure that Azul kept some brandy in her kitchen cupboard and I lifted myself carefully off the bed to take a look. Her cupboards were empty, and so I decided that maybe she'd hidden the stuff in the bottom drawer of her wardrobe. If I had wanted to hide a bottle of booze, that is where I would hide it. And since the room was so sparse, there were few other places that it could be. I half thought and half spoke these conclusions as I looked around the room. When I bent down to search through her drawer, my head filled with blood and I almost passed out. The room spun around and I had to fall to my knees to get low enough to start searching.

'One brassière,' I said playfully, my head still turning around and around, the sun setting on my back.

'One silk dressing-gown.'

I was taking the items one by one from the drawer and naming them, because, I thought, when you are crazy, really, really crazy, you can do whatever the hell you want to do.

'One pair of knickers. One linen shirt. One something I don't know what the hell it is. One pair of stretch pants. One notebook.'

I laid all of these things out on the floor, filled with an urge to empty the drawer with both hands to get to the bottle that I was sure was in there. Instead I searched slowly, drunk with fear and with horror, but smiling nevertheless. When I was sure that the drawer was empty, I began to replace all the items of clothing, naming them a second time as I did it, until I just had the notebook in my hand.

'Baxter,' the notebook said. I looked again. On the waxy

front cover of the notebook, Azul had written the word 'Baxter' in green ink.

'Baxter,' I said with wry amusement. And then, all of the fun went out of my face. I opened the notebook and began to read, cross-legged on the floorboards, shifting position to ease the pain in my stomach but unable to stop myself from reading. After I had read the whole thing, from front cover to back, I was sick in Azul's sink, and my vomit was pink with blood.

'*There are some press people around*, Miami Herald, Tampa Courier, *maybe even the* National Enquirer . . .'

Through the buzzing in my ears, I could hear Baxter's voice. I could hear him talking to me in his Spanish room, telling me that Farmer would feed this story to the press like candy. I still had my head in Azul's sink, looking at my own blood swirling into the plug.

'*. . . how a cop taught a writer how to commit a perfect murder and then he goes ahead and does it. That would look real pretty, wouldn't it, Mr Stone. And just to sweeten it, the victim is a movie star.*'

I splashed my face with the rusty water that dribbled from Azul's tap. But Baxter's voice wouldn't go away.

'*There are some press people around*, Miami Herald, Tampa Courier, *maybe even the* National Enquirer, *and they'd just feed out of the hand of anyone who offered them a story . . .*'

I went back to the wardrobe and looked again at Azul's notebook. I was kneeling in the very place where I had found Scarlet's body and that irony took its place right there amongst all of the others, making me want to laugh out loud. Now that I knew who Azul really was, now that I knew which story she'd really been working on, I didn't even feel angry, or betrayed. It was just another piece of

349

wire, another pain to add to all of the others. Azul wrote very well. She was a better writer than I would ever be.

Tom Baxter, Chief of Police, Key West County, does a nice line in public relations. Ask him the way to the shrimp docks, he'll tell you. Ask him for a fishing licence, a marriage licence, a waiver for hunting 'gators and, hell, no problem. Ask him the best way to commit a murder, and he'll tell you that too. You don't believe me? Ask Mr Karl Stone.
   I did.

And on and on.
The piece was written twice. Once funny, wry, the second time dark and ghoulish.

Karl Stone came to the sunshine of Florida's tropical island from the fog and mist of London. And with him, he brought a secret . . .

Then she lost faith. This opening sentence had a line through it. Beneath it:

Karl Stone came to Key West from the fog of London to write a murder mystery. Now the mystery is, did he commit a murder for real? The only man who knows the answer to that is Chief of Police Tom Baxter because he's the guy who helped him to plan it . . . [crossed out] . . . who acted as Stone's murder consultant . . . [crossed out].

And on and on.
I put the notebook back at the bottom of Azul's drawer. I wondered if Azul had let Farmer put his hand on her ass too. Then I figured that it wouldn't have been necessary. Farmer had needed Azul and Azul had needed Farmer. But if it had been necessary, Azul would have let him do

it anyway. I realized then that I had known ever since I'd spoken to Baxter that this had been more than a possibility. It had always been a probability. Ever since Baxter had told me that Farmer was planning to use the press to discredit him, I had known that that was the story Azul was really working on. I had known somewhere in my mind that the Scarlet Timberley story wouldn't have kept Azul in Key West. She had been sticking close to me to get the inside story on me and Tom Baxter, and I didn't doubt that in return for being given the story, she'd helped Farmer to build his case. The page of the script that had mysteriously appeared in Farmer's hands, the way Farmer had always known where I was going, what I was doing. At least now I knew who Azul really was out of all the characters she had been. At least I had finally pulled away all of the masks, and even though what I had found was ugly, there was some comfort in stripping those masks away. I walked back down to my room singing 'Streets of Laredo' at the top of my voice, just to let the hurricane know that even now, even after this final twist of the knife I could still remember the words.

I waited for Azul to return to the movie house, not even sure that she ever would return. After all, her work was now complete. I thought that it might be interesting if this time, now that I knew who Azul really was, the beast paid her a visit. It would be interesting to see what would happen if by some chance I bumped into Azul before Farmer had a chance to feed me to the alligators and the fishes.

And after I had contemplated that, I decided that maybe me and the alligators deserved each other.

After darkness had fallen, the rain began.

The rain in Key West comes in big droplets, and it machine-guns the dry earth with a fury that only the tropics can sustain. The sky was filled with electricity, and it rumbled and groaned above my head, the perfect evocation, I thought then, of the pathetic fallacy. I'd learnt that phrase at school and now I kept on running it through my mind, in time with the drumming of the rain, as a kind of anxious nervous tick.

'This thing ends with an electric storm,' I said out loud to myself, 'and that is called the pathetic fallacy.'

The telephone rang in the middle of a drum roll of thunder. My phone hadn't rung since the day Benelli had called me up from New York, and the sound of it took me by surprise. For a long time I let it ring, not wanting to interrupt my tedious repetition of old phrases and my rerunning of irrelevant memories. I had stopped thinking about Azul, cursing her, damning her to hell for making me have faith in her, and I'd begun to think about schooldays. About a small boy I'd punched on the nose one afternoon for no reason, just to see how it felt. I remembered the blood that had poured from his face and the look of terror and shock on the faces of all the witnesses. I had been nine years old and I vowed never to do anything like it ever again.

'Hello?'

'*Aló!* Hey, listen . . .'

The electrical storm made the phone line howl and rattle.

'Hello?'

Another roll of thunder, this time quieter and more distant.

'*Aló!* Hey, you wanna go fish? Good day for sharks today. Nice and hot.'

The crackling on the line made the words hard to

distinguish, but I was sure I recognized the voice of the Cuban café owner. I assumed that the voice was in my imagination, that I was constructing it from the weird banshee chorus that the storm was creating. I half expected him to whisper, 'Hey, you remember me, I'm the only character you got left who ain't turned bad. Well, screw you, ass-hole.' I wondered how much of the noise was coming from the storm and how much was coming from Farmer's bug. Then the voice hit a clearing and I heard it distinctly.

'You wanna go fish today? You know who this is? It's me, wanna-go-fish. You know me, right?'

The voice of the Cuban bar owner was lost again in a swell of electricity. The room was lit by a flash of sickly blue light and it was followed half a second later by a crash of thunder, like an invisible ceiling caving in.

'Hello?'

'Listen. I got some guy here. Says he got an appointment. Wants to see you right away. Says I should say I'm calling from my place but don't say where . . .'

The bar owner's accent was thicker on the phone. After I had stood up to take the call, my belly had started to hurt again, and I thought I could feel blood inside. I could hardly make out what the voice was saying.

'Something something something gringo something something says his name is Harry. Says you'll know . . .'

'What?'

'Says his name is Harry. Don't wanna give second name 'cause you're bugged. That right? Hey, this is some kind of game, right? Like in the movies?' . . . A drawl, then the sound of the Cuban café owner laughing . . . 'Says his name is Harry. He's right here by me. He don't look so good. Hey, your phone really bugged? Iss just like the movies . . .'

Another crash of thunder, hitting simultaneously with a flash of lightning, wiped the connection away and the phone line went dead. Straight away, I wasn't sure that the voice had been real. I thought that maybe I'd invented the whole thing, because a writer hears a lot of voices in his head and only one of them is for real. Then I thought about Baxter and I tried to think this thing through in the way he would have done. Percentages. It was eighty per cent that the call had been arranged by Farmer and that, if I went outside now, down to the café where I had been so many times, I would be walking to my death. Eighty per cent. That left twenty. The twenty came from the name Harry. The way my stomach had turned when the café owner had said the name 'Harry' had hurt like hell, and my kidneys were burning. I was in no condition to go outside, to walk all the way to the café on Salt Pond Key, to dodge the patrol car and sneak out past Carlos and John, but at least I knew that in this weather there'd be no helicopters in the air. I knew that by stepping outside the door, I would maybe be walking out to my death, but that was OK too. Me and the beast could handle ourselves, and I decided that, if Farmer was laying a trap, he'd need a whole fucking regiment and a few armoured cars. Sure, there was some pride in that. I put on my thin linen jacket and my real leather shoes (agony to bend and tie the laces) and I ran and limped down the stairs of the movie house. Outside, Mallory Street was varnished with golden rain in the street light, and the puddles on the sidewalk were swelling into floods.

I sang out loud to myself, '*I spied a poor cowboy all dressed in white linen* . . .' and I lifted my face to the rain, to let the big drops cool my face. A Key West rainstorm will last all night, and then there won't be another drop of it for three whole months. It says so in all the tourist guides. I still had a tourist guide in the pocket of my jacket, there since the first day I arrived, and by the time I reached the café at Salt Pond Key, it was no more than a ball of wet coloured paper.

The café was a different place at night. It was as if all the familiar features that I recognized from my morning visits had been transported into a different hemisphere. It was a reflection of the daytime café in a dark and dirty mirror. And the people who drank there at night were the dark sides of the people who took coffee there during the day. The rain was making my eyes sting, refracting all the electric lights, turning the scene into an image from a dream, smudged and uncertain. I was hot, too, because Key West rain doesn't chill the air, it just makes it suffocatingly damp. I was so hot that I thought I might slip at any moment into delirium and I still wasn't sure how much blood I'd lost into my own body cavity. Whether it was the heat, the rain or the loss of blood, my head felt as if it were balancing on stilts.

All the customers were sitting under a tarpaulin canopy near to the front of the café. They were mostly Cubans, dressed in white linen shirts and khaki pants, kitchen staff from the local restaurants getting drunk and slapping the tables and smoking and doing all the things they couldn't do in their regular restaurants. I'd never heard music coming from the café before, but now there was a cracked sound system playing loud salsa that was accompanied by the sound of rain drumming on the tarpaulin. The fringes of the tarpaulin and the frame of the door were decorated with coloured Christmas-tree lights, and at the far end of the *ramada*, there were four fishermen with leathery tans playing cards in the shadows. I looked all the customers over and tried to see inside the café. I sniffed the air and all I could smell was burning fish and ocean. If this was a trap, I decided, I would smell it right here and now. And I'd see something in the eyes of those Cuban guys slapping the table, in the gestures of the fishermen playing cards in the shadows. Then I thought that maybe my delirium had started already. I imagined that at any moment a movie director would step out from the shadows and switch off the rain and tell the guys to take five while someone touched up the grease on the café windows. The scene was too perfect an evocation of what I would have created myself as the scene for my rendezvous with Harry S. Rose, the sick doctor. Harry S. Rose whose name I had almost forgotten, and who I knew had something to do with Baxter's second possibility. The last remaining ten per cent.

Inside the café, the air stank of fish and burnt bone and fins. The café owner had his back to me, throwing salt on a griddle of burning coals which flashed and spat with sardine oil. My clothes were drenched with rainwater and sweat, and I made two tiny puddles as I stood in the doorway, looking around at the sparse interior of the café, lit by fluorescent light. The café owner turned to me and smiled. He looked sleepy. His boy was leaning back on a chair beside him, dressed in a thick oilskin that was unbuttoned and three sizes too big for him. The boy looked up from a comic he was reading and rocked forward in his chair.

'The guy's in the john,' the boy said, and the café owner threw some more salt on the coals. 'Hey, he looks pretty bad. Maybe I should go check he's OK.'

The café had a Formica bar with stools along it, and I took a seat directly in front of where the café owner was cooking his fish. The boy skipped out through a set of greasy-looking curtains to where I imagined the john must be. I was sure that my dreams had flooded the café, that only half of this was real and I was still getting my breath from the run from the movie house. The café owner turned to me and I thought that I should attempt at least half an explanation. But when I opened my mouth he shushed me.

'Don't need to explain,' he said and he winked at me. Then he poured me a small glass of Cuban brandy and placed it in front of me.

'Here, we get lots of stuff. Coca, rum, illegals. Mostly cocaine. Don't need to explain. I always had you down as a mysterious guy. You on the run?'

'Kind of. Yes. You seen any cops around this evening?'

The café owner liked the question. He shook his head with his eyes narrowed.

'You safe here, my friend,' he said.

'No strangers? New customers?'

'Only the old guy in the john.'

I relaxed. I felt a surge of empathy from the café owner. I could see that he wanted to slap my back and shout out loud that I was a guy on the run and that he himself had told me there were no cops around.

'Sure, you're on the run,' he said. 'I can tell. See it in your eyes.'

He shrugged his shoulders and gave me a ludicrous look of indifference. I could hear his boy shouting somewhere out behind the greasy curtains, banging on the door of the lavatory.

'Hey, mister, you OK in there? Mister. Your guy's here.'

The café owner ostentatiously turned up the volume of the salsa music until it was almost deafening. Then he turned to me and put his finger over his lips. He turned back to flip the line of sardines on the griddle. He wanted so badly to prove that he could be discreet, but I could tell that his curiosity was driving him insane. He shook his head and giggled.

'I could tell your phone was bugged,' he chuckled. 'Tell by the crackles. So what is it, the harbour patrol, FBI, who?'

I picked up the small glass of Spanish brandy and sniffed it. Carlos Tercero, my favourite brand. I put it back down on the counter with the vapour still in my nostrils and I pushed it away. Out behind the greasy curtains, I could hear someone coughing. One of the leathery fishermen came into the bar, dressed in a plaid shirt, jeans and cowboy boots, with his black hair pulled back tight into a ponytail. He glanced at me and the café owner put his finger to his lips again and shook his head. His confidential look was comical. 'Coca,' he said darkly between two salsa tracks, and the fisherman walked out of the café empty-handed.

When the greasy curtains opened, I saw the café owner's son, still swamped in his oilskin, acting as a human crutch for a grey-faced old man. Except he wasn't so old, he was just hollowed out, gutted like a sardine, and the lack of substance to his insides gave him the appearance of age. I would have guessed that he was a sick fifty-five. Very sick. His eyes swivelled inside great sucked-in sockets, and his chest heaved as he walked. The boy eased him into the stool next to mine and winked at me in exactly the same way his father had winked. Harry S. Rose leant forward against the bar and took some deep breaths that seemed to relieve a great pain.

'Cheeezus,' he wheezed, and then suppressed a cough. 'Guess I'm ready for breaking up for parts, right?'

'I'm Karl Stone.'

'Harry S. Rose. Marathon PD forensics. Pleased to.'

He swallowed and another urge to cough subsided. I

waited a few moments for Harry to straighten himself up on his stool.

'Hey, can you turn that damn music down,' he hissed. 'Man trying to die in here.'

Harry chuckled, and some life came into his features. He had silvery blond hair and eyes that had once been blue but were now no colour at all. His shirt looked way to big for him but he had tightened the collar around his scrawny neck with a tie, probably through force of habit. I guessed that Harry S. Rose had always worn a tie for appointments. His pants were tightly belted too, and he looked the way my father had looked just before he had died of cancer. Except Harry S. Rose didn't look so scared. He took my glass of brandy from the counter and swallowed it whole. I tried to remember the name of the old guy in the movie *Key Largo*. The old guy who was sick and dying but who still had the spunk to needle Edward G. and get a beating for it. The name eluded me.

'Baxter's a good guy, you know,' Harry said, suddenly serious, as if we were already halfway through a conversation.

'I know.'

'He's a good guy and I'm glad to be of service to him. You are Stone, ain't you?'

'Yes, I'm Stone.'

'Damn good guy.'

Harry rattled the empty glass on the counter and the sky rumbled moodily above our heads. Now that the café owner had turned the music down, I could hear the constant drum of rain on the tarpaulin outside, and the hush of waves in the distance. And the sound of the card school getting frisky outside on the *ramada*. The smell of fish was getting stronger and I could tell that the smell was making Harry feel sick. He took a tiny sip of his second brandy.

'It's good news, Mr Stone,' Harry said.

'What is?'

'This.'

He seemed to be preparing himself for a swallow dive off the stool. He shifted his position and then bent over sideways, reaching for a macintosh that was crumpled up on the floor beneath his seat. I stood up and picked up the coat and handed it to him. His hands were almost transparent, lined with blue veins like highways on a map. They shook as he took a large brown envelope out of the inside pocket.

'Guess this is the last forensic report I'll ever submit,' he said and smiled at some private irony. 'Curious that it should be like this. In some spik café. No offence, señor. Curious that I should be doing something good for someone.'

I took the envelope from him. My own internal pain (still shifting around my body) suddenly seemed irrelevant next to Harry S. Rose's pain. I could almost see the agony streaking through his limbs and torso as he moved around. From the sound of his breathing I had figured that it was lung cancer. His eyes followed the envelope fondly.

'Guess you'll never know what it took to put that thing together,' he said. 'Did it for Tom.'

'I think I can imagine.'

Harry turned to me and peered into my eyes. I felt like a bit-part player in a huge drama, an epic, the drama of Harry's life.

'You ever seen the angel of death?' he said suddenly, still staring into my eyes. I didn't reply. 'Great tits,' he said. 'Great tits she's got.'

He laughed and took another sip of brandy.

'Hey, you'll have to forgive me, Mr Stone. Pumped myself full of morphine to get here. Did I just call this guy a spik?'

360

'No, not really.'

'Good. I don't use words like that no more.'

I wanted to open the envelope there and then, but somehow I knew that it would be sacrilegious to do it in Harry's presence. I even imagined that inside that envelope was one man's life's work. I wanted to ask Harry what this whole thing was about, ask him about the second possibility, but I knew that I couldn't do that either. Baxter would explain soon enough.

'On the back of the envelope there's some directions,' Harry said. 'That's where Tom'll be to pick up the envelope. Tom's arranged it all. The boy there is going to take you . . .'

Harry began to cough inside his mouth, trying not to let the cough surface.

'Take me where?'

'To see Baxter so you can give him the envelope. It's good news, Mr Stone. Serious. Tom'll be pleased as hell. Bastard might even buy me a drink.'

I thought Harry was going to laugh but he just nodded his head and peered ruefully at the café owner.

'Didn't mean to call the guy a spik.'

'You didn't, Harry. What do you mean it's good news?'

'I mean we win. We win. The good guys win. And Farmer loses. That's what this whole thing's been about. Worked my ass off through purple pain to make sure that Farmer loses. Sure. And he does.'

The café owner served up his sardines, stiff and burnt and still staring out of their sightless eyes. I thought Harry was going to retch at the sight of them slithering on to the large cracked plate that the café owner had laid on the counter, but he controlled himself. His eyes swivelled around to me.

'Went to school with the guy. Farmer, I mean. He was a

cunt then and he's a cunt now. Didn't know that for a long time. But Tom changed things around here. He's a good guy, Mr Stone. When you're dying you'll know what good means. You'll know there's a difference. Good and evil. The angel of death, she's good. Great big fat tits she's got, Mr Stone.'

I folded the envelope in half and put it into my pocket. Harry felt around in his inside pocket and produced a small Cellophane envelope. He handed it to me.

'Here's the sample back,' Harry said. 'Tell Baxter I've finished with it. Tell him to keep it as a keepsake and that he should remember me. Tell him that old Harry wishes him God speed.'

The Cellophane envelope contained a lock of blond hair. Something clicked inside my head. The café owner's son fastened his oilskin and walked over to my stool. He took my arm and whispered confidentially that we should hurry, that the boat was filled with fuel and that we didn't have much time. He looked out at the rain and blew up into his fringe, letting me know that this was going to be a rough ride.

'Boat?' I said.

'Sure,' the boy said, 'your friend who wants the envelope is down on the shore at Fort Taylor. We'd better hurry because the wind's against us all the way. He'll be getting pretty wet too.'

The boy squeezed my arm to let me know that we had to go. Harry was peering without expression into his brandy glass, the tide of morphine finally dragging him out to sea. The Cuban boy explained his father would see that the sick guy got home safely and then led me out to the *ramada*, where the rain was still falling in sheets, and where the lights were buzzing in the damp air.

'Tell me something,' I said to the boy. 'Why are you

362

doing all this for me? Are you doing this for Tom Baxter too?'

The boy didn't want to talk in front of all these customers. He just turned to me and shrugged his shoulders.

CHAPTER THIRTY

As we climbed into the Cuban boy's tiny motor boat, he introduced himself as Billy.

'That's not my real name,' he said, as he pulled the engine cord, 'but you couldn't pronounce my real name.'

On the third pull, the engine fired. The ocean around us was as dark and thick as oil, and blades of orange light shone on it from the lights of the café. The rain was still heavy, and the sound of the rain and the noise of the asthmatic engine on the launch made the boy shout as he grinned at me. I was trying to find a dry place to sit.

'How would you pronounce a name that's spelt X-A-V-I-E-R?' he shouted as he spun the boat around through one hundred and eighty degrees.

'I'd pronounce it Billy,' I called back and the boy laughed. At last I was down in the water of the harbour, the same patch of milky blue water I'd always seen in my dreams, where Laura and Max, me and Sarah would go splashing around one day, shouting out that we loved each other. Now the water was stirred by the wind and it looked forbidding, but I was laughing nevertheless, laughing up at Billy's face. I wanted the wind to blow harder and I wanted the rain to do its worst because the harder the storm blew, the more I could laugh. I had been flooded by a feeling of abandon, a wild fury, brought on by what Harry S. Rose had told me.

'It's good news, Mr Stone,' the wind said as it whistled through the boat. 'We win ... the good guys win,' the wind was saying. I didn't know what kind of good news it was, or what it meant, but I knew that it was good because Harry S. Rose had said so. Salt Pond Key was lit by harbour lights, muzzled by the rain, but soon we had slipped out of the harbour and we were ploughing our way out into the dark ocean beyond Smathers Beach. In the distance I could just make out the lights of tankers skimming the horizon, and the lights of harbour patrol boats heading for the shore. To the north were the lights of houses and stores along Atlantic Boulevard, and the lights of traffic. Billy followed the line of Smathers Beach, rounded the old concrete fishing pier and then opened up the throttle to get us around the Casa Marina.

'People would pay good money for this cruise!' I yelled, grinning and gripping the side of the boat. The wind was whipping my words away. 'You should charge people and take them around the island, Billy. It's beautiful. The whole thing is beautiful!'

Every few seconds I checked that the envelope was still in my inside pocket. And before we rounded Southernmost Point, I took the lock of hair out of my other pocket and laughed at it. I held it up to the light and whooped out loud. Billy, his face inscrutable against the rain, became curious.

'None of my business,' he shouted, 'but what business you in?'

I put the lock of hair carefully back in my pocket.

'You ain't a smuggler, are you?' Billy said.

'No.'

'No, I can tell. You're no smuggler. Not aliens either.'

'No, not aliens. I'm in the movie business.'

'Oh.'

The boat choked on a heavy swell and the engine almost cut. Billy danced around the throttle and the boat picked up its rhythm again. All my life I had been afraid of rough water, afraid of boats and depth, but now I could have jumped out of the boat and pulled it along with my teeth. The urge to rip open the envelope and find out about the second possibility was strong, but I told myself that this time, just this once, I was going to do things the right way. I was going to wait for Baxter because he'd waited right until the last moment to pull this rabbit out of the hat, the way I always knew he would. And he'd waited for this storm too, because this was the pathetic fallacy and this was how it would be in the movies. The rain was warm and I saw a fork of lightning, thick as a tree-trunk, strike the water somewhere down towards Cuba.

'You didn't answer my question!' I yelled as Billy steered the boat through another wave. 'About why you're doing all this.'

Billy sat down inside the boat, controlling the rudder with the crook of his elbow.

'The sick guy gave me four hundred dollars,' Billy said. 'Told me it was real important I get you to Fort Taylor. I said mister I don't run cocaine and he said it ain't cocaine. I said I don't run rum or tobacco either, or coffee, and he said it was just an envelope with some papers. Some papers he don't want the police to see. So I say sure. Four hundred dollars for a trip I do every day, why the hell not?'

He grinned and his teeth shone in the sea light.

'You're working for a good cause too,' I said. 'Really.'

'Sure.'

Billy turned the boat towards the shore, so that we began a gentle arc heading north. Through the rain, I could just make out the silhouette of a high wall set back from the shoreline, and what appeared to be the irregular outline of turrets. The coast we'd been following had been rocky, but I could see now that we were heading for a small sandy bay, tucked in between rocky outcrops, right underneath the high, turreted wall. The whole scene, the lights on the shore, the darkness of the ocean, Billy standing proud over his spluttering engine, still looked like a scene from a dream. It still seemed to be part of my delirium. Ever since the phone call just an hour before, I had felt as if I had been lifted off my feet, sucked up into the funnel of a hurricane, not sure where it would drop me and not sure if it was for real. Or maybe the feeling had begun when the rain had started, when the thunder had started to roll. Maybe the weather was doing this to me. The whole universe tossing me around, picking me up and changing my direction. An hour ago I had been staring at the blank wall of my room, projecting images. Then the rain had come and now I was inside one of those images, the dark expanse of an ancient-looking fortress, the jagged jaw-line of turrets, the swell of the ocean. Billy cut the engine to a gentle chug, and I could hear his voice more clearly.

'This is where they bring the illegals in,' he said, pointing at the sandy bay which seemed to generate its own ethereal white light. 'Best place to come because the poor bastards can swim up to the beach and hide out in the fort till morning. They unload cocaine here too. So they say. And Haitians. Lot of patrol boats round here sometimes, but I guess they don't like this weather. We'll be OK.'

The beach, no bigger than twenty metres across, was now close by. The waves were foaming up in the rain, and I could smell the pungent odour of rotten seaweed. Billy turned the boat parallel to the line of the beach and stopped the engine.

'You can walk in from here,' he said. 'It's OK, only three feet deep here.'

367

I took the envelope and the lock of hair out of my pocket and held them up high above my head as I prepared to jump out of the boat. I was wet through already, so wading through the ocean wouldn't make any difference. I knew that I'd ruin my shoes. I laughed at myself for even thinking about that. Billy helped me clamber on to the side of the boat because he could see that I was in pain when I moved.

'Movie business,' he said wistfully.

'That's right.'

'So what's in the envelope?'

'I have no idea.'

'You're holding it like it's your life.'

'I think it probably is.'

Billy nodded. I lowered myself over the side of the boat and felt the cold water around my legs. There was sand beneath my feet and the softness of the sand made it difficult to get a foothold. Billy held my arm and pushed me towards the shore. I moved slowly.

'You're no smuggler, that's for sure,' Billy said, and laughed. He waited until I'd waded a few feet towards the shore before he started the engine and turned the boat around. By the time I'd made it up on to the beach, the noise of his engine had disappeared, and I was left alone in almost complete darkness, still not quite sure what the hurricane was going to do to me next.

Baxter appeared out of the darkness a few minutes later. I guess he'd been waiting to make sure I hadn't been followed. He was wearing a long raincoat and a leather hat that made him look like a detective from the movies. I was sitting down on a rock, letting the rain dribble down my face and down the back of my neck, and Baxter came and sat beside me.

'You got the envelope?'

I took it out of my pocket.

'You certainly like to leave things to the last moment, don't you, Tom,' I said, and he blinked at me with incomprehension. 'For a while back there . . .'

He flicked his chin at the envelope, a subtle gesture that denoted enormous impatience. I realized that the envelope might be Baxter's life too.

'Harry says it's good news,' I said, and Baxter took the envelope and calmly tore the seal.

'How was he?'

'Sick.'

Baxter bent over to protect the papers inside from the rain. He used his body as a shield and then took a pencil flashlight out of his pocket to read. As he read his face screwed, trying to piece together the words in the darkness.

'I found out something,' I said to the side of his face, to ease the tension. 'Found out about the lady journalist. You remember her?'

Baxter didn't respond. I wondered if he could even hear. The tiny beam of the flashlight illuminated one word at a time, and Baxter was mouthing each word to himself as he read.

'Found out the bitch was working for Farmer all along. You remember her, Tom? The blond lady. The one who was following me all over the island? Farmer was using her to write the story that was going to get you fired. The story about the cop who teaches the writer how to commit a murder.'

Baxter broke off from reading and looked up at me.

'And in return, she was helping Farmer to nail you,' Baxter said, not in the least surprised. He turned back to his papers. 'But I guess you've finally worked that out for yourself too,' he said.

'Wait a minute,' I said, felled at his lack of surprise. 'You mean you knew about her all along?' I grabbed Baxter's arm but he jerked his arm free and went back to his flashlight.

'Tom? You knew about her? Why the fucking hell didn't you warn me?'

'Like I said, I couldn't trust you not to fuck up.'

Baxter read some more, the light from the torch moving quickly across the pages.

'Fucking bitch,' I said to myself and the sky rumbled.

'Sure,' Baxter said. 'Clever fucking bitch too.'

Baxter gritted his teeth and then relaxed. The light from the pencil flashlight hovered on a word which I couldn't read.

'Did Harry give you a lock of hair too?' he said at last. I handed him the Cellophane envelope and he put it in the pocket of his raincoat. He carried on reading the report. Then he switched off the pencil torch and looked up at me.

'Harry was right.'

At that moment, the drumming of the rain was thickened by the sound of an engine somewhere in the distance, out to sea. Baxter looked over my shoulder and, when I turned, I saw the rectangular cabin lights of a harbour patrol boat. Baxter didn't move.

'They can't see us in this light. Visibility's zero. They're just fishing for spiks.'

Baxter put the envelope in the pocket of his raincoat.

'But I guess it might be wise to get away from here . . .'

He was turning to leave but I grabbed his shoulder. The rain had misted up his spectacles and I could hardly see his eyes in the half-light.

'Tom, you're not going anywhere until you explain.'

Suddenly, the beach was illuminated by a frosty beam

370

of light. I could see the rain lit up in its beam. The light was coming from the harbour patrol boat and the beam swept the beach quickly. The beam illuminated Baxter's face for a fraction of a second and we both froze. We heard the engine of the patrol boat labouring and then it changed up a gear. The boat suddenly kicked into life and sped away east.

'Like I say,' Baxter said, 'we'd better get away from here.'

'No. Tell me now. Tell me here. Tell me about the second possibility.'

The rain had plastered Baxter's hair to his head and he looked almost human. I could tell that he was blinking with impatience behind his misted-up spectacles. I hadn't let go of his arm, even when the patrol boat had scanned the beach. I pulled him towards me.

'Mr Stone . . .'

'Now, Tom. This is the perfect place. Tell me that I didn't kill her. Tell me how you know that.'

Baxter blew a dribble of rain from his nose and swept his wet hair from his face. At that moment, with perfect and terrifying timing, there was a flash of lightning.

'I don't know that for sure yet,' he said. 'But your percentage just went down. You're down to twenty per cent, maybe even less. Hell, much less. Let's be realistic.'

I knew that Baxter wasn't being deliberately obtuse. It was just that his mind was racing so far ahead and it was tiring for him to wait for me to catch up.

'The second possibility is the lady journalist,' he said, and the thunder to match the flash of lightning cracked over our heads. 'She didn't just have you fooled, Mr Stone. She's had Farmer fooled too. And me for that matter.'

'You mean Azul?'

Baxter nodded.

'What about her?'

'She's outsmarted you and she's outsmarted me and she's outsmarted Farmer.'

Baxter smiled as if he admired her.

'But she didn't outsmart Harry S. Rose.'

I had been right. This was the perfect place for Baxter to tell me what this was all about. The rain and the lightning and the thunder made the moment glorious, gave it depth and colour.

'First day of the investigation,' Baxter said, 'I took some samples from her to eliminate her. And sure enough, we found nothing at the scene of the murder. But when Harry did the forensic analysis on Caroline Lisson, he noticed something. There was a match. A genetic match between the hair samples we took from the lady journalist and the blood and hair we took from Caroline Lisson. No one but Harry S. Rose would have been that thorough.'

'Tom, for Christ's sake, what are you saying?'

'What I'm saying is that according to these test results, it's eighty per cent sure that the lady journalist is Caroline Lisson's daughter. There is a direct genetic match . . . And her name isn't Azul. It's Mary. Mary Hope.'

CHAPTER THIRTY-ONE

It was hilariously difficult to get off the beach and back on to the road that led away from Fort Taylor. There was a sandy path that led up a sheer incline, and the rain had turned it into a series of rivulets and waterfalls. The rocks and sandstone wouldn't take a foothold, and Baxter and I kept on slipping back and sliding as we tried to get away from the beach. The exertion made us both breathless, and the pitch darkness meant that we were climbing blind.

'Mary Hope?' I hissed, grabbing at a clump of spiny grass to haul myself up.

'Recognize it?' Baxter said.

I remembered the name from the Chase Manhattan bank statements. Four hundred dollars a month raised to a thousand dollars a month. Baxter held out his hand and hauled me up through a gurgling waterfall of mud and sand.

'I came across it when I was looking for next of kin,' Baxter said. 'Weingartner at the Chase Manhattan told me that Mary Hope was Caroline Lisson's daughter. Illegitimate. Born back in Kansas. Mrs Lisson had the baby adopted, but when she got rich, she set up a trust fund for the kid she'd abandoned. The Mary Hope Foundation. Then Weingartner told me that, now that Mrs Lisson was dead, the whole of the estate would go to the illegitimate daughter.'

'Wait, wait, wait a minute,' I said.

'It's simple enough, Mr Stone.'

'No, wait a minute. I got my shoe caught in this damn hole.'

I had to get down on all fours to free the heel of my shoe from what appeared to be a rabbit hole in the sand. We continued our climb in the darkness and Baxter grunted and groaned as he tried to give me a full explanation, shorthand. He said that since Mary Hope was Mrs Lisson's next of kin, he was obliged to try and trace her after the murder. He found out that she was a freshman at Texas State University, but when he called the university, they said she'd skipped classes a month before and that they didn't know where she'd gone. It was right around that time that Harry S. Rose had called and asked how come he'd got two different samples of Caroline Lisson's hair, one blond, the other dyed brunette.

'I told Harry that the two samples were from different people. One from the victim, the other from the lady who was calling herself Azul. He said if that was so, why was there a match on the genetic fingerprints?'

Baxter said he realized then that he had a daughter who'd gone missing and a lady journalist whose genetic make-up was coming up close to the make-up of the victim.

'It didn't take a genius,' Baxter said, catching his breath as he waited for me to clamber up a sand bank.

It was then that Farmer had taken Baxter off the case, just when Harry was in the process of sending the two samples up to Miami for a more thorough analysis.

'Jesus, that lady was smart,' Baxter said, and he lost his spectacles to a waterfall. He sat down on a clump of grass to wipe the mud off them.

'She knew that Farmer was after my ass,' Baxter said. 'So she offered her services as a journalist to take the story to the *Enquirer*. That way she took herself out of Farmer's line of investigation. She also got herself the job of helping to make sure it was you who got nailed for the murder. So she plays Farmer off against you and you off against Farmer. And she comes out of it with ten million dollars. That's what the Lisson estate is worth. Ten million dollars. Come on, my ass is getting cold.'

Something big and black, probably a bat, flew directly into my face and I nearly fell back twenty feet. Baxter shook his head.

'Can't have been a bat in this weather.'

'It was a bloody bat.'

'It was a branch, Mr Stone. Come on, we're almost there.'

A few moments later, we were up on the grassy verge beside Whitehead Street. Twenty yards up the street, there was a car parked with its lights off. It seemed to be empty.

'Tom,' I gasped, still hurting from the climb, 'you've got to wait a minute. I'm hurting. Tell me again about Azul.'

'Mary Hope.'

'OK, Mary Hope.'

'It's the second possibility,' Baxter said. 'It's Harry who should take the credit. He's a hell of a guy you know, Mr Stone. You say he was real sick?'

'Real bad. Listen, Tom . . .'

'Mr Stone, we've got a lot to do tonight.'

'Listen. Wait a minute. Are you saying that you think Azul, Mary Hope, you think that she killed Scarlet?'

'Hell of a motive, Mr Stone. Ten million dollars.' Baxter clapped his hands together, a brief moment of triumph. An uncharacteristic gesture. 'Can't ignore a motive like that. And she's concealed her identity from the start. That's if we're right about her. Like I say, a hair analysis is only eighty per cent. But that's just the start.'

'But Azul said she was at her hotel when the hurricane hit. She said she had witnesses.'

'Sure,' Baxter said.

Suddenly, there was a flashing light. The parked car flashing its headlights three times. Baxter waved his arm at it and the engine fired. The car cruised closer. Baxter waited for it to pull up, and through the sloshing wind-screen wipers I saw Carmelita at the wheel. She wound down the window.

'Good news?' she said.

'The best,' said Baxter, and he handed her the envelope from the inside of his raincoat. Baxter said something to her in Spanish and she smiled bravely. Then she drove away, leaving us alone.

'She'll be in Miami before dawn,' Baxter said, peering at the red tail lights. 'By ten, if the right people get to see it, they'll have to put me back on the case.'

Baxter looked to be very proud of the red tail lights in the distance. He clapped his hands together again. Then his triumph subsided when he turned to me.

'What's wrong, Mr Stone?' he said. I was hurting inside, still trying to put the pieces together.

'She said that she had witnesses,' I said. 'Two cleaning ladies at the Flamingo Key Hotel.'

Baxter said that she had told him that too.

'Didn't think about it at the time,' Baxter said, that note of admiration back in his voice, 'but she was smart about that too. Those hotels on the ocean hire a lot of illegals to clean rooms. Almost all illegals. Every damn one of them calls herself Concha Gonzales. No SS numbers, no tax, no records. She knew that it would take a genius to find the two women who were working her floor of the hotel when the hurricane hit.'

Baxter caught his breath. I'd never seen him so animated.

'So . . .' I said.

'So, like you said once, Mr Stone, I'm a genius.'

Baxter laughed out loud and said that if we hurried we'd know for ninety-nine per cent sure before midnight.

CHAPTER THIRTY-TWO

'Before I returned, the spirit had left him
And gone to its maker – the cowboy was dead.'

'Will you quit singing that damn song,' Baxter said, as he
eased a length of coat-hanger wire into the rubber gums of
a station-wagon window. I wasn't singing so much as
breathing the song under my breath, to ease my anxiety,
to deaden the pain inside my stomach. As I sang, the
words hung in clouds of breath. The wind from the ocean
was blowing cold.

'Go gather around me a crowd of young cowboys . . .'

Baxter glared at me. The rain had eased a little but it still
hung like a huge mosquito net over the ocean to the south.
We had come across the station wagon a few hundred
yards from where we'd emerged on to the road from Fort
Taylor. It was an old model, and it didn't take Baxter long
to break into it. He'd brought the coat-hanger wire
specially. When we got inside, the windows began to mist
up instantly. Baxter produced his pencil torch and peered
at the dashboard.

'You ever hot-wired a car?' Baxter said. I told him that
I had and he looked hard into my eyes. There was no time
for me to explain. We swapped seats, Baxter easing his
way over my belly and making me gasp with pain. I used
my thumbnail and the key to the front door of the movie
house to get into the wiring of the steering column, while
Baxter shone his tiny beam of light at my fingertips.

'Isn't this against the law, lieutenant?' I said, and Baxter wiped his window to peer across the street.

'Just make it quick,' he said. 'If we walk any distance in this weather we'll be arrested for sure. I'll return the vehicle when we're through with our business.'

'And what is our business?'

'Please, Mr Stone. Start the car.'

The engine fired and I whispered, 'Good old Ford. Same all over the world.' Baxter tried hard not to be impressed as I pulled away into an ocean of rainwater that engulfed us. The road was almost flooded and the creaky, broken wipers had to work hard to clear a patch of windscreen big enough to see through.

'When I interviewed the lady journalist,' Baxter said, as if he recognized that he owed me an explanation, 'she told me she was at the Flamingo Key Hotel at the time of the hurricane. Said she was with a cleaning lady in her room when the hurricane hit. Farmer took me off the case before I got round to checking her story . . .'

We came to a road junction, and I saw the reflection of a flashing light on the greasy surface of the road. The light was yellow. Baxter mumbled that I should relax. When we reached the junction, I saw that the light was flashing on top of a tow truck, hitching up a broken-down VW.

'So if her alibi doesn't hold, we know for sure,' I said.

'A couple of the guys have been working on my behalf while I was canned. They tracked down the two ladies who were working the third floor of the Flamingo Key when the hurricane hit. If they have no recollection of the lady journalist, then we know for sure.'

'One hundred per cent?'

'Ninety-nine. Point nine, nine, nine.'

Baxter smiled at me and I glanced in the rear-view

mirror. The road behind us was clear. All the roads were clear. No one drove on Key West in this weather unless they had to. No one except cops and tow trucks and guys like us who had urgent business. The road followed the line of the coast, retracing the route I'd taken with Billy in his boat. Baxter mumbled directions, saying 'Straight ahead' each time we came to a junction. After we'd been driving for ten minutes, we reached a turning marked 'Casa Marina' and we drove down a bumpy dirt track that led to the ocean and a sunken harbour, made out of rotten wood and truck tyres. The place was deserted, lit by a single orange street light that revealed just how hard the rain was still falling. It wasn't until we stopped and I slipped the engine into neutral that I realized how wet I was, how I had been sitting in a puddle of water, and how the atmosphere seemed to be two parts rain and ocean to one part air. In the headlights, I saw three boats moored in the harbour, two of them lit from inside by hurricane lamps. Baxter took a piece of paper out of his pocket and checked it with his pencil torch.

'*Santa Anna*,' he said and flicked off the torch. 'They're sisters. Live on a boat called the *Santa Anna*.'

We got out of the station wagon and, as we set off towards the edge of the harbour, I saw a flash of silver and blue and then the outline of a man. A cop, with his hand on his holster, emerged from the shadows beside the boat. I was about to turn and run when Baxter called out in Spanish, and the cop replied in Spanish.

'It's OK,' Baxter said. 'He's one of mine.'

Baxter and the cop had a hurried conversation, all in Spanish. The cop pointed at the boat in the middle of the three, and he showed us to a gangplank that led out to it. The cop shone his torch along the length of the plank and Baxter and I walked uneasily along the beam of light. I could hear someone whispering in the darkness where I knew the boat to be. Then I saw a hurricane lamp swinging in front of me, showing me the way.

'*Tranquila, tranquila*,' the cop hissed behind us, and I heard the voice of a woman answering from inside the boat. Soon we were being shown into the cabin by a shadow who seemed to be mumbling a prayer under his breath. He pushed open a tiny slatted door and we were confronted by two old ladies, sitting upright and prim in hard-backed chairs, both with their hands on their knees and with their grey hair pulled back into tight buns. There was a flickering lamp at their feet that cast grotesque shadows across the tiny cabin, picking out the dark red and orange of their faces. The windows of the cabin were covered with newspaper, and the air smelt of incense and spices.

'*Buenos días, señoras*,' Baxter said.

'*Buenos días*,' they both said in unison. They looked like identical twins, and they seemed to be wearing identical clothes. There was hardly room to stand inside the cabin, and I hung awkwardly in the doorway as Baxter squatted at their feet. Baxter was about to speak when the cop put his head round the door.

'Their accents are pretty thick,' the cop whispered. 'You want me to translate, Tom?'

Baxter said that he'd be fine, but that the cop should stick around. Now there was me, the cop and Baxter all squashed together at the bow end of the cabin, with the two old ladies, licked by shadows, peering up at us. I felt that we were being given an audience by two spirits. Their faces were expressionless.

'*Señoras, una pregunta*,' Baxter said, and the two old ladies both drew breath at the same time.

'*Sí, señor*,' they both said.

Baxter edged a little closer, into the flames of the lamp.

'*Señoras, recuerden ustedes la noche del huracán?*'

On the word '*huracán*', the two old ladies raised their hands from their laps and crossed themselves, mumbling to God. One of them took a tiny piece of lace which she had tucked into her sleeve and dabbed her eyes.

'*Sí o no?*' Baxter said when they had calmed themselves down. '*Recuerden ustedes la noche del huracán?*'

They both peered at Baxter, their eyes twinkling in the orange lamplight. Baxter turned to the cop.

'How am I doing?' Baxter said.

'Not so good,' the cop said, then he cleared his throat. He repeated Baxter's question, and this time the words were almost indistinguishable from each other, or from an exhalation of phlegm. The two old ladies nodded their heads.

'Ask them where they were when it hit,' Baxter said, and the cop asked. The two old ladies both began to talk at once, their voices high-pitched, like the chirruping of finches. They crossed themselves as they spoke and the cop pursed his lips to calm them down.

'They say they were scared,' the cop said. 'They say they were cleaning rooms up at the hotel, one room to the next, like every day, but when they heard the moaning sound, they got scared and they tried to hide in a cupboard.'

The two old ladies seemed to have involved themselves in an elaborate mime of hiding in the cupboard, and the cop said 'tch, tch, tch' to bring them to attention.

'Ask them if they stayed in the cupboard,' Baxter said.

'No, they didn't,' the cop said. 'They just told me that they got out of the cupboard because they needed to go to the bathroom because they were scared.'

'So where did they go?'

'*Adónde?*' the cop said.

382

The two old ladies began to talk at the same time, and this time there was a lightness about their voices. It seemed to be a happy memory. The cop waited a long time before he translated. The hurricane lamp cast an orange halo around Baxter's face.

'They say a lady invited them.'

'Invited them?'

'A gringo lady invited them into her room. They say she was a good lady. A saint. They say she had blond hair like the Madonna.'

Baxter's expression didn't change. The laboratory behind his eyes was filled with gas from broken pipes waiting for the spark.

'Says she gave them some water from her refrigerator. Says that she was a gringo but she had a Spanish name. Her name was the Spanish word for "blue".'

'Blue?' I said.

'Azul,' the cop said. 'The Spanish word for blue is *azul*.'

The laboratory behind Baxter's eyes blew. It blew into a billion tiny fragments, but his expression didn't change. He turned back around to stare at the two old ladies. They seemed to be frightened of the look in his eyes, which I couldn't see.

'*Seguras?*' he said.

'*Sí. Seguro, y entonces . . .*'

The two old ladies began to chatter, a soft, warbling duet, illustrated by sweeps of the hand and by the sound effects of the hurricane. Baxter had stopped listening. So had the cop and so had I. Baxter and the cop were looking at each other in the half-light.

'Does this mean Azul's story checks,' I said at last, but neither Baxter nor the cop seemed to hear me. I saw for the first time the deep walnut tan of the cop's face, his

383

thick bushy moustache, his languid brown eyes which appeared to be filling with tears.

'Ask them if they have papers,' Baxter said at last.

'Tom . . .'

'Just ask them. Just fucking ask them.'

The tearful cop waited a few moments and then asked them the question. The moment the cop spoke, the two old ladies fell silent, struck dumb, and the orange light drained from their faces.

'Tom, is this really necessary?' the cop whispered.

'Just as I thought,' Baxter said. 'They're illegals. Both of them. Fucking illegals. Ask them to show me their naturalization papers.'

'Tom. Please . . .'

Baxter stood up, his head touching the roof of the cabin.

'Tell them both that I know that they are illegals,' Baxter said, and when the cop showed some reluctance Baxter put his face close to his.

'Tell them.'

The cop translated. The two old ladies gasped and put their hands to their cheeks.

'Tell them that they keep their fucking mouths shut or I'll hand them back to Fidel. Tell them that, Ramirez. Tell them that tonight never happened or they'll be washing shit from their clothes with rocks in Havana.'

CHAPTER THIRTY-THREE

We drove in silence, Baxter at the wheel.

The Cuban cop who'd translated followed on behind as we drove through the torrential rain that was threatening to flood the whole island. Rain so thick and heavy that it felt as if the ocean would rise up at any moment to meet the heavy clouds and then there would be no island left at all. Just a memory. Every twenty yards, Baxter's face was lit up by the yellow street lights. The windscreen wipers beat out a rhythm, in time with my thoughts.

'Tom . . .?'

I glimpsed the expression on Baxter's face. I knew that it would be unwise to talk. As we drove past the city cemetery, Baxter pulled over to the side of the road and waited. The cop behind pulled over too and he put his jacket over his head to run up to Baxter's window. Baxter wound the window down.

'You want I should call now?' the cop said.

'Better had,' Baxter said. 'Radio Farmer and tell him that you saw Karl Stone on the beach at Fort Taylor. Say that he was all alone on the beach. I'll wait here while you make the call.'

The cop ran back through the rain to his car. Baxter wound his window up. He explained that as soon as Farmer heard that I was on the beach at Fort Taylor, he'd go down there with a few of his boys to finish me off. He said that the word was that Farmer's plan was to shoot me or drown me and make it look like suicide and that maybe he'd fabricate some kind of suicide note, a full confession.

385

With me out of the way, he'd be able to close the Lisson case and leave no one in any doubt that it had been me who had committed the murder. Then he'd let the press loose with the story that would end Baxter's career.

'Except I'm ahead of him,' Baxter said grimly. The cop car behind flashed its lights, and Baxter pulled away into the rain. I knew the moment we turned into White Street that we were headed for the movie house. I felt that we were still following some plan that Baxter had worked out in advance but that Baxter no longer believed in it. I realized that those two Cuban ladies had shot Baxter's plan to blazes but that we were still trying to fly the wreckage, trying to keep the thing in the air through this storm, even though we both knew that the machinery didn't work any more. Baxter the tail gunner, his jaws clenched, trying to see clearly through the rain, driven on by sheer momentum.

'I'm ahead of him,' Baxter said again, and this time it sounded as if he was trying to convince himself.

Baxter pulled up and parked at the end of Mallory Street. He switched off the engine of the station wagon and began to drum his fingers on the steering-wheel. I asked him what we were doing and he said, 'Waiting.' After a few moments, a patrol car which was sitting outside 1131 and which I hadn't even seen turned on its lights and pulled away.

'There they go,' Baxter murmured and he nodded his head. Then he felt inside the pocket of his raincoat. He looked at himself in the rear-view mirror, and straightened his hair. He took a deep breath and turned to me.

'She carries a pistol, that right, Mr Stone?'

'Who?'

'Mary Hope.'

'You still think her name is . . .'

'Does she or doesn't she?'

'Yes. A Smith and Wesson .38.' I paused, wanting Baxter to explain. He checked the inside of his pocket again.

'You're still sure that she is Mary Hope?' I said.

'She's Mary Hope,' Baxter said.

'But she didn't kill Scarlet? How can that be, Tom?'

I wanted a flash of genius from Baxter. I wanted to feel dumb and slow. I wanted Baxter to be a hundred miles ahead of me, but instead he was right beside me, his face betraying him.

'Is there a fourth possibility?' I said. 'I mean, maybe she really is Scarlet's daughter, I can see that's possible, Tom. Scarlet told me herself she had had a baby. I don't know . . . she met some cowboy in Kansas. She told me that herself. But, Jesus . . .'

Baxter looked out of the window, not wanting to hear what I had to say.

'. . . But, Jesus, you heard what those two Cuban ladies said . . .'

While we had been driving through the rain, the fourth possibility had taken shape in my mind, all by itself. It was that Azul really was Scarlet's daughter, but that she wasn't the killer. The whole thing came together in easy pieces, fitting together perfectly. Mary Hope had come to Key West when she found out that Scarlet was throwing away her inheritance on the phoney movie scam. She'd come to Key West to put a stop to what Benelli had been doing, to blow the scam wide open. That was why she had been following me around the island, that was how she knew so much about Scarlet's finances. And after the murder, she'd stayed around to make sure that I got nailed. That was why she had struck a deal with Farmer

387

to help him make the case. But just because Azul was Mary Hope, it didn't mean necessarily that she was the killer. Hell, we both knew that she wasn't the killer. I tried to put all of this to Baxter but he hissed that I should be quiet.

'Baxter, this is insane,' I said. 'We've got to think this thing through.'

'Shut the fuck up.'

'Tom, you're acting crazy.'

Baxter punched the steering-wheel and then got a hold of himself. There was an irony here that wasn't funny. Not funny at all. Baxter squeezed his hand, the hand he'd hurt punching the steering-wheel, and then he said that I had a choice. If I wanted to wait and think things through that was fine, but I wouldn't survive to see the sunrise.

'This is between me and Farmer,' Baxter said. 'He nails you, or . . .'

'Or you nail her,' I said.

'This is between people like Farmer and people like me,' he said, almost shouting. 'You don't understand, Mr Stone. This is between his way and my way. And he's had his way for too long. Too damn long. It's my time now. You don't understand any of this because you don't belong here.'

The Cuban cop who'd been following us suddenly loomed up in front of the car out of the shadows. Baxter composed himself and opened the door.

'We clear?' Baxter said.

'The surveillance team have gone. The lady's up on the third floor. She's all alone.'

The cop pointed up at the attic room of the movie house. I could see that the light was on, and I could see Azul's silhouette against her ghastly flowered curtains.

'Tom, there are things about that night that I think I

really ought to tell you about,' I said as Baxter got out of the station wagon, but he pretended not to hear.

The three of us ran down the deserted street to the front door of 1131, our footsteps echoing in the rain, our shadows enormous. When we got to the front door, Baxter told me to open it. I had my key in the lock when I saw the cop was almost crying. It wasn't just the rain on his face, or the wind getting into his eyes. His face was broken up with fear and anxiety and there were real tears on his cheeks.

'Tom,' I said, 'just what exactly are you planning to do?'

Baxter jerked his head and I opened the door. We were greeted by the familiar smell of turpentine and rotten wood, and the floorboards creaked under our feet as we took the stairs. I could hear Azul singing in the attic room, off-key, and then her singing stopped when she heard our footsteps on the stairs. I grabbed Baxter by the arm on the landing, where the shadows of leaves were dancing in the light from the skylight.

'Wait a minute, Tom,' I said, 'you're going to arrest her even though . . .'

Baxter brushed past me and the Cuban cop brushed past me too. He didn't look into my eyes.

'Tom,' I hissed, 'how the hell are you going to make this work? She has an alibi.'

Baxter whispered something to the cop in Spanish. The cop grunted.

'If you get this into a courtroom she'll call the two Cuban ladies as witnesses. You won't be able to stop her.'

They were above me on the stairs. When they reached Azul's door, they stood on either side of it. Azul had started to sing again, but this time her voice was uncertain.

Her song was broken up, leaving gaps so that she could listen to the noises on the landing. Baxter pulled a snub-nosed revolver from the inside pocket of his raincoat and he held it close to his body, pointing it up at the ceiling.

He gestured to me to come closer. When I was close enough to hear, he whispered that I should knock on the door. I hesitated and wiped my mouth. My belly wasn't hurting any more and I felt strong enough to stop this thing right now, before it all started to move too fast. I felt that I was rolling down a steep incline. Suddenly, Baxter lowered the revolver so that it was pointing at my head. I felt the heat of it on my forehead, like a hot beam of light. There was a glint from the corner of Baxter's spectacles. The Cuban cop was breathing so hard that I thought he might pass out. Baxter waved the gun at my face.

'Knock.'

'Tom . . .'

'Now.'

I knocked on the door and Azul's singing stopped.

'Who is it?' Azul said.

'Azul? It's me. Karl.'

Azul opened the door and, the moment she did, Baxter pushed his way into the room. The cop followed on behind and I saw that he had drawn his revolver too. Azul stepped back towards the bed, looking from me to Baxter and then back to me again. She was wearing her ancient silk dressing-gown. Her eye was properly healed. She looked sweet and delicate, just the way she had the night when we had made love, but she could have been anyone. I had always known that Azul could have been anyone.

'Karl . . .?' she said, her voice breaking.

'Azul, it's OK, we just need to talk to you about . . .'

Baxter suddenly shouted, 'Shut the fuck up,' at the top

of his voice and the sound of his voice almost brought the ceiling down, almost demolished the walls. The cop was trembling, looking all around the room. Azul began to tremble too, putting her hands to her face, an ugly clawing gesture. Baxter nodded at the cop and he moved around towards the bed so that his line of fire was at right angles to Baxter's line of fire.

'Mary Hope,' Baxter said calmly, 'you are under arrest for the murder of Mrs Caroline Lisson.'

I tried to say something but Baxter told me to tell him where Mary Hope kept her gun. I was silent. Baxter glanced at me and said in an even voice that I had a choice. He said it was me or her. Either Farmer won or he won.

'It's right there in my bag,' Azul said, pointing at her brown shoulder-bag that was lying on the bed.

'OK, Mary Hope,' Baxter said, 'I want you to pick up the bag, take out the gun by the butt and hand it to the patrolman.'

Azul didn't move. The cop swallowed hard. Then Azul walked over to the bed and picked up the bag as if it were alive. She reached inside. There was a deep oiled clicking sound as Baxter and the cop cocked their pistols.

And then, the moment Azul pulled the gun from her shoulder-bag, held limply between her thumb and forefinger, pointing down towards the floorboards, Baxter and the cop both opened fire at the same time, and Azul fell like a thing made of paper, like a creature without bones, on to the floor. The force of the bullets made her spin around, and when she hit the floorboards, she landed in exactly the same place where I had found the body of Scarlet Timberley.

It took a long time, almost ten seconds, for the echoes of the gunfire to stop reverberating through the house.

The sound of the two guns firing so close at hand had almost deafened me, but through the ringing and the buzzing in my ears, I could hear Baxter talking in a calm and deadly monotone.

'When I confronted her with the fact that her real name was Mary Hope, and when I told her that she was under arrest for the murder of Caroline Lisson, she reached for a gun that she had hidden in her shoulder-bag. I called out to warn her to put the gun down but she aimed it directly at me. I was left with no alternative but to shoot her. Patrolman Ramirez was also obliged to open fire.'

Baxter finally lowered his revolver and looked at me.

'Can you hear what I'm saying, Mr Stone? Patrolman Ramirez and I opened fire in self-defence.' He came close to me. Patrolman Ramirez was still frozen in the firing position.

'Do you understand what I am saying, Mr Stone?' Baxter said, and I told Tom Baxter that I understood. I told him that I understood everything perfectly now. And when I looked down at the body on the floor, Mary Hope's face was staring up at me with exactly the same expression I'd seen on Scarlet Timberley's face. Now, as she lay there on the bare floorboards, there was no mistaking the similarity between the two of them.

CHAPTER THIRTY-FOUR

Baxter had been right, just as he was always right about everything. The woman who had called herself Azul Lake really was Mary Hope. And she really was Caroline Lisson's daughter. In the *Miami Herald* and in the *Courier*, they ran a three-page cover story, with pictures of Mary when she was a little girl at high school in Lawrence, Kansas. They said that Mary had been born when Scarlet Timberley was just nineteen years old, and that she'd been adopted by Damon and Valerie Hope, who ran a Kansas dairy farm. They said that Mary had had a promising career ahead of her, and she had won awards for her performances in high-school drama productions. The papers said that if she hadn't gone crazy and done what she'd done, she would have maybe made it as an actress some day.

And since it had been established that Azul really was Caroline Lisson's daughter, and that she stood to inherit ten million dollars on her mother's death, then the Lisson case could now be realistically closed, with the inference being that it was Mary who had committed the murder. It could never be proven now that she was dead but it couldn't be disproved either.

And after I had read about Mary Hope in the *Miami Herald*, I read in the *Key Wester*, on page four or five, that two old Cuban ladies, two illegals, had been picked up on their houseboat and deported back to Havana. It must have been the first thing that Baxter did, now that he was back at his desk. Now that he was back and looking good (so word had it) to take over Farmer's job when he retired in the spring.

The deportations showed some of those who weren't sure about Tom Baxter that he could be firm as well as fair.

Two days later, after Baxter and I had made our statements, after Baxter had been quizzed and believed and exonerated, after the truth about Azul Lake had been established, after the word had spread that Baxter would get some kind of commendation for the work he'd done, after all of these things had happened, I took the wooden alligator, the Indian smock and some copies of a moth-eaten script out of the cellar of the movie house and loaded them into the back of Baxter's Honda.

He'd offered to give me a ride to Tampa airport, to make sure I made my flight. He'd taken the day off especially to do me the favour of making absolutely sure I got to the airport on time. As I loaded the things into the boot of his car, he mumbled, 'What the hell are those things?' and I told him that they were props from the movie *Key Largo*, my favourite movie of all time. I would have told him that these things had been lying around in my subconscious for a long time before I ever set eyes on them for real, but I didn't, because neither of us felt much like talking.

We took Highway One all the way back to the mainland, crossed the beautiful ivory-white bridges, crossed the spines of islands and spits and sand bars, looking out at the fishermen dangling bait into the ocean on either side of the highway. Then we headed north towards Miami and turned off the highway to head west along Alligator Alley.

'We'll take Alligator Alley (a short cut, but an inferior road to the highway) because I think it's quicker,' Baxter said. That was all he said for the whole two hundred miles that we drove from Key West to the first turn off. I didn't say anything at all. We were alone together, totally alone, because a shared secret can isolate two people more surely than any ocean, any river or fallen bridge.

But it was a beautiful hot day.

Alligator Alley cuts through the Miccossoukee Indian reservation, and we stopped off at a roadhouse there to eat an Indian delicacy. Frogs' legs, Southern fried. At least we ordered the frogs' legs. We didn't eat them because we didn't feel much like eating.

When we got back into the inferno of Baxter's car, he found a large dead wasp sitting on the driver's seat. He carefully picked it up by the wing, mumbling that these things could still sting you even after they were dead. He tossed it out on to the highway and after that, we both began to itch with the heat and the sullen air and with the exotic pollens released by the colourful flowers in the mangrove swamps to the left and to the right. We itched in silence, isolated so surely in the tiny bubble of hot air inside his car.

When we were fifty miles from Tampa, I said, 'You know, Mr Baxter, I really believed that you were a good man.'

Baxter thought about that for a further ten miles. After ten miles, he said, 'My father's a good man. He sells peanuts in Orlando.'

He sounded tired and familiar, intimate. Like a brother you don't really care for. Now that the silence had been broken I wanted to tease this brother of mine a little further.

'You know, Mr Baxter, in the movies, we have a thing called the "final cut". Do you know what that is?'

Baxter didn't say anything. A huge ivory-white bridge

three miles long arched up into the sky in front of us. The last bridge before Tampa. I could see that Baxter was gripping the steering-wheel so hard his knuckles were white.

'Having the final cut means you get to make the final edit of the movie. You decide how it's going to turn out. You decide how it's going to end. And all the other endings get left on the cutting-room floor.'

'Make your point, Mr Stone,' he said. I hadn't realized that he had even been listening to me. But I guess that since I was the only other human being on this island, he had no choice but to listen.

'The point is, Tom, that we have the final cut. You and I. Writer and hero.'

Before we reached the long ivory bridge that takes you into Tampa, Baxter pulled over to the side of the highway and began to talk to me without looking at me.

'Mr Stone, I don't ever want you to set foot on my island again. You understand?'

'Because I murdered Scarlet?'

'If I ever see you on my island again, I will have you arrested.'

'Or because you murdered Mary Hope?'

'Do you understand, Mr Stone?'

Baxter checked his rear-view mirror carefully, and then eased the car back on to the highway, so that soon we were high up in the sky on the ivory bridge, lost amongst the rest of the rush-hour traffic.